UNEXPECTED CIRCUMSTANCES

Dear Reader,

I am so glad that you found your way to this little story about Tracy and Marcus. I really enjoyed writing about them. It took a long time for them to open up to me, but when they finally did, I was captivated by what they revealed. That is how I look at the characters, really—as people who have come to me, to tell others their story. Thus, the art of "storytelling." I'd love to meet you one day, dear reader, and find out what you thought about the book and what else you're reading. As I visit with readers, I find that their insights into the characters always intrigue me.

Crystal Downs

CRYSTAL DOWNS

UNEXPECTED CIRCUMSTANCES

ARABESQUE®

UNEXPECTED CIRCUMSTANCES

An Arabesque novel

ISBN 1-58314-574-5

© 2006 by Crystal Downs

www.kimanipress.com

Printed in U.S.A.

To a family that is full of creative,
loving and kindhearted people.
Your support knows no limits.
Your loyalty has no questions.

ACKNOWLEDGMENTS

My first thank-you, as always, goes to God, Who has given me the talent and the strength to follow along the path He has sent me. I would like to thank my parents, Charles and Queen, for their unwavering support, encouragement and belief in my chosen profession. To my babies—Immanuel, Daniel, Linnea and Luke—the sun rises and sets on those eyes and smiles. To my siblings, Cody, Carla and Craig...I'd come back again, if I could have you guys with me. Thanks to Ivan Daniels for the fun times and multitude of creative ideas you've shared with me. Sheree, you're wonderful as always. I love you, cuz, almost as much as I love Uncle Mike. To my cousin, Yvonne Honore-Bennett, Monique was a wonderful example of the great impact one person could have in a short time on earth. She was beautiful. And finally, a big thanks to those with heartfelt words of encouragement that kept me pressing ahead: Christine Smith, Daphne Robinson Durkin, Pamela Sims Nunley, Melody Waller, Nicole Barrett, Tricia Watkins, Connie Toole, Richard and Benita Reid, Darlene Williams, Roosevelt Burnett, Priscilla Coatney, Latonya D. Walker, Celeste Sawyer, Derrick Stinson, Barbara Mitchell, Ozella Carroll and Minna Davidson.

Chapter 1

"Twenty-five," she said relieved, and allowed the weights to slam back into place on the machine. Tracy Middleton snatched up her notebook from the floor beside her and jotted down the number on the last set of her workout. Out of the corner of her eye, she caught the swift movement of a woman she had come to identify as her stalker.

As Tracy moved from the weight room to the locker room, she noticed that the woman, whom she had caught staring at her several times over many days, was following her. Tracy's mind raced as she heard the woman's footsteps behind her on the stairs.

Tracy wasn't sure how long the woman had been watching her and dogging her movements. She had first noticed on Wednesday that when she left her aerobics class ten minutes early to nab a treadmill facing the windows, her follower left too, and occupied a treadmill behind her. Tracy also noted that when she ended her run forty minutes later and moved on to the weights, the lady also moved, choosing a weight machine not far from hers, and kept glancing at her. Ever since that day, Tracy had been monitoring the woman's movements and they always, uncomfortably, coincided with hers. If it hadn't been for the furtive glances, she would think of her as no more than someone with the same routine.

She was an attractive woman who appeared to be in her early fifties, with pretty honey skin and a floppy pageboy haircut. She was incredibly fit, but sort of thick in the thighs and shorter than Tracy.

Just a year ago, she wouldn't have given the older woman a second thought. But after her stint at Chicago Metro Television, Tracy had witnessed the darker side of human nature. Her work buddy, Vivien Marsh, an occasional weekend anchor, told her about some of the disturbing mail that the attractive female anchors received from men *and women* who were fixated on them. In Viv's usual cool manner, she laughed it off, saying, "There are some real kooks out there, girl." But it was one disturbed guy who had created a full fantasy life in his head about Vivien that changed her attitude from amused to frightened. Vivien received all sorts of strange mail and gifts from him. She ignored the packages until the tone had become increasingly threatening. The station manager was finally alerted and called the police when the guy arrived at their building, waiting in the lobby to confront Vivien about her engagement. He had read about it in a community newspaper and came to ask her why she was breaking up "their family." Fortunately in that case, the man was arrested and Vivien had a restraining order issued against him.

Tracy cut a commanding presence at five feet, nine inches, but she knew that she had no real defense against a crazy person. Besides, her intimidating attributes were all feminine. She had always been a physical person, so working on her body was her favorite pastime. Her full breasts; impossibly small, tight torso; curvaceous hips and long shapely legs gave her a figure of a model's proportions, but with a bit more meat on her bones. Her skin was a rich chocolate brown that was so radiantly poreless it appeared to be velvet. Her face was heart-shaped and set off with big brown eyes, thick eyelashes and a prominent cleft in her chin. With her remarkably striking looks, Tracy had become accustomed to strangers occasionally taking a second glance—but this was ridiculous.

Right now, Tracy wanted to take a shower before heading home, but the woman was creeping her out. Out the corner of her eye, she could see her staring at her and she certainly didn't want to take off a stitch of clothing under this kind of scrutiny. This really sucked too, because she liked this ritzy downtown health club. Now that this creep was here, she was going to have to finagle a way to get a premium membership somewhere else. She was already overextended financially, and these high-end health clubs cost a lot—even when you bought a membership secondhand. Vivien, who received all sorts of first-class gifts from companies eager to list her as a patron, had handed over this membership to Tracy. Now that she had gotten used to the luxury of it, she vowed never to go back to the Y.

Tracy opened her locker, removed her street clothes from the hook and stuffed them into her gym bag. Normally, she would never put them in the musty bag, but now she wanted nothing more than to get the heck out of there. She slammed the locker, turned to leave and practically jumped out of her skin. The woman was standing at the end of her aisle.

"Hi," the older woman said, staring at her curiously.

"Oh, hey. You scared me." Tracy looked around her. No one else was in the locker room. She had at least twenty years of youth on the woman, but Tracy mentally plotted an escape route anyway. The sister was in good shape, and you could never tell how strong another person was until you got into a scuffle. "Well, take it easy," Tracy said and turned to go out of the other side of the aisle.

"Uh, Tracy, wait. I want to talk to you for a minute," the woman called, rushing up behind her. When Tracy turned around, walking backwards, the woman was awfully close.

"Whatever you're thinking—Wait, did you call me Tracy?"

"Yes, Tracy. I wonder if you would join me for a coffee or something." The lady advanced on her smiling and Tracy backed farther away. Now, she was certain that she was dealing with some sort of crazed, middle-aged stalker. She stared at the woman horrified. The woman, sensing that she wasn't getting any closer to achieving her goal, stood in place and offered an even larger smile. "I'm Elaine Newell. Please, it'll only take a minute of your time." She extended her hand, but Tracy just gaped at it.

"Look, I'm not into women, if that's what you're thinking," Tracy said.

Elaine clasped her hands in front of her and laughed. "It's nothing like that. I assure you."

A true city girl, Tracy knew that nuts came in all shapes, sizes and sexes. And just because this Elaine-chick looked fairly wealthy, sharp and sensible, it didn't mean she was any more normal than the kook who yelled expletives at her every morning as she left her house. Tracy slung her gym bag over her shoulder. *Is she lonely? Looking for girlfriends?* "Hey, maybe some other day. I've really got to get to work." Tracy turned away from the woman again.

"But you're not going to work. You lost your job, Miss Middleton. Surely you have time for coffee."

Tracy turned back stunned. She had been unemployed for three weeks, but it wasn't the kind of news—and she wasn't the kind of person—to make the papers. How could this stranger know her name and know that she was no longer employed? She stared at her incredulously and Elaine looked back at her with the demeanor of a kindly old grandmother.

"Now, you're just freaking me out. Who are you again?" Tracy squinted at her.

"I'm Elaine Newell, CEO of Cathy Booker Foods and I might be able to offer you a position with my company." When Tracy still stared at her skeptically, she elaborated. "You'd be very well compensated." Elaine's eyes drifted toward a group of women returning from their aerobics class. She cautiously took the few steps toward Tracy and took her elbow. "Please, let's talk in the juice bar."

Tracy was too perplexed to resist. She knew of Cathy Booker Foods, whose chief product was a popular line of canned and frozen soul foods. Since Tracy was currently in no position to turn down a job that appeared to have fallen into her lap, she let her legs carry her along with the woman.

As they boarded the elevator, Elaine made general conversation about the unseasonably warm weather Chicago was experiencing this late in September. Tracy could only utter monosyllabic answers in response to her generic chatter. Her thoughts were still occupied by the strangeness of the entire situation, but she didn't see a reason not to listen to the woman for a little while. They got off the elevator at the floor of the stylish cafeteria and juice bar.

"What'll you have?" Elaine approached the counter and turned to Tracy.

"Uh, nothing for me, thanks." She wanted to make this as brief as possible.

Elaine turned back to the counter girl and handed her a credit card. "Two chai teas, please, and a bran muffin. We'll be over at that table."

Tracy followed Elaine to a table by the windows but far from the few other patrons who were in the bar. It was only eight-thirty on a Friday. This late in the morning, very few members had the luxury of idly hanging around the health club after they finished their workouts.

"Well, this is nice. I finally have a chance to sit down with you," Elaine said, settling into her seat. Tracy placed her bag on the floor and looked at the woman expectantly. The server dropped off their drinks and Elaine quickly signed the credit card receipt. She started to drink her tea. "You should try this. It's really good."

"Look, you mentioned something about a job." Tracy still wasn't sure that the woman wasn't mining for girlfriends, so she pushed her to get to the point.

Elaine chuckled and broke off a piece of her bran muffin. She sat back in her chair, smiling. "I can see you're the direct type. That's good...good. Smart and direct. Just how I was hoping you'd be."

"Um...Mrs. Newell is it...?"

"Please. I insist that you call me Elaine."

"Well, Elaine. Do I know you? How do you know I—"

"Was fired from your job at CMT? How do I know your name? Etcetera, etcetera?" Elaine drank more tea as Tracy nodded slowly. "Well, Tracy Middleton, don't be alarmed. Or should I say don't get any more alarmed than you already are," she chuckled. "But I've been watching you for quite some time. I've also had a private investigator look into your background."

"What?" Tracy's brow wrinkled angrily. "Who the—"

"I know, I know. It sounds pretty crazy." Elaine waved a dismissive hand at her. "But listen...I own a multimillion-dollar corporation and I can't have just anybody work with me as my personal assistant."

"Oh, look"—Tracy sat back and crossed her arms over her chest—"I know you think you've searched extensively into my background and stuff, but apparently you didn't look hard enough. I'm not the personal assistant type. I'm a journalist."

"I'm well aware of that...and you're pretty smart too. Top

of your class at the University of Missouri. I thought you produced some great segments on the news and to top it off, you're very attractive. You should've been in front of the camera. Trust me. You're exactly what I'm looking for." Elaine ate more of her muffin.

Tracy took a sip of her tea, allowing herself time to study the woman across from her. The tea turned out to be a spicy mix that was quite tasty. But she didn't think she could trust Elaine's judgment about everything. "Well, honestly, I don't think you're what I'm looking for. I think I'll just look for another news job."

"That pays as well as nine thousand dollars per month? Plus expenses in the form of your own company credit card. Plus a bonus of half a million dollars if you work out?" Elaine raised her eyebrow and gave her a sly smile.

Tracy was once again astonished. The producer's job at Chicago Metro Television, though short-lived, was the highest salary she had ever made in her twenty-nine years. She was thrilled to have negotiated $72,500 with them. Now, this woman was offering her so much more to be *an assistant*?

"So let me get this straight. You're offering me over one hundred thousand dollars a year to be your personal secretary? Plus another five hundred thousand as a bonus if I *work out?*" Tracy asked, making air quotes. She sat up straighter in her chair and peered at the woman, trying to get a better understanding of her motivation.

"That's right," Elaine said without a hint of irony. "But it's not a secretary. You'd be my personal assistant. That involves more than secretarial duties."

"Oh," Tracy said with sudden understanding. She sat back and looked at her coldly. She curled her lips. "I get it. And these duties involve the bedroom, right?"

Elaine laughed and shook her head. "You young people are so jaded with life. I am *not* gay. I am not interested in pursuing a relationship with you, other than…uh, a professional one."

"'Uh…a professional one'?" Tracy mimicked Elaine's words. "So what's the catch? One hundred thousand is already a generous offer for a secr…personal assistant, or whatever. Why would you also throw in an additional half million dollars?"

"Okay…so I admit, there is a catch." When she saw Tracy's big brown eyes become guarded, she hurried to explain. "But it's not what you think. It's that I have an immediate assignment for you, should you accept my offer."

"And it's not sex, so it's illegal." In her mere seven months in the news business, Tracy had seen a lot of scandalous acts committed by people who looked as clean-cut and wealthy as Elaine Newell. CEOs were dragged away in handcuffs just as frequently as the common criminal these days.

"It's not illegal," Elaine said, avoiding her eyes and twisting her lips. "It might not be ethical, but it's certainly not illegal."

"All right, Elaine, spit it out. What is this covert assignment that you're really offering me? Because I'm getting the distinct impression that the secretary-assistant thing is just the carrot and this little project you're throwing in, is the actual stick." To prove to Elaine that she was completely unimpressed by her, Tracy reached over, pulled a piece off Elaine's muffin and popped it into her mouth.

"That's why I like you. You're a smart cookie." Elaine amiably pushed the plate with the muffin to Tracy's side of the table.

Shrewd move, Tracy thought. This woman was a smart cookie herself, and an adherent of Norman Vincent Peale's *How to Win Friends and Influence People*. Elaine leaned forward on her elbows and crossed her arms. "Okay, here it is. I really do need a bright assistant. This person would have to stand in for me at meetings and attend some of my committees in my stead, help me organize my schedule and manage my staff. You would get to use some of your journalism skills by ghostwriting some things for me and making sure that the external relations staff is on their toes. Plus, you've got the connections to get Cathy Booker some prime media placements."

Tracy drank some of her tea, relaxing a little. "Sounds good, but why not advertise for such a person. I'm sure every girl with that kind of experience would be chomping at the bit to grab that job."

"That's the second part." Elaine swiped her floppy hair out of her eyes and touched Tracy's arm. "The part where you earn half a million. She has to be smart and beautiful and confident…like you…if she's going to catch the eye of my son."

Tracy set her cup down and really started to laugh. She saw Elaine looking annoyed at her, but she couldn't control herself. Tracy eventually settled down, shaking her head like she had just heard a great joke.

"Find something amusing, Miss Middleton?"

"I insist. Call me Tracy." She smiled, noting Elaine's angry look at the mock. "Isn't this a lot of trouble to go through to fix up your son? Kind of expensive, huh? He must be a real looker."

"As a matter of fact, my son Sean is quite handsome. He has no problem meeting women."

"They say a mother's love is blind." Tracy smirked.

Bristling, Elaine reached for her wallet and opened it to a photo of her son. She held it out to Tracy irritably. Tracy took the wallet and stared at the photo.

"Ooh…cutie pie. He's more or less a double for Blair Underwood."

"Who?"

"Never mind." Tracy handed back the wallet. "So if he's so fine, how come his mama is out trying to find women for him? He won't settle down?"

"It's *whom* he wants to settle down with that's the problem," Elaine said, relaxing.

"Oh? A hootchie mama? And you don't approve?" Tracy ate the muffin, unconcerned. This obviously was not her problem.

"Just the opposite. He's engaged to…she's a nice enough girl, but the wrong woman for him." Elaine said, looking down. For a woman who, Tracy could tell, prided herself on speaking her mind, Elaine was tripping over these words. Something was up, and this woman still wasn't leveling with her. "You are exactly the type he used to date. His type…until she came along. And I can't have my company fall into, um, the wrong hands."

"Your competitor's daughter? A real life Romeo and Juliet?" Tracy eyed her levelly, but Elaine didn't respond. "Whatever. I'm not into pretty boys…I go for the more masculine type. Besides, I'm all for love and if these two are in love, who are you to split them up? This really doesn't sound like the job for me." Tracy reached for her bag and frowned when Elaine touched her arm to stop her.

"Tracy, don't be foolish! I'm not asking you to marry him. This would only take a year out of your life, and imagine the money you'd make." When Elaine saw Tracy's steely face, she tried another tactic. "Maybe less than a year. Once you got there, you would turn his head. Just think…six months of work and you could be a very wealthy woman."

"Sorry. No deal." Tracy stood up.

Elaine rose to her feet and gripped Tracy's arm. "Please," she whispered desperately. "All you have to do is come and work as you normally would. I really could use you as my right arm. You've got everything I'm looking for. And if, in the course of your work, Sean sees you and has doubts about this impending marriage, what's the harm?" She spread her hands open as if to show how easy it would be.

"First of all, I don't think your stupid plan would work unless your son is some sort of cad or womanizer, and secondly, you need to find somebody else to do your dirty work." Tracy slung her gym bag on her shoulder and headed for the door. Elaine caught up with her.

"One million dollars." She caught her arm again, whispering, "I'll give you one million, but our arrangement would have to be absolutely confidential."

Tracy pried Elaine's hand off her arm.

"Lady, you really need to get a life. Good-bye." Tracy headed toward the elevator. When she boarded, she was relieved to see that Elaine hadn't followed her. She blew out a breath. *Whew! Talk about your nutcases.*

Tracy stepped out of the health club and onto Michigan Avenue. She was sorry she didn't have that shower. Although the weather was unseasonably warm for September, the underlying breeze from the lake was incredibly cool. It caught the dampness on her clothes and chilled her body. Tracy ran to the self-park garage to retrieve her car. She tried not to think about it, but it really rankled her nerves that a total stranger could readily get as much information on her as she wanted. At least Elaine's ludicrous proposition had one positive effect on her. It strengthened her resolve to stop dawdling and find another job.

Chapter 2

October guaranteed some pretty cold days, but long-suffering Chicagoans were typically hard-pressed to let go of their glorious summer and face the fact that winter was looming. Tracy was no different. She mentally scolded herself for leaving the house in a black cable-knit sweater coat, but the day had appeared to be pretty temperate from her window and she thought this little wrap would do the trick. Now, she questioned the logic of that decision and reluctantly reached to the dashboard and turned on the heater. As she drove her Jeep Cherokee through her old neighborhood, she once again noted the telltale signs of despair—twenty-five-cent potato chip wrappers, sucked-dry cigarette butts and broken beer bottles littered the ground. Adults and children walked or ran the streets with seemingly nowhere constructive to land.

A scowling group of baggy-jeaned, hooded sweatshirt-wearing young brothers eyed her warily as she parked her car in front of her mother's building. Tracy looked at the three-flat walk-up with some disdain. It had been a beautiful property twenty years ago when their little trio moved in, but the latest landlord had allowed the building to carry on in its slow depreciation. The chain-link fence surrounding the property curved where so many angry young bodies had decided to rest their backs. The grass, in the spots where it continued its struggle for survival, was long and brown. And the hedges, which Tracy could remember as being lush and green during her youth, were sparse and unkempt.

Tracy reached into the backseat to retrieve the bag of groceries for her mother. She firmly attached her purse to her shoulder and took a deep breath before getting out of the car. She dreaded passing by the gauntlet of young men, but it was a normal part of her weekly trek. Even though they were on the fence next door, today, their feral gazes crawled over her body as though ogling her was guaranteed in their civil rights.

Most nodded as she glanced at them, but one, Darrel, whom she had gone to high school with, spoke her name. She spoke his back and used her key to enter the building. Tracy pressed the buzzer and yelled out, "It's me Mama," as she climbed the stairs. At least her mother was on the first floor. This was good for Sheila Ward's bad knees, but it wasn't so great for safety. The bars on her windows were in response to two attempted break-ins back in the eighties.

Tracy waited at the apartment door for her mother to undo the locks. Tracy had keys, but her mother needed to unhook the chain. After a series of unlocking clicks, her mother's small frame appeared in the doorway.

"Hey, baby," her mother said, stepping aside and smiling up as she allowed her tall daughter to enter her home. All of Tracy's height came from her father's side of the family. Even Tracy's sister, Tai, wasn't blessed with these elongating genes. Her father's height was what had attracted the young and very short Sheila Ward to the striking Tony Middleton. Unfortunately, his charm was short-lived and his commitment to maintaining a family as a nineteen-year-old was even shorter. He hung in there as long as he could, but Sheila ended up alone at the ripe age of twenty-one with two babies and only a high school diploma. Her bad knees were the result of supporting her girls as a housekeeper for years until she eventually found work as a receptionist in a private doctor's office.

"Hi, Mama." Tracy kissed her cheek, but was unhappy to see her still wearing a robe in the middle of the afternoon. "Why aren't you dressed?"

Her mother waved a hand, concentrating on setting the locks back into place. "I've been in and out of bed all day. I'm not feeling so hot."

"Not feeling well, how?" Tracy could never tell when her mother was actually sick, or whether she was in her hypochondriac mode. As soon as one of her girlfriends told her about an ailment she was having, Sheila would experience the same symptoms the next week. Tracy didn't even want to think about the number of complaints she now had working for the doctor.

"Aw, you know my bronchitis has been bothering me and I think I'm coming down with a flu bug." Sheila returned to her seat on the living room couch, where she had been watching TV. Tracy turned on the lamp. To her annoyance, her mother never opened the curtains and would sit in the dark, watching television. Tracy took the groceries to the small adjoining kitchen. She surmised that the bronchitis was real, but the flu was probably a result of Mrs. Robinson across the hall, whose bout with influenza Sheila had mentioned during Tracy's last visit.

"I brought you some soup and some stuff to snack on and some fruit...bananas, oranges and grapes," Tracy called as she placed the groceries in the proper places.

"Did you get my orange juice?"

"I got your orange juice and your soap."

"Did you get Tide with bleach?" Sheila asked.

"What? You said 'soap'. I got Ivory *soap*." Tracy frowned and came out of the kitchen holding the neat four-pack.

"You know I meant soap powder. I have lots of soap…I think." Sheila tore her eyes away from *Jeopardy* to look crossly at the soap in Tracy's hand.

"Mama, I wish you would call it 'detergent'. You only said you needed soap on the phone." Tracy shook her head and went back into the kitchen. She would have to bring that next time, or maybe her mother would buy it with one of the five twenties Tracy placed on the kitchen table.

"Well, you can never have too much of anything I suppose. I'll get the soap when I get my check." Sheila waved her hand and pulled her robe tighter.

Tracy knew her mother's check was barely a living wage. Mercifully, before the original doctor who'd employed her died from old age, he handed over the reins to a younger partner. But the new physician didn't have as many office hours as his predecessor. Now Sheila only worked on Tuesdays, Thursdays and Saturdays for about five hours each day. She had no savings and Tracy and Tai helped her out with expenses. Tai had married a civil engineer and moved to Minneapolis, but she paid half of the rent, while Tracy handled the everyday expenditures.

"I'm leaving some money for you on the table. It's not as much as I usually do, but it should tide you over until you get your money." Tracy debated telling her this, because she knew what was to come.

"Tracy, I know times are tight for you. Don't be leaving me all sorts of money that you can't afford to part with right now." Sheila stood up and crossed the room to check the amount on the table. "A hundred? That's too much. You already gave me forty last week."

"It's okay. I'm doing all right." Tracy wasn't sure if this was a lie or not. After weeks in the job search, she was beginning to worry about her finances.

"Here. Take back sixty." Sheila held out the money and Tracy waved it off.

"It's cool. I'm okay, Mama." She attempted to look convincing.

"You sure?" Sheila looked doubtful.

"I'm fine." Tracy moved into the living room and removed her sweater coat to get out from under her mother's scrutiny. She sat on the couch and grabbed the remote to turn up the sound. Sheila had a bad habit of keeping the sound low and cocking her head at the television as if straining to hear.

At only fifty-one, her mother carried herself like an old woman. True, she hadn't kept up her body the way she should have, but that was no excuse for puttering around the house with a ponytail and slippers on her days off either. Tracy and Tai talked about it with each other, but they never broached the subject with Sheila. They presumed that she felt ten years older for having so many responsibilities at such a young age. They wanted to see her settle down with a nice man, but years of experience had shown them that she had trouble choosing the right kind of men or even believing she was attractive. The last guy she had was the one back in the eighties who had provided the bars for the windows, but little else.

"You want some orange juice?" her mother called, pouring herself some.

"Yeah."

"So how's the job search going?"

"Going, going, gone. Pathetic." No point in lying about that. Tracy leaned on the armrest with her hand under her chin.

"Aww…with your skills? Somebody should've snapped you right up."

"Well, they're not. But I read somewhere that in this

economy, you can expect your search to take about three months." Tracy tried to keep it positive.

"What month are you in now?"

"Oh!" Tracy smacked her head lightly, conveniently recalling something else. "I forgot to get you candy bars for Alaina's kids. Halloween is coming up too."

Sheila placed Tracy's orange juice on the coffee table and sat down beside her. "Oh, they moved out."

"What? When did this happen? I was just here last week."

"Last Tuesday, before you came. I guess I forgot to tell you."

"Well, who's moving in there now?" Tracy looked sideways at Sheila.

Her mother shrugged and drank her juice. "I don't know. I hope it's not this group that came to look at it yesterday. Girl…it was two fat women, four little kids and a carload of teenage boys. I'm not sure who all is supposed to be getting the apartment, but it looked like trouble to me." She twisted her lips and gave Tracy a look.

"Teenage boys attract more teenage boys. I swear, that Jerry doesn't care who he puts in here. Doesn't he even think about the fact that this is a building full of single women, some retired? Y'all don't need a bunch of boys running in and out of this place at all hours." Tracy fell into her regular gripe about her mother's landlord.

"Well, I'm not sure they were all going to be moving in."

"But still," Tracy said, crossing her arms in front of her chest. She looked over at her mother.

"I know." Sheila picked up the remote and turned the volume back down to the level she liked.

Tracy shook her head sadly. She and Tai really needed to get their mother out of this place.

Chapter 3

"In other news, Mayor Daley has ordered an investigation into the fire that killed…"

You're a rat, Brian. A rat and a creep. Tracy switched from the news broadcast to a movie and pulled the blanket more tightly around her legs. She didn't want to turn up the heat, because her old greystone took a lot of energy to warm up. She picked up the Häagen-Dazs container and found it empty. *Oh, right. Already ate that.*

She didn't know why she tortured herself in the afternoons by watching her rotten ex-boyfriend. But she felt drawn to the local cable news like a gaper to a car wreck. Now Brian Simmons had been promoted to the anchor desk and, according to Tracy's friend Vivien, Brian's new producer on assignments, Millicent Fields, was also bumped up to executive producer. They were also very openly an item at work. Tracy first thought was that she and Brian hadn't been *openly* dating. He always said that they needed to keep their private business private.

As far as Tracy was concerned, his dating Millicent was the last nail in the coffin of the "Brian Simmons Story." But her true disillusionment with Brian was mostly due to the fact that she had found out his true nature only when Vivien also told her that Brian was behind Tracy's firing. Vivien found out from the producer's secretary that Brian went to the executive producers and told them that he couldn't work with Tracy anymore. He said that she was erratic and her instructions were sloppy and that everyone working on the shoots was uncomfortable taking direction from her.

It was a really low blow. After Tracy heard about her firing, she solicited Brian's advice on what she should do to keep her job and asked him to go to the bosses on her behalf to try to help her keep her job. It had seemed like a good idea at the time.

Brian had been with CMT for three years and there were rumors that he might be up for the four p.m. anchor slot when the current anchor went to network TV. Though Tracy was a competent journalist, the position had been her first television news job. Prior to that, she had only done freelance feature work at lots of newspapers and periodicals. Once she joined CMT, she worked hard to distinguish herself at the metro desk to get the chance to produce a few of Brian's slots. Back then, Brian was her biggest advocate. He talked the heads of the station into giving her a chance. Now, Tracy realized that it was probably just his way to get closer to her. Though she was attracted to him, she had been standoffish. She didn't want to mess up her job by getting involved in an office romance. He broke down her defenses with his mentoring and charm.

But once his eye lingered elsewhere, his loyalty did too. Thanks to Vivien's information, Tracy was now figuring it all out. Brian was, no doubt, tired of having Tracy as a producer—and as a lover—when he got a good look at Millicent. And with his powers of persuasion behind Millicent and Millicent's strong background in television, Tracy couldn't compete. It would have been easy enough to get her reassigned, but since Brian was such a coward and wanted to move on without the messiness of having to see Tracy every day, he made sure she was fired.

Life is so unfair. Tracy started to cry, thinking about it. *The mean people prosper, while the nice people get stepped on and tossed aside.*

After she was offered the producer's spot, she had purchased her house. She put most of her meager savings into the down payment. It was just a normal three-bedroom, two-bath greystone—nothing spectacular. But having grown up in an apartment with her sister and her mother, Tracy saw homeownership as proof that she had finally "arrived." Now, after months of being out of work, her mortgage was going to be late, her utilities were outrageous, her insurance and property taxes were coming up, and her car note was due. She hadn't bought a stitch of clothing in ages and couldn't afford to get her hair done—even if she *did* get a job interview. In this tight economy, it didn't make a difference because she never got called for an interview. Even seasoned veteran journalists were hanging on to their jobs or looking for work.

Tracy dissolved into sobs. The worst was the thought of losing her house. "Why? Why is this happening to me?" she yelled into the sparsely furnished room. That was another thing. She had had big plans to refurbish this house, then furnish it from top to bottom, room by room. She had only gotten as far as completing her bedroom and the master bathroom before she was fired.

Her credit cards were all virtually maxed out. Christmas was on the way, and she wouldn't even be able to send anything to her niece and nephews. Her old freelance contacts barely had any work for her since they had found new writers when she went to television. And there was no use pressing them for work now that they were slowing down for the holidays.

Whatever. Guess I just have to keep on keeping on. Tracy wiped her eyes and went to the fridge in search of more ice cream. She dug through the freezer and didn't see any, but her hand pulled out a frozen dinner. Cathy Booker's Big Chicken and Dressing Dinner—*Now with Greens!* Tracy sniffled and blinked as she stared at the box.

Chapter 4

Now, Tracy was in the position of stalker. From the back of the aerobics class, she kept an eye on Elaine. Elaine's watch beeped and she looked at it while keeping up with the vigorous steps. She did a few more moves, then went to get her towel and water. Tracy watched her leave and then followed Elaine, keeping her distance. Even though she practiced this, she wasn't sure what she was going to say. Elaine dashed down the stairs to the locker room and Tracy took the elevator. She had seen Elaine around since their strange conversation and Elaine spoke, but kept to herself. Today, Tracy entered the mostly empty locker room and Elaine looked up from her bench when she saw her.

"Hi," Tracy said, smiling.

"Hi." Elaine smiled and went back to removing her clothes.

Tracy went to her locker and opened the door. *What was I going to say again?* She was breathing hard, uneasy about approaching Elaine, but she knew she would have to act fast. She didn't want to have to converse with her in the shower. This time, a few other women were in the room. Tracy peeled off her shorts. *Just do something.*

"Did you find anyone for that position yet?" she called over to Elaine, smiling brightly to show that she meant it in a friendly way—not mocking. Elaine, in her bra and panties, looked at Tracy, surprised.

"I think I might have someone," she called back and gave a small smile.

"Oh." Tracy couldn't hide the disappointment in her voice. She wasn't thrilled about the *attract my son* thing, but the assistant job could've really made a difference in her life. It was early November and Tracy was desperate. "Well, that's good."

Elaine nodded and removed her underwear. Tracy took off her top, her brow knit fretfully. *Now, what the heck am I going to do?* She tried not to get depressed. "Well...I guess you snooze, you lose." Tracy tried to smile, but it wouldn't hold. She glanced over and Elaine had wrapped a towel around herself. Elaine closed her locker and came to Tracy's row. She leaned against the lockers and stared at Tracy.

"I have a meeting at ten, but I was going to relax in the sauna for a while. You want to join me...or do you have somewhere else to go?" Elaine smirked, cocking her head. Tracy looked down. She knew that Elaine was well aware that she now had the upper hand.

"That sounds good," Tracy said. She watched Elaine go to a sauna room. There were several rooms lined against the wall so that friends could relax together or a person could find one to be alone in. Tracy removed her underwear, put on a towel and entered the sauna.

Elaine was pouring water onto the stones when Tracy sat down on the wooden bench. It felt warm and fantastic in the small room. Although she was tense about this impromptu meeting, she felt her muscles loosening.

Elaine spoke first. "I haven't approached my new prospect yet. Of course, she's not as great as you…but I was looking forward to the money I'd save."

"Excuse me?" Tracy knew this was some sort of manipulation. Elaine must smell her desperation and was going to talk her down.

"You were my first choice but that last figure I gave you was a one-time offer. You passed, so it's gone." Elaine stretched out her legs.

"So you're not paying nine thousand a month anymore?"

"Oh, yeah. That still stands. The million is off the table, though." Elaine cut her hand through the thick air. Tracy couldn't care less about the stupid bonus thing. It would be nice—she could do so many things with a million dollars, but that wasn't what she was looking for. But with this woman, you had to show some gumption.

"So, the second part of the job is off the table?" Tracy asked casually.

"No. If you can achieve my goal by my deadline, you'll get your bonus."

"Of?"

"Half a million."

Tracy rubbed her arm. This felt so wrong. She decided to drop the tough negotiator pretense and just be herself. "I just want to work…to tell you the truth. I don't want to have to seduce anybody. I'm more attracted to the assistant thing."

"But that's my only reason for taking on an assistant…an *attractive, young* assistant. Other than that, I could just use my executive secretary. Besides, I told you, you won't have to seduce anyone. Just do the things that I ask and I guarantee…with your looks, body and brains…he'll be rethinking this Ashleigh fixation. And you'll be a rich woman."

Tracy was quiet. Elaine allowed the silence to stand.

"So when were you looking for this person to start?"

"If that person is you, you tell me. You could start tomorrow or Monday."

When would I get my first paycheck? "Monday is better for me."

"All right. Come by my office tomorrow and we'll draw up a contract." Elaine gathered her towel around her and stood up.

"A contract?"

"Of course. You don't think I'd do this without a commitment, did you? As a matter of fact, you'd better come by my house. I don't think I want to unveil you until the meeting." Elaine sounded so excited, Tracy could almost see the wheels turning around in her head.

"Unveil me?" Tracy was getting worried. This might be more than she had bargained for.

"Relax, Tracy. It's just a figure of speech. Actually…I'm glad you chose Monday. You've got your work cut out for you this weekend to get it together before starting next week. When was the last time you went to the hairdresser?" Elaine laughed a little. "Look, I won't start in on you until our meeting tomorrow. You relax here a while. I'll slip my card into your locker with my home address on the back. Meet me there at two, okay?"

"Um…okay." This was obviously going to be a trip.

"Great. Look forward to seeing you then." Elaine left Tracy in the steam.

Chapter 5

Lord, who am I supposed to be? As Tracy drove to her new office in a brand-new silver Mercedes she thought of her weekend experience as surreal. The car was her "company car," but she was under strict instructions not to mention that to anyone. Elaine had insisted that she meet with Melvin, a personal shopper, who made sure all of the new suits and shoes in her closet were strictly the best designer names. Her crinkly uneven Afro had never looked better in her life and the highlights were to die for. Tracy had had a manicure and pedicure during her Elizabeth Arden spa visit late on Saturday.

She would have to clean up her house later. It was left a mess with all of the bags that needed to be put away. They were full of makeup, jewelry, hose, underwear, briefcases, coats (two cashmere and two fur), perfumes and every other thing that Elaine could think of to deliver to her house on Sunday. Fortunately, Elaine had provided her with a one-month advance on her salary and told her that her company credit card should be ready in a week. Tracy could use the card for meals and travel expenses.

Sunday, she had studied up on the company from the materials that Elaine had given her: annual reports, press releases, company profiles, brochures, glossy product-line photos and descriptions, a notebook with Elaine's calendar and on and on.

Tracy was confident about her ability to perform the assistant duties, but she wasn't so comfortable dressed as someone else. She had grown up a JCPenney, Montgomery Ward and Sears girl. When she became an adult, she occasionally added a suit from Marshall Field's, Carson Pirie Scott or Lord and Taylor, but she mostly trolled the racks at Marshalls, T.J. Maxx and Nordstrom Rack. She had never even seen some of the shops that the personal shopper had taken her to on the Magnificent Mile, Armitage and Oak streets. And the jewelry! He'd picked out an expensive assortment of watches, necklaces and earrings. She even had two evening gowns on order from a couture designer. These things all belonged to the company, unless she wanted to buy them from it. But for now, she kept her copy of the inventory in the desk beside her bed. Not including the car lease, Tracy figured that Elaine had spent more than $200,000 on her over the weekend.

Tracy drove her car to the garage that Elaine told her was used by the company and stopped at the gate. She slid the window down with a touch of a button, looking at the attendant. This woman would be the first to meet the new Tracy Middleton.

"Hi, I'm Tracy Middleton for Cathy Booker Foods." Tracy watched as the woman checked the list. Finding her name, she smiled and leaned out of the booth's window.

"Okay. You been here before?" she asked brightly.

Tracy shook her head. The attendant leaned dangerously out of the booth up to her waist and pointed. The movement wasn't necessary, because there was only one direction to go, but Tracy squinted at her instructions attentively.

"Drive up to the seventh level. You have parking space 712. To your right, you'll find the elevator to take you up into the building. Cathy Booker is on the thirty-fifth floor."

"Okay. Thank you." Tracy rolled up the window and followed the instructions. No one else was around her car as she gathered her briefcase and headed for the elevator.

As she boarded the elevator, she took a deep breath. *Here goes.* People joined her at various floors and she smiled at some uncertainly. She didn't know if any of these were her coworkers. The building housed a lot of corporations. When she got off at the thirty-fifth floor she followed a few others through the glass doors. They went their separate ways, while Tracy stopped at the desk. The receptionist was talking to someone on a headset.

"Joseph, this call's for you on line five…Hi. Can I help you?" she asked Tracy in a friendly voice, but with an unsmiling face.

"I'm Tracy Middleton, the new—"

"Oh, right. Hi, Tracy. Mrs. Newell is expecting you." The young woman punched some buttons and spoke into the headset. "Julia, Tracy Middleton's here for Elaine." She looked back at Tracy. "She'll be right up…Hello, Cathy Booker Foods."

"Uh, thanks." Tracy wandered away from the desk and viewed some of the artwork on the walls. From what she could see, the offices were bright and charming. It was nothing like the gritty chaos of a newsroom or the bleak starkness of some of the non-profits that she had worked for over the years. An older black woman was walking heavily down the hall, finishing off the last piece of a breakfast bar. She smacked the crumbs off her hands and glanced at her watch before looking at Tracy.

"Hi," she said extending her hand a few feet before she reached Tracy. Tracy took the woman's hand and smiled. "I'm Julia Lorrey. I'm Elaine's executive secretary. Please come this way."

"Hi, Julia." The woman walked fast and Tracy rushed to match her step. Julia talked even faster than she walked. Tracy leaned her head forward to catch everything as she tagged along.

"So, I guess you'll be my boss. I heard a lot of good things about you from Elaine. I would introduce you to some of the staff that will be reporting to you, but that will have to wait. You're part of the senior staff and there's a meeting in a few minutes, but Elaine wants to see you first."

They passed a large room of cubicles and turned a corner down another hallway. The décor was soft and pastel. The woodwork was light and there were glass-paneled conference rooms on each side of the room. When they reached the end of the hall, there was a long row of junior-executive offices with glass walls. Tracy smiled at anyone she passed in the hall and couldn't stop smiling. On first impression, Tracy was feeling that this corporate life was definitely for her.

Julia led her through a set of double doors and into a small waiting room. She spoke to a receptionist seated there. "Pam. This is Tracy Middleton."

"Hi, Tracy. Welcome." Pam said and stood to shake her hand. She was very pregnant, probably in her third trimester. Tracy spoke, smiling. She noticed that everyone was so professional looking. Even with her pregnancy, Pam had on a flattering suit and blouse.

There were four office doors, all solid wood. No one could see into these, but most kept their doors open. One was apparently Elaine's because it was another set of double doors and had her nameplate on it. Tracy started toward it, but Julia touched her arm.

"You may as well take off your coat. Your office is right here." She led her to the right of Elaine's door and twisted the knob, but the door didn't budge. "Oh, who locked this? I'll be just a moment. Let me get the keys."

Julia disappeared through Elaine's office. A man came out of one of the other offices, holding some papers.

"Pam, can you get me a copy of the marketing report before the meeting?" When Pam picked up the phone, he glanced at Tracy and then glanced back at Pam. Then Tracy saw his eyes register surprise as he looked back at her. He looked away quickly, knowing she must've seen how her beauty had unnerved him and Tracy watched as he decided to look again and speak.

"Hi." He smiled, crossing the room to extend his hand. She watched as a rush of color left his face. "I'm Marcus. You must be the new assistant Elaine's been screaming for."

"Hi. I guess that's me. I'm Tracy." Tracy took his hand. She thought his blushing was charming. He was the same honey color as Elaine, and his hair was cut very close with no facial hair. He had deep dimples that only appeared when he smiled, and his teeth were perfectly white, straight and the best feature in his smile. He had a soft look to his intelligent brown eyes that all but promised that he couldn't hurt anyone, despite his towering size. Marcus wasn't wearing his suit jacket and, in his shirt and slacks, Tracy categorically liked what she saw. The brother spent some time in the gym and he had the strong upper body and thick thighs to show for it. She didn't usually get flustered around guys, but this time, she felt something grip her in the pit of her stomach. He was really gorgeous. *And he smells good too*.

Fortunately for her, the door to her office opened and Julia appeared. "I'm sorry about that, Tracy. Come on in."

Marcus let go of her hand, and jammed his hands into his pockets.

"Well, welcome, Tracy. I guess I'll see you in a few...at the meeting," he said. His voice was deep yet soft. She noted that he wasn't going anywhere, just watching her.

"Okay. Nice to meet you." Tracy turned on unsteady legs

and just when she felt a little more composed, her office practically knocked her off her feet. As she walked through the door, the pile of the carpet became so lush that she nearly tripped. Julia closed the door behind her.

Tracy's office was really huge. It was decorated in shades of peach, pink and cream. The wood on her extensive desk was a high-gloss birch and was of contemporary style with rounded corners. Her view of downtown Chicago was magnificent and she could see the lake from her window. There was a small seating area with a couch and two chairs to the left, and to the right there was a glass conference table that seated four. In front of her desk were two peach leather chairs for visitors. Someone had made sure the office was filled with fresh, pretty floral arrangements. "This is *my* office?" Tracy dropped her briefcase onto the couch. She removed her coat in a daze, her eyes darting around the room, trying to take in everything.

Julia laughed. "Welcome to Corporate America. You like it, I gather?"

"Are you kidding? I love it." Then Tracy remembered that she was supposed to be some sort of sophisticated executive type and immediately dropped the *golly gee* look on her face. She looked at Julia. "I guess I must appear to be a rube or something."

"No, no. Not at all. Not many companies, especially *our* companies, still go all out like this...but you'd have to know Elaine and the kind of image she's determined to project."

"I think I'm beginning to get it," Tracy said, thinking back on her expensive shopping spree.

Julia took Tracy's coat and gestured to a door to her right. "Your secretary is right through there. Gina is filling in right now. She could be yours permanently, if you like her. But if not, we can interview candidates for you. She's young, but I think she's extremely competent and professional." She gestured to another door to her left. "That leads to Elaine's office. First, you'll pass through my reception area." She took Tracy's coat to a closet. "So, once you get your bearings, come right on in. Elaine is expecting you."

"Julia, how long have you been with Elaine?"

"Forever." She laughed and then smiled. "No really, about fifteen years. We didn't start out like this though." Julia gestured to the opulence surrounding them.

"Is she easy to work for?" Tracy moved behind her desk, but didn't sit.

"Aw, Elaine's a pussycat if you know your stuff. She keeps you on your P's and Q's, but you shouldn't have a problem. She's already been raving about the wonderful assistant she's found. You'll fit right in."

Tracy looked down and fiddled with the fancy pens on her desk. Julia stared at her.

"Look…you'll do fine. I know her, and she wouldn't even hire an assistant unless she thought that person was right. And that person seems to be you."

Yeah, right for her son. Tracy was unconvinced, but she looked up and smiled. She selected a notepad and started toward the door to Julia's reception area.

"Oh! Take her calendar. You, especially, always meet her with her calendar." Julia went through the door.

"Oh, right, thanks." Tracy went to her briefcase and got the binder containing Elaine's calendar. She hurried past Julia, who gave her a thumbs-up and opened the door to Elaine's office. If Tracy's office was huge, Elaine's office was enormous. And her view was magnificent. Elaine's was decorated more like a very classy living room with a big office area by the windows. She had a multitude of seating-area choices. Tracy stood nervously because she didn't see Elaine.

Then Elaine appeared from a door near the office area at the back of the room. "Tracy. Welcome. I was in the bathroom." Elaine gestured toward the couches, looking her over head to toe. "You look magnificent."

"Thank you," Tracy said and sat down on a comfortable floral couch.

"Very, very classy." Elaine stopped at her desk to get her calendar and joined Tracy on the couch. She put on her reading glasses.

"Thank you," Tracy said again, opening her binder to the current day. She wasn't sure what to expect but she wanted to be prepared. The calendar was a typed set of individual sheets that detailed Elaine's schedule hour by hour. They were in a three-ring binder so that, as entries were added to her schedule, Julia could print new sheets of any changes and provide them to those concerned. At the end of each entry were notations detailing her contact person, addresses, phone numbers, dress code or anything else to make Elaine's life easier. Tabbed dividers separated each month and Tracy had noted that Elaine's corporate life was mapped out until May of the next year.

"Okay, we have a meeting in a few minutes, but as you can see from the schedule, I also have a breakfast meeting with the Chamber that I'm supposed to be attending right now. So, I'm going to have to leave…not too long after I introduce you. Sean will handle most of the meeting, but I want you to pay attention to Marcus's report on the marketing team. They should have a more aggressive plan for the East Coast, but if he's still talking only about New York, tell him that I want to see the entire new market mapped out by the end of the week…*with numbers*. None of that theoretical stuff." Elaine paused and stared pointedly at Tracy. Tracy nodded.

"All right. I'll be back here—" She marked a meeting on the calendar at one. "—for the taste testing of the proposed dessert line. I've got a lunch with George Collins that's not on this calendar because I just made it this morning. Check

with Julia for a new page. I want you to talk to the public relations team right after this meeting. They'll tell you what
they're working on. Oh, and get with Julia about the invites
that came in and decide which ones look like something. If
you're not sure what I like to attend, assemble a meeting with
Sean and Julia, they know me best. I want you to join me for
the two o'clock career day at the high school tomorrow. I
already have a speech this time, but next time I want you to
write it. And call Cecelia Ferrell from…"

As Elaine talked, Tracy relaxed. So far, this seemed exceptionally normal. It was too bad about the niggling part of her
job. Every time she mentioned Sean's name, Tracy's heart
leapt into her throat. Listening to Elaine, Tracy knew that
what Julia said was true. Elaine couldn't and *wouldn't* trust
these kind of things to just anyone. She felt more confident
in all of the power Elaine was delegating to her. It was like
she was the CEO when Elaine was away.

Tracy thought back on the way she had talked flippantly
to her when Elaine first approached her and got a knot in her
stomach. She couldn't even imagine speaking to her this way
now. This was a smart and powerful woman. In these surroundings, Elaine didn't even seem as approachable as she did
at the health club or at her house—she was all business.

After her briefing with Elaine, they walked to the executive conference room together. Most of the people were as-
sembled and busying themselves getting coffee and pastries
or talking among themselves. Tracy counted eight people so
far. Elaine sat to the side of the head chair and Tracy took a
seat beside her. Elaine entered into a conversation with the
people on the other side of the table. They were talking about
the Bulls' game the night before.

Marcus entered, now wearing his suit jacket, and threw his
leather folder down on the table next to Tracy. She looked up
at him and he winked, then leaned down and whispered into

her ear, "You'd better follow my lead and get some coffee. Sean is going to keep us here forever."

His breath tickled her ear enticingly. Tracy smiled and pushed her seat back to follow him. They crossed the room to a rather large continental breakfast spread. Marcus grabbed a cup and saucer. Tracy opted for a tall glass of orange juice. Marcus noticed. "I was gonna make this cup for you. You don't drink coffee?"

"Not really," she answered, wrinkling her nose. "Coffee kind of upsets my stomach. Tea or orange juice is my morning routine."

"Oh. Well, Sean will knock that tea habit right out of you. He could put the dead to sleep with his nitpicking." He snickered. "I'll know he's gotten to you when you reach over and gulp down my coffee."

Tracy laughed. "You need to stop."

"Or fall over on the desk. I'm serious," he said, smiling and briefly placing his hand at the small of her back. Tracy felt tingly in the pit of her stomach at the small contact. "You'll see."

Tracy smiled and poured her juice. She narrowly spilled some on her suit when a young woman roughly bumped her arm, reaching past her for a muffin.

"Sorry," the young woman said flatly. She didn't look sorry at all. Instead, she cut her eyes at Tracy. Marcus looked past Tracy at the girl and they exchanged not-so-friendly glances at each other. Tracy raised her eyebrows and took a small plate of grapes and watermelon slices. *What's that about*, she wondered.

"Uh-oh, here goes," Marcus said and placed a pastry on his plate. He jerked his head in the direction of the door. Sean Booker had arrived. He moved through the room with brisk authority and everyone began to settle down. Their conversations tapered off, and those who were away from the conference table returned. He said a general "Good morning" to the room. He was much more handsome in person than his photograph had let on. He didn't really look like Blair Underwood. He really reminded Tracy of Marcus, except he was a pretty milk chocolate. They had similar puppy dog eyes, but Sean looked out of his more severely than Marcus. Thicker eyebrows framed Sean's eyes. Sean was also clean shaven with neatly cut hair. He was tall, over six feet and loosely muscled.

Tracy took her seat. Her stomach was turning over and actually growled. She quickly popped a couple of grapes in her mouth and hoped she wouldn't have to do the whole "tell us about yourself" thing. Her career had been so varied that she didn't know where to begin. Marcus spotted Pam at the door with the report he'd requested. He set his food down next to Tracy and went to meet her. From the head of the table, Sean's eyes followed him all the way back to his seat. Now, Tracy, seeing Sean's severeness, was certain that Elaine's nefarious plan wouldn't work. Sean hadn't looked at her once.

"All right. Good morning. First things first," he said, looking to his right at his mother. "Elaine, you want to introduce the new addition to our table?" Sean looked at Tracy. Tracy looked down at her blank notepad and picked up her pen.

"Yes." Elaine leaned forward on the table and intertwined her fingers. "You all know that I've been saying I need a competent assistant for months now. Well, I've found her and so far, I'm very pleased. This is Tracy Middleton." Elaine paused, touching Tracy's shoulder, and everyone said hi. Tracy smiled and waved a hand to all the faces at the table.

Elaine continued. "Tracy was at the top of her class at the University of Missouri, graduating *magna cum laude*. She has an extensive background in journalism and feature writing, and she was a producer at Chicago Metro Television prior to joining us."

A lot of the scrutinizing faces looked impressed. *If they only knew*, Tracy thought, but she was relieved that Elaine was doing all of the talking.

"It was difficult for me to convince her to leave that glamorous life behind and join me as my Mini-Me, but you can get anything you want for the right price." People chuckled at Elaine's small joke, but Tracy swallowed hard. *Was that a secret dig at me?* She wasn't prone to paranoia, but from what she had seen of Elaine, you could be sure that she would take every opportunity to assert her authority over her. "So, as hard as I worked to find her and get her here, I expect you all to show her the same respect that you would show me. We can start by going around the table and introducing ourselves so that Tracy can get an idea of who's who. Give your names and your titles. Marcus, you start us off."

"Hi, Tracy. I'm Marcus Hansen Booker, I'm the chief operating officer and vice president of marketing and external relations." He ended his little introduction with the kind of smile Tracy had been known to fall for in her past.

So he's actually a Booker. But she still thought it strange for a man to have two last names and wondered what the deal was with that. Was he married and had one of those new fangled marriages where both the husband and wife change their names to reflect their union? She hadn't spied a wedding ring, but not everybody wore one. Tracy had drawn a diagram of the table on her notepad and added each person's name and title onto her configuration as they gave them. This was something she learned to grasp people's names more quickly from her days of reporting.

She looked over at Marcus's notepad after he discreetly nudged her arm and saw that he was making funny notes about everybody as they introduced themselves. He wrote things like "Control freak," "Mr. Macho," and "Drama queen." Tracy tried not to laugh because, naturally, each one who introduced him or herself was looking at her. She met the chief financial officer, the directors of marketing, brand development, public relations, corporate administration, internal relations, manufacturing, external relations, the liaison to the board of directors, Julia, the foundation director, and lastly, Sean. He eyed Tracy levelly and then his gaze crawled over her notepad.

"And that comes back to me. I'm Sean Booker. President. Brand development, administration, and manufacturing report directly to me. Marcus handles what he told you and the rest report to Elaine. Which will be your primary area of focus. But I guess"—he paused, looking at Julia—"you can get her an organizational chart."

Julia smiled at Tracy, nodded and wrote it down. Sean shifted his notes.

"All right. The pressing issues have been whether we're going to produce a dessert line and increasing our presence on the East Coast. Tiffany, you have a taste testing this afternoon, but Brad, let's hear the report from manufacturing. What kind of numbers are we looking at to modify the plants for this kind of production? You have equipment costs and staffing information?"

"Right," Brad said and started handing around packets of his report. "Well, it's all going to come down to which desserts we actually want to produce. If everyone will open their reports to page four, you'll see that I give some figures on…"

Tracy stared at Brad, a handsome Latino, and then looked around the table at everyone. She didn't know if it was because she was happy to be at Cathy Booker or to finally have a job, but everyone—young and old—was very attractive. It could be because they were all well compensated, but these people looked good. She didn't really think that she stood out as any more appealing than anybody else and she certainly didn't feel as comfortably affluent as quite a few of them seemed to be. Plus, other than her skills, her affluence was all an act. Knockoff suits or not, Tracy would love to be sitting here as herself, not Elaine's dress-up doll. Tracy didn't realize she was staring at Sean until he glanced at her and raised his eyebrows amiably before looking back at Brad. *God. I have to watch that.* She made notes on her sheet about what Brad was saying.

Elaine got up and touched Sean's arm. He nodded. She crossed the room and whispered something to Anne, the director of public relations, pointing to Tracy. It was the girl who had rudely bumped Tracy's arm. She wondered what was up with her. Tracy had caught her staring at her throughout the meeting and Anne always looked away with an almost imperceptible roll of her eyes. Marcus had labeled her as a "Psycho" on his notepad. Tracy knew that Elaine told her to meet with Anne immediately following the meeting as they'd discussed. Maybe she would find out what was wrong with the woman during their talk.

Marcus was right. Sean wasn't boring, but he did ask a lot of questions about each point on Brad's report. An hour later, when he'd completely exhausted *all* the manufacturing considerations, he moved on to Marcus. Marcus and the director of marketing both shared the presentation of the marketing report. Tracy was disheartened to hear that the report wasn't as specific as Elaine wanted. They didn't have actual numbers. They recited projections from numbers available to anyone from *American Demographics* or *Target Market News*. She braced herself to deliver Elaine's message to have concrete numbers by the end of the week.

Tracy was startled when Marcus touched her arm while he was speaking to the table.

"…And before you say anything, *Elaine*, you only gave us this assignment last week and we're working on our own numbers. We're using these figures as placeholders until we can get that to you by Friday." Marcus smirked and everyone laughed, including Sean. Anne laughed with a sneer.

Tracy tried a smile, but her humiliation prevented it from holding. She wondered if her role as Elaine's mouthpiece was going to be considered a constant source of comic relief by the rest of the executive staff. Elaine had never had an assistant before, and after Marcus's comment, Tracy now thought that she would be received with barely concealed or open contempt.

Marcus continued with his report and Tracy only half-listened. On second thought, she didn't think she liked him very much. He seemed friendly and on your side, gossiping about what a bore Sean was and writing snide remarks about everyone else. Yet, Tracy saw that it cut both ways. His derision of Elaine had undermined Tracy's authority with the others. She had been planning to be cordial and make friends, but now she found it easier for her to adopt the cold exterior that Elaine wanted. No nonsense. She would deliver Elaine's instructions and not take any guff from anybody. She wouldn't be here if she weren't qualified. *And pretty.* She tried to push that thought down. It floated away easily enough, mainly because Sean was all business and apparently not half-interested in her. She took comfort in that fact and sat up straighter in her chair.

Half an hour later, as the internal relations director talked about the progress on the Christmas party, Marcus nudged her arm, with a small curl on his lips. "You ready for that coffee now?"

Tracy gave him a cold disapproving look and returned to writing her notes about the details of the party. Before she looked away, she saw his smile waver and a quick frown cross his gentle eyes. He got up to freshen his coffee.

"All right. I guess that's everything," Sean was finally saying after the report on the party. He looked at Tracy. "May as well save something for next Monday, or we'll never get Tracy back to this table. I usually don't hold long meetings, Tracy. But we have a lot on our plate right now. We're glad to have you aboard." He looked around the table. "If there's no other item…meeting adjourned." He spread his hands and leaned back in his chair. Immediately, several people stood up and some rushed to the front to talk with Sean, as though he were a celebrity who didn't appear in person that much and you had to grab him while you could.

"Don't you believe it," Marcus said to her. "This one was relatively short."

Ignoring him, Tracy stood and looked across the table at Anne, who was also looking at her.

"Let me take a break in the girl's room and I'll be over to your office," Anne said before Tracy could say anything. Tracy nodded. Marcus was waiting to walk with her to their offices. She rushed past him and he hurried to keep up.

"When are you going to grab lunch? We have a great dining room here, but if—"

"I've got meetings," Tracy said briskly. Marcus noticed the cool attitude.

"I didn't say when. I usually go late myself," he said. His face alternated between a smile and a frown as he struggled with what to make of her sudden distance. Tracy just blinked at him. Julia joined them, since she was going in the same direction, her chatter filling in the empty air between the two.

"Tracy, I'll get you that organizational chart right now. I have all the materials for Elaine, but she'll be expecting a briefing from you. Do you need me to put you on her schedule for this afternoon?"

"No. I'll fill her in on our way to that high school," Tracy answered. They'd entered the lobby to their offices and Tracy went through her office door and closed it. She had seen Marcus staring from the middle of the reception area floor, but she didn't care. She plopped down on her desk chair and took a deep breath. Right now, the pace and the responsibility were overwhelming her. She picked up the phone, intending to call her mother, but replaced the phone when she heard a knock at her door.

"Come in," she called, looking at the door in front of her. She jumped a little when a young woman entered from a door to her left.

"Hi. I'm Gina Callow? I'm your administrative assistant?" She looked professional, but Tracy noticed that she said everything in "up speak," where all her statements were delivered cheerfully as questions. This was usually attributed to young women from California.

"Hi, Gina," Tracy said, standing to shake her hand. "You're not from Chicago?"

"No!" She laughed. "Why? Do I have an accent or something?"

"Something like that. Have a seat." Tracy sat down and gestured to the chairs.

"Oh, I'm not going to take up your time. Anne Duncan is here to see you? I just wanted to see if you needed anything and introduce myself?"

"Oh…well, nice to meet you. Tell her to come on in." Tracy watched as Gina went through her front door and escorted Anne in. Tracy glanced at her watch and wondered if every day was going to be this formal and this packed with obligations. Though she couldn't complain. It certainly beat the unemployment line.

Anne said hello and sat across from Tracy, grim-faced. She had papers in her hands, but she didn't offer any to Tracy.

"Hi, Anne. Elaine wanted me to meet with the public relations team and go over your activities." Tracy smiled. The woman nodded and blinked, but still didn't say anything. She was cute, in a preppy, long-haired, pug-nosed way. She seemed to be Tracy's age, so she didn't think that her coolness toward her could be that Anne thought Tracy was too young to supervise her.

"So...what is your department working on?" Tracy continued with a withering smile.

"What do you want to know specifically?" Anne asked.

This was like pulling teeth. Tracy reflexively grabbed her pen and held it to a notepad.

"Well, are you planning any press releases on anything? This is my first day, so you should just fill me in on whatever you're doing. What kind of requests do you get from the media?" Tracy gave her a steely eye. She could see that this Anne Duncan was going to be problematic. But Tracy was confident in her power here, because she knew public relations pretty well. For years, a lot of her freelance work came from public relations clients.

Anne sighed deeply before handing Tracy a folder that she had apparently created for this meeting. Only she knew why she took such a long time to surrender it. "These are some of the past releases we've sent out, along with some that will go out today and again tomorrow. There's one about your appointment. We could use a head shot for some of the papers. Of course, I could use a complete résumé from you...that bit that Elaine gave us at the meeting wasn't enough," she said, with a sneer, and looked past Tracy out of the window.

"Naturally. I'll bring that tomorrow," Tracy agreed, thinking of a nice picture she had taken for the CMT Web site.

"Where did you go to school again?" Anne asked.

"University of Missouri," Tracy told her.

"Where?" Her brow knit as though she had never heard of it, even though the school had one of the best journalism schools in the United States. Anne was in public relations, so she should have heard of it. Tracy grasped the real meaning of her questioning. The woman just couldn't understand where Tracy came from and how she landed in such a high position.

Tracy wasn't going to play this game with her. And she thought Anne had a lot of nerve trying to take control of the meeting and interrogating her. It took all of Tracy's willpower to suppress her hot temper and not tell this heifer off.

She took a deep breath and answered calmly, "It's all in the résumé, which I'll bring tomorrow."

Anne stayed in Tracy's office for roughly half an hour, with Tracy intentionally prolonging the encounter to ask a lot of questions that seemed to work the woman's nerves. Elaine wasn't the only one who knew how to lord her clout over her inferiors. Not that Tracy felt superior to Anne, but she handled Anne as though she were the tough steed she needed to break to get the rest of the horses to follow along. There was always a leader of the pack in subordinates who was going to give you trouble, and Tracy suspected that this girl was the one. She had figured her right, because Anne fought her all the way.

At least, when she left, Tracy had a full understanding of the directives of the public relations team. Their meeting had been mentally exhausting and Tracy still didn't have any idea what the deal was with her. Judging by her preppy clothes— *who wears a Peter Pan collar, pleated skirt and pearls to work but an old lady or a prep school snob?*—Tracy guessed that Anne's true objection to her was based on elitism. Anne could probably smell someone who was not "of her class" like a pair of stinky sneakers. What really raised Tracy's hackles and caused her to grip the pen in her hand tightly, was that she had never strived to be an imposter. If she were wearing her own style, it would be clear to Anne Duncan that she was the artist and the idealist. She would meet the rest of Anne's public relations staff later that week. At that meeting, she would have to be prepared to counter any defiance from the group, which almost certainly would be encouraged by the attitude of their department head.

At 2:14, Tracy collapsed in her chair, clutching a stack of literature on the corporation in her hand. Her first day had

worn her out and it still wasn't over. She pressed her fingertips to her eyes and tried to remember what she was going to
do next. She dropped the slick stack of brochures and dialed
the phone to get Gina. Tracy had voice mail, but since her
message gave callers her secretary's extension in case they
wanted to talk to an actual human being, Gina was usually the
bearer of some of Elaine's important contacts.

"Yes, Tracy?"

"Could you bring in my messages please?" She whirled her
chair around to stare out of the window behind her desk. She
watched the buildings, gray skies and bustling streets as
though the panorama was created just to soothe her tired
mind. Within minutes, Gina came in and placed several slips
of paper in her hand. "Thank you," Tracy said.

"What time are you taking lunch?" Gina asked, looking at
the scene Tracy was viewing. The question was delivered
more for informational purposes than an invitation.

Tracy looked at her watch. "I don't know…I guess I
haven't worked that out so well yet."

"You should schedule it or, like, every day you'll miss
lunch? You've got to eat."

"Don't I know it?" Tracy said, smiling at Gina's back as she
went out the door. She was sorry to see her leave so fast. A little
friendly banter could break up her workday and ease some of
the pressure. She leafed through the messages to see which
needed to be answered first and turned around to face her desk.

"Are you busy?" Marcus asked. Her door was open, but he
leaned his long, loose body against the doorframe waiting to
be acknowledged. He had an amused look on his face, like he
had been watching her for some time.

"Come in," Tracy said, looking up briefly. He had removed
his suit jacket again and she glanced at the chiseled muscles
that were evident under his neatly starched beige shirt. She
looked away quickly and occupied herself by reading the

messages. Too much eye contact with him was guaranteed to make her stomach quiver unnervingly. And moreover, she was sure that if she looked at him outright, he would be able to tell that she found him extremely attractive.

"You won't believe it, but I completed the East Coast marketing report early and I thought I would run it by you," he said, striding through her office and taking a seat in front of her desk.

"Elaine will be back at about four, you can give it directly to her," she said, flipping through the notes for a third time. Flustered by his presence, she wasn't retaining one name or any meaning.

"True. But you would know if it's up to par and give me some pointers before I get yelled at." He gave a small smile, which she missed entirely. "If it's missing something, we'd still be able to fix it by Friday."

"All right, leave it there. I'll work it in," Tracy said in a bored voice.

Marcus placed the report on her desk, but remained seated. He stretched out one leg and leaned his arm against the chair. After trying to ignore him for a few more seconds, she looked up.

"I can't look at it now," she said, wondering why he wouldn't leave.

"If you haven't had lunch, maybe we could grab something and go over it now," he offered, watching her. His sensitive eyes were having the effect she was afraid of.

"I don't...I have so much to do." Tracy shook her head sadly.

"You've got to eat. Even Elaine has lunch." He wouldn't be deterred so easily.

"I know. Judging by her schedule, she's having it in some of the finest places and with some of the top people in the city," she said, relaxing a bit by remembering how approachable he had been at the meeting.

"Exactly, and you don't want to be accused of working

harder than even Elaine." He smiled. His mocking observation made Tracy recall the joke he made at the meeting earlier. She cut her eyes at him, not sure whether this was another veiled jab at her.

"Right now, I've got to return some phone calls, so if you'll excuse me," she said brusquely, moving her chair closer to the telephone and spreading the messages out by it.

The smile faded from Marcus's face and he leaned forward in his seat. He thought he knew why she had suddenly become aloof. He cleared his throat. "Look, Tracy, um, I tend to joke around and stuff. You know, to relieve the tension in the workplace. But if I offended you with that crack I made at the meeting, I sincerely apologize."

"Don't worry about it," Tracy said, but her expression didn't soften.

"No. Don't say 'Don't worry about it,' and then still hold it against me. I'm trying to clear the air here." He watched her face. When her eyes connected with his, Marcus dropped his gaze. He plucked at a crease in his slacks. As far as he was concerned, she was just too pretty. He had met her before and though she didn't give any indication that she recognized him, Tracy had never quite left his mind. To have to work with her every day and keep it professional was going to be a challenge. By coming into her office, he didn't know if he was rising to that challenge or giving up on it already.

"Seriously, everything's fine. We're cool." She shook her head, feeling silly for becoming touchy over such a little thing. She liked his straightforward manner. It was the way she always dealt with adversity herself—just confront any conflict head-on.

"We might have started off on the wrong foot, but why can't we grab a bite and go over this real quick? You got a boyfriend or a husband or something who's going to pummel me if you eat lunch with me?" Marcus worked in the question awkwardly and stole a fleeting look at her. He was a little disturbed by his clumsiness. He had never been smooth with women, but he wasn't usually this obvious.

"No. Nothing and no one like that. Just a lot to do." Tracy caught the gist of his line of questioning, but didn't bother to be more direct as to whether she was currently involved with someone.

"Like what? This is your first day. What could you possibly be working on that's more important than my report?" Marcus asked, teasing.

"Well, I have to return these calls for one thing. Then I have to bone up on the company and read all this stuff," she complained, placing her hand on the stack of brochures. Now that he'd gotten her to open up, she launched into a litany about her workload. "Not that I didn't read a whole bunch of stuff before I got here. Then I get here and…no, there's more. When Elaine gets back, I have to go over the speech with her for some high school's career day. And I took this with me from the taste testing, but I have to fill it out and turn it back in. Now you waltz in and want—"

"Whoa, whoa…hold on a minute," Marcus said softly, holding his palms out to her to calm her down. He was quiet until he had her eyes. He stood up and came around her desk, talking all the while.

"You were a producer at CMT. I know you've handled more things under a tighter deadline than this."

"Yeah, but here, I'm out of my element," Tracy whined. She watched him approach. Then he kneeled down right beside her, facing her desk. He picked up her messages, and started sorting through them.

"Let's see…Grunwald…Elaine doesn't want to talk to her," he said, tossing the note over his shoulder. It fluttered onto the floor. "Francis is just trying to confirm the high school career day." He placed that one down on her desk.

Tracy looked at him incredulously, but a little smile was creeping onto her face. "Chaplin has her cell phone. He's obviously trying to avoid her by calling your number." That one went over his shoulder too. "Anderson is from our plant. He calls about the same thing every month. Tell Gina to tell him to fax his report," he said, placing it on the desk. He squinted at the last note, holding it close to his face to read Gina's loopy handwriting. "And this one is from Elaine telling you to add something to her calendar, and she doesn't want you to join her at career day anymore."

Notes sorted, he put his hand on the stack of literature. "All this is about individual products and stuff. Who assigned you these?"

"Anne gave most of it to me. The other bit I got while I was at the tasting over in manufacturing. I thought I should read them," Tracy said, shrugging.

"Screw that. What have you read already? Annual report, marketing prospectus, financials?" he asked, looking at her. She nodded, loving the gentle way he was taking charge. His voice was so soft and calming, his cologne smelled good and he looked fantastic this close to her. She had to prod herself to pay attention to his words and not his lips. Her stomach twirled giddily.

"That's all you need to know. This is the kinda junk we put in our in-box and don't look at unless someone asks us about it." He grabbed a Post-it note from her supplies caddy and stuck it on the stack. He took a pen and scribbled, "Gina, please file" on the pile, reached for a rubber band, and after securing the stack together, he tossed it to the end of her large desk.

"Now," he said, taking the food survey in his hand. There were only ten questions. "Would you say that Sample A was better than Sample B?" He read the first question to her, looking at her in an overly serious way that was meant to be funny.

Tracy, who had been sort of astonished by his behavior,

now laughed at Marcus's efficiency. "I don't remember now, which was A or B or what," she told him honestly, throwing up both of her hands and sitting back in her seat.

"Yeah, you should've done it right then." He nodded, barely able to contain his smile. He crumpled up the survey and expertly tossed it in the wastebasket. "But since you didn't, it doesn't make a difference. We do consumer taste testing to determine if a product is going to make it to the market. They just hand those out to make us executives feel useful." He clasped his hands together and turned to her. "What else?"

"I was going to read Elaine's speech for career day, but now since I'm not going—" She shrugged, carefree, getting into the spirit of his impromptu stress relief.

"Who cares, right?" he finished for her and placed the speech within the items for Gina to file. "Now, that just leaves my report. Read it tonight. Tell me what you think about it tomorrow. It's not due until Friday anyway. Okay?" He touched her arm and rose to his feet. She felt electricity pulse through her body.

"No, I've got an hour before Elaine comes. I'll tell you what I think about it in a minute," she said, looking up at the man who was standing over her.

"See, that's what you're doing wrong. Don't put pressure on yourself to review it just because I barged into your office, asking you to take a look. If I said tell me tomorrow, run with it. You don't see me rushing to Elaine with it, yelling 'I got it! It's ready!' She'll get it when she gets it." Marcus cut his hand in the air and walked to the door.

Tracy smiled at him and happily held her face with both her hands. "Thanks, Marcus."

After he pulled the door open, he leaned against it and said, "Call Francis and confirm career day…then relax, Tracy. The job is not that hard." He winked. Before he disappeared, he intentionally closed the door behind him, indicating that she was not to be disturbed.

She smiled for a long time after he left, playing his actions over and over in her mind. How could she relax working so closely with a man like him day after day?

Chapter 6

When Tracy arrived home after six, she parked the Mercedes in the garage next to her Jeep and entered her house through her back door. She started peeling off her coat once she got through the door. Tracy could barely wait to take off her "costume" and put on some sweats and socks. She glanced at her watch. *Too late to watch Brian the Rat.*

Having been out of the workforce for a while, the day had drained her energy, but she was determined to work out. The only thing she had eaten all day was some fruit at breakfast and desserts at the tasting. She hoped that they would choose the sweet potato pie, caramel and lemon cakes for production. They were delicious, even with the preservatives and stuff. She kicked off her shoes and stared into the not quite empty fridge. *I have to go grocery shopping. Maybe pick up something for Mama too.* She closed the refrigerator door and thought that, all in all, she had had a pretty good day. Elaine seemed to be a normal boss, and now that Tracy was on board, she never mentioned the entice-Sean thing.

The phone rang and Tracy dashed on the hardwood floor to grab it in the living room. The sprint reminded her, once again, that she needed to get a phone for the kitchen. Before she reached the phone, she stopped dead in her tracks. *Scratch that. Elaine is a nutcase.* Someone had been in her house. Instead of taking anything, they'd left more clothes. She angrily pushed aside the new suits on her couch, kicked the new boxes of shoes at her feet and picked up the phone.

"Hello," she snapped. She glanced down at a beautiful pair of black pumps that fell out of their box and rolled her eyes.

"What's wrong with you? Today was your first day at work wasn't it?" It was her big sister, Tai. Tracy sat down, stretched out her legs and started to unbutton her suit.

"Yeah. What's up, Tai."

"Congratulations! Congratulations!" Tai sang her own song with the two words. Tracy laughed.

"Thanks."

"That was fast! First you're all sad and outta work, and then Mama told me last night that you were starting a new job today. I started to call you last night, but it was after nine and I said, that fool is probably asleep." Tai smacked her lips jokingly.

"You were right. I was," she sighed, picking up the shoes to examine them. *Jimmy Choos, big deal.*

"So you must not like it. You sound all dry." Tracy knew that she wasn't giving Tai much to work with, but Tai was trying to keep up the enthusiasm.

"No, I like it. I'm just a little tired. I just got in," Tracy said. She felt bad about not allowing Tai to enjoy this happy moment with her, so she perked up a bit. She dropped the shoes back into their box along with the bad mood. "Girl! You should see my office. It. Is. Phat!"

"Really?! What's your job at Cathy Booker? Mama didn't explain it well."

"I'm the special assistant to the CEO," Tracy told her.

"What? Like a secretary?" Tai sounded offended. Tai was a bank teller on maternity leave from her job. She had taken some secretarial classes at a community college as an adult, but she had been working since she was a teenager. She also made cakes for special occasions. Most of her clients were from her church, or referred by church members. All Tai knew was that she and her mother hadn't scraped to put Tracy through school for her not to use her degree, no matter how tough the job market.

"No. It's more like I manage her staff when she's away. Well, even when she's there. I have all these meetings, and I call her personal contacts, and I'm in on some of the decision making," Tracy explained, making more of her taste testing than it was, trying to distinguish her position from that of a secretary. "Oh! And I write too. Speeches and stuff."

"Well, that's good. Do you have a secretary?" Tai fished, trying to see if it really was an important position.

"Yeah girl. I make over a hundred thousand a year." Tracy thought that should put an end to *that* speculation.

"Say *what*?!" She could hear Tai screaming, "Kevin! Tracy done hit pay dirt with her new job! She's making more than you! Way more!" to her husband in the background. Tracy heard Kevin say something in reply. Tai replaced the phone to her ear. "Girl, Kevin says do you think you can hang on to *this* job long enough for us to visit you at it?" She started laughing.

"You and Kevin both know where you can kiss it." Tracy kissed teeth, but smiled proudly.

"Oh, my God! Girl, I'm proud of you. That is really great," Tai said.

"Thanks."

"Any cutie pies at work?" Tai asked, but before Tracy could

answer, she could hear Kevin saying something and Tai answer him. "Shut up, I'm talking to my sister. This here is girl talk." She turned her attention back to Tracy. "Anyway, he's talking about what does that have to do with her new job?"

"Everything!" they both said together and burst into laughter.

"So any prospects?" Tai pushed. Tracy's mind immediately went to Marcus. Her mind offered an image of Marcus looking strangely at her whenever he encountered her in their shared reception area and the unassuming way he had handled her workload. After his visit, she did not let the pressure of the multitasking stress her out again.

"There are definitely some beefcakes just walking around and looking as fine as they want to. The president is pretty handsome too, but he's almost off the market," she added quickly.

"'Almost off' ain't off," Tai said flippantly.

"Shut up. You didn't feel that way when Kev was almost off the market."

"Girl, I wish some hootchie mama would have tried to steal my man. I'd have sent that chick home crying. But Kevin wasn't no president. In that case, I know I would've had to stay on my toes…lose some of this fat, get my nails done, and wear my sexy stuff." Tai laughed.

Tracy laughed too, but felt uncomfortable with the picture Tai was painting. *Isn't that what I'm doing?*

"So, you're big-time now. You're going to have to update your wardrobe. Look like you belong. If you're making that much as an assistant, some of those people must be really rolling in the dough." Tai was suddenly filled with serious sisterly advice.

"I know." Tracy couldn't even tell her own sister about her situation. She sighed heavily. There had never been a point in her life where she couldn't tell Tai everything.

"How do they dress?" Tai asked, concerned.

"Oh, *definitely* designer duds. Girl, everybody looks good,"

Tracy said, thinking back on the people at the conference table and the others she had spotted in the hallways.

"When do you get your first check? Kev and I can loan you some money to get some new outfits and whatnot until you get paid," Tai offered.

Tracy looked at the pile next to her. Seven new suits. She looked at the boxes on the floor. Five more pairs of shoes. "No. I had a little savings left and I got a few things over the weekend."

"Nice things?" Tai had grown up with her. She knew quite well that Tracy had a preference for the eclectic.

"Yeah. I got some very nice suits and shoes," she said. At least it wasn't a lie.

"Well…you and I don't know Gucci from Pucci, but these people sound like the real deal. When you get your check, go hit some of those stores on Michigan Avenue. You got to *represent*."

"I'm fine. I look like I fit in."

"Well, lil' sis, you keep on making us proud and maybe we'll get down there to see you and Mama soon."

"What? I don't get to talk to my babies?" Tracy asked with urgency in her voice because Tai was obviously wrapping up their conversation. Hearing her little nephews would really make her day and take her mind off the call she had to make next.

"Kevin is giving them a bath right now."

"All of them?" Tracy said.

"The boys…and the baby is asleep. Plus, she can't talk no way."

"But she could listen," Tracy said hopefully.

"If she were awake," Tai said yawning. "But we'll be down there soon. Maybe we'll come after Christmas. But I'll have them call you on Saturday."

"Look…Tai. I'm making enough now to take more re-sponsibility with Mama. You and Kev got the kids. I could do her rent too."

"Tracy, give yourself some time to get on your feet. I know you been struggling with the house and all. We're all right for now. Put something away until you're sure this job is going to work out."

"But, she's got to move you know," Tracy said, reminding Tai of their mother's plight.

"I know it. She told me about them fools that moved upstairs. Teenage boys...who sit out on the front stoop," Tai agreed.

"What?" Tracy didn't know about them sitting on the steps. But their mother always did share more troubling things with Tai than she did with her. That's why Tai was also more protective of Tracy. "Then, this job has *got* to work out. We've got to get her out of there."

"We'll talk about that when I get there. It's gonna take the two of us teaming up on her to get her to leave that apartment. Maybe you should start looking around so we can offer her some alternatives. Maybe something closer to her job," Tai said wearily.

"All right, that's cool." Tracy felt better now that Tai had offered a plan. She wanted to push them to a resolution, but she didn't want to do all the heavy lifting. It was enough stress on her that she had so many new responsibilities at work.

"All right then, later."

"Love you girl. Bye." Tracy hung up the phone and looked around. *How the hell did Elaine's cronies get into my house?* She got up to check the doors. They were locked and not broken into or anything, but she had a bone to pick with Elaine Newell. She went to her briefcase and picked up her cell phone, where she had programmed in Elaine's number. She dialed.

"Tracy, hi," Elaine answered. "I guess you received the suits."

Tracy was taken aback by her casual attitude about the whole thing. "What the hell is this? Just because I work for you doesn't give you a right to break into my house," she said.

"Calm down, nobody broke into your house. Melvin used your key."

"My key? How did you get a key to my house?" Tracy's face was hot she was so angry.

"From your purse," Elaine said, like it was an everyday occurrence. "Look, Melvin found some more things that he thought would be perfect for you and I told him you were busy in meetings and just to get—"

"You are really unreal! You have a lot of nerve!" Tracy yelled into the phone with her hand on her hip.

"You're making a big deal out of nothing. Melvin's not going to steal anything. Maybe we should talk about this when you're in a calmer mood," Elaine said, condescendingly.

"Oh! How would you like it if I entered your house to drop off stuff without your knowledge?"

"I would expect it. You're my assistant and I trust you completely," Elaine said, unfazed. "Just to show you how much I mean that, I'll have a key ready for you tomorrow. Come and go as you please. I have an indoor pool that you can relax—"

"That's not the point," Tracy said more calmly, thrown by Elaine's compliance.

"That's *exactly* the point. You're in an entirely new world now, Tracy, and you have to stop thinking Third World. I expect you to be the kind of person who walks through that door, sees those suits and thinks, 'Oh, Melvin must've dropped these off.' The same way I would if I came through the door and saw some papers from you. I'd simply say, 'these must be the reports I was expecting from Tracy.'"

"The difference there is that you were *expecting* my papers. What if you woke up and I was sitting at the edge of your bed? Is that First World or Third World?"

"Point taken," Elaine said with a sigh. "It won't happen again. If he finds anything in the future, I'll tell him just to hold it in your name at the shop."

"Enough with the clothes already. You've already purchased enough clothes for me not to have to repeat the same outfit for at least a month." Tracy plopped onto her couch. Elaine didn't say anything. "Besides, I don't think you're going to get any satisfaction from my secret mission anyway."

"What makes you say that?" Elaine sounded suddenly concerned.

"I'm not Sean's type. He barely even looked at me." Tracy wasn't complaining, she was just stating a fact.

"Oh, I know my son, and he's definitely interested," Elaine said, obviously pleased.

"You don't know that. You were gone most of the day. I saw him in the executive meeting and that was it. There were no googly eyes or even a second glance." Tracy pushed the issue because if she was going to lose this good job over this stupid stuff, it had better be before she got too attached to the steady paycheck.

"Trust me, there are signs," Elaine said coyly. "You just have to know how to read him. But I was meaning to talk to you about Marcus. I see signs from him too…and need I remind you, he is not your target?"

"Sean is not my target either," Tracy said, finding herself again. Sheila didn't raise her to be some rich woman's plaything, or her son's. Plus, she didn't appreciate being told not to talk to Marcus. If she wanted to keep things cool between them, it would be *her* choice, not Elaine's.

"I'll let that comment stand because I know this isn't easy for you. You're a self-made woman and intelligent, and used to doing things your way…on your own terms. That's why I like you. You remind me of myself at your age. That instinct is how I built an empire." From the sound of it, Elaine was moving around her house. "But this is just a little exercise in thinking outside the box. You've got to leave your comfort zone to make big things happen, Tracy. Look what happened when you took a chance with me. You have a great job with a lot of power and a lot of money. All you have to do is keep on being yourself, and keep that sharp temper under a lid, and this will be the easiest half million dollars you'll ever make in your life. Who knows? A few years down the line, I could be looking at you as my biggest competitor."

Tracy thought about her words. She certainly hoped she wasn't like Elaine, because that could mean that she could potentially end up like Elaine—a controlling, cynical busybody. But on the other hand, Elaine was happy with Tracy's progress so far and all she had done was show up and do her work. If the rest of this silly commitment was going to be like this, maybe she could hang in there until the end.

"Whatever," was her eventual answer. "But tell Melvin not to buy me any more clothes. I've got a salary. I can buy my own clothes."

"I'm afraid he's found a couple more coats and some gowns for you, but I'll tell him that that's enough." Elaine chuckled. "He loves your stature and your figure. He said it's like dressing a supermodel. I guess he got carried away. He doesn't get to do that much with me anymore. But I was really something when I was your age...."

"Anyway..."

"Okay. Well, I'll see you at work tomorrow. What's on my schedule for the morning?"

"Your women's board at the Art Institute," Tracy said by rote, then realized that Elaine must know what she had to do first thing in the morning. She was just testing her.

"Great. Have a good evening."

"'Bye." Tracy put the suits away before changing for her workout.

Chapter 7

On Thursday morning, Elaine called Tracy to ask her to attend a meeting with Sean for a tour of a small company that produced a top-notch canned greens product Cathy Booker was interested in purchasing. Elaine claimed she loved her DuSable Museum board meetings and couldn't attend the tour, but she wanted Tracy there as her eyes. Tracy figured it was Elaine's way of pushing her closer to Sean, but she didn't argue. Obviously, Sean could fill Elaine in on the details of the company, but it was smarter to send two representatives just in case one forgot some of the more important details in the presentation.

It was only her fourth day at work and though she had become more comfortable in her knowledge of her job, she felt sort of nervous about the encounter. As far as Tracy was concerned, Sean was rather intimidating. She chose a gray pin-stripe suit, black stockings and black shoes, topped with a gray cashmere, full-length coat with a tie belt. The wind chill was bitter cold, but Tracy didn't have the nerve to wear one of the fur coats. It just seemed too pretentious; plus, she still wasn't sure where she stood on using the fur of animals for her own warmth.

Once she arrived at the office, Julia told her that the limo was waiting downstairs to take her to the plant. She dropped her briefcase, took her notepad and noticed that a key to Elaine's house was indeed left on her desk. She picked it up and went down to the limo.

When she entered the car, she sat alone. She wished she had thought to grab a tea. At least that would be something to do with her hands. She watched nervously as the chauffer opened the door for another passenger.

"Good morning," Sean said as he sat in the car. He had carried his coat and placed it on the seat between them. Tracy thought she should have done that. The car was really warm. His cologne smelled nice.

"Morning." Tracy instinctively moved closer to her side of the car and unbuttoned her coat.

Sean pulled some papers from his briefcase and began to look through them. He took out his pen and marked various sections. This was exactly what Tracy expected. He totally ignored her. She watched the city go by from the window. It was going to be a long trip. The company was a few miles out of Chicago in the southern suburb of Sauk Village. She thought of saying something, but he seemed really focused on his work. *May as well be comfortable.* She removed her coat and as she was struggling with the sleeve, Sean helped her.

"Thanks," she said. He nodded and went back to his notes. With nothing better to do, she marked some thoughts on her notepad. She should've brought Elaine's schedule. There was always something to plan there. But she wrote down the things she could remember about what she needed to do for the day.

They had made it to the expressway before Sean spoke.

"So what do you think about Down-Home Grown's prospectus?" he asked.

"Oh...I didn't have a chance to look at it. Elaine just told me this morning that I would be attending this meeting." She hated being unprepared. If Elaine wanted her to make an impression on Sean, this was a pitiful way of going about it.

"She didn't brief you on our position?" Sean's brow creased.

"No. I only know what's on her schedule. Where it's located...who her contact is...you know...basic stuff. She told me that you're thinking about acquiring them, but that's it." Tracy was sure that Sean gave her a look that said, *What good are you, then?*

"I'm pretty certain that we'll acquire them, but I don't want to look too interested. I wanted you to do most of the questioning. As the president, I was going to play it kind of detached. But if you don't know anything about the company, I guess I'll have to step in with questions."

"Sorry. I didn't know—"

"It's okay. I put the blame on Elaine. She knew, as the CEO, that there was no way she was coming. The president and the CEO would look like we were ready to buy. She should've gotten that report to you. Here, try to bring yourself up to speed on it now. I've marked some of the more pressing issues. If you can get those down, we should be all right." Sean handed her his papers and she made notes on the things he'd marked.

His phone rang and Tracy had no choice but to listen to his conversation.

"Hey, baby...No, I'm on my way to a meeting with Down-Home Grown...No, with Elaine's assistant, Tracy...What?... Anyway. No comment..." He smiled.

Tracy cringed. His fiancée had to have asked something about her. Out the corner of her eye, she glanced at him. It was the first time she had seen him smile. He had nice teeth, with cute pointy canines. She also noticed that his eyes were nice too. They weren't hazel, but they were lighter than the average brown. And his eyeballs were very clear, reflecting that he didn't abuse his body. Tracy thought his girlfriend was one lucky sister. Good black men were hard to find and she had one that was cute, confident and very successful. Brian was the only white-collar boyfriend Tracy had ever had. But Brian had been well aware of the ratio of successful black men to their female counterparts and he made the most of it—living like he was God's gift to women.

"So where are you going to be tonight? You coming by my place?" He looked at his watch. "I'll be there by seven…Please, don't start that again…I can pick you up." He rolled his eyes and glanced at Tracy. She pretended to really concentrate on her paperwork. "We'll discuss it when I get home. Now is not a convenient time…Okay…Love you too. Bye-bye."

Sean put the phone away. He still wore a small smile on his face. "Sorry about that."

Even though Sean intimidated her, Tracy wasn't the shrinking violet type. "Were you talking about me? I think you were." Tracy tilted her head with a mockingly mean look.

Sean flinched and then scratched his forehead, smiling a little. "My fiancée has a few insecurities. She asked me if you were pretty."

"Oh…so 'no comment.'" Tracy looked back at her pad.

"What could I tell her? That you are? Very pretty? I don't think I'd be able to go to work after a revelation like that. Or she'd tag along with me every day." Sean shook his head. "No, a question like that is best avoided."

"Uh-huh…but as a woman, I can tell you that she has her answer. You could've said no. I wouldn't have known what you were talking about. But since you said 'no comment,' she'll probably be in the office tomorrow to check me out." Tracy shrugged. It was easy for her to open up if someone talked to her honestly. Her ability to connect with people on whatever level they spoke to her was what made her stand out as a reporter and get the real story.

Sean squinted, thinking about what Tracy said. "You're probably right. I've no doubt raised her hackles. I'm already in the doghouse for not giving her a key to my house."

"What?" Tracy couldn't help it. She was shocked. "She's your fiancée and she doesn't have a key to your house?"

"Don't tell me you're taking her side?" Sean groaned, relaxing. He unbuttoned his jacket and turned more fully to Tracy. He was happy to have a young woman on the executive level that he could talk to candidly.

"I'm not taking sides. It's just that you don't trust people much, hunh?"

"Does it smack of issues of trust?" Sean asked seriously.

"Of course it does." Tracy chuckled because it was so obvious. She thought that Sean probably didn't do much soul searching. He no doubt led a charmed life and, without therapy, there was no reason for him to dig any further into his motivations for anything. "So when you get off work tonight, she couldn't be waiting for you at your house?"

"Well, no, but it isn't really a problem. I mean…we'll be married soon and then we'll share everything, including a home. She's only started complaining about it lately," he explained.

Tracy shook her head sadly and wrote down some more questions on her notepad.

"What?" Sean asked. Tracy shrugged.

"Look. I just got here and I love this job. So, I don't want to get in any trouble with the big boss." Tracy looked at her notes.

"My mother is the de facto big boss. So as long as she's happy with you, you can talk to me any way you like." His eyes twinkled at the prospect of her opening up to him.

"Yeah, right." Tracy playfully rolled her eyes.

He pressed. "No. Tell me. What are you thinking?"

"Well, it's no wonder she has insecurities. You say it's not a problem, but it is a problem for her or else she wouldn't keep bringing it up. You're not married yet, and you seem to base your intention to share everything on a piece of paper and a couple of I do's. You won't let her fully into your life until you're legally obligated to do so. If I were her, I would feel like you're holding on to your bachelorhood until the very last minute." Tracy looked at him. He looked out his window, squinting at the passing scenery.

"I don't feel like that's what I'm doing. Naturally, I'm only seeing her." He turned back to her and opened his hands, expressing his confusion and frustration.

"Well, I'm just telling you how it feels to us…as women. If you're committed only to her and you're going to marry her, why can't she have a key to your house? Elaine gave me a key to her house this morning and I'm only her employee."

"You sound like Ashleigh," Sean muttered under his breath.

"She's right, though. Do any employees have a key to your place?"

"No. I don't think I could do that. I think you're right about the trust issues," he conceded.

"Cleaning service, even?" Tracy tried her hunch.

"Oh. I guess they do have a key." Sean looked embarrassed, either at his pampered lifestyle or that he had forgotten that someone did have a key and it wasn't his fiancée. "Maybe I do have other issues. I guess I should stop on the way home and have a key made."

Tracy smiled to herself as she continued making notes.

"Are you engaged or living with somebody? Or, I don't see a ring, but you could be married."

"Me? No-no. I'm not seeing anyone. I'm just full of lots of unsolicited advice."

"I solicited your opinion. But I can't believe an—"

"Please don't start that 'an attractive girl like you' stuff. Relationships are difficult and not everyone is blessed with such pressing issues as 'will he give me a key to his place before he marries me' and 'is Elaine's assistant pretty?' Some people have real problems to deal with…relationship-ending problems." Tracy looked at Sean and he looked stunned. *Damn. Not making a good impression here.* "Look, I've got a big mouth and most of the time I'm good at controlling it, but sometimes it runs off by itself or it's just big enough for me to stick my foot in it."

Sean shook his head and, incredibly, started to laugh. "Don't apologize. I asked for your opinion and I definitely got it." He chuckled again, and adjusted a pleat in his slacks. "I guess I should've expected you to be like this. You would have to be a shoot-from-the-hip kind of person to deal with my mother."

"Now you can see why I live alone. I don't know how to behave in proper society." She shrugged and offered a smile.

"By no means am I proper society. Well, Tracy…I can see that your addition to the staff might shake things up." Sean smiled to himself.

"Is that good?" Tracy cocked her head at him, not sure whether it was a gibe, as if she was the colorful ignoramus whom everyone tolerated in the office because she was funny.

"Are you kidding? That's great. We could use some fresh blood on the executive level. There's Elaine, Marcus and me. And we all know each other too well to make any headway. Of course, there's Gretchen, the CFO, but she's housed over with accounting." Sean clasped his hands together and dipped his head at her. "Now would you please study the materials? I want you to ask the questions about the operations, and I'll handle the administration. Actually, I think your not being prepared might work in our favor. Your questions will appear more natural and come from their presentation."

"I'm glad you said that. It puts me more at ease." Tracy had something else on her mind and before he clammed up, she decided to ask it. "Were you opposed to her hiring me?"

Sean sighed. "She's only been asking for an assistant for about…a year, maybe. Six months? I'm not that good with time frames. I realize that she's getting older and needs help, but I was initially opposed. Not to *you* specifically, but to the fact that this person would be privy to our most confidential decisions and inner workings. As you can see, besides the support staff, you're the only non-family member in our office wing. But when Elaine gave me your background, in news and all…I thought she made a good choice."

"Thank you. So Marcus is your brother?"

"My cousin. But we grew up like brothers." Sean turned serious and seemed to want the personal conversation to end. "Study my notes please."

"Believe it or not, I've got it." Tracy nodded confidently.

"What? That fast?" Sean looked doubtful.

"Yep." Tracy looked at the papers. "Of the things you've marked. I've got that down."

"Really? How many different products do they offer?"

"Five. Collards, mustards, turnips and two varieties of mixes, one including kale and all flavored with turkey. They began their company in 1982 with mustards and collards shipping to locations in the Midwest and the South. Now they have a limited showing in the West and a strong presence on the East Coast, which is probably your main reason for wanting to acquire them. Each variety is offered in a sixteen-ounce size and everything but the mixed with kales is offered in a thirty-two-ounce size. They have this main plant in Sauk Village and another in northern Wisconsin. Down-Home Grown has 243 employees and the company is on its second ownership and run by a father and son. What else do you want me to know?" She was showing off now.

Sean quizzed her on their daily output and a few more points about Down-Home Grown and Tracy knew most of the answers. Since she was a quick study, Sean asked her to look over the financials.

When they arrived at the company to take a tour of the plant, they were instructed to wear paper hats and shoe covers. At least Sean looked as ridiculous as she did in the unflattering getup. Tracy proved to be worth her salary, asking the right questions at the right moments with such flair that Sean winked at her behind the owners' backs.

Tracy thought that he was really something to watch in action. The sharp shrewdness that he displayed in the office was even more acute in his dealings with outsiders. Tracy saw the owners trip over themselves trying to impress him. They offered all sorts of information about their operations that they seemed not to have planned to share, in hopes that Sean would maintain his interest in buying them out. Sean was noncommittal when he left, but with a date to get back with to on his final decision.

Tracy and Sean had a more natural rapport on the way back to the office and discussed everything from Down-Home Grown to the latest news. They arrived back downtown in time for lunch.

"You want to continue this conversation over lunch?" Sean asked as they exited the limo.

"That sounds good," Tracy said. There were some things she could do at her desk, but talking to Sean seemed a lot more interesting. She was learning a thing or two from him about how to operate a giant corporation and how to conduct yourself in these settings.

"There's a great Italian place right down the street from us. We could hoof it," Sean said, indicating the direction with a quick touch on her elbow.

"It says in your bio that you worked at Baldwin-Richardson Foods before joining your mother at Cathy Booker," Tracy said. She watched the eyes of people as they passed and she could tell by the prolonged stares that they must have made a striking couple. Not that she cared. *Right?*

"Yeah. I cut my teeth in the salt mines so that no one could say that I was just an inexperienced heir. Even though I have my MBA and have worked in various positions in the company since I was nineteen, people talk…you know."

"I know. You could be the most experienced person in the world, but people always want to cry nepotism at the drop of a hat."

"Not that it falls under that category, but yeah, that's what it would've been. I notice that more black CEOs' kids feel the need to justify their position by starting somewhere else than whites'. We're more critical of ourselves I think," he confided.

"Of each other too." Tracy nodded.

"What do your parents do?" Sean looked over at her. "Are they in business too?"

Tracy's penchant for identifying with his position had led Sean to believe she had gone through the same thing. She shook her head with a small smile on her face. "No. I didn't know my father. My mother works as a receptionist in a doctor's office."

"Oh, so she was a single mom?" He seemed interested and not judgmental.

"Yep. For most of my life. She had to struggle to raise us, but I think she did a fine job. Now, I'm trying to get in a position to take better care of her."

"From what I've seen, she's done an excellent job. How many siblings do you have?"

"One. A sister. My sister, Tai, lives in Minneapolis. She's…" Tracy almost stopped dead in her tracks, but managed to keep her feet moving. Brian Simmons was crossing their path as he exited a cab, right on the street in front of her. He came out of the cab with a woman and placed his hand at the small of her back. It wasn't Millicent. He glanced at them before going through the door of a restaurant. Tracy thought she saw his eyes widen at the sight of her.

Sean touched her elbow. "This is the place... You were saying?"

It was the same place Brian had gone into. Tracy stood still as Sean held the door for her. Several diners went through the door before her and thanked Sean for holding the door. She could see Brian helping the young woman take off her coat. He looked past Sean to try to see Tracy. She jumped back, out of his eyesight.

"So am I going to be reduced to a doorman, or are you eventually going to go in?" Sean frowned at her. In that brief moment, Tracy had forgotten where she was and whom she was with.

"Um...I just remembered that I really do have a lot of stuff...meetings and stuff that I have to do...." She glanced at her watch. "Yeah...right now. Sorry. I don't know what I was thinking. Look, you enjoy your lunch and I'll see you back at the office." She didn't wait for his response and turned on her heels to make quick tracks away from the restaurant. She had made three or four substantial strides before Sean caught up with her.

"Whoa. Wait a minute. What's going on? Hate that place? Don't like Italian all of a sudden?" He matched her quick pace, his breath making puffs in the wind.

"Sean, I'm sorry. I just better get back to work." She watched her shoes as she walked.

"Well, I'm not going to eat alone." He looked at her curiously. Even though she wouldn't make eye contact, he noticed that her face was cloudy. "You look like you've seen a ghost." He glanced over his shoulder at the now fading restaurant to see what he might have missed.

"I think I did. And there's no way I'm going in there to see it again," she said, waving a hand in the brisk air. She didn't mean to tell him the truth, but seeing Brian had thrown off her professional demeanor. Sean's brow wrinkled as he thought back on their progress. He recalled an attractive couple crossing their path.

"Was it the guy or the girl?" he asked quietly.

"What?" Tracy looked up from her shoes at Sean.

"I remember a couple just when you stopped talking. So which one were you trying to avoid?" He didn't look at her and stuffed the hand that wasn't holding his briefcase into his pocket.

Tracy smirked and shook her head, thinking about Brian. "Him...she's just the flavor of the day." She looked at Sean earnestly. "Look, I'm sorry if I overreacted, but I really don't want to see him."

"He have a name?" Sean's eyebrow rose.

"Yeah. 'Ratface' is my favorite," Tracy said seriously. Sean laughed. Glancing over at him, she laughed too. She was so caught up in the moment she hadn't realized she had said this to her boss.

"So he's one of the problems that women might have that's more serious than 'will he give me a ring or not?'" Sean watched as Tracy nodded. "We could've gone somewhere else."

"No. Maybe some other time. I lost my appetite," Tracy said. Because she was walking so fast, they had made it back to the office sooner than they'd gone down the street.

They were entering the lobby just as Anne and some other young women, mostly other directors, were going out for lunch. Their conversation got quieter as they spied the two top executives. Anne pretended to be buttoning her coat and not really looking, but she said something under her breath to a girl named Alice that made her laugh and look at Tracy.

As they passed, they stopped talking and Anne said, "Hi, Sean," childishly snubbing Tracy. At least the other women said a general "hi" to both of them. They weren't foolish enough to pick a fight with someone who had the president's and CEO's ear. Obviously, Anne felt some sanction to do as she pleased with no fear of reprisal. Tracy had had such a good day talking to Sean that she thought of asking him what the girl's major malfunction was. But, after her running from Brian, she thought the question would make her out to be some silly woman. She could just imagine him thinking "rrroowr" and doing the cat-scratching thing with his hand in a paw. It was unfair how some men reduced just about every disagreement between women to a catfight, even if there were legitimate observations of intentional disrespect.

As they entered their office foyer, Tracy and Sean were laughing with each other about how well Sean had handled Down-Home Grown's owners. Marcus was leaning behind Pam at her computer. They looked up as they saw Sean and Tracy come in. Before separating to go to their respective offices, Sean lightly touched Tracy's arm. "We'll have to do this again sometime, but with the expectation that you complete your lunch with me. After all, I am your boss," Sean joked.

"Yes, sir." Tracy smiled and gave him a brief salute before turning into her office.

Chapter 8

Sean was still smiling as he removed his coat and hung it in the closet. When he walked out of the closet, Marcus was waiting to talk to him.

"What's up, Marc? I didn't hear you come in." He moved to pick up his briefcase and place it on his desk.

"Have a good meeting?" Marcus asked through hooded eyes.

"Yeah...we should wrap with Down-Home Grown by the first of next year." Sean sat at his desk and glanced at Marcus. It wasn't like him to come in with no purpose, so he continued talking until Marc was ready to get to the point. "Their plant looks good...of course, we'll need to visit their other plant after Christmas. You could do that, actually. Take Brad, so manufacturing can get a better idea of the expected changes."

"What? I don't get to take Tracy?" Marcus said sarcastically.

"Excuse me?" Sean cut his eyes at Marcus.

"You two seemed awfully friendly. Laughing and promising to meet again for lunch soon." Marcus crossed his arms over his chest.

"I don't think I like what you're implying. I'd advise you to tread carefully here." Sean stared at Marcus.

"Or what? Risk termination?" Marcus said, sneering and taking a seat in front of Sean's desk, slinging his leg over one side of the chair. Sean's phone buzzed.

"Yes?" Sean said, pushing the intercom and never taking his steely eyes off Marcus.

"Hi, Sean. If you're back, I could come in." The disembodied voice of his secretary boomed from the speaker.

"Lila, give me a minute. I'll call you in." After getting her agreement, Sean cut off the phone. "Marc, if this is about what I think it's about, you need to get a grip. And you don't have the right to question me."

Marcus snorted and looked to his right at a painting on Sean's wall without responding. He absolutely had a right to question Sean, knowing his history with women while they were growing up.

"She's my subordinate. I've never been accused of any impropriety with employees and I don't intend to start now. You seem to forget that I'm engaged to be married," Sean said, unsnapping his briefcase and pulling out some papers.

"*You* seemed to forget that, if you ask me," Marcus said, the cloud not disappearing from his face. "And, as I recall…you never felt any woman was off-limits if you wanted her."

Sean had been holding his report, planning to make notes on the meeting, but he put it down on his desk. He leaned back in his chair, his hands resting folded in his lap, and devoted his full attention to Marcus. "I wonder…you've read a lot into a brief encounter that you witnessed and you seem pretty hot about it. I think at this point, I should remind you that she's *your* subordinate as well."

"I know that, Sean, but you don't see me chatting her up." Marcus's eyes locked on Sean's.

"Was I chatting her up? I was talking to an employee. Ending a pleasant morning with Elaine's assistant." Sean raised an eyebrow. "Your interest is troubling though. Or should I say your jealousy?"

Marcus stood up, speaking just as evenly as Sean. "You can play the innocent role with me, but I know you. I'm just making sure you're not backsliding into your old ways. Tracy is just the type of girl you would stick on your arm—"

"Back in the day maybe, but—"

"The *day* was just seven months ago, before you met Ashleigh," Marcus countered.

"The end result being that I *did* meet Ashleigh and I'm marrying her. I didn't expect that pretty girls would cease to exist just because I've narrowed my choices down to one. I *do* have something called 'self-control' and I should be able to interact with Tracy without the third degree from you. If you're going to fly off the handle every time you see us together, you'd better exercise some restraint or find another job. We're all going to be working together, Marc, and I don't want to have to have this conversation with you again." Sean leaned forward on his desk.

Marcus took a deep breath and headed for the door.

"Marc," Sean called out.

With his hand on the doorknob, Marcus turned to look at him.

"We don't have a policy against employees dating and you've made your interest in Tracy quite clear. But I would advise you against pursuing a relationship with her. These kinds of things can get messy. Remember what happened between you and Anne Duncan? You're the one who could use some guidance in viewing Cathy Booker as your personal dating ground."

"That was a long time ago and she pursued *me*. I haven't

looked at an employee since," Marcus said, irritated at Sean for reminding him again about his short-lived relationship with Anne.

"Yet...now Tracy's caught your eye?"

"I won't even dignify that with a response." Marcus shook his head.

"You don't have to. It's pretty obvious with this pissing contest of yours. But anyway Tracy's not over some guy that broke her heart."

Marcus was convinced that Sean threw that out calculatedly to further rile him. The cousins had a long-standing competitive relationship and, on occasion, couldn't resist pushing each other's buttons.

"Oh? So she shared this with you during your *innocent* lunch with an employee?" Marcus released the door handle and fully faced Sean, crossing his arms over his chest.

"We didn't have lunch...and yes, she did." Sean let it stand at that, not sharing anymore on the subject. "You're obviously attracted to her, but what did you think you were going to do about that?"

"I don't have any intentions, Sean, and my attraction is irrelevant. Tracy is obviously a very beautiful woman. I'm just making sure that the policy is hands off. On both our parts."

"Works for me." Sean opened his hands innocently.

"Cool," Marcus said and left. Hot blood and testosterone had compelled Marcus to barge in and challenge Sean, but he was now having second thoughts about his impulsive actions. Despite his assertions that his attraction was irrelevant, his interest in Tracy was exposed, akin to wearing his heart on his sleeve. Like a fool, he only had himself to blame for revealing his hand to Sean.

Before Ashleigh, Marcus knew that Sean was not one to be trusted around a girl that he liked. The major rift between him and his cousin, besides the psychological stuff created by

Elaine, was that Sean seduced the one girlfriend Marcus had genuinely loved. And he would never forgive him for that. But he would have to take comfort in the belief that Sean didn't know if he was truly interested in Tracy or had just come in to stir up one of their periodic confrontations.

Marcus left Sean's office and returned to Pam, who was assisting him in creating a pie chart. Just as Sean had intended, one thought remained with him. *She's not over some guy who broke her heart.* He hoped it wasn't true. Because he knew exactly the guy Sean was talking about. Brian Simmons, the anchor on CMT. Marcus had met him a little more than two years ago, when he was just a star reporter.

He and Brian served together on the board of a small community hospital that was desperate for corporate support and publicity about their health programs and free services. They gravitated to each other because they were the two youngest members on the hospital board, the others being in their fifties to seventies. Both men were really too busy to carry on a friendship in any way women would consider substantial, but for them, bonding over their love of sports moved them beyond the realm of associates.

In fact, it was at the annual golf outing, when he and Brian were matched in a foursome with a couple of older guys that their friendship began. He and Brian shared a golf cart and got to know each other. After that, Brian would invariably invite Marcus out to a "just the guys" sporting event. Marcus didn't often get to return the favor, because as a television personality, Brian was far more likely to have complimentary box seats to the Cubs, Sox, Hawks, Bears and Bulls games. They talked about girlfriends, but never brought them along.

The day he met Tracy was not as Brian's girlfriend, but as a producer at CMT. He recognized Tracy the moment she had walked into their offices at Cathy Booker, and he wasn't truly surprised when she didn't seem to remember him at all.

About a year ago, Cathy Booker Foods and CMT were two of five major sponsors for a community event for kids. It was the first of what would become an annual day of go-kart racing for African-American children in the Chicago housing projects. A large oil company provided the go-karts, Cathy Booker provided the food and CMT was there to cover the event. The other two sponsors were an R&B radio station and a kids' cereal brand.

Tracy had turned his head the moment she walked onto the scene. He remembered that she emitted an air of smart, uninhibited confidence. Unlike the way she presented herself now, back then she had a funky style that let you know she was one of a kind. She wore ragged-bottom faded jeans with a nice designer blouse, Dr. Marten's boots and cool ethnic jewelry, long before he began to see it on other women.

She had arrived to prepare for the interviews long before Brian, just checking out the event and chatting with the other event organizers. Marcus had talked to her for a while that beautiful, breezy summer day. He made general conversation about how much fun the kids were having at the event, all the while checking out her flawless skin, funky hair and perfect body. He was working his way up to asking for her phone number and suggesting they get together sometime, when Brian finally got there. They greeted each other jovially and Brian told her that they were buddies. But with Brian's arrival, Tracy was primed to get right to work. When the crew arranged the major sponsors for an on-air interview, he was surprised to find out that she was the producer of the segment; she seemed too young and relaxed to be the one running the show. Watching her in action was like watching a maestro conduct an orchestra. She skillfully executed the arrangements of the broadcast like a production master.

After they finished a couple of live broadcasts, she and the crew stuck around to join in the fun before returning to the station. Marcus had to return to manage the Cathy Booker booth, but he made frequent glances in her direction throughout the event. Tracy and Brian paired off and it was evident to Marcus that Brian was more to her than a star reporter. Marcus watched her interact with him and her whole demeanor changed. Her face lit up like Brian was the only man in the world, which probably attributed to the reason Tracy didn't even remember that they had met.

He remembered how, after Tracy had already gone back to the van with the crew, Brian had stopped by the booth before leaving to give him a handshake and plan to meet again.

"All right man, I guess we're out of here," Brian had said, gripping Marcus's hand and pulling as only a black man can.

"All right, take it easy. So, what happened to your beautiful producer? I'd rather say good-bye to her," Marcus joked clumsily, trying to find out if she was involved with him or just infatuated. He had never heard Brian refer to his girlfriend as anything more than "the woman" or "my girl." He didn't think he had ever heard a name.

"She went back with the crew. I would've rode with them, but I have to go and interview this brother on the west side for a story I'm working on," Brian told him, then moved closer to him, stretching his arms above his head. He said in a rather low voice, "You know that's my girl. Tracy."

"No," Marcus had said, trying to suppress his disappointment. "That's your woman? Why didn't you say so when you came over?"

Brian had shrugged. "We keep it under wraps at work and all, and I didn't know who was around, but yeah…that's her."

"Well, you did all right for yourself. I'd scream it to the rafters if I was her man," Marcus said, figuring that honesty was the best way to hide his envy.

"Yeah, but you know how these sistahs are. You act like you

like them just a little bit and they're ready to start telling you what to do. Swear you're ready to march down the aisle. Tracy's fine, but I'm keeping it loose…keeping my options open." Brian smacked his fist into his palm, and as a demonstration of his words, he allowed his head to rotate along with a passing young woman's big booty in tight jeans.

"I hear ya," Marcus said, but didn't mean it. Even though he had been burned in the past, he still believed in giving his all in a relationship. If it failed, it failed, but at least he had been willing to fall in love. After Brian had left with promises to get together for a Cubs game soon, Marcus racked his brain for any references Brian had made to Tracy and came up with very little. When he saw him again, true to his word, Brian acted like a free man, chatting up women like he didn't have a care in the world, or a beautiful, intelligent, sexy girlfriend.

Marcus didn't understand how Brian could be so indifferent to Tracy, when she had remained on his own mind for months afterward.

Now he glanced over at Tracy's door and saw that it was open a crack. He walked to the middle of the foyer and debated whether he should go in or not. Throwing his shoulders back, he pushed the door open, intending to say something flippant about her morning with Sean. The mischievous grin he'd adopted faded from his face when he saw Tracy standing with her back to him at her office windows. Her arms were wrapped around her body in a self-embracing hug. As he watched her, he was alarmed at the incredibly happy and content body language. At this point, he became concerned that what had happened at their lunch was more than Sean let on. Was he too late again? He leaned against her doorframe, crossing his arms over his chest.

"Got a minute?" he asked, placing a million-dollar smile on his face as though he wasn't bothered by how blissful she looked after her outing with Sean. Tracy whirled around, startled that she wasn't alone. "Or, am I interrupting?"

"Oh, what's up, Marcus?" she asked, unconvincingly trying to establish an air of professionalism. She couldn't make eye contact with him and busied herself looking through her briefcase as though she were trying to find something. In the presence of Marcus, Tracy felt strangely ashamed at musing about how much she was beginning to love her new job. She had this beautiful office. She had just held her own in a site visit with her boss, and had even made an embarrassing gaffe over Brian, and it wasn't held against her. Despite the crazy plan of Elaine's, and although she would have never sought a position like this on her own, she really thought she fit into this kind of corporate environment. The only thing she had to watch out for was her attraction to the man in front of her. From head to toe, he was pure temptation. Hands reassuringly on some paperwork, she looked up to watch Marcus stride assertively across the room to sit in a chair in front of her desk.

"You look pleased. Everything go okay with Down-Home Grown?" He folded his hands together between his knees, striving to look innocently interested.

She looked at the small dimple in his cheek before answering. "It went great actually, we talked to the father and son owners. You should've seen the way Sean handled them, he—"

"So you and Sean look like you had a good time," Marcus said, not really sure what he'd intended to find out when he had decided to come into her office, but he was certain that he didn't want to hear about Sean's magnificence.

Marcus only became conscious of the fact that he had rudely interrupted Tracy when she cocked her head at him suspiciously, and didn't say anything. "Oh, sorry…you were talking about the brilliant Sean?" Though his nature was usually lighthearted, his words dripped with bitterness. He had been second fiddle to Sean for as long as he could remember, and with Tracy singing his praises—this fine, sexy woman that he truly desired—he could no longer conceal his resentment.

Tracy lost her enthusiasm for the story after Marcus cut her off. Accustomed to getting half of the story from intuition, she was beginning to understand that all wasn't as lovey-dovey between Sean and Marcus as their shared last name would imply. "He is brilliant actually, but obviously, you don't want to hear that," Tracy stated in her usual honest manner.

"No, no…please elaborate," Marcus said sulkily. Now that she admitted that she liked Sean's mind, at least, he was reluctantly willing to find out how much more she found interesting about the boy.

Tracy shook her head sadly at their whole, messed-up family. She was famished and mentally exhausted from being thrust into an intimate situation with Sean, studying the materials so fast, being put on the spot to ask questions at Down-Home Grown and seeing Brian, that she let out a sigh. Marcus was not about to add to her stress. She was determined not to lose her good mood though and perked up. She would just have to turn the tables on Marcus and pick his brain. Maybe she could figure out what was going on here…in the entire place. "All right, if you're going to grill me, at least let's do it over lunch."

Marcus's dour face turned to unbelieving surprise. He cocked his ear toward Tracy. "Say again?" He watched as she emerged from behind her desk, placing her small purse on her arm.

"Today's your lucky day. You get to show me this beautiful cafeteria I've heard so much about." She stood over him because he still wasn't moving.

"I thought you ate with Sean," he said, sincerely unaware. His history with Sean told him that just because Sean said that he and Tracy hadn't had lunch didn't necessarily mean it was true.

"We didn't have a chance to get lunch," she explained and rolled her eyes, exasperated that he was still in the chair. "And you and I won't get a chance to either if you don't get up outta that chair."

"Oh, right," he said, rising to his feet. "But you didn't hear all that about the cafeteria being great from me." He went and opened the door for her, his mood dramatically improved. "We'll be lucky to find anything palatable up there."

"You always got jokes," Tracy observed, twisting her lips at him. "But I suspect you're not as cynical as you pretend to be."

"Unfortunately, I really am." He smiled. As they entered the outer office, Marcus called rather loudly to Pam, "We're going to grab some lunch. We'll be in the cafeteria." She barely glanced in their direction and gave a little nod. His comment wasn't made for her benefit anyway. Marcus looked toward Sean's office, but his efforts at one-upmanship were thwarted when he saw that Sean's door was tightly shut against his triumph. He knew it was juvenile, but Marcus could only hope that Sean would see them together when they returned. Sean aside, the opportunity at hand was the attractive lady beside him.

"Why are you always cracking on the company and, uh, everybody?" she asked, her eyes narrowed at the memory of the ire he'd raised in her when he made that quip about her at the meeting. "You must like Cathy Booker. It's your family's corporation," Tracy said, trying to summon her old interviewing skills to get to the bottom of their family's dynamics.

Marcus looked at her and for a second she caught something serious in his briefly wrinkled brow. He pressed his lips together and then looked at his shoes. "Yeah, my *family*," he said, barely audibly. The elevator arrived and he stepped aside to let the people out and Tracy in before entering. They weren't the only two on it, so she decided to hold her questions until they sat across from each other at lunch.

The cafeteria was, in reality, quite nice, covering the entire floor and offering stunning views of downtown Chicago with the same kind of floor-to-ceiling windows that were in the Cathy Booker offices. Fifties' diner-style seats and tables were in the center of the room, radiating out from a rather large and varied salad bar. Around the perimeter of the room opposite the windows, there were different hot food stations from which to choose. Tracy spied Mexican food, an American grill offering hamburgers, hot dogs, Polishes and the like; and then there was the standard meat-and-potatoes kind of dinner. She even saw that Cathy Booker Foods had its own station offering a sampling of soul foods to the building's other tenants.

"I guess we should patronize the company," she offered, gesturing toward their corporation's service area.

"Please." Marcus sucked teeth and then twisted his lips in disgust. "I'd rather eat glass than select a Cathy Booker meal on my own time."

"See, there you go again," she said, nudging him. "You don't want the other workers in the building to hear you saying that. They'll think something's wrong with the food, instead of the truth."

"What truth?" Marcus asked, dumbfounded.

"That something's wrong with you," Tracy chided him. Marcus had to smile at his bad attitude.

"Look, if they had to eat it at every function that we had with guests, year in and year out, they'd sympathize with me completely. Look at all the people standing in line…not one of them is a worker for CBF." He pointed a finger at the gathered crowd of mostly white men with their trays.

"Well, I'm going to try it. Usually you just get it frozen. I've never had it fresh."

Marcus knew better. She had eaten the food fresh from their kitchens at the go-kart event where he first met her. It remained vivid in his mind because it ticked him off when she passed a plate to Brian that Marcus had prepared for her himself. As an executive of the company, he wasn't in the habit of serving plates at events. But he couldn't find a way to mention that to her without looking like a chump. "Okay, pick a table. I'm going to get a burger."

Tracy grabbed a tray and got in line at the Cathy Booker counter. The food had the familiar look of a soul food buffet: greens, macaroni and cheese, smothered chicken, turkey and cornbread dressing, fried chicken, pork chops, green beans, mashed potatoes, ham, black-eyed peas, rice and gravy and a chicken gumbo. Her mouth watered at the vast selection as she waited in the long line. She was hungrier than she thought, but she kept changing her mind about what she was going to get. When she finally got to the front of the line, she chose the turkey and dressing with green beans. Marcus walked up while she was waiting to pay for her order. He pulled her arm to get her out of the line.

"What?" Tracy smiled, not sure what he was up to.

"You don't have to wait here. You're an executive with the company." He escorted her to the cashier. They stood behind the people who were paying for their food.

"Hey, Franklin," Marcus called to get the man's attention and pointing at Tracy over her head.

"What's up, Marcus," he said, noticing them and smiling broadly. "Who you got there?"

"Tracy. Elaine's new assistant," he told Franklin.

"Hi," Tracy said, smiling.

"All right. Okay, welcome to the family," he said, nodding at Tracy. "I'll definitely remember you next time you come through."

Marcus pulled her away, showing her to the table he'd secured. "You were actually going to pay for that?"

"I didn't know. I wanted to support the corporation," Tracy shrugged, setting her tray down.

"You support the company enough by just working here every day. Nobody has to pay to eat at our own counter," he told her. He waited for her to sit before sitting across from her.

He pushed one of the plastic glasses of iced tea he had retrieved to her side of the table. Tracy thanked him. "It usually works out because people who work at CBF would rather eat elsewhere."

"I prefer to call her Cathy," Tracy said. She sampled a bite of her food. It was really good, like someone had made it at home. She dumped the little cup of cranberry sauce on her dressing and mixed it in.

"Who?" Marcus smiled. "The company?"

"Yeah. Men love acronyms. But women usually like the personal touch. I work for Cathy. CBF sounds so cold and heartless," she said.

"You don't know Cathy," Marcus teased. He bit into his burger. "She seems nice now, but once you get to know her, you'll see that CBF fits her personality."

"Are you confusing Cathy with Elaine?" Tracy squinted at him.

"Cathy is Elaine and Elaine is your Cathy." He ate some of his fries, then picked up his burger again, biting a large chunk. It was juicy and he needed to hold it over the plate to prevent it from soiling his clothes.

Tracy shook her head. "I don't see it that way," she said. She couldn't accept Marcus's assertion, or else she would feel trapped. In her mind, she had to separate her feelings about Elaine from her job with the corporation. "All of these people…how many employees do we have?"

"Over three hundred," Marcus said, wiping his mouth and hands with a napkin.

"Right, over three hundred employees, who have taken the company beyond Elaine's original concept. You heard what that guy said. That guy Franklin, he said, 'welcome to the *family*.' Not to mention the consumers. We collectively shape Cathy," she said. She put another forkful in her mouth. She pointed to her plate with her fork. "This is really good."

"That's how they want the employees to feel, but the real deal is that Elaine and, worse, Sean run the show. You, me and the 298 others don't shape anything," Marcus said, unimpressed.

Tracy narrowed her eyes at him. "What is the deal with you? You are so negative."

Marcus looked surprised and embarrassed. Tracy watched as a wave of emotions crossed his face. Clearly, he didn't think of himself in that way. He chewed his hamburger for a while before answering.

"No, I'm not negative," he said, offering a feeble smile. "You've got to understand…I've been here from the beginning. I've worked with Elaine and Sean to build Cathy Booker Foods since I was a teen. Even before that."

"Then you're Cathy too. You also influenced the company," she said brightly and ate more of her turkey.

Marcus was shaking his head before she could finish her entire thought. "Naw…you just don't understand." Having finished his burger, he sat back and stretched out his legs. He occasionally ate one of his remaining scattered fries.

"So tell me. Why don't you consider yourself part of them? Sean said you grew up like brothers." She was finally getting to the real reason she had asked him to lunch. Well, part of the reason. After his considerate performance the other day, she was actually eager to see more of him. Professionally, of course, she told herself.

He nodded. "My mother was Elaine's sister. She died when I was eight."

"Oh, I'm sorry to hear that. Then Elaine raised you?"

"Raised?" Marcus said, contemplating the word. He looked out the window. "I'd say…Elaine was kind enough to take me in. Sean was…not so kind."

Tracy paused with her fork on the way to her mouth. "Wow," she said, returning the food to her plate. In her years of working with the news media, she had heard a lot of stories, but the way Marcus had singularly summed up his familial relationship staggered her.

"Wow is right," Marcus said quietly. He wiped his mouth with a paper napkin, crumpled it and dropped it on his tray. He placed his elbows on the table and leaned forward with his head resting on his clasped hands. His soft, brown eyes bore into Tracy's. His body language told her that he was open to any further questions she had in mind.

"You make it sound like you were Cinderella," Tracy said, her voice low and seriously concerned. She hated stories about child abuse or maltreatment. Even though she considered Elaine a devious creep, she didn't want to believe she could abuse a child. "Did she…" Tracy swallowed hard, not really even knowing how to ask.

Marcus could see where her thoughts were going. "I wouldn't say so much that she made me work hard and that stuff. She made both Sean and I work hard. You have to understand, Elaine was a single mother, now with two little boys, trying to be an entrepreneur. We had to hustle her food back when she was selling plates out of her car. No, her attitude towards me was…" Marcus searched his brain for words. "It was more like…indifference. Sean mattered and I didn't matter as much. You see?"

Tracy's reference was her own single mom. They had hard times, but their household had always been filled with love. "Why do you think she was like that?"

Marcus peered at her. "You mean why do I feel that way?"

"No. I've accepted that she was like that," Tracy said, quickly trying to squelch any misunderstanding that it was all in his mind. "I mean why do you think she acted that way towards you?"

"Oh," Marcus said, sitting back. "That's simple. She couldn't stand my mother."

"Her own sister? Weren't they the only two?" Tracy asked, naively attributing her own family values to the situation.

"Yeah, but as far as Elaine saw it, she was better than my

mother. My mother was a free spirit. She was an artist…a writer…a dreamer," he said, looking down and running his fingers along the edge of the table. He suddenly looked up at Tracy, inclining his head forward. "She had me out of wedlock, by the way."

"And Elaine didn't have Sean that way?" She asked, unconcerned with his revelation.

"What, are you kidding? No way," Marcus said, looking at Tracy as though she should know better.

"Elaine's first husband died. He was an artist too. A jazz musician," he said, stretching out the word "jazz." "Elaine would tell you he was a loser. I remember him as really nice. Real cool." Marcus was looking out the window as if trying to resurrect images of the man.

"How did he die?"

"Drug overdose…heroin," he said softly, as though it had happened just days ago. "According to Elaine, he and my mother got what they deserved."

Tracy raised her eyebrows. "What? Were they together?"

"No, no. Nothing like that. My mother was killed by one of her boyfriends," he looked at her through hooded eyes. "But, y'know, according to Elaine, they led that bohemian lifestyle. They were bound to end up that way."

"She told you all of this as a little boy?" Tracy's eyebrows twitched, annoyed at what she was hearing.

"I knew what happened to my mother," he said, looking at his hands.

"I mean, she bad-mouthed them to you?"

"All my life—at least, my life with her. And, I would end up just like them," he said with a sigh. Tracy crossed her arms in front of her chest and sat back, thinking. Marcus simply watched her.

"That's emotional abuse," she finally said.

"Hey, I survived," Marcus said, lightening his mood and

picking up his tray. Apparently, he'd had enough of this walk down memory lane. Tracy followed his lead, gathering her things and rising. He took her dishes and she walked with him to return the trays.

"But you know what's interesting?" Tracy asked. They walked toward the elevators.

"What's that?"

"That Elaine despised artists and yet she married one." Tracy pushed the button and turned to him.

"I know. Isn't that something?" Marcus said, raising an eyebrow. "I've thought about that."

"Did Elaine do anything creative?"

Marcus kissed his teeth and twisted his lips. "Please. Elaine doesn't have one creative bone in her body. Even her food is the same old soul food everybody made in black households. Sean and I would fill our orders on lonely bachelors who didn't know how to cook." His face brightened abruptly as he thought back. "You should've seen the dishes my mama would cook. She'd try them out on me and nine times out of ten…it was the best thing I had ever tasted."

Tracy smiled at his use of the word "mama." She knew he had been happy with his mother. The two of them were probably best friends. What was more heartbreaking was that he'd known a mother's love and had to go into Elaine's household, where he met a cold reception.

"I think she was jealous of your mother," Tracy said. Uncharacteristically, she continued talking when they got on the elevator, despite the other ears around. "Did your mother hate Elaine?"

"No. My mother was her older sister. She loved Elaine and always wanted the best for her."

"What was your mom's name?"

"Karla," Marcus said distantly, as though comforted by the word. "Karla Hansen."

They exited on their floor.

"So that's Elaine's maiden name, Hansen," Tracy murmured to herself.

"No. Their maiden name is Booker. Hansen was my father's last name," Marcus explained, opening the door to Cathy Booker for Tracy. He nodded a greeting to the girl at the reception desk. Now, Tracy was confused. Walking in front of him, she glanced over her shoulder at him with a wrinkled brow.

"I told you my mother was different. She wanted to give me my father's surname, so I'd always know I had other family. But she didn't want me to walk around with a different last name than hers. So, she legally changed her name."

Marcus Hansen Booker, Tracy thought. Now she understood why he had the two last names. Marcus was so open and easy to talk to that Tracy felt she knew him better over one lunch than any man she had ever known. She stopped outside the doorway to their executive offices, wondering one more thing.

"You seem like an intelligent guy. If Elaine was like that, why did you come to work with her?" she asked in a low voice. "You could've done anything in life."

Marcus stood over her, smiling kindly—the way you would at someone who was just too slow to grasp a simple concept. He put his hand on her shoulder and looked into her eyes. "I am a smart guy…and a very rich guy," he whispered. He winked at her and went inside the office.

Tracy remained fixed in place. *Of course. Why didn't I think of that?* Cathy Booker Foods was privately owned and the major shareholders were Elaine, Sean and Marcus. She tended to think of Elaine as rich and the guys as well off. But Marcus was unquestionably a multimillionaire himself. Aside from the support staff, Tracy was the only one pretending to be wealthy in this little scenario. She felt stupid for asking why he worked there. Where else would he have worked that would have rewarded him so greatly at such a young age? She walked into their office area and looked towards Marcus's door. It was open, but Pam was already in with him. He looked out the door at her and smiled.

Tracy moved slowly in the direction of her own office, her mind spinning with all the information Marcus had revealed. She was beginning to like Elaine less and less. Before, she had at least admired Elaine's business acumen. But after hearing Marcus's story, she thought that Elaine's achievement came without regard for anything else—like common human decency. She also resented the fact that Elaine thought she was like her. Tracy was more of an artist herself than a business-woman. She identified with Karla and her carefree lifestyle and raising your child in a household filled with love. Why would Elaine take a person like her and try to remake her? There was way more to this messed-up situation than Tracy had ever considered. She had forgotten to ask Marcus about Sean. She wondered how Sean was "not so kind."

Chapter 9

The phone was ringing as Tracy walked through the back door. She ran through the kitchen to the living room.

"Hello?" she said, out of breath.

"Hello? Tracy?" It was Brian. Tracy was taken aback. She sat down on the couch, too stunned to speak and not sure whether she should just hang up.

"Tracy? Hello, are you there?"

"I'm here, Brian. What do you want?" She decided to hear what he could possibly say to her, but she didn't have to be nice.

Brian cleared his throat and chose to ignore her foul mood. "What's up, girl? I haven't talked to you in ages."

"And why are you calling me now?"

"I think I saw you on the street today. If that was you, you looked good. I thought I'd call to see how you're doing. What are you up to these days?" There was no sense of irony in his voice.

Tracy pulled the phone away from her ear and stared at it

with a frown. *Is he serious? Does he actually think he can call me up and chat like old friends?* "Brian, I'm busy. What is this about?"

"What?" Finally, his voice seemed to betray that he wasn't as confident as he was making out to be. "As much as we shared together? I can't call a friend to see how she's doing?"

"First of all, we were never friends…we were a couple. And secondly, if it will get you off the phone any faster, I'm doing great."

"Tracy, Tracy…" he said exasperatedly. She could visualize him shaking his head and smirking at her anger as though she were an incorrigible child. "Why can't we be civil? Have you seen me on the news lately? I've finally made it to an anchor spot."

"Well, I'm sure you're very proud of yourself, Brian," she said, not even addressing whether she had seen him or not. She was furious that she could hear the smile in his voice. *Self-satisfied prick.*

"Why are you being so rude to me? I just called you to catch up with you…and maybe meet for drinks or something. As close as we were to each other, we should be able to keep in touch. Talk about what you're working on…y'know."

It suddenly occurred to Tracy that Brian didn't know that she knew all about his backstabbing and his maneuverings to replace her with Millicent. And even more telling about his ambitious nature, she surmised that he saw her dressed to the nines and walking with someone looking equally successful, and he probably wanted to know if she landed in a position that could be of some help to him—either now or in the near future. She could tell by the submissiveness in his attitude that he was obviously concerned about not burning his bridges.

Tracy would be wise to consider the same. With Brian rising at the station, he might be someone she should keep in contact with. But she was too much of a hothead to go in for that sort of phoniness.

"And what would Millicent say to all of this *friendly meeting* with your old girlfriend?" she asked, narrowing her eyes.

Brian was quiet for a second. "Oh…so you heard about Millicent? Who do you keep in touch with at the station?"

"Someone who also told me that you orchestrated my firing." Tracy felt heat rush to her face. In retrospect, Tracy thought that she had not been in love with Brian, but she could have been, if he'd allowed their relationship to grow naturally. Instead, he was playing her the entire time they were together. So she had to attribute the deep feeling she had for him at that time as an infatuation. Love would have never felt that bad. Now he had the audacity to just call her house and attempt to reenter her life—it was infuriating.

"I—I…don't know why anybody would say that.. Who—"

"Brian…don't try to lie to me. I know for a fact that you told the producers that you and the crew couldn't work with me." Her breath was coming hot now, and she could feel a knot in her throat. But she wouldn't give him the satisfaction of making her cry.

Brian was quiet. Tracy allowed the silence so that she could get her voice under control. She had been a rising star at the station and this is the man who had ruined it for her, with a twist of the knife in her heart to boot. She waited for him to respond.

"Tracy," Brian said, measuring his words. "You know that's not true…I've been nothing but an advocate on your behalf."

Straight-up lying! Tracy was livid. She had a mind just to hang up on him.

"Look, we ought to meet and sort this stuff out. I don't know who's telling you these kind of lies, but I think we need to talk face-to-face," Brian said in a soothing yet patronizing voice, as though he were dealing with a mental patient.

That did it. Tracy's hothead got the better of her and she slammed the phone down. His call was a perfect reminder of why she shouldn't get involved in another office romance, no matter how much she was vibing on Marcus.

Chapter 10

After three weeks, she could no longer fool her body. Trac
was a morning workout girl. By the time she came home
from work on Monday and Tuesday, she was flagging in her
exercises. Two days of trying to manage evening workouts a
home convinced her to check out Cathy Booker's fitnes
center. She also needed an alternative because she didn't have
the great machines at home that most health clubs offered. If
the fitness center turned out to be nice, she could free up
couple of hours after work. It would also be more convenien
than parking at her club, working out, showering, getting
dressed and traveling north to the office. Elaine could do i
because she was the big boss—she could arrive when she ar
rived—but Tracy didn't have that luxury.

As she left her car, she inhaled a breath of air and smile
to herself. She wondered how Elaine would feel if she saw
her arrive at work with navy Lycra pants and double tank top
under her coat. *Probably send Melvin out to Fatigues to bu*

*me some new workout clothes and more athletic shoes than I
can shake a stick at.* Her suit was slung over her shoulder. She
got off the elevator at the office and unlocked the door. As she
walked through the darkened rooms, Tracy marveled at how
different the office felt before everyone arrived. It was only
seven-thirty and the spaces were quiet and sparkling clean
from the maintenance crews. She unlocked the doors to the
executive offices and was surprised to see the lights on and
Elaine's office door open. She was drawn to a light inside and
peeked her head through the door. Julia was sitting on Elaine's
couch leaning over a McDonald's Big Breakfast on the table.
She looked around startled at Tracy.

"Oh." Julia laughed. "You scared me."

"Hey…Elaine in?" Tracy asked, looking around the room.

"No. I usually get in early. Sometimes she calls me in the
morning for stuff. It's easier for me to put my hands on it if
I'm here already," Julia said and went back to eating her
breakfast. "You going to work out?"

"Yeah, I thought I'd give the fitness center a try." Tracy
moved through the room to get to her office.

"Oh, yeah, it's really nice. You'll like it," Julia called after
her. "You're doing a great job, by the way. Elaine's very happy
with you."

Whatever. Tracy dropped her suit and briefcase on the couch,
pulled her shoes out of the athletic bag and went out through
her front door. As she made her way to the top floor, she thought
about how dedicated Elaine's staff was. If she entrusted
someone with responsibility, she expected him or her to handle
it without her having to micromanage. Tracy longed to be in a
position to show Elaine that kind of enthusiastic loyalty to
Cathy Booker Foods…without the burden of her mission.

When Tracy got off the elevator at the fitness center, the
number of people taking advantage of all the machines surprised her. There had to be more than twenty people working

out. The workout area disappointed her, however. The room was brightly lit, but Tracy liked windows and this one didn't have any. Instead, there was a wall of mirrors. At least there was a great variety of machines. She decided to warm up on one of the few treadmills to start. Just as she stood on it and tried to figure out the unfamiliar monitor, her secretary, Gina, approached.

"Hi, Tracy." She was cute in her workout gear.

"Oh, hey Gina," she responded, squinting at the controls.

"Um…you're going to work out?"

Tracy's eyes looked sideways at her, saying, "Isn't it obvious?" "Yeah."

"Well…there's an executive gym through that door?" Gina said, pointing.

"That's okay. This is fine." Tracy started to push the buttons.

"Um…" Gina had a frown on her face and was looking at Tracy strangely. "Well…"

Tracy stopped programming in her routine. "What's up?"

"Um…you should check it out?" Gina smiled and shrugged.

Something was up. Tracy looked around at the others. A lot of them had an eye or two on her, even as they did their exercises. Anne was there on a rowing machine. She made a face and shook her head to herself, but Tracy could tell it was about her. Tracy pushed the buttons to turn the machine off. She suddenly understood. It was the same principle as why the executive bathrooms were separated from the rest of the staff's. Subordinates wanted to be able to talk freely in their own spaces without being overheard by management. She was management. Worse—she was Elaine.

"O-kay," Tracy said picking up her gym bag and taking her CD player off the treadmill. "Right through there?"

"Yeah. I heard it's nice," Gina said, relieved that Tracy was complying.

"Okay, thanks." Tracy smiled. She wondered if the others had given Gina the duty of getting rid of her with some sort of secret hand signals or a jerk of the head or something. No matter which way you cut it, she was no longer just one of the gals.

When she went through the indicated door, it slammed shut behind her with a loud clang and she found herself confined in a stairwell. She became suspicious that this was all a joke on the new girl. Now, she was too embarrassed to go back through the door and face her suspected tormenters, or even to try the door to see if it was locked. So she allowed her feet to carry her up to the next level, hoping she would find the promised executive gym. Besides, she didn't really think that Gina would be involved in a cruel trick on her boss. When Tracy opened the door, she was reassured to see a bright gym with floor-to-ceiling windows. There were lots of machines, plush carpeting, wood paneling and nobody around. Best of all, there were four unoccupied treadmills facing the windows.

"This job is making you paranoid, girl," she said aloud, shaking her head at her thoughts of office bullies. She made strides toward one of the treadmills, but nearly jumped out of her skin when she heard a voice coming from the corner.

"Paranoid? How?" the deep, yet subtle voice asked. It was Marcus, wearing shorts, a tank top and gym shoes. He was sitting on an exercise bench in the back of the room.

"Oh, I didn't know anyone else was here." She watched as Marcus went over to the light switch near the door.

"That's obvious, talking to yourself and all. But you're just in time to spot me," he said, glancing at her as he walked. "I usually don't turn on the lights. The sunlight is enough for me. But with the winter, I guess I should turn them on. So, who's making you paranoid?"

"Off is fine. It's bright enough in here." She put her bag by a treadmill and stood on the machine to figure out the buttons. Marcus turned the lights back off. Their prior shared confidences and the fact that no one else was in the room, permitted her to be up-front with him. She jerked her thumb in the direction of the stairwell. "I was summarily kicked out of the other gym. When I got in the stairwell, I thought they were pulling my leg about there being another gym for executives."

"Oh, yeah…I'm the only one who really uses this gym ever since Elaine had it installed, but I got the same evil eye when I tried to join the others." He returned to the free-weight bench and started to remove some weights and replace them with larger ones.

"I'm serious. I want you to spot me for this set. I wanted to see if I could increase my weights, but was afraid to try it alone. I was thinking about promoting somebody to be an executive, just so I'd have someone to join me," he joked.

"Look, I want to start warming up," Tracy complained, glaring at him.

"Come on, woman, this is only going to eat into your workout for a few minutes." Marcus grinned and waved his hand, beckoning her to come over. She didn't move. "Seconds," he amended and cocked his head. Tracy rolled her eyes and crossed the room. Marcus lay down on the bench and gripped the bars.

"How much weight is this?" Tracy asked, standing over him.

"Three-fifty."

"You know, if you can't do this, I can't pull it off your neck." As he started to pump, she held her hands over the bar, waiting pointlessly to assist.

"I've got it," he said through the strain of pushing the heavy weights up, his brow crinkling under the pressure. From her vantage point, Tracy's eyes were drawn to his body. The muscles in his chest and arms were defined during his workout and his entire body was glistening in a light coating of sweat. She saw the fine hairs on his big chest and her eyes traveled down his torso. His thighs were tight and thick from the exertion. The boy was fit and exceedingly her type. But she had to admit that he would be anybody's type.

She focused on the wrinkles in his brow and could only imagine how that exertion and concentration could be applied in another, more intimate setting. It had been a long time since a man had touched her, and despite her resolve not to get involved with co-workers again, her fantasies had all recently featured Marcus Hansen Booker. Even after spending time with the smart and attractive Sean, she wasn't as affected as she was with Marcus. But to encounter him in this position made her pulse race and her stomach quiver.

Marcus placed the weight bar in the holder. "Two more sets," he promised, peeking past the bar at her face to offer a feeble smile. He rested a few beats and then lifted the bar again.

On his last set, Tracy's gaze crept leisurely over his masculine body, as though conducting research for her next daydream involving him. Her eyes automatically lingered on his promising groin area before traveling up his body again. Tracy's face and the back of her neck were growing warm by the time she sought that view of the erotic exertion on his face again. When her eyes arrived at his face, he was staring at her during his pumping. She was startled, and so thrown off balance that she accidentally placed her hands on top of Marcus's on the bar, momentarily adding her weight to his load.

He guided the weights into their rest and gently grasped the bottom of Tracy's forearms. Her eyes were captivated by his gentle "come here" expression while she felt the heat from his touch. With his palms flat, he rubbed up her arms to her elbows and she felt herself leaning forward on the now stable bar. Marcus's arms reached past the bench to embrace the sides of her legs. He seemed to marvel at the feel of her strong female figure, so neatly defined in the form-fitting pants. Tracy snapped out of her lustful stupor and took a step back. His knowledgeable hands had felt entirely too nice and too comfortable for her to continue to allow his welcome exploration of her body.

Unexpected Circumstances

"Um...I better start warming up," she said very quietly. She left him and returned to the safety of the treadmill. *What the hell was I thinking about doing? I've been down this road before. No matter how totally attractive Marcus is, dating a co-worker, especially one in a higher position, is not a good idea.* She didn't look at him, but she could feel Marcus's eyes on her as she snapped her headphones over her ears and climbed on the treadmill. Her hands were shaky as she programmed in her routine. As she started running, she could see his silhouette reflected in the glass. He had moved on to a machine to lift weights from the front. She turned up the volume on her CD player and tried to concentrate on the cityscape.

Marcus completed his program by rote. The only other person in the room occupied his mind. He felt a bit embarrassed for acting upon his desire and touching Tracy's thighs. His actions were exactly the kind of behavior he had recently warned Sean against. Unless he was misreading her signs, he was pretty sure that, this time, she was attracted to him, too. He shouldn't have touched her though. He was in no position to pursue her for a relationship. He was her superior and a stockholder in the corporation. He made a mental note to himself that any future advances would have to come from her. Yet, he wondered if he should mention his gaffe and apologize. He'd never been particularly interested in a co-worker before, and he realized that he could land in the sexual harassment zone if he wasn't careful. That stuff with Anne Duncan was just an unfortunate mistake that, in the end, deepened the rift between him and Sean.

Cathy Booker had no policy against office dating because, like most American corporations, the people on their staff spent a lot of time at the office. You had to expect that the workplace was generally a good place for hardworking singles to hook up. They'd had some incidents in the past where they had had to reprimand a couple or two for carrying on their disagreements in the workplace. But they could boast more marriages than nasty breakups. Early in their formation, Sean had actually devoted an entire meeting with the managers about the differences between consensual relationships and unwanted advances. The basic premise was that a person of power should not pursue his or her underlings. Despite what he had said to Sean about "hands off," it was easy for Marcus to convince himself that Tracy wasn't really his subordinate. She worked for Elaine directly and he considered her an equal.

Marcus really wanted to develop a relationship with Tracy. He didn't delude himself that he categorically desired it to be "hands on." They'd had a nice lunch together, but he wasn't sure whether she was interested in him romantically, or whether she was just interested in discussing his upbringing. He searched his brain and realized that he had done all of the talking.

But when their eyes had connected over the weight bench, he thought he saw in hers the same thing he was feeling. They wanted each other, not just physically, though there was a dangerous sexual tension in the air every time he was close to her. Even now, as they worked out on their separate sides of the room, Marcus could actually feel her presence. Over these past few days, he could tell when she entered a room even before he spotted her.

He completed his routine and marked his sets in his notebook. He glanced over at Tracy before leaving the gym. Smart, beautiful, confident and *sexy as hell*, she was the woman he'd been looking for—but he had to learn to rein in his impulses and watch himself in the future.

Chapter 11

Julia had assured Tracy that it was okay to use Elaine's shower, but as she turned around in front of the mirror to see how flattering the black suit was to her butt, she heard vigorous knocking on the door, immediately followed by Elaine calling to her.

"Tracy? May I come in please?"

Before she could answer, she heard Elaine twisting at the knob. Good thing it was locked. Tracy screwed up her face at her reflection and looked at her watch. It was only 8:14 A.M.

"Tracy?" More knocking.

Tracy placed her hands flat on the sink and rolled her eyes at the door. She reached over and flushed the toilet to signal to Elaine that she was really being unbearable. *Can't a girl have some privacy?* "Just a minute, Elaine. I'm coming out." She gathered up her workout clothes and shoved them into her gym bag and then heaved a big sigh before opening the door. Elaine was standing so close to the door that Tracy had to squeeze by her to get out. As she passed, she observed that Elaine's lips were twisted and her arms were folded across her chest like she was exceptionally annoyed.

Not wanting to get Julia in trouble, Tracy accepted the blame. "I thought it would be all right if I used your bathroom to freshen up after my work—"

"I don't care about that," Elaine said, uncrossing her arms to wave a hand in the air. "Sit down, I need to talk to you."

"Okay," Tracy said, placing the gym bag over her shoulder and starting to go to her office. "Let me just go get your calendar."

"No-no. This won't require my calendar. Have a seat."

"Oh? Okay." Tracy smoothed her skirt and sat down heavily, her gym bag fell onto the couch next to her. Elaine sat opposite her, on the edge of her chair, the frown still etched upon her forehead but her eyes were focused on her own hands.

"Look, Tracy…I'm going to need you to step up your game plan," Elaine blurted out so fast that it took Tracy a minute to understand what she was talking about. But she still played the innocent role.

"My, uh, game plan?"

"Come on now, I don't have time to play your 'I'm so innocent' games right now. Last night I had to endure a *grueling* dinner with Sean and that…that woman, and I'll be damned if I'm going to let her just waltz into my family without a fight!" Elaine's voice grew increasingly louder as she spoke.

Tracy narrowed her eyes at Elaine. She wanted to slap her. *I'm so innocent games* resonated in her ears. And the fight she was so willing to wage didn't impress Tracy either, since hers was such sneaky, underhanded mess. "Did you pull him aside and tell him you don't want him to marry Ashleigh?" Tracy asked with as measured a voice as she could muster.

Elaine answered her with a cold stare, then posed her own

questions. "Are you enjoying a steady paycheck? Or is this all a little too much for you?"

Tracy dropped her eyes, and lost a little bit of her tough posturing. She had forgotten that Elaine could give as well as she could take. In a verbal or mental battle, Tracy was convinced that this woman would always come out on top. "Well, I don't know what you mean by step it up. You said that all I have to do is just do my job and dress the part and the deed would be done on its own."

"Yes, well…I can see that we're running short on time," Elaine said, rising to her feet. Alarmingly, she sat on the other side of Tracy's gym bag, as close to her as possible. Tracy leaned her back against the couch, not liking the feeling of an intimate strategizing session—when in truth, that's precisely what this powwow was.

Elaine continued in a lower voice. "After the managers' meeting today, I want you to get with Sean and tell him that you would like his help in putting together a big bash for my sixtieth birthday. Tell him it will be a surprise party and that you don't want to be caught discussing it at the office. You'll need to involve Julia at some point to make it look legit, but I want you to have some one-on-one time with him first."

Elaine's face was so intense. With the ease of actually working on real projects, Tracy had forgotten how serious Elaine took all of this Ashleigh stuff. She tried to concentrate on what Elaine had just said instead of thinking about the good money a therapist could make on this crackpot.

She played the words back in her head; *'Meet with Sean and plan a party.'* She could do that. "Okay. When's your birthday? And is this a big thing or a small, private affair?"

"First of February. It's on the calendar. Of course, it should be a big bash. Don't mention my age on the invites though," Elaine said, relaxing against the couch as well, now that her burning instructions had been passed along.

"All right, I'll try to get with him soon," Tracy said, rising and adjusting the gym bag on her shoulder.

"No. Do it *today*." She anxiously sat up again.

Tracy screwed up her face at the pressure. How was she supposed to do this naturally if Elaine was dictating all of the parameters? But she didn't want to get into a fight with her and wanted to retreat to the comfort of her own office as soon as possible. "Fine. Today."

Elaine relaxed again. A silence stood between them until Elaine stood up and went to her desk. Tracy rose too, picking up her gear and heading for the door. "Bring back my calendar. Let's talk about my day before the meeting. I'm supposed to fly out to Boston tonight," Elaine called to her back. Tracy's shoulders stiffened as she opened the door.

"Okay, let me just put away my stuff and I'll be right back in," she said as sweetly as she could muster, while she passed through Julia's office.

"Marcus was looking for you," Julia said without looking up. Tracy's expression must have broadcast her annoyance at that trifling woman and her trifling job, because Julia had a strange look on her face. "Everything okay? You look like you got chewed out," she said, getting ready to go into Elaine's office now that the coast was clear.

"It's all cool. Nothing I can't handle," Tracy said, at the same time as she was wondering if that was true.

"Trust me Tracy, it happens to all of us," Julia said sympathetically.

Tracy nodded. *Not this. This is my own personal hell.* It was too soon to walk away from the kind of money she was making now. Another thing that was pressing on her mind was that she wanted to impress Tai by having the money for a down payment on a house for their mother when she arrived for Christmas. She knew she would just have to grin and bear it. There were people out there with worse problems than having to flaunt themselves in front of a handsome man, at a mighty good salary to boot.

When she went back into Elaine's office, it was like a whole new personality had taken charge of the woman's small body—the one who was all business and focused on her corporation. Once they had gone over her schedule, Tracy unenthusiastically followed Elaine into the conference room, trying to push her prime directive to the back of her mind.

She felt it would've almost been better to attend the meeting directly after the morning's first encounter with Elaine. At least then she had adrenaline rushing through her veins as motivation to approach the inscrutable Sean.

Upon entering the conference room, Sean's was the first face Tracy saw across a room full of people. And worse yet, he was watching her movement through the room. His eyes seemed to take in her entire outfit, down to the shoes, before returning to the paperwork in front of him. Tracy started to sit in the same seat she had taken before, but when she saw Marcus's portfolio sitting next to the spot, she sat down in a chair two seats to his right, directly between two other people. She was yearning for a good, strong cup of tea, but she waited until Marcus had left the refreshment table before going to serve herself.

Tracy had no real reason for avoiding Marcus, other than the fact that she was so damned attracted to him that she found him an unneeded distraction right now. She zoned out while waiting behind the last few stragglers at the breakfast table, until she heard Sean clear his throat and tell everyone that he wanted to get started. When she turned from the table with her tea, she was surprised by the setting. Marcus had moved his portfolio to another seat, placing him directly across the table from her. Returning to her chair, her eyes connected with Marcus's. She smiled at him and he nodded to her, but quickly looked away. Tracy looked down, self-consciously. She figured he was embarrassed about what had happened in the gym this morning. Tracy thought she would have to talk to him to put his mind at ease that she hadn't been offended. She would tell him once the meeting was adjourned.

The meeting was made doubly long with the combination of Elaine and Sean. They were like a tag team, with Sean questioning everyone's reports at length and Elaine adding criticisms and micromanaging suggestions. After Tracy had completed her report, with surprisingly little comment from either Elaine or Sean, she looked at Marcus. He watched her, strangely, like he was not really seeing her. Maybe he was thinking something over. Tracy indicated that she needed to talk to him after the meeting. He nodded absently, but he looked at Elaine and didn't look back.

During his report, Marcus delivered his information unenergetically and handed out the graph Tracy saw him and Pam working on all week. It was a very thorough analysis of their markets and what was popular in each area. It was such detailed work that Sean didn't have any questions. Elaine had one, and Marcus must have given her a satisfactory answer, because she said, "Good work, Marcus."

When the meeting was finally adjourned and everyone stood up, Marcus jumped up so fast that Tracy was scrambling to collect her things. "Marcus," she called. He was leaving with Kerry, the human resources director. She called to him again. He turned to her vacantly, as though he didn't know who she was. "I need to talk to you," she said. Instead of answering, Marcus nodded and looked at something behind her. Tracy frowned and turned around to see what he was seeing. Sean was standing directly behind her. Her stomach lurched nervously.

"Tracy, can you come into my office for a minute?" he asked, briefly touching her arm.

"Oh, uh, sure," she said, surprised. It was unusual for Sean to approach anybody after a meeting. Normally, everyone was clamoring to meet with him. She glanced at Elaine, who

gave her a barely visible nod. She looked for Marcus, but h
had disappeared.

Tracy became more nervous as she followed Sean into h
office without his talking to her in the corridor. She didn't kno
what he might have to reprimand her about, but she felt one wa
coming. Or worse, he might have figured out Elaine's plot an
was going to talk to her about her involvement in it. After sh
crossed the threshold, he waited to close the door behind he

"This won't take long," he said, turning to her once the do
was shut. "Elaine's birthday is coming up and I need you t
help me to plan a large surprise party for her."

Tracy wanted to burst into tears, she was so relieved
"Fine," she said.

He moved to his desk, but didn't sit. He stood over i
flipping through his calendar. "She's going out of tow
tonight, but she'll be back tomorrow…hmm, how about nex
week?" he said, looking up at her. "You have her calendar?

"Oh…right." Tracy snapped out of her stupor, pulling th
notebook from the stack she was carrying and balancing
in her arms.

"I'm sorry. Have a seat," Sean offered, noticing the awk
wardness of her paper shuffling. "It's just that I'm runnin
between meetings, that I—"

"No, I've got it." Tracy found the right pages in th
calendar. "She'll be gone to California next Wednesday an
returning on the following Tuesday."

"Does she leave in the morning?" Sean raised his eyebrow

Tracy flipped back through pages to find the answer. "N
Wednesday afternoon."

"Good. She's going on a business trip with Howard. Let'
do it that Thursday at seven, at her house. I'll be leaving
meeting up in Wilmette at around six or six-thirty."

"Okay." Tracy wrote it on her own calendar. She woul
enter it into her PDA later. "You need me for anything else?

"No, that's it," he said, penciling the appointment in on his calendar.

As Tracy left, she considered what Marcus had told her about Sean and Elaine. They thought a lot alike. Elaine woke up thinking she should have a surprise birthday party and so did Sean. Tracy left his office feeling a load off her back. She looked over to Marcus's office and his door was closed. Tracy went to Pam's desk.

"Is he in?" Tracy asked, nodding toward Marcus's door.

"He's in a meeting."

Tracy regarded the closed door with some trepidation. She felt a knot in her stomach that something was wrong. His reactions at the meeting had been uncharacteristically cold. But then again, she could be making it all up in her head, the way she had just done while walking down the hall with Sean. But she and Marcus were closer than she and Sean. In this case, her intuition felt right.

"Could you tell him that I want to see him when he's got a minute?" she finally asked.

"I'll let him know, but he said he's taking off early today," Pam said, but was looking at Tracy rather curiously.

"Ask him to stop by my office before he goes," Tracy said. She went into her office, dropped her things on her desk and slumped down on her couch. She kicked off her shoes and closed her eyes. She had a lot to do, but she needed a moment to herself. Her phone buzzed, indicating an inside call. She ignored it. It was probably Elaine. It was too soon after her inquiry at Pam's desk to be Marcus. Besides, if it was Marcus, she wanted to see him in person. It buzzed again and again before the person finally gave up. A minute later, just as Tracy was standing up and stepping back into her shoes, Gina came in.

"Elaine is trying to reach you? I called your line." She walked over to check the telephone.

"The phone's fine. I was ignoring it," she told Gina.

Gina smiled knowingly. "Call her on her cell phone," sh
said, leaving as quickly as she had come. Tracy pressed h
fingertips to her temples, walked over to the desk and dial
Elaine. As the phone rang, she stood looking out the windo
Outside, the temperature had dropped another few degre
and the people scurried to and fro with a purpose. No one di
lydallied in weather like this, when the wind slashed acro
your face and swiped the words from your mouth.

"Hello?" Elaine answered. She sounded as though she w.
in her car with several other people. Tracy should have know
where she was going, but she hadn't retained much inform
tion when they'd gone over her schedule that morning.

"Hey, Elaine."

"Well? Did you do it?" Elaine asked, once she recognize
Tracy's voice.

"No. He did it actually," she said. She put her palm again
the window and examined the imprint her warm hand mac
against the cold glass. Then she wiped it away.

"Who did what?" She didn't understand, but Tracy ha
known she wouldn't.

"That's why he was calling me into his office after th
meeting. He wanted to get together to plan your surpris
party." Tracy paced the floor. This was the first time she ha
ever had to report on this other part of her job, and she foun
it very unpleasant.

"Oh, that is a *good* sign, Tracy. That's a great sign," Elain
squealed with delight. "You're practically on your way
easy street."

Tracy held the phone to her ear. How was she supposed
respond to that? Yippee? She had an overpowering need
really look for another job and get away from this crazy broa

"Are you still there?" Elaine asked, the glee still eviden
in her voice.

"I'm here," Tracy uttered, blasé.

"Aren't you happy?"

"I'm thrilled," Tracy said dryly.

"Well, I can see you're getting into one of your little moods. I'll see you in the office tomorrow morning. Put me through to Julia. No, as a matter of fact I'll call her directly," Elaine said huffily and hung up. Marcus never stopped by her office and Tracy didn't see him for the rest of the week.

Chapter 12

That morning in his office, Marcus had tied his tie while looking over the bustling city traffic from his windows. He had showered downstairs in the men's locker room, thinking the entire time about what had happened between him and Tracy. In the confines of his own space, he had finally come to a determination that he should either apologize for touching her, or he should clear the air between them. He should tell her that he met her before and knew her ex-boyfriend, Brian. Back then, he thought Tracy was his ideal. The more he got to know her, the more he felt he was right. Either way, he figured he had to have a discussion with Tracy about what had occurred.

He picked up his jacket from the chair and then put it down and glanced at his watch. Not many people around at this time of day. He had to catch her before the meeting so that the conversation wouldn't be hanging over his head all day. Marcus's stomach growled from a combination of no breakfast and mounting nervousness. *Well, here goes,* he thought, swallowing hard. He left his office and crossed the executive corridor to Tracy's. Her door was ajar, but he knocked anyway. Not hearing anything, he pushed the door open. "Tracy?"

Julia came through the door connecting her office with Tracy's. She had Elaine's calendar updates in one hand and several slices of an orange in the other. "Good morning. Don't you look nice. But you always do," she said, placing the papers on Tracy's desk.

"Thanks…uh, you seen Tracy?" he asked, anxiously rubbing his hands together.

"Yeah, she's in Elaine's bathroom. She was using the shower, but she should be out by now," she explained while passing by him to exit through the other door. "Go through my office, but you better be quick. Elaine was also looking for her."

"Cool," he said, going through Julia's reception area. He pushed the door open to see that Elaine had already beaten him there. She was so intent on knocking on the bathroom door that she didn't see Marcus standing prominently in her doorway. He watched Elaine for a minute, thinking she was being rather obnoxious. Couldn't she wait for the woman to come out of the bathroom before harassing her with work? He knew she was this way with him and Sean, but she still considered them "her boys" and she would talk to them any time she damn well pleased. She had said as much. He looked at his watch. Yep, still too early to be gunning to meet with someone. Not wanting to talk to Elaine first thing in the morning himself, he turned and went to the window behind Julia's desk, deciding that he would wait a minute to see if he could grab Tracy when she came through to get Elaine's calendar.

From the open doorway, he only caught snippets of their conversation, mostly on Elaine's part. She had a tendency to talk loud when she was keyed up about something. But, he thought he heard her open by saying she needed to talk to Tracy. His heart sank. Elaine could be very hard on people who reported directly to her, and he feared he might be about to hear her tell Tracy that she just wasn't working out. But what he heard instead made him stop looking out the window and move closer to the doorway.

A frown grew on his face. He was not really sure what to make of what he was hearing. What did Elaine's having dinner with Sean and Ashleigh have to do with Tracy? And what was this so-called game plan that she had to step up?

He heard Julia moving around in Tracy's office and decided it was time to leave. Snooping wasn't really his thing anyway, and he had heard more than enough to know that this conversation was not meant for anyone else's ears.

"Did you get a chance to talk to Tracy?" Julia asked, coming back into her office.

"Nah, she was having a private conversation with Elaine," he said, not making eye contact with Julia. "I'll catch up with her later."

Marcus went back to his office and closed the door. He sat at his desk and stared at a blank computer screen. He wasn't sure what he had heard, because he couldn't hear Tracy's side of the conversation. But from what he caught before Julia had come in, he knew it wasn't something good. Moreover, he had grown up with Elaine and was acquainted with her knack for crushing her enemies to achieve her aims.

This was the first time he had ever heard that Elaine didn't like Ashleigh. On the few occasions he had seen her with Ashleigh, she always acted so nice to her. Now that he considered it, he should have realized that Elaine was being overly nice. It wasn't like her to suppress her feelings. However, in this case, she probably didn't want to alienate her precious son, Sean. Marcus should warn Sean, but they did not have that kind of relationship. Besides, he couldn't care less about Sean and Ashleigh. You reap what you sow.

No. He was more concerned about Tracy. From what he'd

heard, Elaine was trying to intimidate Tracy into doing something against Sean and Ashleigh. And worse, she was holding her job over her head to make her do it. But he wondered why a bright girl like Tracy would stand for such an assignment. When he got to the meeting that morning, he had considered sitting next to Tracy and attempting to get her to confide in him. At the last minute, he decided to distance himself from the entire scene and observe all three of them from the other side of the table. Maybe he had not done a good enough job of explaining to Tracy how deceitful Elaine and Sean, for that matter, could really be.

Chapter 13

Finally, it was Saturday. Tracy jumped out of bed, washed her face, brushed her teeth and went downstairs in her short nightshirt and house shoes. Opening her pantry, she perused two shelves full of cereals. She had everything, from the super-sweet cookie kind to the healthiest grains, to oatmeal and Cream of Wheat. Tracy pulled a box of sugary Corn Pops down from the top and went to the fridge to grab a quart of milk. She looked carefully at the missing child's face on the carton of milk, determining that she didn't know her, before she sat down to eat and consider her options of what to do for the day. She had to stop by her mother's. That could wait until the afternoon, leaving her with a stress-free morning.

Typically, this was the one day in her weekly schedule that exercise wasn't on the menu, just in case she actually went out partying for the weekend. But given her current workload, carousing wasn't very likely to happen. Therefore, exercise was one of the first things she thought of doing. Breaking out the old elliptical trainer and putting in a good hour might be just the thing to relax her mind.

Must be the craving for some sort of physical release, she thought, smiling to herself. Her mind drifted to Marcus's beautiful, manicured hands and what they would feel like on the most sensitive parts of her body. She had been thinking a lot about him since she had joined Cathy Booker Foods. It had been a long time since she was in close proximity to such a hottie, especially at work.

Sure, she had been attracted to Brian while she was at CMT, but it wasn't because he was handsome. To tell the truth, he wasn't particularly that good-looking. He was just polished and had an air of confidence and power that she couldn't resist when he asked her out. Brian was also kind of short. They could see eye to eye, and that wasn't her type at all.

In contrast, Marcus was taller than her. He gave the impression of being honest with his emotions, in touch with his feelings and totally open with his life. Even though he was rich, he had retained some of the free spirit that his mother had instilled in him during their short time together. Tracy could really imagine a life with Marcus. She could imagine a household that was stress free and loving. She thought of their little kids with dreadlocks running around, exploring projects from science to art to films…whatever they wanted to do.

It did trouble her that he was acting so strangely at the meeting and she had been unable to catch up with him before the weekend. But his absence just caused her mind to dwell on him more frequently. She hoped that he wasn't thinking she was offended by his touching her at the gym.

As to her erotic fantasies of Marcus, she had to laugh at herself. She couldn't think of Marcus without her mind eventually putting him in her bed. She had heard and read all the studies about how much men thought about sex during the day, but she wondered if the scientist had really done their research on the number of times women dwelled on the matter. Maybe the women's numbers were depressed because, whenever they did those studies, women were lying.

She knew she would lie. If some lab coat was asking her to rank the amount of time she spent thinking about sex, compared to other topics, she would put work at the top of the list, and running the household and all that other crap and then, put sex somewhere near the end. But not dead last because she wouldn't want to come across as frigid.

Yeah, the more she thought about it as she scooped another big spoonful of cereal and milk into her mouth, she knew the women of the world were, likely, skirting the issue. Thinking about sex or having it—men weren't in it by themselves. Uh, except the gay men and brothers on the down low.

After she placed her empty bowl in the sink and vowed to start thinking less frustrating thoughts, Tracy looked around her nearly barren kitchen and thought that maybe a day of home shopping might be just the thing to lift her spirits. With her new job, she could afford to pull the credit card out of hibernation and get some decent furniture. She wanted to go to Ikea, but the closest one was in Schaumburg and she certainly didn't look forward to all that traffic and road construction, or the crowds. Driving long distances was definitely not in the plan for today.

Or she could stay at home and clean up. Some dust bunnies that had probably sprouted babies were gathering in the corners of her living room. She was usually so exhausted when she came home that she had gotten into some bad habits, like peeling off her clothes and leaving them on the floor of her bedroom and going over papers while watching television and leaving all of the paperwork lying around. But it was such a gorgeous day, a bit cold outside, but sunny and enticing.

She leaned her body against the sink with her arms crossed and came to the conclusion that she would go shopping closer to home. She could hear the telephone ringing in the living room and on impulse she started to dash for it. But she suddenly put on the brakes and stood in the hall listening to it ring. Tracy didn't even want to look at the caller ID, just in case it was Elaine. She didn't want to feel guilty about not taking her call. Plus, she should've been out of the house anyway. So she sprang into action, running up the stairs to take a shower, get dressed and get out the door.

When she came back downstairs, clad in a burgundy jogging suit, gym shoes and a short suede jacket, she grabbed her portable CD player and keys off the kitchen counter. But after she had opened the front door to leave, curiosity got the better of her and she went back in to look at the name. Vivien had called her. She dialed her back with some trepidation. Tracy didn't really want to hear any more about Brian. But she did want to tell Viv about his calling her the other night, like they were old friends. She knew if anybody could understand her indignation, it would be Viv.

"Hey, what's up, girl?" Vivien answered.

"Hey, Viv, nothing much. I was getting ready to head out."

"Oh, where're you headed? Steve is out of town and I was thinking we could hang out today. You could tell me about your new job and I need to tell you about the drama around here," Vivien said in such an upbeat and gossipy way that Tracy was intrigued.

"I'm not really going anywhere. I was going to walk around Washington Park. Y'know, just to get out the house," she told her, willing to do whatever Viv had in mind instead if she could leave as soon as possible.

"That's cool. Let me get my stuff and join you there. Look for me over by the baseball diamond in about twenty minutes."

"Aiight," Tracy said, trying to be funny.

"Aiight, later," Viv answered, trying for the same slangy tone, but her speech pattern was just too proper for her to produce the same effect. She and Tracy laughed at Viv's pitiful Ebonics before they said a final good-bye. After hanging up the phone, Tracy was eager to get out the door and get on her way. Elaine had a proven track record of being more than a little overbearing, and wouldn't have a problem disturbing Tracy with minutiae on her days off. Not that Tracy minded so much. After all, she was the woman's assistant, but she was opposed to having to deal with the office first thing in the morning. She didn't want to hear any of that Sean stuff right now either.

She pumped up the volume on her CD player, enjoying the images of summertime that Shaggy evoked in his songs, and hit a brisk pace in her stride toward the park. She lived about seven minutes from the park and Viv lived about fifteen minutes away by expressway, in a newly developed area of yuppiedom on the near west side. Tracy had no delusions that she would be walking around for a while before heading over to the baseball diamond to look for her girlfriend.

The day was cold, not cold enough to take your breath away, but chilly nonetheless. She increased her walking speed to warm up faster, but she didn't want to burn herself out. Then, come to think of it, she may as well get her real workout in now, because once she was joined by Viv, their intense gossiping session was bound to slow her down. Their chatter was usually filled with so many hand gestures and laughter that they just had to stop in their tracks to talk. She expected this one to be extra intense, given the information she had to share about Brian's call. She couldn't imagine what Vivien wanted to tell her.

As she reached the park, she saw the usual die-hard walkers and joggers. Plus, this time there was a bunch of guys playing flag football in the middle of the grass. It hadn't snowed yet, and the dirt path surrounding the park was hard as concrete. She walked on the grass to give her joints a break and sang along with Shaggy. Following a spell that would make a lesser woman throw herself in front of a Metra train, Tracy had to admit that life was getting pretty good. Now, she thought, if she could only add the right man to the mix and get out of this scheme of Elaine's while retaining her job, she could be really happy.

This has to be by divine order, Tracy thought as she slowed her pace. A real cutie pie was running toward her waving his hands. She looked at the CD player in her hand and pushed the pause button so that she could hear what he was saying.

"Tracy! Whazzup?" he asked, crossing the grass grinning. It was Marcus. She had an urge to smooth her hair and then thought better of it. Had she put on makeup? Or earrings?

"Hey, Marcus," she said, breathless, her heart beating faster than from the exercise.

"What are you doing here?" they both asked together and then laughed.

"I'm over there playing football with the fellas," he explained, pointing unnecessarily to the only people playing football in the park. "We're the only fools stupid enough to have a league that starts in the winter and ends in the winter. What about you? You live around here?"

"Yeah, I have a place over there on Drexel." She gestured in the general direction of her house as though she thought, heaven forbid, he might want to come over. The place was a mess.

"So…you're out walking?" Marcus asked the obvious, stuffing his hands deep in his sweatshirt pockets. She hadn't recognized him when he first approached her because of the hat. Actually, she had never seen him in anything but a business suit. Here he was, wearing a blue skullcap with a Bears logo on the front, navy sweatpants, gray T-shirt, zip-up sweatshirt with a hood and knit gloves with the fingers cut off.

"Um-hm." Tracy nodded, her grin matching his. *Where are my words?* She knew she was acting funny, and her stomach chimed in with flip-flops. Seeing him like this, so cool and sporty, was right up her alley. Plus, with him being the latest object of her desire, her gaze crawled over his face. He was so sexy with his little dimple and whatnot.

Marcus was also clearly checking her out, from her funky Afro to her spotless sneakers. He liked her fresh and casual look and was about to comment on it when he was distracted by his teammates calling from behind him. He turned around and yelled, "Would y'all chill, I'm coming!" He turned back to Tracy. "Look, we only got a coupla more plays. You gonna be around?"

"I'll be here…continuing on my walk," she said shrugging. *Why didn't I mention I'm meeting Viv?* She mentally scolded herself for planning to ditch her girl.

Marcus reached over and tugged on the sleeve of her jacket. "Why don't you stick around? Wait for me? Like I said, we've only got a few more plays and then I'll be through. You can watch us play."

Tracy playfully cocked her head and twisted her lips. Why did guys always think whatever girls had to do wasn't as important to them as standing around waiting on or watching them? Must be something they learn as early as grade school. It just so happened, she convinced her inner feminist, that her main reason for being here wasn't exercise, but to get out of the house. And, if single people were completely honest with themselves, running into a hunk or babe always trumped every other endeavor. "Okay, I'll check you out…see if you got any game," she answered, smiling.

"Good, I've been meaning to talk to you. And, as to my game…you'll see why they're calling me back. I'm the whole team," Marcus boasted and ran back to his football game.

Once his back was turned, Tracy's hand went up to fluff her hair and check for earrings. She had on some small diamond studs from the previous day. But she knew she

wasn't wearing any makeup and there was not a thing she
could do about that unless Viv arrived soon and had some in
her bag. Even though Viv was a few shades lighter than Tracy,
she might have some mascara. In her opinion, if Tracy had
one makeup must-have, it would be mascara. It always
brought out her big eyes.

A big shout went out from the guys on the field over a play,
and Tracy realized that even though she was watching, she
wasn't paying attention to their game. Football wasn't really
her sport anyway. So even if she had been concentrating on
the action, she wouldn't know what was going on. She had
been showing off when she said she would see if he had game.
*As a matter of fact, are you even supposed to say "got game"
for football?* She, Tai and her mother were all basketball fans
and spent many nights yelling at the television screen, or
running in from the kitchen to see what had happened when
there was an uproar.

Marcus seemed to be some sort of running back or something for his team. Tracy knew some of the terminology, but
didn't know how they scored it and who was what…other than
the quarterback. She turned Shaggy on again, but this time she
didn't sing along. Her mind was preoccupied with Marcus's
comment about wanting to talk with her about something. She
looked over toward the baseball field and didn't see Vivien
yet. With all the bare trees from winter, she had an unob-
structed view of the entire park. If this had been summer, she
would have had to walk over to get a better look.

Plus, she could see the parking lot next to the field and if
Vivien were there, Tracy would've spotted the huge, red
Hummer that Steve had bought. It was a standing joke between
Viv and her husband that, although she protested the purchase,
whenever he was out of town, she left her Jag in the garage and
drove his behemoth everywhere. She looked at her watch. Vivien
should be arriving soon, but she didn't want to go over there.

Her patience was rewarded. The fellas were slapping hands and congratulating each other on a good game. Marcus ran over to Tracy.

"Did you check out that last scrimmage?" he asked before he reached her, smiling broadly. Due to her lack of attention, it wasn't exactly the question Tracy wanted to hear.

"Uh, yeah. You were good. So you all won?" She began walking slowly on the footpath on the way to the baseball field. Marcus fell in step beside her. They strode along, throwing frequent glances at each other. They walked so close together that their arms occasionally touched.

He laughed, throwing his head back in the air. She watched his breath on the wind. "We lost! You didn't know what the hell you were looking at, did you?"

"I did too," she lied, smiling.

"Nah." He shook his head. He bumped his arm into hers. "No, you didn't. Be honest."

"So I didn't. So what?" she admitted, chuckling. She waved her hand, dismissing the entire sport. "Who cares about football anyway? Basketball is the real game."

"True," Marcus said, grinning and looking at his feet. "I play that better than I play this. And I don't play either that well. Truth be told, I'm the reason we lost."

Tracy squinted at him. She really liked this man. It was highly unusual for a guy to admit he lost the game, especially when she didn't know pigskin from pig's feet. "What happened?"

"I dropped the ball," he said, glancing at her. "The final touchdown. I fumbled it and the other team got a turnover. But at least I recovered my footing enough to tackle him before he ran it back."

Thanks to her zeal for basketball, Tracy could figure out what had occurred. She knew about turnovers. "Poor baby," she teased, poking out her lip and rubbing his back. Marcus pretended to sniffle and put his head on her shoulder. Tracy was in heaven. Her legs nearly gave out. She wanted to pull him back when he moved his head away. They walked alongside each other wordlessly for several steps. Marcus cleared his throat, causing Tracy to glance at him.

"I've been meaning to talk to you," he said. His face had turned solemn all of a sudden.

"Yeah, I was looking for you, but you left the office early Wednesday and I hadn't seen you since," Tracy said, reminded that he didn't stop by her office before leaving and he had been acting kind of funny before he left.

"Yeah, well…" Marcus started and then cleared his throat again. Tracy thought she knew what he wanted to say.

"If this is about what happened at the gym, I wasn't…um, offended or anything, I just thought…" She struggled for words herself. Her eyes darted to Marcus, who appeared confused about what she was talking about. "I thought, y'know, I should get back to my workout."

"Oh, right. I'm sorry I touched you…I was out of line," he said, shaking his head and looking at his shoes. In truth, he had forgotten about his momentary error in judgment. He looked in the opposite direction, embarrassed. "But, you know…I came up to apologize to you and you were, uh, in a meeting with Elaine."

"Don't worry about it," Tracy said hastily, wanting to end this awkward conversation and return to the ease they had enjoyed. She gave a self-conscious smile and waved it off.

"Anyway, I wanted to talk to you about Elaine," he said, finally getting to his point. Even in the best circumstances, Tracy flustered him. And with this more difficult subject matter, it was all he could do to keep his hands from shaking. He stuffed them in his pockets.

"Elaine," Tracy said dully. She was disappointed that Elaine was what he had been meaning to talk to her about. She didn't actually believe that Marcus was going to blurt out some declaration of love, despite her fantasies, but she thought it would be something more along the lines of her and him. The last thing she wanted to think about today was Elaine.

Marcus stole a glance at her, but mostly kept his gaze forward. "I told you a little about Elaine when I was coming up, right?"

"Oh, yeah, how could I forget that?" She nodded. Picking up on his tension, Tracy fidgeted with her compact disc player.

"Well, it gets worse," he said, so low that she almost missed it. Tracy waited, not daring to look at him. She braced herself when he cleared his throat again. This time, he actually coughed into his hand. Good at reading unspoken signs, Tracy knew this was something difficult for him to say.

"Marcus, if she abused you, I'm not really sure I want to know," she said, looking at her feet. All the moisture in her mouth was gone and she felt queasy on the stomach. "For right now, I have to work with this woman and I'm already struggling to like her."

Now Marcus looked at her outright, surprised. He smiled and chuckled lightly, then shook his head. "No. I told you, she didn't do anything like that. God, I couldn't tell you anything worse about Elaine than you're already thinking, huh?"

Tracy, embarrassed, smiled weakly at him and shrugged. "Well, you were saying 'it gets worse' all dramatically and whatnot. I didn't know what to think. Shoot, I don't know the woman."

"Okay, my bad," he said smiling, still amused at Tracy's low opinion of Elaine. "No, her thing is more mind games, intimidation and schemes. You should have heard the things she would say and do to eliminate her competition. I didn't mean to be 'dramatic,' as you put it, but she can do some underhanded things." Marcus looked off into the distance, remembering.

"One time, another lady on our block decided to sell plates

to the bachelors and at some of the businesses where Elaine was already providing lunches. Elaine snuggled up to one of her regulars and told him that he could eat for free if he just started a rumor that Mrs. Adams's food had made him sick. He did. That worked a little bit, but the sistah could *cook*. The other fellas told him that it must've been something else he ate.

"Sean and I knew because he came around all the time, thinking they had something going on, but she played him to the left. We heard them talking. Then Elaine had the bright idea to go into business with the woman. Elaine convinced her that she had the business savvy to take them far, which she does, as you can see. But she knew all along that she wasn't going to take *her* far. They teamed up and, indeed, Elaine started to get some businesses to accept their catering services for large events and she placed their baked goods at several local joints. Actually it was Mrs. Adams's cakes and pies that they sold. Naturally, Elaine stole the entire company and most of the lady's recipes to form Cathy Booker Foods."

"What?" Tracy said, shocked at the story. She stopped in her tracks and looked at him. When she saw the mild look on his face, she got annoyed at the theatrics of his story. It was so corrupt that Marcus had to be making it up for some reason. He continued walking, so she matched step with him. "And why are you telling me this?"

"Mrs. Adams wrote it off as a bad business deal with an unscrupulous woman. She went back to supplying her regular clients, but she no longer had some of the stores…since they were accepting Cathy Booker cakes and pies now. I think she began to grow more and more destitute. One of her young relatives told her she should sue Elaine after the CBF brand started showing up in the grocer's freezer, but Elaine out-lawyered them and even had Sean and I testify that the recipes our mom used were her own. We were just kids," he continued, ignoring Tracy's question. He looked at her and her eyes were narrowed at him, unconvinced. He nodded, but couldn't help smiling at her disbelief. "It's true."

"What? Are you for real that Elaine is that wicked?" Tracy asked, confident he was pulling her leg. He nodded. She decided she would still think on it. "And anyway, like I say, what is your point?"

"Point being, Elaine is a user and she can't be trusted." He stopped and turned to Tracy. He touched her arm. His soft brown eyes bore into hers. "You don't want to get caught up in one of her schemes. To this day, I regret what we did to that woman."

Tracy's heart leapt in her chest. She ran his conversation over in her mind, recalling that he did say he had come to apologize to her and she was in a meeting with Elaine. He must have heard them talking. She opened her mouth to say something and then closed it. She felt like he was looking at her as if she should confess.

"Well, you can bet I wouldn't get…get involved in one of her schemes," she said breathily. She could feel her heart pounding.

Marcus nodded solemnly. "I figured you were too smart for that," he said, but his eyes narrowed at her in that annoying way.

She looked away, and saw Vivien's Hummer pulling into the parking lot by the baseball field. Before she joined her girlfriend, she wanted to get to the bottom of Marcus's knowledge about her deal with Elaine.

"Did you think I would?" Tracy asked, afraid of the answer. But she wasn't one to lie awake at night mulling over something without having found out as much as she could about the circumstances.

"I don't know." Marcus looked at the Hummer several yards away from them. "I wasn't snooping. Like I said, I was waiting for you…but I got the impression that Elaine wanted you to find out something on Ashleigh, or whatever… " He kicked at the hard ground, watching the puffs of dirt his feet

made. Tracy thought his face looked redder than from being
bitten by a cold wind. She waved to Viv.

"That's my girlfriend. We're supposed to be walking together," Tracy told him.

"Oh, yeah? She's that anchor on...from your station,"
Marcus said, starting to walk with her to meet Vivien.

"Vivien Marsh," she said, still reeling from how close he
had come to understanding her shameful secret. "So, you're
right. Elaine does want me to do something like that, but I can
handle it. I've just been putting her off," Tracy lied, thinking
fast. Even though they were yards away from Viv, they spoke
quietly to one another as though she were in earshot.

"Elaine won't put up with that for long. She'll pressure you
until she gets what she wants. She might even threaten you
with losing your job. Why don't you let me talk to her for you?
I think I can get her off your back."

If only he could, she thought sadly. Then she was suddenly
hopeful. "How?"

"What does she want you to do? Find some dirt on
Ashleigh? Break them up?"

"Basically," Tracy said. No point in going into detail on
Elaine's off-the-wall plan when she didn't really understand
it herself. All she was looking at when she agreed to do
Elaine's dirt was a steady paycheck.

"I haven't had a confrontation with Elaine about anything
for years. She does her thing and I do mine, but I might have
some things I could say to her that would shut her up."

"And allow me to keep my job?" Tracy asked, doubtfully.

With a tilt of his head and a twist of his lips, Marcus
signaled that he wasn't sure on that note.

"Then, no. Let me handle it," Tracy sighed. "You're not
supposed to know about it in the first place. And secondly, I
wouldn't want her to think I ran to you to cry on your shoulder.
I'm a big girl. I got myself into this mess and I can get myself

out." She heard her mama's voice in her head, echoing the same sentiment.

"She can be pretty vindictive, though," Marcus told her. "And you don't want to get in a mess between her and Sean."

"I don't and I won't," she said hurriedly. They were almost to Vivien. "I've got it for now, but you hold that thought. I'll let you know if it's more than I can deal with."

"Hey, girl," she said brightly, hugging her good friend. Vivien looked at Marcus over Tracy's shoulder. He smiled, waiting to meet her.

"What's up?" Viv immediately released Tracy and held a hand out to Marcus. "And who is this handsome fellow?"

"Marcus Hansen Booker," Marcus said before Tracy could introduce them. He shook her hand. "How you doing?"

"Good, good. I'm Vivien Marsh," Vivien said, staring at Marcus and smiling broadly. "And who is Marcus exactly?" She looked at Tracy with raised eyebrows.

"I was going to introduce you if you'd given me a chance," Tracy scolded Viv. "Marcus is one of my bosses at work."

"Boss? You're too cute to be a boss. A girl could get in trouble at work with a boss like you," Vivien flirted. Tracy was mortified. You would think that someone with as much decorum as Viv exhibited on television would know how to act in public.

"Nah, Tracy's being gracious. I'm not her boss." Marcus smiled. "We're co-workers."

"But Booker…you're one of the owners, right?" To Tracy's dismay, Viv continued in this line of questioning.

"Yep," Marcus said, pressing his lips together. "The little one."

"Ooo…do they get much bigger than you?" She exaggerated looking up into Marcus's face and she actually reached out and touched the muscles in his arms.

"Vivien!" Tracy said, embarrassed. "You're a married woman."

Marcus took it all in stride.

"I meant ownership-wise," he explained, knowing darned well that she knew that in the first place, but he played along.

"Calm down, Tracy, I'm only asking for you," she said over her shoulder to her friend. Then she stage-whispered to Marcus: "You know she's not seeing anybody. In case you were interested."

Tracy watched for the ground to open and swallow her up. Even knowing Vivien had a playful personality, Tracy had never seen her behave like this before. Then again, the only love interest she had to talk about at that time was Brian. And Tracy could guess by the way she was acting with Marcus that Viv had never really liked Brian.

"Is that right?" Marcus asked conspiratorially, unable to hide the smirk on his face. He was enjoying the way Vivien was making Tracy squirm. She was always so in control and unflappable. "So you're saying she's available?"

"Free as a bird," Vivien said, taking his arm and leading him back along the path he and Tracy had walked. Tracy rushed to keep up, walking on the other side of Marcus. "And what about you? Are you married?"

"Nope. I'm free too," he said, raising his hands.

"Ooo...so you two can tell your grandkids that you met at work... " Holding on to Marcus's arm, Vivien leaned past him to look at Tracy.

"Actually, I met her before, but she doesn't remember," Marcus told Vivien. Tracy stopped shooting daggers at Viv with her eyes and she gaped at Marcus.

"Where was this and how could *anyone* not remember meeting you?" Vivien said, suddenly very interested. Tracy was frowning and nodded her head in agreement.

"Do you remember the first go-kart event for kids in the housing projects?" Marcus said, addressing Viv. It was easier to tell this to a third party without looking stupid. "Exxon, Cathy Booker and CMT were the sponsors?"

"Yes." Vivien nodded. He peered at Tracy, watching as she searched her mind and the recognition dawned on her face.

"We met there," Marcus said to Viv, but still looking at Tracy. He turned his face back to Viv. "She didn't even notice me, she was so sprung on a guy named Brian at the station."

"Oh, yeah, a real loser. That's ancient history, though," Viv said. "But you remember her?"

"How could I forget?" Marcus said so matter-of-factly that Vivien winked at Tracy. Tracy glanced away.

"So what do you do at the company? What's your title?"

Tracy tuned out while Marcus explained his position to Vivien. She was stunned. Had she been so infatuated with Brian at the time that she didn't even see other men? Even totally gorgeous, eligible men like Marcus? She did recall meeting and talking to a guy from Cathy Booker. She didn't remember much more than that, and she certainly couldn't put Marcus's handsome face on that guy. She had been such an infatuated fool, completely wasting her feelings on what—Viv was right—was a total loser.

So when I met Marcus for the first time, he was expecting more. Like recognition of some sort. Why didn't he say something? Tracy thought about that and came to the conclusion that she must have been totally dismissive of him. She thought she remembered someone calling her from Cathy Booker.

She wasn't consciously aware that she had put her hands over her face and was shaking her head, until she felt Vivien grab her arm. She had gotten between them and was linking her arms with both of theirs.

"So what are you two doing today?"

"We ran into each other in the park, Viv. We're not together," Tracy said, hoping that this would signal her to lay off the matchmaking stuff. Didn't she mention that he was one of the bosses?

"Oh? I thought when I was driving up that you guys came together. Strolling along, talking *privately*," she said, stressing the last word.

"Yeah, we were discussing a situation at work. A serious situation," Tracy said sarcastically. She wanted to either dump Viv and talk to Marcus unaided about his disclosure, or dump Marcus and talk to Vivien about all the things she was trying to sort out in her mind. But one thing she was certain of was that she couldn't take the two together for much longer. Vivien saw that Tracy was losing her patience with her shenanigans.

"Well, my husband's out of town and I love nothing better than puttering around with the house all to myself, so I could just get out of your way," Viv said. Tracy squeezed her friend's arm tightly. She had decided she needed to talk to Viv more than Marcus.

Marcus took his cue. "Nah, you ladies go ahead and do your walk thing. I think Tracy was looking forward to seeing you before I came along and brought her day down with work junk."

"No, it wasn't like that. You can join us," Tracy offered insincerely.

"I've got stuff to do. I should be over at gym now. Gotta meet my little mentee soon," he said, pulling his arm away from Vivien's. She let him go reluctantly, heaving a huge, dramatic sigh.

"You're a mentor?" Tracy asked, impressed. How did he find time to mentor a child?

"Yeah, to a teenager. His name's Claude. He wants to work on his lifting today," he explained. He backed away from them, looking at Tracy. "So, I'll see you in the office. We'll talk about that other stuff later."

"I think I'm done talking about that for now," she said. She couldn't imagine having to bring up that stuff to Marcus again. He was trying to be helpful and she was in the position of lying to him the whole time. She felt queasy in her stomach again, like she was going to throw up. She hoped he would drop it.

"Okay, I'll leave it alone if you feel you got it under control," he said, shrugging. She nodded.

"See you later. It was nice meeting you, Vivien," he called out before turning and making up the distance to his truck in a brisk run.

"See you Monday," Tracy said.

"Nice meeting you too, Marcus," Vivien yelled at his back.

"Girl, he is superfine…and his eyes, so sweet, so sensitive. Just like a little puppy," Vivien said. "Lord, if I wasn't in love with my husband, I'd give you a run for your money on that one."

"I'm not thinking about him like that," Tracy lied. She was too despondent about her discussion with Marcus to get excited with her girlfriend over him.

Vivien kissed teeth and looked at Tracy. "Girl, please, I could tell from the truck that you were sprung. And you know he's sprung on you too."

"What makes you say that?" she asked, smiling in spite of herself.

"Come on now…" Vivien pulled her, their arms were still linked. "He said he met you before. He said how could he forget you. He said he was free too, not just single. He said he was *free*. How many more signs do you need?"

"He was probably just being nice to your nutty butt," Tracy retorted, but actually felt more hopeful that Viv had seen something that she was looking for. When she first saw Marcus in the park, her feelings were along those lines—that maybe today could spark something with them. But when he started in on the stuff about overhearing her with Elaine, she was sure that his actions had been the icebreaker for what would be a tricky conversation for him.

"Ah, don't try and play me. I'm not going to tell you any more about why I think he likes you until you admit to me that you like him." Viv pressed her body into Tracy's, making her veer off the path.

Tracy twisted her lips into a smile and leaned her head to one side. They looked at each other and started laughing. "Yeah. You know I like him."

"See! I knew it. You're trying to act all cool." They pushed against each other, picking up the pace in their walk. "Girl, if you like Marcus, you can't play it coy. As fine and as rich as I know he is, women are probably throwing their panties at him when he walks out the door every morning. You got to throw your hat into the ring. Let. Him. Know. Men aren't mind readers. You have to spell it out. I bet you he's yours if you want him." Vivien poked a well-manicured nail into the air to emphasize her words.

"Where were you with all this advice when I was dating Ratface?" Tracy asked, amused.

"You were so hooked on that silly little man it was all I could do not to slap you. My advice would have been to run the other way. Do you think you were ready to hear that back then?"

"I guess I wasn't, if I didn't even see Marcus the first time I met him," Tracy admitted. "Oh, and you wouldn't believe who called me the other day."

"Ratface," Vivien said drearily. Ignoring the fact that they were just talking about him, Tracy looked at Vivien, surprised that she knew. Or surprised that she wasn't surprised. Vivien nodded. "I figured he was either going to talk to you or had talked to you or something, because he was all up in my face the other day asking if I still talk to you."

"What! What did you say?" Tracy stopped in her tracks.

"I said, 'No I haven't talked to Tracy. How is she doing these days?'" Viv said, putting on the face she used to deceive Brian. They laughed and continued along the trail. Vivien filled her in on the goings-on at the station. It seemed Brian and Millicent's relationship hit a snag when she found out that he had been applying for jobs in New York without even discussing it with her.

Tracy told her everything that he had said in the phone call, embellishing her reactions in the way you can only do with your good girlfriends. She wanted to tell Vivien everything about Elaine, but kept up the lie she had told Marcus about Elaine wanting her to get dirt on Ashleigh. She needed Vivien's advice, but felt too guilty to tell her about the real deal between them, especially about the money. Without all the facts, Viv told her she should take Marcus up on his offer and allow him to help. Tracy knew that wouldn't work because of Elaine's vindictiveness. At least Vivien promised to start asking around for a position for Tracy.

Chapter 14

Marcus walked around the perimeter of Elaine's indoor pool, gazing at the artificially warmed water, and for a moment he considered stripping down to his most natural state to complete several laps. But after tossing his shirt aside and peeling off his jeans, he opted to keep on the blue briefs he was wearing underneath his clothes.

He hadn't seen any staff when he passed through the house, but Elaine's home was big enough for servants to be lurking anywhere and not be seen until it was too late. He had let himself in, having kept the keys to the place even after he moved out to go to college. Even though she never seemed overly enthusiastic about having to include Marcus in her small family, she had never minded his having access to the house and coming and going as he pleased. Besides, everyone who knew the security code had keys to her house, including staff.

Once he reached the deep end, he dove into the pool in such a smooth entry that the water barely rippled around him. His rock-solid body became one with the soothing liquid until he surfaced in a perfect breaststroke. With each lap, he resurrected images of the daring eyes and the dazzling, smooth, chocolate skin of Tracy Middleton. His mind created a montage of each encounter they'd had all the way back to the first time the saw her at the event with Brian. He was deluding himself that he could remain a co-worker with her.

Beyond the point of playing games now, Marcus wanted to spend more time with her. He couldn't keep relying on the workday to provide him with his fill of Tracy. He had thought about calling her after seeing her in the park because of Viv's strong hint that she was available and would be interested in him. But he lost his nerve after finding her home phone number and dialing everything except the last digit. He tried to recall if she expressed interest or just mortification at Vivien's chatter. Thank God, she was through with Brian. Marcus hadn't seen Brian himself in the time that Tracy had been working at Cathy Booker.

Marcus knew he would just have to make it clear that he wasn't the kind of man to fall into the category of "just friends" with a woman he found desirable. Actually, it was more than desire that fueled his drive to have Tracy in his life. He craved her, the way a starving man yearned for food. He was hungry for her, and yet, he had no idea how he was going to go about jumping from his work-buddy status to something more serious. His mind was working against him, already presenting him images of the next phase, which made him unable to concentrate on the task at hand. He found himself frequently fantasizing about going places with her, working out together, laughing at inside jokes and, his favorite vision…making love with her.

He was surprised at his trepidation. He was no Casanova, not like Sean. But since he'd been an adult, he was usually pretty relaxed with women, simply asking them out and seeing where the relationship went. But something about Tracy was holding him back. It could be that, in her position, she represented Elaine, though that didn't seem very likely. He was pretty sure that his real apprehension was that he wanted something more from Tracy than he ever had with those women in the past. And Tracy didn't pull any punches. He would have to be straight up with her if they were to have a relationship. There could be none of his stupid jokes to offset his true feelings.

There was also the fact that the last time he was in a serious committed relationship, Sean had seduced his girlfriend. And oddly, his intuition told him that Sean could be on the radar screen here too. He stroked harder in the pool, trying to relax his mind and work out some of his tensions so that he could receive an answer as to how to proceed. Divine intervention would be welcome at this point.

Tracy was uncharacteristically nervous as she pulled onto Elaine's estate. This was it—her first real one-on-one encounter with Sean in a casual setting. Although she hadn't seen anything from Sean to indicate that he was interested in her as more than an employee, she worried about whether Elaine could be right: that all this plotting on her part was working to lure Sean away from Ashleigh and toward her. As she turned off the engine, she wondered what she would do if he really was attracted to her. What if he tried to make a pass at her tonight? She wasn't sure how she would react. Of course, she wasn't going to sleep with Sean, but would she allow him to kiss her? Job or no, she was certain she wouldn't let it go that far. Her nature was to tell him off, slap his face or some other exaggerated move to let him know that she was not that kind of girl.

The outfit she had chosen wasn't particularly alluring. The cream cable-knit turtleneck sweater with camel, brushed-corduroy jeans and brown boots could not be mistaken for anything but a casual getup.

Gripped around the steering wheel, her hands were shaky. She would have to calm down and relax her mind before facing Sean, lest he mistake her trembling for desire. There was nothing more attractive to a man than the thought that he made you nervous when you were around him. Tracy turned on the ignition and thought about just fleeing the scene. She would call him tonight and say she couldn't make it. Maybe they could meet at the office. Since Elaine was out of town, there would be no way she would overhear their plans for her party. Yeah. That's what she would do. She turned on her headlights and started to turn around in the drive, when she saw Sean open the front door.

He was waving at her as he stepped out onto the pavement. She rolled the passenger-side window down when she saw that he was coming to the car. "Hey, Tracy, I see you made it."

She took a deep breath and turned off the engine. "Yeah, I was just trying to figure out where to park," she said, leaning over to look at him.

He leaned into her window. "That's what I figured. I saw you drive up, but thought you were confused because you didn't see another car. I'm here. I just put my car in front of the garage, around the side there. You can do that, or you can leave it here, but come on in. It's cold out here."

"All right," she said to his back. He returned to the house. Now that she had actually seen Sean, she relaxed a bit. He was the same old Sean that she always encountered, friendly but exceptionally businesslike. She had let her imagination run wild just moments before, until she had just about talked herself out of completing the task. Besides, now she saw that her plan to flee would not have worked because Sean had seen her in the driveway, possibly the entire time she was sitting there. She shut off the engine, scooped up her attaché and exited the car. Tracy wrapped her coat tightly around her against the winds that tried to blow her away in the short distance from her car to the house. She had to applaud Sean for coming outside without a coat in this bitterly cold weather.

He stood at the door and shut it behind her when she was safely in. "Cold out there, isn't it?"

Tracy cut her eyes at him, still holding her coat closed at the neck. "Whoo," was her only reply.

"Let me take your coat," he said, holding his hands out in the event she would ever release it. She gave one last shiver and allowed him to take her wrap to a nearby closet. She looked around the foyer while he was talking. "I was thinking, we're supposed to get some snow tonight. Maybe I should put your car in the garage for you. So when we get through, you won't have to clean snow off your car."

Tracy threw a hand at him, dismissing the thought. "Nah, it's cool there. Cleaning snow off my car is one of my favorite parts of winter."

He shook his head in disbelief. "You can't be serious."

"Oh, yeah." She nodded briskly to emphasize her bizarre declaration. "I love it. Especially when it's dark outside and the snow is still falling around you. It just makes the world seem so quiet and peaceful," she said whimsically, seeming to Sean like she had been transported to that very space and time.

"You are a person all your own, Tracy, I'll give you that much." He gestured toward the living room, before leading the way himself. Tracy had been to Elaine's before, but she didn't know if he was supposed to know that. "In that case, I promise to let you clean the snow off my car if we get enough."

"No, no. I don't want to take any work away from your driver," she countered, dropping her attaché onto the coffee table and settling into the longest couch in the room. Sean stopped on his way to a well-stocked bar in the corner and cocked his head at her.

"How spoiled do you think I am?" he asked with a mock-offended look on his face. "You think I would have someone sitting there for hours while we planned the entire event?"

"Well," Tracy said, looking into the crackling fire and stretching out her legs, "not to say spoiled, necessarily, but I'd call it accustomed to a certain level of comfort and convenience in life."

"Aw, see, you're just like everybody else," Sean said with a little disappointment in his voice. "I drove myself here, thank you very much. And for your information, we didn't come up as spoiled rich kids. Marcus and I were well into our teens when Elaine started the company." He continued to the bar with a frown on his face. "We've known hard times, Tracy. Even while Cathy Booker was in its infancy, we would have to figure out how to pay distributors just to keep the trucks rolling and get our product onto the supermarket shelves. There were times when we had to hold the paychecks. Marcus and I would have to convince the large chains to carry our food, while—"

"All right, all right, my bad," she said, raising her hands in the air. She could see that her comment had really offended him. "I didn't mean to rile you up. It was just an innocent and maybe foolish statement on my part."

Sean's features softened. "No, it's not you. I just get tired of people looking at the life I have now and assuming we've just been lucky in life somehow. What would you like to drink?" he asked, holding up ice tongs with two tumblers in front of him.

"Uh, nothing, thanks," she lied. She wouldn't mind having a rum and cola, but she didn't know if it was appropriate.

"Don't be like that. This is a more casual meeting. Just you and me planning Elaine's party and if we're going to discuss Elaine all night, I'm going to need a drink and you're going to join me…even if it's soda. So, what'll you have?"

"Oh, cool, then I'd really like rum and Coke. Or Cherry Coke, if you have it," she said relaxing. The situation didn't seem like Sean was going to turn into a wolf and attack her, so she could be herself. Feeling rather warm, she reached down to unzip her boots, but stopped and looked at Sean.

"Mind if I take off my boots?"

"By all means. Elaine doesn't really like people wearing shoes in her house," he said, coming from behind the bar.

She just noticed that Sean was in his socks. He must have removed his shoes in the foyer. "What? You should've told me at the door. I would've taken them off once I came in." She quickly removed her boots and took them back to the front door.

"It's no big deal. I'm sure if you left some stains on the carpet, the housekeepers would remove them before Elaine got back. I have to go to the kitchen to get the pop. I'm not sure if she has Cherry Coke, though."

"Yeah, but it's a matter of principle," she called down the hall to him. "Some people don't want you to wear shoes in their house for spiritual reasons. You know…keep the evil and all that stuff from the world out of their home."

He turned to face her before going to the kitchen. "Trust me, for Elaine, it's all about dirt."

Tracy shrugged. She thought that Elaine must have really wanted her to join her staff, because she didn't recall her asking her to remove her shoes when she came over for their first meeting. Or, did she? It was such a whirlwind of activity at that time that her memory of the whole day was like a hazy dream. She met Elaine, Elaine talked a lot, they signed some papers, she met Melvin, who took her shopping, and on and on.

Before sitting back on the couch, Tracy wandered around the great room. In all honesty, even though she had been to Elaine's house before, tonight was like seeing it for the first time. Much like the offices at Cathy Booker, everything here was in light tones. Clearly, Elaine used the same interior designer for both spaces. As opposed to their offices, which were modern, the home was decorated with soft colors of peach, cream, teal and tan that captured an overstuffed Florida design. It was very country clubby, light, airy and comfortable. Her pictures and paintings were just as innocuous, with scenes of ships on the ocean, lighthouses, seashells, sea horses and the like. Behind the bar where Sean had been standing, was a full-size aquarium filled with brightly colored tropical fish. The fireplace was a peachy-pink marble, the same marble as the three steps that led down into the sunken living room. Even the plants were of tropical varieties, small palms that stretched over the furniture in spots and floral arrangements with birds-of-paradise in them. Tracy suspected that the summer look of the room added to her feeling hot. She felt she should be here in shorts and a T-shirt. Sean returned with a regular cola.

"This do?" He held up the can.

"That's fine," she answered, sitting down in the cushy seat. "I guess Elaine would rather be in Florida."

Pouring Tracy's drink, Sean looked up at her and then looked around the room. "Do you think?" he joked. He made himself a scotch and water. "Actually, she has a home in Florida with the very same design. It's like walking into this one, just in another town with a different floor plan."

"Wow. That says a lot about her personality."

"What?" Sean brought the drinks over on a serving tray and set them down on the cocktail table. There were even ice tongs on the silver serving tray. Tracy smiled internally at the formality of it all. Heck, if you came to her house, you would have a drink in hand before the ice had a chance to cool the liquid. She forced herself not to show even a smirk at the risk of offending Sean's image of himself again. She focused on what he was asking her.

"You're a good judge of signals. What does it mean that

Elaine has duplicated the same design in all her dwellings?" He sat down on the couch, leaving a large section between them, and picked up his drink.

It means she's a control freak that has to have everything exactly her way. It means she doesn't like change, even the change of her son getting married, she thought. But Tracy wasn't going to fall into that trap, talking about Elaine to her child or about one boss to the other. No matter how relaxed she was, she didn't forget her position. "It means that maybe we'd better plan her party with a tropical theme," she answered minimally and reached for her case. Sean raised an eyebrow.

"You got out of that one rather smoothly," he said, a small smile tugging up the corner of his mouth.

"My mama didn't raise no fool," Tracy said, pulling out her notepad and an array of paper samples and spreading them out on the table. She focused her attention on them, reminding herself that she was dealing with a smart group when it came to Elaine, Sean and Marcus. Their brains worked much like hers in evaluating even the things you'd left unsaid.

"I'd love to meet this mama of yours sometime. Compliment her on the great job she's done."

While reaching in her bag for a pen, Tracy glanced over her shoulder to wink at Sean in agreement, but the look she briefly caught in his eye was all *wolf.* She smiled instead and looked back at the materials in her hand. "All right...unless I'm going to be here all night, we'd better get started."

"Yes, ma'am," Sean said, setting his drink on the tray and reaching beside the couch for his briefcase. He placed it on his lap and unsnapped it. "I got a list of Elaine's closest friends from Julia and the business colleagues that she wouldn't mind seeing at her party. But we better go over them meticulously to see if either of us knows any reason why anyone shouldn't come. Relationships can change at the drop of a dime with Elaine, and you and I might have information about someone that she might be on the outs with lately. There's copies for both of us."

He tossed the lists on the couch between them. Tracy picked up some of the paper samples that matched the colors she saw in the living room and spread them in the same place.

"Cool, and I brought samples of the designs and stuff that might be good for her invitation. Foil, embossing, fonts, colors, textures, theme…I want to decide all of this stuff tonight."

"I hear you. We got real work to do, not to mention that we'll have to do it all over again for the staff Christmas party," Sean agreed.

"I ain't on that committee," Tracy said flippantly, shaking her head and throwing her hand like she was shooing away a fly.

"Oh, yes the hell you are. In the final stages, you and I have to attend the meetings. I'm monitoring the budget. You have to represent Elaine."

Before, she was joking, but now she really was irritated. "Why the heck are people always saying I have to represent Elaine? I have to represent Elaine," she mocked. "Shoot. You and Julia and Marcus all know her better than I do. I just met the woman. Why am I always the one assigned to be her mouthpiece?" She snatched up her drink and took a gulp.

Sean just smiled and said lightheartedly, "Pressures of your job getting to you already?"

She looked at him surprised, both at his response and at her own outburst. He had hit the nail right on the head. That was exactly what she was feeling. It wasn't the pressures of the real job she was angry about, but the secret one. Plus, her words must have tipped him off that she resented Elaine. She looked down into her glass and then placed it back on the tray. Chagrined, she picked up her copy of the potential guest lists. "Oh, whatever. Let's do this thing."

"No, no. Now, if you've got some concerns, we can address them," Sean said, still smirking at her.

"All right Sean, don't be a mean winner. You caught me at a low moment. I'm over it. Let's please move on." She put a fingernail on the first name on the list and called it out. "Lacey Anderson, any objections?"

Sean wasn't saying anything, so she looked up at him. He was laughing silently and actually holding his stomach. She twisted her lips, smiling at the same time. "Don't laugh at me."

"Woo…Tracy…you are so funny," he said through chuckles. "I wish Ashleigh could be more like you. You are so direct. I always know what you're thinking. It is just too cute."

Even though she was smiling now with Sean, Tracy felt her stomach turn over. Could it be? Elaine's harebrained plan really was working on him. Simply by her being herself? She didn't know whether to jump for joy or cry at the wretchedness of it all. On one hand, soon she could count on half a million dollars being transferred into her account. But on the other, she wanted to like Sean and not believe that a smart guy like him could fall for one of his treacherous mother's meanest tricks. And she was the instrument of the trick. The smile dropped from her face and she took a sip of her drink.

Luckily, before she fell into true doldrums, Sean got back to the work at hand. "Okay. Lacey Anderson…no objections."

"Barbara Antoine?" Tracy continued.

"No," Sean replied, propping his drink on his knee as they continued down the list of two hundred business associates. After they completed the list, only checking off four people that they could label as questionable, they reviewed all of the design options for the invitation and narrowed it down. Then, after narrowing down a location, they reviewed menus, finally deciding that neither of them was good at that and that Julia could handle the details of the food. Finally, after two hours and each on their third drink, they were working on a theme for the party.

"I think that it should be 'Sixty and Sexy,'" Tracy said,

giggling before she could even get the words out. Sean, who was sitting on the floor in front of the couch, knew she wasn't serious, but looked up at her anyway.

"Elaine will have our heads if we put her age on this invite. Besides, that's a dumb theme anyway."

"Why? You don't think Elaine's sexy?"

They both laughed. "Please. Spare me," Sean said. He suddenly jumped up from the floor. "Ooh, I know. We could make a theme off of one of her favorite songs."

Tracy watched him, perplexed, as he went to the CD changer. Elaine had more than two hundred CDs loaded into it. He switched it on. The first song that came on was "Love's Gonna Last" by Jeffrey. "Ahh, now we're talking," Sean said and started stepping by himself. "We could have some good stepping music, a live band and whatnot."

Tracy lay back on the pillows of the couch, rubbing the sweat from her glass before taking another swallow. She smiled as she watched him dance. Sean was so stiff and proper at work that it was amusing to see him behave like this. "True, we could have all that. But that still doesn't bring us any closer to a theme."

"Steppin' on Into Sixty," he said in an announcer's voice. They both laughed again, knowing that they had reached the silly point of this meeting. They were nearing the brain-drain point when no more work would be accomplished. Sean crossed the room and took Tracy's drink out of her hand and tried to pull her to her feet.

"Oh, no…" she protested. "I cannot step."

"Come on," he said, tugging her hand. "I'll lead. I'll show you."

"No way," she said, but allowed herself to be pulled to her feet. He led her out in the middle of the living room where there was no furniture underfoot. Without looking down, she tried to get into the groove of the music and follow his movements. It became evident that years of dancing to rap music didn't provide the skills needed to step with a partner. Tracy did okay when it was just the bop, but when he tried to steer her body away from his and back again, she actually bumped into him.

"Oh, my lord, you are really pitiful at this," he agreed, not giving up on trying to twirl her.

"I told you," Tracy said, laughing at herself. She released his hand and started to return to the comfort of the sofa.

"Okay, give me both your hands. We're gonna have you ready by the party." He took both her hands in his and started with the basic foot movements, which Tracy was following fine. But when he tried a more complex move, she was lost. The alcohol and the unusualness of the situation caused her to start laughing. Sean dropped her hands. "You're hopeless."

Now Tracy was challenged. She grabbed Sean's hands. "No, wait…try me again. Start with the foot thing. I got that. But then tell me what you're going to do next…and do it slower."

"Okay." Sean took her on as a pupil again. "One, two, one, two, then…"

They were counting, laughing and looking at their feet and didn't notice Marcus staring at them from the top of the steps. He was shirtless and barefoot, with a towel around his shoulders, but he was wearing his jeans. "Is this a private lesson, or can anyone join?"

Tracy and Sean's heads whipped around, and they stopped laughing and dancing.

"Marcus," Sean and Tracy said within seconds of each other and instinctively moved apart. It was Sean who asked the question on both of their minds. "What are you doing here?"

Marcus moved into the room and pointedly looked at the tray of drinks. He wiped his head with the towel. "I thought I heard music, so I came to investigate." After he'd finished his laps, he had relaxed, floating around the pool and thinking when he heard music coming from somewhere in the house. "Imagine my surprise at this little scene."

"I meant, what are you doing here in the first place?" Sean asked, going to turn off the CD player.

"I was swimming laps in the pool. And what were you two doing?" he said, picking up Sean's half-empty glass and taking a sip. "Is this your cozy little hideaway?"

"Look, there's no cause for that kind of talk," Sean said, his nostrils flaring angrily. "You can rag on me, but your assumptions are particularly insulting to Tracy."

"That's okay," Tracy said, gathering up her paperwork. "I'd better be going anyway."

"No, you stay right where you are. I believe Marcus owes you an apology." Sean held out his hand in a stop gesture at Tracy.

"Yes. Don't leave, Tracy," Marcus said derisively, turning to her. "I apologize for interrupting what promised to be a glorious evening for you. I'll just get out of your way." He turned from them and headed up the stairs and down the hall.

Sean dashed to the top of the hall. "Yousonofabitch. You'd better come back here."

Far down the hall, Marcus stopped and turned to face Sean. He pointed at him with his entire right arm. "No, Sean," he called back calmly. "Don't call me that. We both know who's the real son of a *bitch.*"

Marcus put his arm down. He and Sean stared at each other silently.

"And if you really want me to come back down that hallway, say it again," Marcus challenged. Sean watched Marcus for a moment longer before he turned his back to him and rejoined Tracy in the living room. He gathered their glasses, putting them back on the silver tray.

"I'm so sorry about that. There's no reasoning with him when he gets like this," he said quietly, not making eye contact with Tracy. She wondered if he was explaining Marcus's actions or why he had backed down all of a sudden. "You don't have to leave because of his idiotic remarks."

"It's all right. Like I said, I'd better get going. They say a snow is coming in, and…" She stopped and looked out the window. It was snowing heavily and it must have been the entire time she had been there, judging from the amount of snow on her car and the ground. "Ooh, it's really coming down."

Sean joined her at the window. "Yeah, that's pretty bad. And you have how far to go?"

"Far. Back into the city," she said shaking her head. Why did she come all the way up here to Wilmette, knowing that a snowstorm was on its way? But when she thought about it, the forecasts hadn't been for this much snow. Three inches had probably fallen already.

"Give me your keys. I'll go start your car for you," Sean said, turning to her. She went to her purse and dug out the keys.

"Thanks, Sean. I'll clean up here," she said, placing the keys in his hand.

"No, don't worry about it. I'm sure the cleaning staff will be here in the morning." He went to the foyer to get his coat.

"If they can get through. It's no problem…just a couple of glasses," she said sadly. Even though she hadn't done anything, she really felt dirty right now.

"Leave it," Sean insisted before he went out the door. Once he was gone, Tracy took the glasses and dashed down the corridor to the kitchen to place them in the dishwasher. That done, she started to search the house for Marcus, calling out his name. Of course, he didn't answer. Every fiber in her body told her that she needed to catch him before he left.

She ran up the stairs to the second level and found him dressing in one of the guest bedrooms. He had already put on his undershirt and his shirt. His shirt was still unbuttoned and he was furiously unfurling his socks. He glanced up at her when she entered the doorway, her form a shadow to him. The room was lit by moonlight from the wide-open curtains. He hadn't bothered with the lights.

"Marcus, it's not what you think. We were planning Elaine's birthday party," she explained, her voice shaky as she crossed the floor to him. Sitting on the bed, he jammed his foot into a sock and in his anger, lost track of the other one.

"I didn't mean to insult you," he said looking around for his sock. "I meant to compliment you. You have excellent taste in men. Just ask Elaine. She'd tell you Sean is the best there is." Each word spewed from his mouth like venom.

Tracy felt like she had been slapped. She blinked and watched him search in vain for his sock, too angry to see it right near his leg. She picked it up and handed it to him. He snatched it from her hand.

"Really, it was innocent," she continued. "We were planning her party and trying to think of a theme…Sean was playing around when you came in, but we hadn't been like that all night. It was just that we were tired, and—"

"You don't have to explain it to me, Tracy. Why waste your time with little fish like me when you can have the big kahuna? Be Sean's whore if you want to, what do I ca—"

Before he could get the word "care" out of his mouth, Tracy had slapped him right across it. Her chest was heaving rapidly from her anger. She didn't know why she cared to explain herself to him anyway, but she did. He stared at her, angry and stunned.

"I don't have to take this from you. Go screw yourself," she spat at him, turning on her heel. Before she could get out of the room, Marcus leapt from the bed and made two broad steps across the room. He grabbed her arm hard and turned her to face him. "Let go of me," she shouted, trying to break free, but he held her steady by both of her arms now. "You don't know me! You have no right to call me a whore!"

"I'm sorry," he said huskily and urgently, his chest rising

up and down with adrenaline. "It just made me crazy seeing you with him. I thought I would...that I would..."

He pulled her to him and pressed his lips against hers. She resisted, the hot tension still in her shoulders and her hands pushing against his hard chest. He let go of her arms, and hastily squeezed his arms around her back, pressing his entire burning and hungry body against hers. Her mouth finally gave in to his, matching the urgency of his kiss, while her hands slid up his undershirt until they met flesh. She continued her exploration up his body until her arms were wrapped around his neck, drawing his head harder against hers, so that they could devour each other in the wet kiss each had been longing for. All night, she had been wishing that this were an intimate evening with Marcus instead of Sean. And this same night he had been thinking of how he could get Tracy in his arms, just like he was holding her now. The entire time they were longing for each other, they were in the same house and didn't know it. His hands roamed her back and her tight waist. Hers took in every inch of his neck and head like she could never get enough of him. Their tongues pressed solidly against each other's, both vying to get deeper into the other's mouth and neither wanting to come up for air. A warm, fluttering responsiveness began at the bottom of Tracy's stomach and continued to burn in her crotch and thighs. She felt the equivalent passionate anticipation press against her body from Marcus. Now that their actions had fully spoken the desire that they had held for each other for such a long time, they were able to ease their tight embrace and kiss each other softly and sweetly. Their need evident, they pressed their cheeks together.

"Marcus," Tracy sighed in his ear, as though his name held all the meaning in the universe. "You know I wouldn't be with Sean," she told him, her heart breaking at the thought of hurting his.

"I can't stop thinking about you," he finally had the

chance to tell her. "I came here to figure out how I was going to tell you that, and then I saw you with Sean. I just thought I would lose it."

"Sean, Sean…screw Sean," she said in a soft voice and looked into his eyes. "I've been thinking about you all night. Only you."

He put his hands on her shoulders and stared at the moonlight reflected in her big, brown eyes. Her words washed over his body like a long awaited rain. "Say it again, Trace."

"I want you, and nobody else," she said slower, adding more sincerity, and sealed her pledge with another passionate kiss. They were falling into each other again when they heard Sean calling her name. They unhurriedly disconnected their bodies until they were joined at the hands. When they heard Sean's footfalls coming down the hall, they let go of each other's hands and Marcus sat on the bed to resume his dressing.

Sean entered the doorway and turned on the light. Tracy turned to him, while Marcus concentrated on tying his boots. "My car all warmed up?" she asked, striving to put an airiness in her voice.

Sean ignored her question and looked from one to the other, knowing something had gone down. "That lipstick is not exactly your color, Marcus," he said coolly, staring at his cousin. Marcus stood up and turned from Sean so he could wipe it off. Tracy passed by Sean and went down the stairs to gather her things and put on her boots.

"I'll see you at work," Marcus said, shouldering past Sean, who was intent on standing in his way. When Marcus got in the hall, he called to Tracy. "Tracy, wait up."

She stopped on the stairs and looked up at him until he drew even with her.

"It's snowing pretty bad out there. If you're going back into the city, you better let me get my car from the garage and follow you out," he said, as they walked down the stairs together.

"Thanks, Marcus," she said, not daring to look too deeply at his eyes. Her pulse was still racing and her thighs were still lit up from their contact.

Sean came down the stairs slowly behind them, his face gloomy. Marcus didn't say anything as he went to gather his coat from the pool room and, from there, retrieve his car from the garage. Left alone with Sean, Tracy went over the night in her mind. Everything had happened so fast, that she hadn't had time to think about the consequences of her actions on Elaine's grand design. First, the evening was going exactly the way Elaine had intended, and Sean seemed to be falling for her. Now, Tracy knew that her presence was having the exact opposite effect on Sean. He probably despised her. Nevertheless, she felt compelled to make conversation.

"Thanks. I saw that you even cleaned off my car. I thought I was supposed to do that for you," she said brightly.

Sean's mind was preoccupied, but he responded. "I've decided that I'll just stay here tonight." There was no luster in his voice. He spoke as though all the energy had been drained from him. He plopped down on the couch.

"You better call Ashleigh and tell her you're all right. If she's watching this snow, she's probably worried sick about you." What was she doing? Okay, so she didn't want to follow Elaine's game plan anymore, but did she have to drive him into Ashleigh's arms?

"Ashleigh knows where I am. You don't have to concern yourself with Ashleigh," he said sarcastically, shooting a look of daggers at her.

"I'll go wait in my car until Marcus pulls around," she said in a low voice.

Tracy was stung and her face must've shown it, because Sean's softened a little. "But, that's a good idea. I had better check on her." He reached into his briefcase and brought out his cell phone. As Tracy was putting on her coat, she heard him saying, "Hey, you still up? Yeah. I'm stuck at Elaine's. I was having a meeting with her assistant. Planning her birthday party…"

So, she had been reduced to Elaine's assistant again, huh? Tracy told herself that she didn't care, but it did bother her. She didn't need to be at odds with Sean at work. She had to think about what she was going to do. She had totally ruined Elaine's plan and she didn't know if she would be out of a job soon when word got back to Elaine. All this drama, just as Tai was about to come down to Chicago for Christmas.

She sat in her vehicle and pressed her fingers to her eyes. This was more than a woman in her twenties should have to bear alone. Too many emotions in one night. She wanted to tell the whole story to Tai or her mother, but she knew what either of them would say—she never should have gotten herself in a mess like that in the first place. If it wasn't just a job for her own skills, she shouldn't have taken it. Plus, if she told her sister, Tai would want to confront Elaine and tell her off. Tracy was too embarrassed to tell Viv. How could she explain going from being a television producer to the plaything of some rich woman. Her thoughts were accompanied only by the noise of the windshield wipers. She wanted to cry. Even with her eyes closed, she could tell when the light from Marcus's car was shining through her rear window. She put her car in drive, ready to pull out, when she saw him coming from his car and gesturing for her to roll down the window.

"You have a hands-free device on your cell phone?" he asked her, holding up a phone that was attached by a small wire to his ear.

"Yeah," she said.

"What's your cell phone number? We can talk as we drive in," he suggested.

Tracy listlessly looked in her purse for her phone.

"You have to find your phone in order to tell me your number?" He smiled.

"No...but Marcus. I don't want to talk on the way home. I just want to be alone with my thoughts," she told him honestly, while she wrote out her number on the back of one of her business cards and handed it to him. His face became suddenly serious.

"What thoughts? Now, I definitely know we have to talk on the way back," he said, taking the card and putting it in his coat. "You having second thoughts?"

"Well...yes and no," Tracy said and looked down into her lap.

"Unlock the door. I'm coming around," Marcus said, going to the passenger's side. Tracy really didn't want to do this right in front of Sean's eye. Marcus had to knock on the window before she decided to let the window down enough for him to hear her.

"No, Marcus, let's just go...I really have to think things through," she said, mustering up as much plea as her worn-out brain would allow.

"Not without me, you don't. Tracy, please...open the door."

Tracy sighed and was about to do just that, when her weary mind coughed up an alternative. She put the car in drive and started on her long way back home. From her rearview mirror, Tracy saw Marcus scrambling to get in his vehicle and follow her. At the first stop sign off of Elaine's property, the phone rang. She held up the phone so that he could see it and she turned it off and then threw it back in her purse. She wasn't mad at him, but what she said, she meant. She needed a moment to process all that had happened. He had no idea what she was going through and he couldn't talk her through it.

Tracy felt that she really couldn't afford to lose this job. She didn't have any savings yet in the bank and she was just climbing out of the debt she had incurred when she was so broke. She could see herself happy in a relationship with Marcus. He was just the kind of man she wanted. And needed. But she could just imagine Elaine's face if she came out as a couple with Marcus. Elaine would blow her stack, fire her on the spot and probably, just to be spiteful, say that Tracy owed her for all of the money she'd spent on her. Tracy drove slowly down winding suburban roads that, unlike the city proper, weren't plowed or salted. She would have rather been driving her Jeep.

At the first two-lane stop sign, she was relieved to see that Marcus didn't pull up beside her and try to talk. He remained dependably behind her, but she could see from his body language that he was not pleased at all. This had been one of the happiest nights of her life. Tracy thought it could've been for Marcus too. Yet, that vicious Elaine was in the way of everybody's happiness. Hers. Sean's. Marcus's. Ashleigh's. *Was Elaine just put on earth to make everybody miserable?* Because she was certainly doing a good job of that.

Elaine was no enigma. Tracy could even see her underhandedly saying worse than she owed for her clothes and jewelry. She could claim that Tracy had stolen company property, used credit cards for personal use…whatever. If wronged, Elaine was the type to start a smear campaign that could keep Tracy out of the job market for years to come, until she was lucky enough to find an employer who wasn't within Elaine's reach. Tears sprang from Tracy's eyes as she realized that she was in too deep. She might be smart, but she was just a kid compared to Elaine. Making a deal with Elaine was like getting in bed with the mob. You don't easily get out because they can always change the rules of the game.

She looked in the rearview mirror at Marcus's silhouette. That was where she should be—riding along in the car with Marcus, talking and joking and smooching at red lights. Instead, she was certainly making his life miserable. She swiped at her eyes, because the water was making stars of all the lights. The car swerved too close to a guardrail and scraped against it. She over-adjusted and her car spun away from guardrail and far out into the road. Tracy slammed on the brakes and the car spun around, skidding toward the opposing traffic's lanes and narrowly missing an oncoming car. Her car finally came to a stop with the rear end sticking over both halves of the road. It was late and the weather conditions were so bad that not much traffic was on the highway. As she tried to figure out what happened, Marcus was pounding on the window. She opened the door and burst into tears. She cried into her hands, surprising herself even while she was doing it. Now she knew she was stressed out. It wasn't like her to get so emotional over a little scare like that. The other driver had pulled over and come to her door too.

"Is everything okay?" he asked Tracy.

"It's fine, I'm with her," Marcus told the man.

"Okay. Be careful. The roads are slick from here all the way to the drive," he warned. Marcus nodded and thanked the man for his concern.

"It's all right Trace. You're all right," he said, wrapping his arms around her shoulders and giving her the squeeze that she needed. She rose up and hugged his neck.

"Marcus, I'm sorry," she sobbed onto his shoulder.

"Sorry for what? You got nothing to be sorry for." He hugged her tightly. "Now scoot over and let me move your car out of the road. We're going to have to spend the night at Elaine's. These roads are too dangerous for us to make it back to the city."

"What are you going to do about your car?" she asked, alarmed, but did as she was told and moved over to the passenger's seat.

"I'll move it onto the shoulder and leave it. We can get it in the morning." He closed the door and drove her over to the northbound lanes, the direction back to Elaine's.

"No. Someone could hit it out here or you could be jammed

in by the snowplow." Regaining some of her composure, Tracy wiped her eyes.

"Don't worry about it," he said, turning on the hazards. He waited until the road was clear and ran across the street to maneuver his car closer to the guardrail. Tracy turned on the radio to a light jazz station. She still didn't feel like talking to Marcus about their evening, and maybe the music would clue him in to keep quiet.

Marcus returned to the car and methodically adjusted the seat and mirrors to his preference. That done, he looked at her. "You okay?"

Tracy nodded, put her hands to her cheeks and closed her eyes. "I'm fine. I don't know why I lost it."

"It's all right," he said soothingly and rubbed her back. "That kind of thing is really scary. I know my heart was in my throat just watching it."

"Yeah, but I just overreacted."

"Nah, you never know how you're going to react in a situation like that," he said, putting the car into gear and steering it slowly back onto the road. Maybe it was because of the near accident, but whatever the reason, Marcus didn't really say much on the way back. When they pulled up on Elaine's property, Marcus put the car in the garage, having taken the garage door opener from his car. They entered through the house.

"I'm sure Sean will be thrilled to see us," he quipped. Tracy snickered nervously, worried about the reception they would get from Sean. They didn't call out to him, but traveled through the house and found him stretched out on the couch in the great room. A half-eaten sandwich sat on a plate on the cocktail table. He sat up when he saw them.

"What happened?" he asked, looking at Tracy.

"None of the roads are plowed. Tracy had a spinout," Marcus explained. "We're going to stay here tonight."

Sean rose to his feet. "I'm sorry that happened to you. I

should have suggested that you stay here," he said, ignoring Marcus and talking only to Tracy. "Are you okay?"

"Just a little shaken up," Tracy said lowly and looked at her feet.

"Are you hungry? Let me fix you a sandwich," he said, moving toward the kitchen.

"No, Sean. Thanks, but I really just want to go to bed," she explained, unbuttoning her coat.

"I'll show you to one of the bedrooms," Marcus said, moving to take her coat.

"I'll settle her in a room, Marcus. I think she's had enough excitement for one night," Sean said, cutting his eyes at Marcus. Marcus opened his mouth to respond, but Sean cut him off and exerted the authoritative manner that Tracy had always seen. "Why don't you fix her a sandwich, anyway? She hasn't had anything to eat all night."

"No, really…don't fuss over me. I wasn't hurt or anything. Just show me to a room," Tracy said, harsher than she had intended, worn down by their sibling-slash-cousin-slash-whatever rivalry.

"It's not a problem," Marcus conceded, noticing her irritation. He placed Tracy's coat in the closet and removed his coat and shoes. "Sean is right. You should put something in your stomach."

Marcus went to the kitchen, while Tracy followed Sean upstairs. The rooms were arranged in a circle around the stairwell, so that the doors of each bedroom faced the hall. The master bedroom was at the end of the hall. One guest bedroom was at the top of the stairs and there were two on each side of the stairs, making six bedrooms in all. He escorted her to the largest guest bedroom at the top of the staircase, the one where she had found Marcus earlier in the evening.

"You shouldn't have to change the sheets; the maids usually keep the linens fresh," Sean explained, turning on the lights and walking through the room. "But if it's not to your liking, this is the linen dresser. Right here is your bathroom. There's a towel closet in there."

"Thanks, Sean," Tracy said. She walked into the spacious bathroom, noting the whirlpool tub, and then came out and sat on the bed.

"No problem," he answered. He stood in the room for a second, watching her, and then clasped his hands together. "Well...I guess that's it. Marcus will bring up a tray, I suppose."

"Oh! Before you go, I don't have anything to sleep in," she said, thinking of taking a long hot bath but remembering that she didn't have anything to change into.

"Oh, right," Sean said, snapping his fingers as though he should have thought of everything. "If you don't mind wearing some of Elaine's things..."

"At this point, I'll take anything."

"I'll go see what she has." He turned and left the room. Tracy stood up and stretched her back, then went into the bathroom and began to run water in the tub. She walked back into the bedroom and removed her jewelry by the dresser. Sean returned to the doorway, looking sheepish. "On second thought, you'd better go look through her things yourself. I wouldn't know what you'd...be most comfortable in."

Tracy chuckled at his embarrassment. "Fine, I guess it's that way."

"Yeah, her bedroom is at the other end of the hall." He pointed. "There are guest bathrobes in the towel closet."

"Cool, thanks." Tracy approached Elaine's bedroom with some trepidation. The ivory double doors and long, curved, brass door handles reminded her of the extravagant way her office was set aside from the others at work. Once inside, Tracy stood in a room that was opulent and sizeable. She didn't know how a man could sleep in the space. It was so overwhelmingly a lady's boudoir. The room was furnished with a king-size canopy bed with a crocheted lace topper, a chaise longue trimmed in fringe in the corner, a vanity table, a writing desk, two large armoires, a dresser, a cream-colored loveseat and thick angora carpet. Even with all of the furniture, Tracy had plenty of floor space to peek through a set of double-pocket doors, which led to the master bath. Elaine had his and hers showers, sinks and toilets, and a huge Jacuzzi tub that was at the top of three small marble stairs.

"Now, this is the life," Tracy said, shaking her head at how the other half lived. She went back into the bedroom and opened one of the armoires. It held a flat-screen television. Tracy opened the other and found the drawer with Elaine's sleepwear. She chose a pink satin pajama set. She held it to her nose, cringing at the faint, sophisticated smell of Elaine.

Upon returning to her assigned room, she found that Marcus had left a tray with a hot bowl of vegetable soup, a turkey sandwich, a glass of milk and a carafe of water. As a nice added touch, he had pulled a pretty purple flower from one of the fresh arrangements around the house and placed it in a small glass of water on her tray. Sean must have been the one to lay an extra blanket out for her, along with a thick terry-cloth robe. One thing Tracy could give Elaine credit for was that she had trained her boys well. They knew how to take care of a woman.

Chapter 15

Downstairs, the two men avoided each other, preferring to stay in separate wings of the house. Marcus had opted to hang out in the game room and shoot pool, while Sean surfed the Internet and watched television in the den. There was nothing they could say to each other that wouldn't spark an argument and they were too keyed up to sleep. The only thing they had in common was that both of their thoughts were on Tracy.

Despite the fact that he was engaged to be married, Sean found Tracy exceedingly attractive. Marcus had been right in their confrontation in his office when he said that Tracy was just the kind of woman he would have dated when he was out there. But Sean could point to a noticeable difference. Tracy was smarter, vivacious and more straightforward than any of the women he'd had in his life. He had gone into this evening without any intentions of seducing Tracy. He had seriously met with her to plan Elaine's party. Well—maybe aggravating Marcus was part of it—but he wouldn't have done anything improper. Yet, as the evening wore on, he was beginning to have doubts that Ashleigh was the right woman for him. He was too intelligent not to apply psychoanalytical thought to his actions. He was willing to admit that part of the reason he was sitting up tonight thinking about Tracy was because he was sure she was dating Marcus or into Marcus or something. All he needed to know was that Marcus had gone ballistic when he saw them together. He also knew that they had kissed. He could tell when he walked into the room. Even though he was lying about seeing lipstick on Marcus, his cousin had wiped it away.

Sean was jealous. Ideally, the kiss was how his evening with Tracy should have ended. Granted, she knew he was engaged, but given a choice, why would she choose Marcus over him? No one else had. And, he'd put that to the test, time and time again.

Growing up, Sean was always seducing the girls that Marcus had a crush on. Sean chuckled to himself at the memory of it. Poor Marc would pine away for a girl in school, wondering if he should tell her he liked her or send her a note. Sean would just swoop in and ask the girl out, then relish the dejected look on Marcus's face when he brought the girl by the house to make out in the basement. He was done with them in about a month, moving on to the next conquest. And, no matter how Marcus tried to hide it, it was always easy for Sean to tell which girl he was digging. He was like that, always wearing his heart on his sleeve. He did have his regrets about the last time he'd done this to Marcus. He was a grown man and going to marry that girl.

"What was her name?" Sean muttered to himself. *Hillary, Harriet, Haley?* Something. He was wrong to sleep with her while Marcus was out of town on a business trip for the company. But Marcus had been walking around so smug that he'd finally found love. Sean felt he had to show him that the girl was no more than common street trash. "Hannah," he said aloud. She was a dancer with the Joffrey Ballet in Chicago. She had been a sweet lay and brokenhearted when she found out that Sean had used her with no intention of continuing a relationship.

Anne Duncan, on the other hand, wasn't pretty enough for Sean to be bothered with. Sean toyed with her just enough to make her think that she had a chance with him. Marcus dumped her after Sean "innocently" mentioned to Marcus that Anne was calling him all the time. The workshop on sexual harassment put an end to her annoying phone calls.

But Tracy was another story. Tracy was clever and stylish. She had shown that she could handle herself. Given time, she could run the business just like Elaine. They would be a true power couple if he decided to go that route. Ashleigh was smart, but she wasn't as quick as Tracy…and no one would really want to see her running Cathy Booker Foods. He loved her he supposed, more than he'd loved any woman. She was meant to be his trophy wife, the one who represented him at societal functions. Sean shook his head in a quandary. He would just have to see if he could entice Tracy without leaving Ashleigh. Tracy worried him though. For the first time in his life, he wasn't sure that the old Sean Booker charm was enough.

Chapter 16

Tracy turned over in bed and looked at the clock. One-twenty-six in the morning and she still wasn't asleep. She had taken a bath, eaten her soup and part of the sandwich and watched a little television before turning out the lights at around midnight. She stood up and paced the floor in the dark. In all that time, she had avoided thinking about what to do about her predicament. She went to her attaché case and took out her pad and pen. She turned on a very small lamp on the desk that illuminated the room only minimally and lay on her stomach on the bed.

The best way she could think things through was to write it out. She wrote "pros" on one side of the pad and "cons" on the other, not really sure what she was listing the pros and cons of. Under pros she put "Marcus," then her salary, then the skills she was gaining at work. Under cons, she wrote "ELAINE" in capital letters. She heard a faint knocking on the door and her heart jumped.

"Tracy...you awake?"

She looked back at the clock radio, then turned over her notepad.

"Tracy?" the voice called again. Through the door, she couldn't tell who it was. It had better not be Sean. She jumped up and put on the robe and turned out the lamp. She crossed the floor and opened the door a crack to see Marcus in a gray T-shirt and pajama pants standing in the hall.

"Marcus," she said, exasperated, but stepped aside and let him in. She quickly shut the door behind him.

"Were you expecting someone else?" He meant it as a joke, but even in the dark, Tracy could clearly see the wrinkle on his brow.

"Don't start that again," she said, returning to sit on the bed.

"Sorry, just joking," he said quietly and sat down beside her. "Were you asleep?"

"No, I couldn't sleep," she admitted. Tracy fidgeted with the pen she found under her leg.

"Me either." He nodded and looked at her. "We have to talk. I didn't want to go back to the office tomorrow without—"

"I know," she cut him off. "I was thinking the same thing."

"So...you go first." Marcus lay back on the bed with his feet still touching the floor. His hands were folded across his stomach. He gazed at Tracy in the moonlight. Tracy stretched out next to him on her side, leaning on her elbow and propping her head up with her left fist. The positions they'd adopted were just right for a whispered, intimate conversation.

"You're the one who initiated this talk. You go first," she countered, just to be stubborn. Marcus sighed heavily and rubbed his right eye.

"Well, I think I told you everything. I can't get you out of my mind. I like you. I want to be with you and you can take that as far as you want it to go," he said softly. He raised his open hand indicating that it was as simple as that. "That's it for me in a nutshell. You're the one having doubts and whatnot."

"That's because I stand to lose more," Tracy explained, taking his hand. She had wanted to touch him ever since he came in the room.

"Lose? Like what?" Marcus swung her hand back and forth.

"My virginity for one thing," Tracy said, laughing before Marcus even figured out it was a joke. He laughed too, glad that she was alleviating some of their tension. He squeezed her hand.

"Could you be serious for just one moment? Please, Miss Tracy Middleton?" he teased her.

"Okay. Okay. Seriously…my credibility," Tracy said. "Elaine will hit the roof if she finds out I'm dating you. She did not hire me to cavort with the men on the executive staff." *Only Sean*, she thought and her stomach felt queasy.

"Forget Elaine. I can handle Elaine," Marcus said with more conviction than she had thought him capable of, regarding Elaine.

"And the rest of the staff…I have to be their boss. As much as I hate to say it myself, I have to be Elaine in her absence. How am I supposed to get their respect if I'm all googly-eyed over you?"

He pulled her hand into his chest. "You googly-eyed over me?" he asked, his voice gentle and teasing.

Tracy shrugged, smiling. "Maybe."

"Yes?"

"Maybe."

He pulled her arm until her face was over his and closed his eyes for a kiss. Tracy obliged, pressing her lips to his and letting go of his hand so she could touch his muscular chest. A benefit she recalled vividly from their last embrace. This time, there was a series of gentle kisses. Marcus placed his arm around Tracy's back and pulled her chest on top of his. He broke their kiss to talk directly in her face.

"So, are you trying to tell me we shouldn't do this?" He kissed her lips. "Or this?" He kissed her neck. He felt really good. Tracy could feel her body responding to his caresses.

"Yeah, Marcus, I'm saying we shouldn't," she said, tearing herself away and sitting up. Marcus sat up too, surprised that she was actually saying no.

"Why not?" he asked, more like a petulant child than a grown man.

"Are you hearing me? I could lose my job," she said, enunciating each word in the last sentence. Marcus twisted his lips and cocked his head at her.

"You honestly think…Elaine would fire you because you and I were dating?"

"Honestly? Yes," she said, standing up and pacing around the room. "And although you're all lovey-dovey now, are you willing to have me move in with you? You gonna take care of me? Because I'm gone be honest, I have bills, brother. Bills like you can't imagine."

Knowing her history as a television producer and recalling the grand way Elaine had introduced Tracy at their first meeting, Marcus smiled at her dramatic representation of her life without Cathy Booker Foods. "Yeah, sistah, I'll take care of you and your bills," he joked.

Tracy's head whipped around, angry at being mocked. She became icily calm. "Well, bottom line is, we can't see each other."

"In the office," Marcus added, not allowing her bad mood to infect his. He walked to where she was standing and she moved away, but he followed her.

"Or anywhere," Tracy said with finality, snapping her head.

"Anywhere, but the office," he said again, catching her and holding her from behind. She tried to pull away, but he held her firmly.

"No. I can't lose this job," she whined, starting to chuckle.

"Cool. So we agree that we'll see each other everywhere, but the office. Keep it on the DL?" Marcus squeezed her affectionately and whispered it in her ear. She laughed and turned around in his arms.

"I give in. I mean, I give up," she said. Tracy draped her arms around his neck and kissed him, pressing her body against his. He opened her belt so that he could hug her inside the robe. Feeling the slickness of the satin pajamas helped him to outline her figure. Their tongues united in a way that meant they'd reached an understanding.

"So, what about tonight?" Marcus asked with lustful eyes.

"What?" Tracy played dumb. In response, he started backing her toward the bed. "Ohhh, no."

Tracy shook her head, but Marcus continued backing. When the back of her knees bumped the bed, she slipped out of his grasp and sat down, instead of his desired outcome, which would have been for her to fall back fully onto the bed. He ended up standing with his torso in front of her face.

"This works for me too," he said, rubbing her hair. They laughed. Tracy pushed him square in the stomach and stood up. She turned him around as he was trying to kiss her again.

"Out," she ordered. "You have to get out now. I'm not about to have sex in Elaine's house, especially with Sean right down the hall."

She had successfully pushed Marcus all the way to the door. He paused with his hand on the knob and turned his head over his shoulder. "So, if Sean wasn't here, you would—"

"Get out, you," she said, laughing, and pushed him out the door. She watched as he ran halfway down the hall. He turned around and ran back to the door and gave her a quick kiss.

"Good-night. Sweet dreams," he whispered.

"Good-night. Now go before you wake up Sean," she whispered back. She closed the door and walked back to the bed with a huge smile. She twirled around on the balls of her feet and fell on the bed, giddy with love.

There was no need for them to worry about waking Sean. He had gone to get a bottle of water from the fridge. From downstairs in the shadows, he'd caught the scene of Marcus leaving Tracy's room.

Chapter 17

By breakfast, a few of Elaine's staff had made it through the snow. At least the cook was there, and had prepared a sumptuous buffet for them in the dining room. Tracy and Marcus where already eating, talking and laughing with each other by the time Sean came downstairs. They were surprised to see him in a full suit, ready for work. They were both wearing the same clothes from the night before.

"Morning," Sean said and went to the buffet to get a plate.

"Morning," they said together. When his back was turned, Marcus pointed at Sean with his fork and mocked his professional attire. Tracy stifled a laugh.

"Uh…Sean?" Marcus said.

"Yeah?" Sean paused to look at Marcus with the lid to one of the serving platters in his hand.

"Um, how is it that you have on a suit? Are you wearing one of Howard's?" Marcus asked, meaning Elaine's husband. He and Tracy giggled like schoolchildren.

"No, you know damn well I would swim in one of Howard's suits," Sean said, impatient with their silliness. He continued to fix his plate. "I keep several suits here, just for this kind of emergency. As you can see, I'm the only one prepared for work. Were you two planning on going to work today?"

"Yeah. We thought it was going to be a three-way casual day in the executive offices," Tracy said brightly. She stuffed a forkful of French toast in her mouth.

"You know, we haven't had a casual day since that time we were expanding our offices," Marcus said to Sean. Sean set his plate on the table and went to get coffee.

"And we're not *going* to have a casual day until the next time we're expanding our offices," Sean said sourly, pouring himself a cup. He returned to the table and looked at his watch before he sat down. "We've got a meeting today. I expect you both to look…better than you look now."

Marcus raised his eyebrow at Tracy. She put her fork down and looked incredulously at Sean. "We have to get Marc's car and I'd have to go home and change," she whined.

Sean shrugged unconcernedly and ate his eggs. "Wear one of Elaine's suits."

"No way," Tracy said, shaking her head. She pushed her plate away.

"Suit yourself," Sean said. He chuckled. "Actually, that fits. *Suit* yourself."

Tracy looked at Marcus, who was eating his food like he didn't have a care in the world.

"What are you going to do?" she asked him.

"I have a couple of suits at the office," he said, unfazed. He was used to this kind of hardnosed attitude from Sean and Elaine and knew to be prepared.

"So I'm the only one left in the lurch?" She looked from one to the other and got no response. Tracy threw her napkin from her lap onto her plate and stood up.

"You're not leaving now?" Marcus asked, becoming alarmed. He snatched up his coffee and gulped it down. "I need a ride."

"You can ride in with me. I called for a car," Sean offered. "You too, Tracy."

"No thanks," Marcus said flatly. He found the prospect of riding in with Sean about as appealing as Tracy had the suggestion of wearing Elaine's clothes.

"I'm not leaving. I have to make a phone call," she said dashing to the front door. She had placed her belongings by the door when she came downstairs that morning. She dug into her purse for her cell phone. She had two options. She could phone Gina and ask her to run by her house and get a suit. Or…she dialed the pre-programmed phone. *I'll show that Sean.*

"Hello? Whoever you are, do you know what time it is?"

"Melvin. I'm so glad you're in," Tracy said, ignoring his bitchiness. She talked fast. "This is Tracy with an emergency. I need something that screams 'I'm a businesswoman' to knock their socks off for the meeting today at ten. But you have to deliver it to the office. I got stuck out without a lick of clothing."

"Fabulous. I've got just the thing. It'll be there before you," he said excitedly and hung up without saying good-bye. Tracy nodded with satisfaction, and put on her coat and hat and picked up her bags. She started back to the kitchen and met Marcus, who was coming down the hall. "You ready to go?" she asked Marcus.

"Yeah, let's get out of here before we have to hear any more orders from Sean," he said, touching her arm and passing by her to get his coat. "He's being a real jackass today."

They went back through the house to the garage, bypassing the kitchen where Sean was. Fortunately, the roads were plowed and salted when Tracy drove Marcus to his car. With the road plowed, they were only ten minutes away from where he'd left it. She pulled behind it. Just as she predicted, his car was too plowed in for him to move it in time for work. Marcus decided that he could call someone to retrieve his car for him and ride in with Tracy.

"So, how are we going to play this?" Marcus asked when they were closer to the office.

"You mean us?" Tracy asked, not surprised that he was back on the topic of them. He had avoided it all morning, talking about Sean and news and whatever. But now that they were alone for an extended period of time, he wanted to make sure she wasn't backing out.

"No, the meeting this morning," Marcus said sarcastically, cutting his tender eyes at her. "Of course us. What else would I be talking about?"

"Well, what's to discuss?" Tracy snatched a glance at him. "We don't play kissy face in the office."

"Right, we established that. So, should we come in together?" he asked, smiling.

Tracy thought about it for a moment, drumming her fingers on the steering wheel. "I guess so. Sean already knows that we left together. It would look pretty silly if we tried to pretend like we weren't together."

"Yeah, if you go into the office and I wait a few minutes, that would be a definite flag that we've hooked up," Marcus agreed, looking out of his window at the beautiful snow-covered city. Even now, a light snowfall was continuing to dust the car windows. Tracy shot him a look.

"We didn't hook up," she admonished him.

"Yes, we did," Marcus said mildly, looking over at her.

"When? In your dreams?" Tracy asked flippantly.

"That too. But I think we have a question of semantics here." Marcus gave in. "So what would you call it?"

"Oh, never mind," Tracy said. "Let's go out tonight."

"My thoughts exactly. Where do you want to go?" Marcus asked, eager to please. Tracy just glimpsed him for a moment.

"You decide. Surprise me," she said. He smiled and returned to looking out of his window. He was thinking that the restaurant called Opera was a good place to take her.

By the time she got to her office, it was 9:37 and the meeting was scheduled for 10:00. This was her first time coming into the office after such a bad snowstorm, but judging by the way he'd acted in the morning, Tracy didn't think Sean was the type to allow for much flexibility in the schedule.

She was comforted to see a wardrobe bag lying on the couch in her office, with several other smaller bags around it. The suit Melvin had delivered to her office was more perfect than she could have imagined. It was a fully lined, deep red, wool suit made in a thirties style. The skirt was long and straight with a fluted pleat in the back and the jacket was a button front with a scalloped bottom and thin brown crocodile leather belt. She had a cream-colored shell underneath. The entire outfit fit her body impeccably and snugly.

But Melvin hadn't stopped at the suit. When it came to fashion the boy was fierce. He thought of everything, including the accessories. He had sent brown crocodile pumps matching the belt, along with a brown crocodile clutch and brown stockings that matched her flesh. She found a thick, hammered-copper bracelet, a sharp, floral brooch and demure copper earrings. She even saw a collection of MAC makeup in colors to complement her outfit. Melvin had left a note saying, "I don't know what coat you have on right now, but I suggest you leave today wearing the one in your closet." Excited, Tracy rushed to the closet to find a stunning, full-length, brown sable coat. She shook her head at the opulence of the item and knew that she would have to send that back. There was no way she could pass that off as something she could afford on her salary. Tracy snatched up the items and went to dress in Elaine's bathroom.

When she finally finished dressing and getting her hair just right, it was about five minutes after ten. She grabbed her materials and rushed into the meeting, where Sean was already talking.

"Due to the inclement weather, we're missing a couple of faces around the table today," he was saying. His speech staggered a bit when she walked through the door and took a place at the table beside Marcus. Sean could barely regain his thoughts as he watched her walk all the way to her seat. "So, um…so, we're missing some people, but as you can see from the agenda, it's not a day for individual reports. I'm just going to give you an update on some of the things we've been working on and we can discuss the merits of each."

Marcus would've been troubled by Sean's blatant attraction to Tracy if he had noticed it, but his eyes were riveted on her also. He had just left her moments before and here she was the most stunning woman he'd ever seen. Marcus was sitting to the right of Tracy so that he had to look past her to see Sean at the head of the table. He didn't bother with Sean. Knowing that this beauty was his woman had taken his mind into dangerous territory.

The mild fragrance of Tracy's perfume filled his nostrils and entered his brain, teasing him into thoughts of how she would look in his office with her arms wrapped around his shoulders and his encircling her tiny waist. Marcus leaned against his hand and unconsciously stroked his finger down his jawline as he gazed at her back. When his eyes lingered on her waist, he forced himself to look at Sean and try not to think about her too much, lest he find himself in a state of arousal that wouldn't allow him to leave the table at the end of the meeting. Instead, he focused on the words in Sean's tedious presentation.

Sean talked about the progress they were making in acquiring Down-Home Grown, and then he began to discuss the effectiveness of advertising their frozen dinners on the new video checkout screens at Jewel and Dominick's, the test areas' largest grocery chains.

Aware that no one was required to give reports in this meeting, everyone relaxed and took notes. Marcus's eyes had drifted to Tracy's back again when Sean abruptly looked at him and asked him for consumer projections on the Down-Home Grown's product line and how they would perform if they were introduced into the markets that Cathy Booker Foods had currently penetrated. Marcus was surprised and caught unprepared. Only last week, Sean had mentioned that he would eventually want them to develop such a report. Marcus sat up straight in his chair and looked across the table at Lisa Hodges, who was part of his marketing team. He had assigned her to be the project director of the assignment, but they had only had one meeting on the topic. She shook her head almost imperceptibly. Her reaction wasn't necessary. Marcus knew they couldn't have produced such a massive report in such a short period of time.

Marcus cleared his throat, and leaned over his notepad. "We don't have that report yet."

"Why not?" Sean asked irritably, his brow wrinkling.

Lisa looked at Marcus, and not one to shirk responsibility, decided to answer. "Well, we were just given this project last week and there are a lot of considerations—"

"I'm asking Marcus," Sean rudely interrupted her. He glared at Marcus. The others around the table fidgeted with their pens and some coughed. Tracy doodled on her notepad. The exchange was making them uncomfortable. It wasn't like Sean to get snippy with employees in front of the entire group.

Marcus eyed him steadily, the only one seeming unruffled by Sean's attitude. He had been startled to be called upon, but now that he saw Sean was trying to pick a fight with him, he wasn't fazed in the least. "We haven't received the report on their complete product line yet. Until we get that from them, we can't move forward with our projections," he explained, sitting back in his chair and stretching his legs out underneath the table.

"Even when we do receive it from them, it's going to take at least three weeks to fit all of their products into a diagram of all of our markets. Then we have to do a comparison on how well they'll perform based on the sales of our competitors with similar products. That doesn't even include package redesigns, change of ingredients or elimination of certain brand names. So, what are you asking about, Sean?"

Sean looked down at his notes. He knew Marcus was right. What he was asking for was impossible to produce within a week. But who was Marcus to be sleeping with Tracy when he wanted that privilege? The image of Marcus coming out of her room smoldered in his brain. That was his true reason for attacking. As a consequence, he wouldn't easily back down. "I guess I'm asking if you called them to at least move that along?"

"I called them, but they said the report wasn't ready. Brad and I are scheduled to go to their plant next week. I'll push them to have it available by then," Marcus told him.

"Get it before then. I want you to be prepared at the meeting," Sean snapped, feeling the power of his position. He glanced at Tracy to see if his firmness was having any affect on her.

Tracy squirmed in her seat, her eyes glued to the doodles she was making. She was growing uncomfortable at the men's obvious rivalry and had to speculate that it was just a continuation of last night's conflict. She suspected that it was now set in an environment in which Sean felt totally confident.

"With all due respect, Sean...our projections as to how DHG's product line will be received in markets that they're not even in yet have no bearing on the meeting Brad and I have with the plant supervisors. That information is for our internal use to create financial projections of the profitability of our acquiring their company. So, are you telling me that I have to be prepared to tell them how much we're going to make on the deal?"

Sean glowered at Marcus, knowing he was beaten by his cousin's quick mind. It was not that he couldn't have connected the dots to arrive at the same conclusion, but he had allowed his jealousy to make him challenge Marcus in front of the staff. He foolishly thought he could back Marcus into a corner by calling upon him to give a report for which he was unprepared.

"All right, we've got the Christmas party meeting in a few minutes," Sean said, looking at the clock on the wall. "I'll note that you don't have the information, but it will be ready once you get the information from them."

Marcus simply shrugged. He had said he wouldn't have the report for several weeks after they received the information, but he didn't want to continue their argument.

"If there isn't any other business," Sean said, pausing for a moment to see if anyone would speak. No one did. "The meeting is adjourned."

Everyone stood except Sean. Even the few who were staying for the second meeting wanted to stretch their legs, get coffee or run to their office before continuing. Tracy stood up to walk with Marcus to the door. She gave a little jump when she heard Sean call to her.

"Tracy, you're a part of this meeting," Sean said, only half scolding. He had a twinkle in his eye, recalling her objections to the group.

"Oh, I know. I left my things, I'm just going to run to my office," she explained. Marcus waited to walk out with her. When they passed out of Sean's sight, they felt free to speak.

"What was his problem?" Tracy asked, twisting her lips and frowning. "Asking you for a report that he knows is impossible to produce in such a short time frame."

"Nothing," Marcus said evenly. "That's the real Sean. It was just the first time that he exposed his true nature to everyone."

"Well, if that's his true nature, I feel sorry for Ashleigh," Tracy said under her breath. She thought the best thing Elaine could do if she didn't like Ashleigh was to let her go ahead and marry Sean. "Anyway, where are we going for lunch?"

"Come into my office for a minute," Marcus said mischievously, his eyes inviting her in. They were standing outside of the executive lobby. Something told her that he wasn't asking her in to discuss their lunch plans.

"Oh, no," she said, smiling. "Tell me out here."

"I have some menus and stuff we can look at to decide." His devilish smile gave his true intentions away. Tracy shook her head, declining his invitation. He reached out his hand, intending to tug her arm and guide her into his office, but he thought better of it when he looked around at all of the employees mulling about. He dropped his hand and gestured toward his door with his head, intent on making his daydream of kissing her within the confines of his office come true.

"You're breaking our deal," she said in a low, singsong voice. "I've got to get back for the Christmas party committee." She unenthusiastically turned from him to head back into the conference room.

"All right, I'll pick a place on my own," he said. His eyes were glued to her glorious, womanly posterior as she left his sight. It took a minute for him to realize that she had waved a hand in the air to acknowledge that she had heard him.

Tracy found that they didn't really need her at the meeting. Kelly, the internal relations director, had completed most of the work in preparing the party. Better still, she had run the entire thing by Elaine before she left town. It seemed that Tracy's only function in the meeting was to listen and take notes. The session didn't last more than twenty minutes. When it was over, Tracy started to gather her notebook and notepad, but Sean asked her to stay. He waited until everyone had exited and the door was closed to the conference room before speaking.

"I'm a little concerned about what happened last night at the house," he said, leaning forward over his notepad.

"Wh-what do you mean?" She frowned at him, considering all the events that had occurred at Elaine's.

"Are you and Marcus involved with each other?" he asked, more to the point.

"No," Tracy answered quickly, becoming nervous. She had thought that if Sean were going to discuss this, he would've done it at the breakfast table with both her and Marcus.

Sean sat back in his chair and observed her. "Are you sure? Because I did see him coming out of your room late last night...or should I say, this morning?" He watched her closely for her reaction. Tracy's big eyes grew larger before she could regain her composure. She knew Sean had guessed that they kissed, but she didn't know he had seen Marcus leaving her room. Now, she realized that he thought they'd slept together. She quickly searched her mind for words that would put his presumptions to rest.

"Well, if you also saw him enter my bedroom, you would know that Marcus was only there for a minute. He only came in to check on me and to apologize for the things he said during his argument with you. You know, the false assumptions on my character," she said, hoping that he would grasp her meaning that he was now jumping to conclusions.

Sean folded his hands on his stomach, averting his eyes from her. She was so beautiful and he found her so sexy that he thought it showed on his face. He had to admit that he hadn't seen Marcus enter, but he had witnessed him run back to the door to kiss her. He had been fuming all morning, thinking that they had made love right under his nose. At this point, he wasn't sure what had occurred. He had to believe her story because she asserted that he could have seen Marcus enter the room and leave in a short time.

"Cathy Booker doesn't really have a policy against employees dating. So, if you were to see him, we can't stop you. I only mention it because I'm concerned that my cousin has a tendency to think of the women in our company as his own personal dating pool."

Tracy's brow wrinkled, but she kept quiet. Sean pressed on, determined to throw out what he considered his ace.

"You've probably noticed that he and Anne Duncan are chilly with each other even now. This is the end result of a bad breakup in the office," he said, pausing to see that his words were having the desired effect on Tracy. She dropped her eyes and her chest was rising and falling anxiously. "I can't have every other woman walking around with a bad attitude because they dated Marcus and it didn't work out. Especially after seeing the way you reacted to that guy we saw at the restaurant, I gather that you're not the type to remain friendly with an ex."

There was no way to respond to his advice and Tracy struggled to maintain eye contact with him. If his lecture was meant to discourage her, it worked. She was stung by the news that Marcus had dated Anne. No wonder the chick acted so evil toward her, Anne had identified her as competition from day one. Tracy was so caught up in finally getting into the relationship phase with Marcus, that she hadn't considered how she would take it if they broke up. Plus, Sean's reminder of her situation with Brian really struck a chord. That had been a clandestine affair too.

Sean leaned forward and touched her arm. "I'm talking to you because I feel you have a bright future with this company, Tracy, and you don't want to ruin that by getting a reputation at the office. You work directly for my mother, and I know that's not what she had in mind for you when she chose you."

His words were so accurate that she had to wonder if in reality he did know what Elaine had intended for her. "I said nothing was going on. He and I had a discussion, that's all," she said quietly.

Sean sat back, satisfied. "Okay. I'm glad to hear it. I guess that's it then."

He gathered his stuff. Tracy stood up and picked up her things, her face burning in humiliation.

"If Elaine calls you before me, tell her I need to speak with her and transfer her to me," he said to her back. Tracy nodded and left. She went back to her office, glancing at Marcus's door before she went inside her own. She wanted to go in, but with Sean coming seconds behind her, she didn't want to get caught talking to him. She dropped her stuff and sat down at her desk, swiveling her chair to look out the window. The phone rang and Tracy suspected who it was.

"Hello," she said with no energy.

"Hey, you, I saw Sean come back. So I figured you were back too," Marcus said cheerfully. "I would come into your office but the way you look today, I think we need to meet in a more public place."

"Marcus, it really isn't a good idea that we see each other," she said, worn-out from her encounter with Sean. She knew she should do this face-to-face, but it was already difficult enough without seeing heartbreak in those deep and sensitive eyes.

"At the office," Marcus joked with her like he had last night. When she didn't say anything, he became worried. "What happened?"

"This time I'm serious. Sean kept me after the committee meeting and lectured me about office romances and worse," she said, turning around to face her desk and leaning on her elbows. Marcus was quiet, so she continued. "And check this out…he saw you coming out of the room last night and he thought we'd slept together. Can you even imagine what he must have thought of me? Sleeping with you in Elaine's house?"

"But that's not true. I'll tell him," Marcus said, feeling the anger rise in his chest.

Tracy pressed her fingers to her forehead. "No, Marcus, you're not hearing me. You always want to solve my problems for me. I straightened that out. What I'm telling you is that exactly what I *said* would happen, *did* happen. My reputation is under question, not yours."

"Trace, I told you that I think we should date openly in the first place. It only looks bad if we're sneaking around." He stood up and paced his office, desperate to persuade her to at least give them a chance. He couldn't accept that the woman he had sought for so long could slip away from him so quickly and that he was powerless to prevent it. He didn't know how he could undo the damage done after only one brief meeting with Sean.

"Plus, he's right. Last night I was caught up in the moment, not thinking about what would happen if we broke up. I don't know how I would react." In her own space, Tracy stood and watched the snow growing heavier outside her window.

How could dating openly solve her problem if Marcus wasn't aware of everything that was going on? And what would he do when he found out? Surely Elaine would rush to tell Marcus why she had hired Tracy in the first place if she felt her plan was threatened. Then, Marcus would never look at her the same again. She would be left without a job and without him.

"So, let me get this straight, you're breaking up with me to avoid the awkwardness of our breaking up?" he asked in a reserved voice. He knew she had a strong will and he didn't know how he could reach her.

"I'm not breaking up. I'm rethinking our getting together," she said mildly. It was not that she wasn't affected. It was just that since she had to be the heavy and do the breaking up, she tried to make it seem less serious.

"Tracy, don't do this," Marcus said flatly. "I don't know what Sean said to you, but we need to go to lunch and talk this over."

She just thought of something on her own that was troubling her mind. "And what about Anne Duncan? You didn't tell me you dated her. Who else have you seen at the office?"

"Who told you that? Sean?" Marcus asked, instead of answering a question he viewed as unnecessary.

"Why? Shouldn't he have told me?" She waited, listening to his breathing. "What's there to tell?"

"Nothing, Tracy," he said finally. Of all the low-down, underhanded things to do, Marcus couldn't believe that Sean would stoop to something like this. "It was nothing between me and her."

"Did you make love to her?" Tracy hoped not.

Marcus would've used more crude words to describe his dealings with Anne, but that would give Tracy the impression that he used women to satisfy his own needs.

"It was a mistake," Marcus said, avoiding the question. He was sure Tracy knew she had her answer.

"I've got no claims on you. I just want to know. Did you two go out a few times or did you sleep together?" She hated the thought of the snobby, frumpy Anne having seen Marcus naked and holding him close. "Speak up, Marcus."

"Okay, Tracy, I screwed her. Is that what you want to hear?" he said in a very weary voice, tired of her pestering.

"You make it sound so casual. So who else are you seeing in the office?" Tracy continued, not happy at all with the information, but she'd asked for it.

"You gonna get mad at me about other women, and you're not even dating me?" Most of the time, Marcus was seething at Sean for putting Tracy on this track of questioning. But now he directed his anger at her.

"No, I'm not mad. I just think Sean has a point—"

"He doesn't," he insisted angrily. Marcus wanted nothing more than to confront Sean about his talking to Tracy, but he didn't want to betray her confidence. He could punch his lights out. He had probably embellished the tale of Anne and him, making their relationship out to be more than the few weeks it was.

"Yes, he does, Marcus. We went over this scenario ourselves last night." Tracy picked up some papers off her desk and put them back again.

"And we agreed to keep it out of the office," Marcus reminded her.

"In the excitement of the moment…yeah. But in the light of day I didn't think about if we didn't work out and we have to continue to work together. Look at how you and Anne behave."

"No, Tracy, that was just a…bad judgment on my part." He didn't want to explain over the phone that she was a rebound fling after he broke up with Hannah. "Let's meet at the coffee shop down the street. We've got to discuss this face-to-face."

"How is that going to be any better? Let's put this relationship on ice for a minute."

There was an extremely long pause before Marcus spoke again. She was just about to call his name into the receiver. "Until when, Tracy? It's now or never."

Never? Tracy was worried about the prospect of losing him forever. But then again, she couldn't be backed into a corner by Marcus's demands. "I guess I'm saying let's wait until I'm not working here. I've been down this path before and it hurts."

"I'm not Brian," Marcus said quietly.

"I know, but, look, Viv is going to find me another job and when I'm working there, we can see if we still want to be together," she offered, but it didn't go over well at all.

"I can't force you to be with me and I really shouldn't have to beg you to see me." He hung up.

She came out of her office in time to see him storm out of his door, slamming it shut and telling Pam he was going to lunch. Tracy called to him, but he left without looking in her direction. It was just as bad as she had expected. Pam was gawking at her and Sean came through the doors to their offices a few seconds after Marcus left. She had just escaped his noticing the ruckus—the very actions he'd just warned her against.

Pam told Tracy that Gina was trying to reach her. Elaine was calling on line one. Tracy went back into her office and found that Elaine wanted an update on what had happened with the planning for the party. Tracy, in no mood for her schemes right now, told her "it went fine" and hung up.

Chapter 18

It was the week before Christmas. As agreed, Tai and Kevin had come down to Chicago for the holiday, with their three children in tow. They planned to stay for their entire vacation of three weeks. Having two extra bedrooms in her home, Tracy had wanted them to board with her. It would give them the chance to discuss their arrangements for their mother. But Tai thought it would be better to settle her family in at their mother's apartment. Tracy figured that with her Christmas bonus, she had saved $15,000 for a down payment on a home for Sheila. Come to find out, she didn't want a house. It was too much responsibility for her to keep up the yard, keep up periodic maintenance, handle emergencies and fix things that were broken. She said she wasn't young anymore and didn't have a man around to help her. Kevin, Tai and Tracy were planning to move her to a new, larger apartment in a safer neighborhood. Tai figured that if they stayed at Sheila's, they would be right there to start packing up her things.

Tracy arrived at the apartment to pick up her mother, who was going to be her date for the company's Christmas party. She had spoken with her sister on the phone since she had arrived the day before, but hadn't yet had a chance to see her in person. As usual, she used her key to access her mother's entryway, but knocked when she got to Sheila's door. She smiled broadly at hearing all the loud talking inside and then the sound of all the locks being undone. Tai answered the door with the baby on her arm.

"Ooo…look-a here, would ya?" Tai grinned and held out her unoccupied arm for Tracy to fall into. Tracy squeezed her sister tightly, wrapping her arms around her and the baby. She was so happy to see Tai that she had to fight back tears.

"I'm so glad to see you. I really missed you," Tracy said, her face smushed against her sister's shoulder. They rocked together, neither wanting to release the other.

"You know I love you, right?" Tai said soothingly to her. Tracy felt tears welling up in her eyes. "And I'm proud of you and I keep you in my prayers *every* night."

The boys screeched Tracy's name and came running from the hall to hug her legs. She reluctantly let go of Tai and bent down to squeeze their small bodies. They had grown a lot since the last time she saw them.

"Hi, Sam. Hi, Lucas. How are you?" she said, overjoyed to finally be holding her nephews in her arms again. They said, "Fine," and then their voices competed with each other's to give her an account of something they found interesting about their trip to Chicago. Tracy made the appropriate amazed faces at their youthful chatter and responded as though their conversation was just as significant as anybody else's.

"Y'all get off her. You better not get anything sticky on Tracy's coat," Tai said, moving to close the door. After kissing the boys and acting interested in their children's stories, Tracy stood up and reached for the baby.

"No, girl, you don't want to mess up your nice clothes," Tai said, walking to sit down on the couch. Tracy stepped i front of her.

"Girl, you better give me my baby!" Tracy insisted, reachin for the little girl she had only seen in pictures until now.

"Hello," she cooed. "Hello, Madison, I'm your auntie." Th baby blinked at her and she started to smile. Then realizin that the woman was a stranger, her face crumpled and sh decide that crying was the better reaction. She reached for Ta on the sofa and Tai reached for her, but Tracy held on, tryin to calm her niece.

"I'm Auntie Tracy, hmmm? You don't know Aunti Tracy?" she spoke softly to Madison.

"Hey, hey!" Kevin said coming from the bathroom dow the hall. "It's the bigwig." He was holding open his arms lon before he reached her. Tracy just had time to surrender th baby before being enveloped by Kevin's bear hug. After while, he pulled back to look at her, holding her hand up s that he could get a good look. "Check her out, with her fu coat and all," he said to Tai.

"I know it. Don't she look nice?" Tai nodded in agreemen adjusting the baby on her shoulder. "Take off that coat, an let me see what you got on underneath there."

Tracy did as instructed, revealing a deep-purple, fitte evening gown with rhinestone spaghetti straps. She had rhine stone sandals and a small, purple satin purse. Her bracele necklace and earrings were real diamonds.

"Oh, heavens, you look nice," Tai said, almost breathless "That looks real classy too. Is it some designer stuff?"

"Yeah, not my usual knockoff crap," Tracy said, waving he hand like she was an expert now at distinguishing fancy clothing

"You look real pretty, Tracy," Kevin said. "It doesn't loo like you and Mama even going to the same event."

"What do you mean?" Tracy frowned, confused. Las

week, she had brought over a black Prada dress for Sheila and matching accessories. She had sought Melvin's advice, but purchased everything with her own money. She looked at Tai, who snorted, rolled her eyes and finally fixed them on the television set. Tracy looked back at Kevin, who shook his head and looked at his shoes, smiling. Alarmed, Tracy hurried down the hall to her mother's room. The door was closed and Tracy knocked at the same time she opened the door. "Mama?"

"Hey, baby. I'm almost ready," Sheila said, standing in front of her dresser's mirror and clipping rhinestone earrings to her ears. Tracy's heart sank. Instead of wearing the gown she had bought for her, Sheila was dressed in one of her church suits, a lavender, three-piece crepe with rhinestone accents on the shoulders. Her hair was in a cute upsweep with curls falling around her face. Tracy looked at the shoes. No. She wasn't wearing the strappy mules she had purchased, but tacky silver, low-heeled pumps and sparkly silver stockings.

"Mama, why aren't you wearing the outfit I sent you?" she whined.

"I tried that stuff on and felt like a harlot," she replied, waving the thought of the outfit away with her hand. Tracy racked her brain to think of how a full-length, long-sleeved, black gown that had an ornate crew neck could look, in any way, provocative.

"Besides, I think this looks much better."

No, it doesn't, Tracy thought. *For a church revival maybe, but not a corporate party.* She prayed to God she wasn't going to wear one of her big hats. Tracy went to her closet to retrieve the outfit, which was right in the front. "How did it look suggestive?"

"It was hugging all on my breasts and hips, showing everything God gave me," Sheila said, dramatically pointing to her form.

Tracy looked at the tag in the back of her mother's suit.

"This is a size up from your size, and they run large anyway. I can't believe it looked that bad."

"Well," Sheila said with a huff, picking up a large handbag "I didn't like it."

"Try it on for me," Tracy pleaded.

"Unh-uh, Tracy. Now, I'm wearing what I'm wearing," she said, getting annoyed that Tracy didn't think she had any fashion sense. "You don't waltz in here and tell me what to wear."

She stared at Tracy crossly. Tracy looked back, hurt and defeated.

"Now either I'm going as myself, or I'm not going," she told her, placing a defiant hand on her hip. Tracy put the dress back in the closet.

"All right, Mama. Your outfit is fine," she said, overpowered by her mother's will and ashamed of having tried to change her mind. She noted Sheila's comment about going as herself and thought that her objections to the dress had nothing to do with its fit at all. It was that the style was out of her comfort zone.

Tracy had gotten so wrapped up in this "dressing the part" that she had forgotten that her own manner of dress was all a big lie. While Sheila was going to the party as herself, who was Tracy going as?

"I know my outfit's fine," Sheila said, reaching for her coat. At least she was wearing the new black wool coat Tracy had bought her. Tracy helped her put it on. "And you look really elegant, by the way."

"Thanks Mama." Tracy managed a weak smile and kissed her mother's cheek. They entered the living room together.

"All right now, look out for the fine Middleton women," Kevin teased.

Sheila strutted and Tracy smiled broadly, picking up her coat and clutch.

"That's right. Don't y'all go out there picking up no men

You two look so nice, you gonna close the place down," Tai chimed in, standing to lock the door behind them.

Sheila chuckled before providing her last-minute instructions. "There's plenty of stuff in there to snack on, but go ahead and eat more of the leftovers if y'all get hungry. And I put out some towels and stuff for the kids' baths. Tracy has a cell phone, so call me if you don't know where anything is—"

"Mama," Tai called out to stop her prattle. "Go to the party already. Don't I know how to find things in this house?"

"I got her," Tracy said, slinging her arm around her short mother's shoulders and leading her to the door. "I'll see you when we come back."

"No, you won't either, 'cause we'll be gone to bed," Tai said, kissing her sister's cheek and then her mother's. "Have fun."

The Drake Hotel was one of the most glorious on the Magnificent Mile. It had an old-world charm about it with modern conveniences. When Tracy and her mother entered the reception area, she saw lots of familiar faces from the job, but not anyone she worked with directly. Everyone looked so festive and joyful, chatting with each other in various groupings. So many people were here with their dates that it was no wonder that Tracy recognized even fewer faces in the crowd than she usually did around the job. She led her mother to the coat check area, where they left their wraps and got tickets. Tracy turned around and looked at a sign informing them on what level they would find their Christmas party. Apparently, other companies had decided that The Drake was the perfect place to regale their staff.

"This is really nice," Sheila said, looking around the large space. The lobby was decorated with Christmas trees, holly, poinsettias, lights and sprigs of mistletoe. Soft, generic Christmas music played in the background.

"This *is* beautiful," Tracy agreed, looking around at the finery. She touched Sheila's arm. "Come on, let's go find out where we're sitting and then I can introduce you to Elaine."

She walked through the crowd and around a corner as directed by the sign. Finally, she spotted a table that was being staffed by the internal relations people from Cathy Booker Foods, along with their volunteers. She started to go to Kelly, the head of the department, but heard her name being called. She looked around a bunch of heads to see her secretary, Gina.

"Hi, Gina, I didn't know you were going to be working the table tonight," Tracy said, happy at last to see someone she knew. Gina leaned across the table to hug her. She was gloriously attired in a gold, knee-length evening dress.

"Yeah. I volunteered at the last minute. So, is that your mom?" she asked, smiling at Sheila.

"Oh, yeah." Tracy reached back to pull her mother forward. "Mama, this is Gina, my secretary. Gina, this is my mother, Sheila."

They shook hands and exchanged pleasantries before Tracy asked Gina if she knew where they were supposed to be sitting.

"It's open seating," she said, looking at Tracy like she must have been testing her. "We're just here to give out your gifts. Hold on, let me get yours." Gina left to retrieve a couple of gift bags from the ones lined up behind the long table.

"Right," Tracy said, embarrassed at her lack of understanding at the protocol of Corporate America. At CMT, they held the Christmas party at their station, with the offices gaily decorated. Gina returned with a red bag for Tracy and a green bag for her guest. Her mother, who was surprised at receiving anything, immediately opened her gift bag and started inspecting her booty. There were some fancy chocolates, a bunch of CDs, a rolled-up Cathy Booker Foods T-shirt, coupons for free products, a Santa figurine and loose Christmas candies.

"All this stuff is for me?" Sheila pulled out the most expensive item in the bag, a crystal picture frame. "I'm going to put my picture of the grandbabies in this."

Tracy looked at her mother's stuff rather than opening her own bag and moved away so that other people could check in.

"Well, let's go in," she said nervously. She touched her mother's back. As she approached the entrance to the ballroom, the sounds of a live band, laughter and loud conversation were increasing.

Tracy and Sheila joined a snaking line with other employees who were waiting to mount three wide stairs. Even with her height, it was difficult to see what the holdup was at the top of the steps. She stood on tiptoes and peered over the crowd's heads to see that a receiving line was formed at the door. Tracy spied Elaine at the doorway in a beautiful red St. John gown with a beaded bolero jacket. Her hair was in her usual pageboy, but it was all curly and bouncy. She could just see a man beside her, that she assumed was Elaine's husband, and beside him, she could see Sean. She stopped looking, her heart thumping uneasily. This was it. She would have to come face-to-face with Sean's fiancée, the woman she was competing with by no fault of her own. What really made her nervous was the prospect of seeing Marcus here with a date. She hoped he was alone, but did not think that her wish would be granted on that one. Hadn't Vivien said that women probably threw themselves at him the moment he walked out the door in the morning?

Tracy chatted with her mother to take the edge off of her nerves. It had been weeks since she had kissed him at Elaine's house and though he attempted to convince her she was being silly once or twice after that day, she stood her ground and wouldn't see him one on one.

The line was moving slowly, yet they were almost to the front now. Her foot was touching the first step. Her whole body was tense and shaky at the same time. To see what she was about to face, Tracy peered over the heads of the people in front of her to view the entire receiving line. Her heart sank at what she saw. First, there was Elaine and her husband, Howard. He was a big guy, much taller than Elaine, a bit on the heavy side and mostly bald, with hair around the edges of his scalp. He was a distinguished-looking older gentleman with a mustache and goatee. Then there was Julia, standing a little behind Elaine at her elbow. Then Mr. McClain, the chairman of the board of directors and his wife. And next was Sean, with the real shocker, Ashleigh.

Why hadn't anybody mentioned to her that Ashleigh was white? Not only was she white, but she was also fair skinned and had blond hair. She was about the same height and dress size as Tracy. Her dress was a blood red, as were her lipstick and fingernails. She looked pleasant enough, but Tracy now saw what the big deal was about Ashleigh for Elaine. She didn't want Sean to marry a white girl and she was using Tracy as a pawn to eliminate this threat from her life.

Before she had a chance to be furious about Elaine's cowardice, she spotted Marcus at the end of the line of greeters. Her heart pounded in glee to see that he was standing alone. Finally, Tracy and her mother were in front of Elaine. The others in line had moved forward to shake hands with Sean and meet his fiancée. Elaine put on an extra-bright face when she saw Tracy.

"Well, hello," she said. To Tracy's horror, Elaine was reaching out to embrace her. They didn't have that kind of relationship, but they hugged briefly, pressing their cheeks together in a mock kiss.

"Elaine this is my mother, Sheila. Mama, this is my boss, Elaine Newell," Tracy said, her introductions done cursorily.

"Nice to finally meet you," Elaine said, grasping Sheila's hand. Sheila echoed the same before Elaine gestured to the man beside her. "This is my husband, Howard."

The man shook Tracy's hand and smiled disinterestedly. He had met so many people that he was already looking beyond her to the next people in line.

"Howard, Tracy is the new assistant I'm always raving about," Elaine said, drawing her husband's attention back to Tracy.

"Oh, so this is the one. How're you doing?" He shook her hand again, now that she was somebody to be recognized.

Elaine leaned into Sheila. "Now that I found Tracy, I don't know how I managed without her. Did she tell you that I absolutely adore her?"

Tracy wanted to gag at Elaine's bogus claim, but she smiled and alternately observed each woman.

"I figured something like that because I barely see her anymore," Sheila said, smiling broadly and touching Elaine's arm in camaraderie. "And thank you for these gifts. They're so beautiful. I already know what I'm putting in my picture frame. I told Tracy that I already had my Christmas."

"Oh, you're welcome. Enjoy the party," Elaine said, with a frozen smile that didn't reach her eyes. She dismissed Sheila as though she was too insignificant to continue to converse with. Tracy narrowed her eyes at Elaine's shallowness. Whatever her mother's shortcomings, Sheila was twice the woman and mother that Elaine could ever be.

"That reminds me. Julia," Elaine said, reaching her hand over her shoulder to Julia for an envelope. "For all your hard work," she said, as she handed the envelope to Tracy.

"Thank you," Tracy said blithely. She took the Christmas bonus and stuck it in her gift bag. It was her time to move on down the line. She braced herself to move ahead and greet Sean and Ashleigh, stopping briefly to acknowledge Julia and introduce her to her mother. She did the same with the board chairman. When she finally turned to face Sean, he was leisurely examining her entire form with a pleased look on his face. Within a matter of seconds, his eyes crept over her breasts, waist, hips and feet before returning to her face. It wasn't the first time she had caught him leering at her recently. She took the lead in speaking.

"Hi, Sean," she said, reaching out her hand. Rather than shake, Sean clasped her hand between both of his and smiled.

"Hello, Tracy, you look…lovely," he said. The way he said the last word led Tracy to believe he was thinking of another, more provocative depiction. Aware that Ashleigh was watching, she gracefully pulled her hand from his grasp. She still had seen no real signs that Sean thought of her as anything more than eye candy, but his attention was making her feel uneasy. She presented her mother. "This is your mother?"

He took Sheila's hand in the same manner he had captured Tracy's. This action allowed her to shake off her discomfort and tell herself that his special treatment was all in her mind. "I'm very pleased to meet you. So, you're the woman who's given Tracy all that sage advice, huh?"

Charmed by Sean's interest, Sheila laughed shyly. "I don't know, what did she say?" she asked, tilting her head at him. Her schoolgirl behavior prompted Tracy to take into account that Sean was a very attractive man.

"Well, let's see… 'My mama didn't raise no fool' is the one that comes to mind most readily." He smiled. At complete odds with Elaine's boredom with Sheila's down-to-earth manner, Sean seemed genuinely fascinated with her.

"Then that's me, I suppose." Sheila grinned at her feet, flattered that Sean was holding her hand for so long. Tracy glanced at Marcus and was surprised to see him smiling delightedly as he watched her mother.

"This is my fiancée, Ashleigh Webb," Sean said to Sheila, releasing her hand so that she could shake Ashleigh's. "This is Tracy Middleton and her beautiful, young mother. Tracy is Elaine's assistant."

Ashleigh wasted little time greeting Sheila, her overly wide blue eyes focused on Tracy even as she met the older woman. Just like her intended husband, Ashleigh promptly scanned Tracy from head to foot without an attempt to hide her assessment. "Yes, I've heard of Tracy. I'm glad to finally meet you," she said, offering Tracy a limp-fish handshake.

"Nice to meet you too," Tracy said, dropping the woman's hand and swiftly moving forward. Ashleigh showed every sign of wanting to engage her in conversation. Tracy wanted to cut her eyes at Elaine, but decided that there would be time to deal with her later. Was she really opposed to the woman or to her whiteness?

Her move forward had placed her directly in front of Marcus. As Melvin would say, he looked fabulous. Sean and the two older men on the receiving line had opted for the standard tuxedo. But Marcus was wearing a three-piece Sean Jean suit that looked just as formal, if not more, than their garb.

"Tracy." He nodded in greeting, as though he couldn't manage any more words. The slight smile he gave her and appraising look told her everything she needed to know about how good she looked tonight.

A wide grin crossed her mouth, in spite of herself. Her stomach swooped up and down again as she looked into his eyes. She extended a hand to shake with him. "Hi, Marcus, it's good to see you."

Having none of that formal stuff, Marcus took her hand and pulled her into his body. He gave her a generous hug. His chiseled, fragrant body became the entire room for Tracy in that moment. She felt like she would never let go.

"Merry Christmas," he whispered near her ear, sending thrills down her spine. He released her and she returned from the time warp she was in, blinking at the man before her. His heart had pounded in his chest as urgently as hers. It was all she could do to reach back for her mother and push her toward him.

"This is—" Tracy started with a croaky voice, but was glad that Sheila had decided to interrupt.

"I'm Sheila Middleton, Tracy's mother." She extended her hand and gazed at Marcus in a perceptive way. She knew her headstrong daughter very well, and anyone who could reduce her to a weak-kneed mass within a matter of seconds was worth scrutinizing.

"Sheila Middleton," Marcus said, the words sounding so much more significant transmitted by his deep, soft voice. He took her hand in his the same way Sean had, but fixed his docile eyes on her like he was trying to see Tracy in her features. "Very pleased to make your acquaintance. You're exactly how I pictured you from what Tracy's told me about you."

Understanding that this man was the object of her daughter's desire, Sheila nodded at him, wondering why she had never heard about him during Tracy's Saturday visits. "Well, it's good to finally meet you…" she trailed off, waiting for his name.

"Marcus. Marcus Hansen Booker," he told her, leaning forward so that she would be sure to hear him over the gay noise filling the room. "Don't tell me she's never mentioned me."

"Oh, I think she has," Sheila said, thinking she had in manner more than words. Tracy could tell by Sheila's enthusiastic smile that she was on to her. She was eager to leave Marcus's company, lest her mother start in on a line of questioning akin to Vivien's in the park.

"We'd better grab a good table before they're all gone," Tracy said, instinctively pulling her mother's arm so that Marcus released her hand.

"You're both welcome to join us at our table. After all, you're an executive too," Marcus offered before she could flee.

At the same time Tracy was trying to say, "No, we'll mingle with the rest of the staff," Sheila was asking, "Which table is that?" Marcus chose to answer the one more favorable to his appeal.

"We're at that one over by the stage. The only one with a number on it," he said, touching Sheila's elbow and directing her eyes to where he was pointing. He looked at Tracy when he added, "But, if you don't sit with us, I'll be making the rounds too."

"Enjoy the party," Tracy heard him call after her as she whisked her mother away.

Tracy barely had a chance to scan the lay of the land; she was so busy putting distance between them and Marcus before her mother embarked on her questions. As soon as they were out of his earshot, Sheila piped up.

"So, who was that?" she asked, smiling up at her daughter with bucked eyes.

"That's Marcus. He's one of the owners. He's the COO and vice president of marketing and external relations," she said rapidly, aware that that didn't answer her question. "Let's find a table."

"Let's go to the one he's sitting at. You know you want to," Sheila said, hoping Tracy would confide in her.

"No, I don't. I couldn't imagine sitting there with Elaine all night. I came to relax and have fun," Tracy said, rolling her eyes at the thought. But she looked at the table and saw that it already had an occupant. An attractive young woman with a deep sienna complexion like a Native American was sipping on a cocktail as she watched the band. She was short and her hair was jet black, straight and hung to her shoulders. She was wearing a cream sheath that flowed over her body like liquid, her nipples prominently on display.

Tracy's heart raced and her face felt flush. She was sure that the woman was Marcus's date. She led her mother to a table across the room from that one, but with a good view of it so that she could confirm her suspicions once everyone was seated. After settling her mother in, Tracy made a beeline for one of the open bars. She lined up behind the few people waiting there and glanced across the room at the offending woman. She could kick herself for being so stupid as to believe that anyone as handsome and rich as Marcus would be here without a date. Or for flattering herself into believing that he was still carrying a torch for her when she had hugged him.

"Could I have two glasses of merlot please," she asked, after reaching the front of the queue. Though the drinks were free, she dug in her purse for two dollars to drop in the tip jar. As she walked back to their table, she pushed her melancholy to the back of her mind and decided to cheer up. She could be getting way ahead of herself. After all, she had jumped to false conclusions before. And wasn't it her who had called it off with Marcus even before it began? Did she expect him to remain faithful to her when she wouldn't even discuss the possibility of a relationship anymore?

"Here you go, Mama," she said, placing a drink in front of Sheila before she sat down. She vaguely greeted a husband and wife at the table who were talking with her mother. The rest of the seats were empty so far. Tracy sipped at her drink and dared to look at the woman again. The girl was swaying to the music and occasionally glancing around the room. Tracy never saw her look in the direction of Marcus, but she was sure she was right about the reason she was parked there. Naturally, she wouldn't be in the greeting line. As Marcus's date, she had no status in their company. Other "plus ones" in the receiving line were either the spouse or soon-to-be spouse, like Ashleigh.

As she watched, an older man joined her, but left a few seats between them. He sparked up a conversation and they laughed. Tracy guessed that the man was Julia's husband. She counted in her head for the ten-seat table: Elaine and Howard, Mr. McClain and his wife, Sean and Ashleigh and they had invited her and her mother. She could only draw one conclusion, the last couple had to be Marcus and Miss Nipples. She sipped at her wine and resolved that she would stop looking over there. It was only making her miserable. She looked at Marcus, who was capably performing his duty of greeting the staff. *Just like he greeted me,* she thought bitterly.

Sheila had finished her pleasantries with the couple and turned to Tracy.

"What's wrong with you? You got your lip all poked out," she said, frowning. Tracy tried to clear her face.

"Nothing. I'm just getting bored, that's all," she said, placing her glass on the table.

"Well, why don't you go around and talk to your friends? I'm fine here. I'm enjoying myself," Sheila said, patting Tracy's leg. She added the last bit because she didn't want to be a drag on Tracy's evening and also because it was true. Sheila had never been to a gala event like this. A fancy Christmas party at a downtown hotel and her daughter was an executive? She was in heaven.

Because I don't have any friends. Tracy thought of herself as pathetic. She glanced around at the roomful of people and realized that she had not had a chance to bond with a single person at work, except Marcus. How could that be? At every other job she ever had, she made friends quickly and easily. There was something about Elaine and working for Elaine that just infected every aspect of her life. While Sheila thought she was trying to figure out where she wanted to go and visit, Tracy was actually looking around the room again to see who else had come without a "real" date. She loved her mother, but she would have looked ten times more impressive with a man by her side. She was relieved to see that some women had brought their girlfriends and some men had come stag. But that premise wasn't true for the other executives whom she saw from day to day and at Sean's weekly meetings. All of them were with members of the opposite sex.

Even Anne Duncan was with some stuffed shirt who appeared to be about as snobbish as she. At the moment she was huddled with her work buddies, laughing and talking. Tracy was becoming more and more depressed as she sank within the depths of her mind. She had to cheer up for her mother's sake. She didn't want Sheila's party experience to be ruined by her sorry daughter. She looked happier and more vibrant than Tracy had seen her in ages.

"I haven't been at the company long. I don't really know anybody," Tracy said honestly. It was Sheila who had introduced her to the man and his wife at their table, and he worked in research and development.

"We should've sat at the table with the ones standing up there at the front. I could tell you like that Marcus." She smiled and inclined her head toward Tracy, nudging her arm.

"Mama, please keep your voice down," Tracy whispered, embarrassed. She couldn't go around saying in front of other employees that Tracy was pining for Marcus.

"They can't hear us," Sheila said, looking across the table at the couple, who were deep into their own conversation. "Besides, they're not listening anyway. But the way you two were acting with each other, I wasn't sure if I should step aside and give you some privacy."

"There's nothing between us. We're just co-workers," Tracy said in a near whisper. "I think he's got a girlfriend. Plus, he's my boss."

Tracy loaded up on the explanations as to why there was nothing between Marcus and her in hopes that Sheila would drop the already demoralizing topic. More than anything, it was the sad look in Tracy's big eyes that really made the other woman ease up on the teasing. She hadn't really expected her to share confidences with her. Both of them had always done their real talking to Tai. Tracy usually kept things inside, but Sheila had hoped the prospect of romance would encourage a deeper intimacy between them.

"Well, we could've sat there because…aren't those the ones you really work with?" Sheila asked, struggling to understand the office politics of her daughter's job.

"Yeah, but…we're…staying…here," Tracy said, growing

mpatient with the continual pestering to move. She looked
up and smiled amiably at another couple, who had asked if it
was okay for them to join the table. "Please do."

She was required to introduce herself and Sheila and
explain where she worked at Cathy Booker before she could
return to a private conversation with her mother. This time,
she was going to stick to her guns and *be positive*. "It's really
lovely here, isn't it? I don't think I've ever been to anything
this nice." She looked around and inadvertently caught the eye
of Anne, whose face became one of scorn and hostility once
she realized she was looking at Tracy. Tracy averted her eyes
toward the band which was now accompanying a talented
singer who was doing a jazzy version of "I'll Be Home for
Christmas."

"I know. Ooo…I can't wait to tell Louise and Juanita about
this," Sheila exclaimed, talking about the other women in her
building. The couples at their table had risen in unison. It
seemed that it was time to go to the buffet.

"Mama, you want to go get some food?" In her sour mood,
Tracy had completely forgotten about the food.

"Oh. Yeah." Sheila rose, surprised herself that she hadn't
even considered the food. Tracy moved toward a long, decora-
tive buffet table that was intentionally in the opposite direction
of the one she saw Anne Duncan rushing to with her boyfriend.
She picked up a plate and leaned to look down the table to see
what was on the many service platters. The food looked succu-
lent and, thankfully, not from their kitchens. She turned back
to give a plate to Sheila, but was brought up short when—for
one, Sheila had her own plate and second, the nipple girl was
standing right behind her mother. Worse, she was waving her
hand in a "come on" gesture to someone near the door.

Tracy couldn't even breathe, let alone walk as she turned
back to the buffet. She didn't dare look in the direction that
the girl was gesturing, but knew that the line at the door had

tapered off and Marcus and the others were free to leave i
they wanted. Elaine and the board chairman were the ones the
staff really wanted to greet. Even as she turned with her bac
to the girl, she was facing in the direction of the doorway.

Sure enough, Marcus was striding across the ballroom
toward them. Tracy uncovered a serving platter with trembling
hands and picked up the tongs to scoop up jumbo shrimp that
at the moment, she knew she couldn't force past her lips. Her
mother was saying something to her, but her ears were primed
to the conversation behind Sheila. By rote, she dumped some
of the shrimp on Sheila's plate.

"Are you coming to the table now, or do you want me to
fix you a plate?" the woman asked Marcus. In her peripheral
vision, as she leaned over an uncovered tray of rolled sand-
wiches, Tracy could see that Marcus inclined his head to the
short girl and stood closely at her side.

"I think I can leave now. Elaine and Sean can handle it.
Nobody really wants to meet me," he said jovially. To Tracy's
horror, Sheila was looking right at them and joining in their
conversation.

"I wanted to meet you," she joked and laughed in her cute,
bubbly way. Tracy heard Marcus laugh with her, and felt she
had to ditch her. She moved past the next two trays without
even opening them up, but she was still stuck in a long line
of people serving themselves.

"Oh, you forgot our forks, Tracy," Sheila called to her.
Tracy swallowed hard and ignored her mother. She had no intention of passing by Marcus and his date to retrieve some
damned forks. She would eat with her fingers if she had to.

"I'll get them. You'll need napkins too," Marcus said,
leaving his date's side. With him gone, Tracy glanced at Sheila.

"I'm going to see what's up there," she said, in a voice that
didn't sound like her own. She didn't wait for a response or
even an acknowledgment. Tracy skipped in front of several

people in line and stood in front of a platter that wasn't occupied by anybody. The dish was meatballs, her least favorite food in the whole wide world, but she grabbed the tongs and picked up three of them. When she closed the lid, she felt Marcus pressing closely against her back. His hand reached around her body, encircling her to place a fork on her plate and drape a napkin on her arm. Her breath caught in her chest and she was lucky her hands didn't tremble all the food onto the floor.

"Your fork," he said enticingly in her ear.

"Th-anks," she croaked. Her mouth felt as dry as the Mojave.

"And I didn't get a chance to tell you how absolutely amazing you look tonight," he whispered. Tracy's chest rose up and down rapidly, which was a relief, since a moment ago she felt she couldn't breathe. She had no response, but started to turn her face toward him. He was standing so close to her that she very nearly bumped her face into his. She turned her attention instead to putting the napkin under her plate. He returned to his date, and she felt her back become a few degrees cooler with the warmth of his body missing.

Tracy couldn't even pretend that she was going to eat now. She walked straight from the buffet to their table and set down her plate. She went back to the open bar and ordered a rum and Coke and another merlot for her mother. Even if Sheila wasn't ready for another drink, Tracy thought she would have no trouble consuming it for her. She brought these back to table and started drinking her cocktail. She looked over at the buffet table to see Marcus and the girl filling each other's plates with their finds. Marcus occasionally touched the small of the woman's back. She was annoyingly cute, with the compact body of an athlete, like a gymnast or dancer. Her arms were muscular in just the subtle way Tracy wanted to get hers and her butt rounded out in a way that really set off the silkiness of her dress. It didn't even need to be said that her breasts were perky. How else could she go out without a bra and have her chest sit up so erect?

Sheila returned to the table perplexed as to why Tracy had left her. "You barely got anything, baby," she said standing over her. "There were desserts at the far end of the table."

She placed her plate down and touched Tracy's shoulder. "Do you want me to go back and get you some? There's all sorts of pies, cookies and cakes."

Tracy shook her head, feeling numb. "No, Mama. Sit down and enjoy your food. I can always go back for more."

Once seated, Sheila frowned at the meatballs on Tracy's plate. "What did you get that for?"

"Hmm?" Tracy said, half lost in her own thoughts. When she processed what Sheila had asked her, she stared blankly at her plate. "Those are for you."

"Oh, thank you, baby, but I got some," she said. Satisfied that everything was okay, she began to eat her food and meet the new people who filled out their table while they were away.

Elaine made her way to the mike and the room quieted down. She greeted everyone and welcomed them to the party. She announced that there would be door prizes throughout the night and to search in their gift bags for their raffle tickets. Sheila was thrilled by the prospect of being awarded more gifts. Tracy just wished the night were over.

Next, Elaine gestured to the band for everyone to applaud the great job they were doing and she began a speech about the past year at Cathy Booker Foods. She talked about their expansion and the introduction of several new products and their plans for the future. She introduced the board of directors, thanked the entire staff and pointed out several individuals from various departments for special recognition. Tracy remembered being required to stand at some point about something, but had only gotten to her feet with prodding from her mother.

With Marcus's table in direct view of the stage, she had been watching his affectionate exchanges with the braless woman. He leaned into her, putting his arm around the back of her chair and whispered in her ear for conversation during Elaine's speech. He scooped food from his plate to hers and vice-versa. He threw his head back laughing and other silly lovesick behavior that Tracy found hard to stomach. Really, she felt sick. She put down the cocktail and gulped at her water.

Elaine was wrapping up her speech with more instructions for the staff to find their raffle tickets. Even if they didn't receive a prize she hinted that Santa would be on his way soon. At least, Tracy had been paying enough attention at the committee meetings to know that that meant each person was going to receive a wrapped gift from the man they had hired to play Santa. She could no longer sit around waiting for Elaine to leave the microphone.

"I'm going to the washroom," she told her mother, jumping up and going to the back of the ballroom. Cathy Booker had secured a very nice ballroom that was self-contained, with bathrooms in the back of the hall, meant for their party only. She passed a line of windows draped in thick velvet curtains and noticed that it was snowing outside on the adjacent balcony.

Tracy just barely made it inside a stall before the flow of tears began to slide silently down her face. Her crying didn't rise above a sniffle. She didn't know what she had expected Marcus to do if she said she wouldn't date him, but she hadn't expected him to flaunt another woman in her face. *You know that's not what he's doing.* He had to go on with his life. Was he actually supposed to remain celibate and wait for her to find another job so that they could start seeing each other? Of course not. But common sense didn't make her heart hurt any less.

Tracy heard applause and she was aware that Elaine's speech was over. She knew that the bathroom would soon be flooded with other people who had waited politely for the address to come to an end. *Damn it*. In her haste, Tracy had forgotten her purse. She pulled copious scoops of tissue off the roll, dabbed at her eyes and blew her nose. She couldn't leave the stall with these red eyeballs. She decided to wait until the major crowd had passed through before emerging to fix her face as best she could. Thank goodness these stalls went all the way to the floor. No one would know it was her waiting in the toilet.

She held her place through a large group of women coming through to use the facilities. Someone even tried her door at one busy point. Soon the flow tapered off, but she could still hear a few people outside the door. After a while, a conversation attracted her attention.

"…and did you see Miss High and Not So Mighty?" It was Anne Duncan. Tracy would recognize that snide voice anywhere. Her heart jumped. She knew Anne was talking about her. Who else did she loathe as much?

"Yeah, who was that she came with?" another asked, ready to laugh.

"Her mother?" several of them exclaimed together in vicious amusement.

"Yet once again, she's wearing an overly pretentious outfit," Anne said. "That dress is probably couture. She's spending all her money on designer names and expensive shoes. Just like a hoodrat, she'd rather look like a million dollars than have a million dollars."

"You said you saw her salary, Greta, how much does she make?" one witch asked the other.

"A little over a hundred thou," she answered. Tracy thought Greta probably worked in human resources, which was supposed to be confidential about salaries.

"See what I mean? She just got here and that dress is at least three months' salary," Anne said. "And look at her mother. Obviously, she doesn't spend any of her money on her. What the heck is she wearing? She looks like she thought she was going to a church function."

Anne's minions laughed, so she continued her tirade. "Oh, and you should see the way she looks at Marcus during the executive meetings, like he's going to be impressed by all her extravagant stuff." Tracy swallowed. Did she noticeably stare at Marcus, or was this one of Anne's mean-spirited characterizations for her friends?

"She probably thinks that he wants her," one of the women observed.

"Oh, I think she thinks everyone wants her," Anne said flippantly. "Even Sean."

"She can't believe Sean likes her," someone said, incredulously. "Did she see his girlfriend? Sean and Marcus could buy and sell her a million times over. She's not even in their league."

"I'm telling you, girls from the hood think that everyone is impressed by the trinkets and baubles that they're impressed with," Anne said. Tracy had to wonder where she got this information on girls from the so-called hood. If anything, she was describing Elaine. This is what Elaine had prescribed as the way to woo her son. Tracy had found him more impressed by her direct manner than anything else. "Let me use that comb," Anne said to someone.

"I've never met her, but my friend Gina works for her and said she's basically nice. She had a good job before. She could've got all that stuff when she was working in television," a new voice said. Tracy thought this person could be someone decent, except for the fact that she hung around with Anne.

"She didn't make that much there," Anne said glibly. Her words were distorted as though she were applying lipstick. "It's a third-rate station and I think they have, like, a bunch of news producers."

She was wrong. There were only a handful, and before Brian had worked his evil magic, Tracy was considered one of the best.

"I'm gonna go. I think they'll be calling the first raffle prize soon," said the Greta voice.

"I'm right behind you," Anne said. All of their clicking heels faded away and she heard the door shut quietly.

After a moment, it was completely quiet in the bathroom. Tracy's heart was pounding out of hurt and fury as she left the stall. At least their unanticipated gossip had quelled her tears. She grabbed some paper towels and wet them in the sink. With trembling hands, she repaired her makeup and blinked her eyes rapidly until the redness had cleared a little. She intentionally inhaled and exhaled deeply to bring down her pulse rate. She tried not to look at her dress, or the diamond jewelry that adorned her body. She wanted to snatch it all off and leave it on the floor. But she couldn't start thinking those thoughts until she was safe in the comfort of her own home. She had to get a grip, just make it through this evening and allow Sheila to enjoy her first corporate Christmas party.

She put the soggy paper in the trash and went to grip the door to leave the bathroom. She took a deep breath and then pulled. Tracy wasn't concerned that Anne and her cronies might see her leaving the bathroom and realize she had heard their entire conversation. Let them squirm, because, regardless of whether they thought she was "not so mighty," she was an executive of the company and she could have their jobs in an instant.

She walked back toward her table with her head held high, sticking close to the edge of the wall. The singer with the heartbreakingly smooth voice had just begun a sultry rendition of "Have Yourself a Merry Little Christmas." The words tore into Tracy's soul as she drew closer to her mother, who was sitting there in her little church suit, having the time of her life. Sheila was laughing her infectious laugh with the other revelers at the table, and holding her and Tracy's raffle tickets in her hand.

"Have yourself a merry little Christmas. Let your heart be light. From now on our troubles will be out of sight. Have yourself a merry little Christmas. Make the yuletide gay. From now on our troubles will be miles awaaay…" the woman crooned as velvety and jazzy as Diana Krall.

Tracy glanced at the table where Marcus was sitting with his arm around his date's chair. Their eyes met across the vast room. Tracy held his gaze for a while, with her chin stuck out and shoulders back as she made her way further into the ballroom. *So, he isn't even in my league, huh?* She suddenly stopped and looked at her shoes as if they offended her. She turned around and went back the way she came, all the nasty words echoing in her mind.

Not about to get trapped in that bathroom again—where she had heard untruths about herself that she never would have imagined possible—she dashed behind the curtains. Finally, tears blurring her vision, she found what she was looking for: a door leading out to the balcony. She slid it open with all her might, tearing a fingernail off at the base, and rushed out into the bitterly cold night. She ran all the way to the edge of the thick, stone parapet and screeched her sorrow in the wind. Giant snowflakes fell at a snail's pace around her and delicately began to coat her body. She neither cared about that, nor her frigid surroundings. She simply allowed herself to cry at will.

Who did everybody think she was? Who the hell did everybody think she was? She was just a person…a woman, trying to make her way in the world. And all of these evil, hateful, manipulative people were tearing away at her bit by bit. She couldn't answer her own question, because she didn't even know who she was anymore. She wrapped her arms around her stomach and doubled over crying.

Before she knew it, a jacket was being placed over her shoulders and secured in place by Marcus's strong hands. He turned her body into his and she allowed it. She didn't even have the strength to resist. She smashed her face against his chest and poured out her grief.

"Shhh. Tracy. Shhh," he was saying as he enfolded his arms around her tremulous body. His soothing, kind voice simply increased her anguish and she let out another wail. He smoothed her hair and rubbed the cheek nestled against his chest, feeling powerless in the face of her tears.

"Sweetheart, what's wrong? Tell me what happened?" he pleaded with a cracked voice.

"I…I…I just can't do it anymore," she sobbed, her throat raw. "I can't…I can't…"

It was not an explanation and she couldn't say any more. Yet, it was all he needed to hear to make his heart ache in rage over whoever or whatever had brought her to this state. He squeezed her body tightly, trying to absorb all her sorrow. She had once angrily accused him of always trying to solve all of her problems for her. She was absolutely right. After he met Tracy, he knew why he had been placed upon this earth—to keep this woman in the same cocky, spunky and happy state in which God had brought her forth. His mission, his personal goal, was to see that she never knew the kind of pain she was experiencing right now.

He rocked her body gently hoping to quiet her weeping, while he pressed his lips to her hot forehead. His comforting embrace seemed to last forever before her crying had reduced to shaky snuffling. Finally, he was able to pull her away from his body and gaze down into her tear-stained face.

"What happened, sweetheart?" he asked again, pulling a handkerchief from his breast pocket and wiping away her tears. His voice was aching with emotion and his eyes looked sadder than Tracy had ever seen them. Tracy took the cloth from his hands and wiped her own eyes. She wiped her nose and backed away from him.

"Everybody here is so phony," she said in a shaky, fractured voice. "And, they're nasty…and mean." She began sobbing again. Marcus moved to hold her once more, but she stepped away from his grasp. She wanted to pour out all of her complaints without them being stifled within his chest. But her words were rambling and stilted by intermittent sobs. "And they scheme and…everyone is just using you, and…and you're with that…Sean's girlfriend is…everybody is so shallow." Only her last thought was delivered coherently. "I hate this job!"

She covered her face with her hands and doubled over in tears. Marcus could stand their separation no longer. He draped his arms around her back and drew her into him again. His chest hurt and his breathing was rapid. He did not know where to begin in providing verbal reassurance, because he didn't know what had triggered her crying. Still, he had to try to make things better, so he spoke about himself.

"Don't even think about Candace. She is a non-issue," Marcus whispered, tenderly. Tracy assumed he was talking about his date. He pressed his warm, wet mouth to her forehead. "How could she be anything to me…when I only want you?"

She drew back her head to look up into his eyes. Snow covered his hair and shoulders and she blinked through flakes on her eyelashes. Marcus gazed down at her and faintly wiped at her tears with the back of his fingers. He held her chin in his large, square hand. "I'm sorry I ever brought her here. I only did it to make you jealous…make you change your mind about seeing me. I'm truly sorry because it backfired on me…miserably." His head was so close to hers that the icy puffs of words floated all over her face.

"No." Tracy shook her head, sniffling. She was not persuaded that he wasn't just being kind because he had found her in such a state. She had been with a duplicitous boyfriend before and was aware that they could lie right to your face. "You were staring at her. You didn't even look at me the entire night."

"Tracy, are you kidding?" He smiled a little, amused at her foolish assumptions. "I don't have to look at you. I'm aware of where you are in a room every second I'm around you." His soft eyes bore into hers, allowing the meaning of his statement to sink in. She dropped her eyes.

"You think I chose that exact moment to come to the buffet table because I was summoned by her? I came because of you, sweetheart," he whispered. "I wanted to be near *you*."

He put his hands on her shoulders. "I don't know how to make it any plainer to you, that I think you're wrong in keeping us apart." One of his hands left her shoulder and swept the snow from her hair. "Your mother is delightful, but we—you and I—should have been in there together tonight. Then, whatever happened to make you so sad, probably wouldn't have happened."

Marcus took a step closer, while drawing her body toward him. He was pressed against her when he told her, more categorically, "No. I *know* it wouldn't have happened, because I wouldn't have allowed anything or anybody to hurt you."

Tears flowed anew from Tracy's eyes. This time they weren't from sadness, but from the devastating impact of his words. She couldn't believe she had brushed off his first sentiments as anything resembling the deceitfulness of Brian. No man had ever spoken to her like this before. No one, male or female, had ever laid bare their emotions like this to her. She obeyed the overwhelming urge to throw her arms around his body and clutched him tightly. "I love you, Marcus Hansen Booker," she murmured into his broad chest, squeezing her eyes shut. As she had felt earlier in the evening, the little space within his arms was her entire world. Now she knew it was also her safe place to land.

Marcus wasn't sure he had heard her utter the words he had fantasized her saying from the moment he had knelt beside her desk in her office. He squeezed her, hoping his ears had not deceived him. His only response was to lift her chin and brush his lips enticingly against her satiny mouth. Tracy succumbed to the teases of his fleshy lips and her entire body grew limp as his tongue performed its now urgent entry into her mouth. A moan, filled with unspoken longing, escaped his throat and vibrated their kiss as his hands pressed flat against her back. The breath from their nostrils provided a halo of steam around them. Marcus felt Tracy shudder in his embrace and reluctantly released her mouth. He kissed her lightly, pressing his torso into hers.

"I don't want to leave you tonight," he said huskily, gazing at her big eyes framed in lush snowy lashes. His awakened body told her exactly what he meant. He whisked fresh snow off her downy hair. She obliged, knocking the flakes gently from his shoulders.

"I'm with Mama," Tracy said, but she wanted the same thing. She suddenly stiffened and became very alert. Tracy glanced in the direction of the ballroom. "Mama!" she cried, pulling herself out of his arms. "She must be worried sick."

Marcus caught her arm before she could dash back into the ballroom. "Hold on. A few more seconds is not going to kill her."

Tracy looked around at him with fire in her eyes. She didn't know how he did things in his pathetic family, but she was not the kind of child to cause her mother any prolonged suffering if she could help it. Worry about what happened to your child was at the top of the list of all mothers' greatest fears.

"Marcus, let go." She tugged her arm, but found it firmly gripped.

"Wait, Trace. I know you want to get to your mother, but stop and think for a minute. How are we going to play this? Go in all snowy, yet sweaty? With you wearing my jacket and your face all a mess? I really don't give a damn, but you're the one who's always urging caution," he said calmly, even in the face of her irritation. "How is your mother going to view that?"

Face all a mess, was the most resonant phrase for her. Tracy stopped struggling and Marcus released her arm. Her hands dashed to her face, wide-eyed at what she felt there. Her skin was all wet from the snow and from her tears. She guessed that her foundation was probably gone, as well as her lipstick. He was right about how they would look. She was convinced now that she was going to see Marcus romantically, but she wasn't prepared to "out" them by walking through the curtains together in a disheveled state.

"What are we going to do?" she asked, ready for him to assume his role as problem solver.

Marcus walked farther along the balcony until he found a door closer to the bathrooms. He tried it and it opened a little. He jerked his head for Tracy to come over. She hurried to where he was.

"You go in here and go right into the bathroom. I'll go back through the other door and find your mother and send her to you," he said. Tracy was about to dash through the door. "Wait, give me my jacket."

Before Tracy took off his jacket, she surprised him by pressing her lips hard against his, one hand holding the back of his neck. "I love you," she whispered and shrugged out of his jacket. She handed it to him and prepared to dash through the doorway. "And tell Mama to bring my purse."

A stunned Marcus, recovered quickly and grabbed her shoulders before her foot crossed the threshold. His eyes were naked to her as he stared down into her face.

"Say it again," he whispered rapidly with no air in his lungs. This time he had heard her clearly, but he couldn't believe it was happening.

Tracy had no problem cooperating. "I love you—" she attempted, but before she could complete the last word, he covered her mouth with his and hugged her with all the muscles in his body. He peppered her face with kisses, and finally, pressed his cheek to hers.

"Oh, I love you," he said in her ear. "I thought you'd think I was foolish…because…" he swallowed hard. He couldn't adequately express his feelings and there wasn't really time. *Because we haven't known each other that long. Because we'd never dated or even made love. Because we never even see each other outside of work. Because. Because. Because.* There were a thousand reasons why they shouldn't be professing their love to each other right now. Except, he knew that they were helpless in the face of the celestial power that had thrust them together and made them sure that this was true.

Tracy dominated his every waking thought. He felt her presence in any room that they shared. She was the star in all his fantasies. The only thing he could remember about most dreams was that he was with Tracy. His stomach flipped and his nerves were on edge every time he first saw her. Tracy was the only one whose welfare he cared about above his own. It hadn't even been like this with him when he was going to marry Hannah. No. Tracy was his destiny.

"Call me tonight, after you drop off your mom," he told her, talking quickly. "I'll take Candace home, but I want to see you. Tonight."

Tracy smiled slightly at the insistence in his request. He didn't even need to tell her when. She knew that she couldn't end a night like this with anyone else or even alone. She had to end it with Marcus. She quickly pressed her cheek to his and dashed through the door.

Fortunately, she entered the hall just a few steps from the bathroom. She came through the door, a shocking sight for the four or five women scattered at the long row of mirrors. Someone gasped at her tousled and snowy appearance. She ignored them and went to pull handfuls of paper towels from the dispenser.

"Tracy," she heard someone cry out in a shocked voice, as she moved in front of the mirror. Her reflection was worse than she thought it would be. Tracy looked over to see Pam approaching her with serious alarm on her face.

"Hi, Pam." Tracy smiled brightly and turned back to the mirror to begin wiping her face.

"Oh, my lord," Pam said, putting her purse down beside Tracy and grabbing some paper towels herself. She returned to Tracy and began toweling snow and water out of her hair.

"What happened to you?" she asked concernedly. Tracy's makeup had run together. Her hair was a wet and icy mess. Her dress had various dark spots of moisture on it, particularly around the hem. Moreover, any exposed skin, especially her shoulders, arms and cleavage, were splattered with drops of water.

"I went out for some air. But it's cold out there!" Tracy exclaimed, smiling, as though her only problem was that she was surprised by the weather conditions. She couldn't deny that she sounded like a mental patient, but she didn't give a hoot. Two of the ladies took this crazy explanation as their cue to vacate the premises. They scurried out of the bathroom without looking back.

Pam turned to watch them go and glanced at the final two inhabitants. They were way at the other end of the ladies' room and seemed to have lost interest in the weirdo. She wiped Tracy's shoulders and back, leaning in to ask her quietly, "And how does Marcus look? As bad as you?"

Tracy's hand stopped wiping off what remained of her makeup and she stared at Pam's reflection. Then she stared at the real Pam, her mouth agape. Pam looked at her with a knowing smile and then busied herself with the back of Tracy's hair.

"What? H-how did you know?" Tracy's voice came out in a whisper.

"Oh, please," Pam said, lifting Tracy's hair in the back to

wipe her neck. She kept her voice low as she explained. "I might have been the only one who saw you go out the curtain, because my husband and I sat this far back. You know I wasn't going to sit anywhere near that crazy Elaine," she added as an aside, pausing to twist her lips at Tracy in the mirror. Tracy smiled and nodded. "I saw you go behind the curtains and I was going to put down my food and go see what was wrong. But you know how long it takes me to get out of a chair in this condition," she said, referring to her third trimester of pregnancy. "And anyway, who did I see leave his hootchie-mama and come rushing across the room, with a worried look on his face, but Marcus. He went right through the curtains and I thought…hmm, I guess I'd better just sit my big butt down then."

Pam carried away the wet towels and got some fresh ones. The other ladies had left, but Tracy waited for Pam to return so that she could talk quietly with her. She knew she had gone undetected in this very bathroom. "Pam, you can't say anything to anybody," she whispered.

"Please. I already knew you two liked each other, or were seeing each other, or had a thing or something." She threw her hand up at Tracy before trying to tackle a wet spot on her hip. "I've worked with Marcus for four years, and I've never seen him as keyed up, distracted, forgetful and preoccupied as he's been since you arrived. Plus, what about that whole door slamming thing y'all did a couple of weeks ago? I ain't stupid."

"Well." Tracy gulped. "Do you think anybody else knows? And what about tonight, did they see him running across the room tonight?"

"No one else in the office seems to know. I'm pretty keen on office gossip and you know, with ours being separate from everybody else, people don't really know what happens in our area unless we tell them. I keep my mouth shut," she said, bending and holding the paper towel to Tracy's hip. "You're going to have to go to the hand dryer to get these out. They're not too wet."

Tracy touched the spot and found it only damp. Pam chuckled and rose up, touching her stomach and looking at Tracy. "I over-dramatized that Marcus running across the room stuff. He was hurrying, but not so obvious. I only noticed you because I work with both of you. I was looking at you because I hadn't spoken to you tonight and I was going to say hi and introduce my husband. Most people didn't even bat an eye," she assured Tracy. She turned to a hand dryer and turned it on. "Come over here and stand close. I bet these will blow right out."

Tracy looked at Pam and felt a powerful urge to hug her. She was so nice and normal and cool. She didn't know why she hadn't taken the time to get to know her before now. This woman could have been her office buddy all along.

Chapter 19

Luckily, Marcus had found the cigar that the board chairman, Chuck McClain, had given him early in the evening. McClain loved cigars and was always trying to extol the virtues of his latest find to Marcus, ignoring the fact that he didn't smoke. He had also handed him a book of matches and said, "Try it when you get a chance and tell me what you think."

After Tracy left, Marcus walked out onto the balcony and tore the packaging off the cigar, bit the end, licked it and broke a tip off it before he lit it. He wanted it to look like he'd been smoking awhile. He coughed, but smoked it enough to produce a decent burn. Just as he suspected, it was nasty. Yet, smoother and less stinky than he'd thought it would be. He spit the nasty saliva onto the terrace and put the cigar out. Now he entered the ballroom a little closer to the middle, cigar in hand for all who had seen him emerge from behind the curtain. *Just been out for a smoke*. He walked back to the men's room to check his condition, smiling at the memory of Tracy's visage before she'd left him.

He placed the cigar on the sink, looked in the mirror and judged the damage as not so bad.

"Marcus, you must be a true cigar enthusiast to brave this weather," Bill Landers, from shipping, observed at the sink beside him.

"The board chairman gave it to me and asked for a report. I had to try it," Marcus joked, shrugging his shoulders. Landers laughed and left the washroom and Marcus was alone. He grabbed some paper towels and wiped off his head and face. Most of his dampness was hidden in the deep black color of his suit. You would have to touch him to know that he was wet. He wiped off his shoes and threw the towels away. He had to hurry to send Sheila to the bathroom for Tracy.

When he emerged in the ballroom, he made a beeline for Tracy's table, but didn't see Sheila. The DJ was playing during the band's break and most of the people were gathered on the dance floor. She should have been easy to spot. He moved closer to the crowd of dancers doing the electric slide and looked through them for Sheila's lavender-colored dress. When the crowd turned in unison, he saw his date, Candace, dancing with the others. She smiled and beckoned him to join her. He shook his head slightly and managed a smile in her direction before realizing that Sheila wasn't there either. He went back to their table to see if their things were there and saw that everything was gone. This he found worrisome. His eyes scanned the room, looking at each buffet table, open bar and corner. Nothing.

He looked around the room to see if he could find Pam and send her into the ladies' bathroom to look for Sheila. He felt bad because Pam was really pregnant, and her husband probably wouldn't like to see some bigwig ordering his wife to get up, go in the bathroom and find somebody. But Pam was the one person he knew he could trust. As he scanned the room for Pam, he spotted a flash of lavender beyond the entry door and hurried in that direction.

Marcus stopped at the top of the stairs. Sure enough, Sheila was standing in the lobby looking around feverishly. Worse, she was accompanied by Sean, who had a comforting hand on her back. Sean looked around and saw Marcus. His face abruptly became stony. Marcus took the three stairs rapidly, focusing on Sheila.

Upon seeing him, she moved forward, her brow knit and her eyes sad, yet hopeful. She was clutching all their belongings in her arms. It appeared she had won a door prize in addition to her Santa's gift.

"Oh, hi there. Have you seen my daughter? Tracy Middleton?" she said, as though Marcus might not remember which girl she was talking about. He half-expected her to say, "She's about five nine, small frame, dark skin." Even as she asked, she was already looking past his shoulder as though ready to find her without their help if his answer was no. He now understood Tracy's urgency in getting back to her mother. His own mother's long absence from him had dulled his senses to how frantic Sheila would have been.

Before he could answer, Sean piped up snidely, "Yes, maybe you can help, Marcus. Tracy is missing and her mother is really worried."

Marcus narrowed his eyes at Sean before turning pleasantly to Sheila. "Um, yeah. I think I saw her go into the ladies' room. She was looking for you." He wanted to give the instruction about bringing the purse, but he did not think it prudent with Sean standing there. Besides, she seemed to have everything with her. He just didn't want her to put that stuff down before joining Tracy.

Sheila's small body sprang into action, but as she placed her foot on the first step, she turned to Marcus. "Oh, I checked the bathroom three times. Uh, when did you see her?"

"Just now," Marcus said mildly. "Like...a few minutes ago."

"Thank you, thanks," she said quickly and climbed the stairs gingerly, favoring her knees.

Marcus started to follow her back into the ballroom and felt Sean touch his arm. He stopped and looked at his cousin. Sean rubbed his fingers together at the moisture he retrieved from Marcus's jacket.

"Just a minute, Marc," Sean said, his eyes boring into his. "Where have you been for the last half hour?"

Marcus didn't think it was that long, but he allowed Sean his dramatization. Marcus pulled the extinguished cigar from his pocket. "Went out for a smoke," he said, casually as though it were an everyday occurrence.

"Since when did you start smoking?" Sean crossed his arms over his chest and leaned back into his legs.

"Since Chuck pressed a cigar on me and asked me for the umpteenth time to 'give it a try, tell me what you think,'" Marcus said, imitating McClain's voice on the last bit. He chuckled. If he became angry at Sean's suspicions he would look guiltier than if he played it like he had no idea what all the ruckus was about.

"But he does that to us all the time. Why did you decide to smoke it tonight?" Sean watched Marcus, ignoring his attempt at humor.

Marcus shrugged. "Why not tonight?"

Sean unfolded his arms and put his hands on his hips. "Where was Tracy coming from? Her mother and I searched the entire ballroom."

"I don't know. I saw her by the buffet table." He raised his hands. "I barely paid it any attention. Why? How long had she been missing?"

Sean dropped his eyes, which was always an indication to Marcus that he was on shaky ground with his facts. "I'm not sure. Her mother won one of the raffles about fifteen minutes ago and she started looking for Tracy not too long after that."

"Oh, well. Good thing I saw her. Next year, we should have the party in a more intimate setting, so this kind of thing doesn't happen. Can you imagine if we invited kids? Someone could get lost," Marcus completed his silly observation, which he knew infuriated Sean, and turned to go back into the ballroom. This time Sean didn't stop him.

Marcus wasn't eager to join his date, but the sooner he found her, the sooner he could get this evening over with and see Tracy. Candace was still dancing with the crowd on the floor. Marcus sat at the table and watched Elaine engage in conversation with Ashleigh. Of course, neither of them would do the electric slide. They seemed to be getting along fine enough, but Elaine had that pasty look on her face when she turned to him.

"Where have you been?" she asked, hitting his leg.

"Tried one of Chuck's cigars," he said, sticking with the script. "What happened to him, by the way? I was going to tell him how I liked it."

"Oh? How did you like it?" Elaine asked, overly interested. She must have been conversing with him to avoid talking to Ashleigh.

"I didn't." he said, flatly, leaning back in his chair. Elaine laughed heartily, surprising Marcus.

"You're very funny, but please don't tell McClain that. He might pull a power grab on us just for your saying that. He convinced Howard to go out with him and smoke one of those wretched things." She laced her hands together in front of her face with her elbows on the table.

"When? I didn't see them," Marcus said, worried that he and Tracy had missed being discovered by mere minutes.

"Ages ago," Elaine said and rolled her eyes in a way that let him know she didn't appreciate being stuck here talking to Sean's fiancée. This was the first indication she had ever made to him that she didn't like Ashleigh, or at least, she found her boring. "They went out front. Where were you?"

"On the balcony. Sean should be back, he was helping Tracy's mother find Tracy," Marcus said, venturing into dangerous territory to see what Elaine knew.

"Better him than me," Elaine said glibly.

"Why do you say that?" Marcus asked, looking at her.

"Did you talk to her mother?" she asked in a lowered voice, inclining her head to him.

"Yep. Seemed nice. Real cute," he said, feeling his temper beginning to rise. He always kept his conversations with her brief in this way.

"Cute? Is that what you'd call it?" Elaine cut her eyes at him. "I'd call her more…tiresome."

She chuckled at her mean joke and glanced at Marcus for his concurrence. He had been so good at playing it cool up until now. The right way to play it would have been to laugh, but he fixed her with a cold stare. He had never struck a woman in his life, but Elaine was coming dangerously close to being his first. Either she or someone like her was the reason Tracy had been crying about all the mean, shallow and evil people at Cathy Booker.

His face must have looked as furious as he felt. Elaine's chuckle tapered off and her eyes turned from amusement to hesitation within a matter of seconds.

"Don't get me wrong. Tracy is a wonderful addition to our offices. I'm just saying that her mother Sheba is—"

"Sheila," Marcus corrected sharply. She gaped at him, surprised by his anger. His eyes dared her to continue her sentence. Elaine dropped her eyes and fiddled with her napkin.

"Well," she said, opening her hands, "I hope they found Tracy."

"They did." Marcus looked away from her out to the floor. The group dancing had broken up, but rather than return to the table, Candace was on her way to the bar. He saw Sean approaching and was eager to leave before Sean could begin another interrogation. He looked at his watch. "I think I'm going to make it an early night," he told Elaine, but was watching his date's progress across the room.

"Can't wait to get her alone?" Elaine said, following the direction of his gaze. Marcus ignored her question. He looked at the five empty wineglasses in front of Candace's plate. Sean sat down next to Ashleigh with a sour look on his face. Ashleigh immediately started fussing over him.

"You were going to call the next raffle," Elaine said. "You can't leave now."

"Sean can do it," he said.

"Why? Where are you going?" Sean asked, staring at him resentfully. He pushed Ashleigh's hand off the thigh she had been rubbing.

Marcus finally looked in their direction, leaning on his elbows over his plate. "Home."

"Where's Howard? He can't really be enjoying Chuck's company that much," Elaine said to no one in particular, but kept her voice down because McClain's wife had returned to the table.

Sean looked at his watch. "It's almost nine-thirty. What's the rush?"

"What's with you and the questions?" Marcus said, getting tired of playing nice with Sean. "Call the next raffle already. Is that so hard? Hell, why don't you call all the rest of them together and then you can leave yourself."

"I think that would be a good idea, honey. Then we can do one dance and leave too," Ashleigh said to Sean. He cut his eyes at her.

"Did I ask for your opinion?" He snapped. Her eyes registered hurt and then she grew indignant. She tossed her napkin on the table and stood. She angrily strode across the room. Elaine raised her eyebrows and smirked at Marcus, holding her head away so that Sean couldn't see her amusement.

"Uh-oh, now look what you did. Your grumpy mood has affected everybody," Marcus teased. It soon became evident Ashleigh was going to the nearest bar.

"I'm not grumpy. I just think that if we have to stay, everyone should have to stay," Sean said. Marcus thought the picture of a spoiled child would be complete if he had folded his arms over his chest and poked out his lip. Marcus shook his head. This was his family, a bunch of bickering, unhappy, selfish people.

"Do you hear yourself?" Marcus was about to mock his words, pouring on the baby talk, when he saw Sean's eyes fix on something across the room. He knew what it was before he turned his head to see what had suddenly grabbed his cousin's attention—or should he say who. Way at the back of the hall, Tracy and Sheila were leaving the bathroom corridor and making their way toward the door. She had emerged from the ladies' room as radiant as ever. Pam was waddling closely behind them and they stopped at her table to meet her husband.

Marcus scrutinized Sean, who didn't even notice he was watching him. In that instant, it became clear to Marcus. Little things had kindled his suspicions before, but now he was certain: Sean liked Tracy. Marcus didn't even have to look at her. Sean's eyes were a clear indicator of Tracy's progress across the large hall. He had always gotten everything he wanted and now he wanted her, fiancée or no.

Candace returned to the table with her drink. She smiled at Marcus and told him that she ran into somebody she knew, and blah, blah. He had tuned out and was peering over her head at Tracy's departure. Before she left through the door, she glanced to the front of the room at his table. He wanted to signal the "call me" thing, but he knew she would be in touch with him after she dropped off her mother. That was probably what her look meant. He leaned over to Candace, interrupting her chatter, and told her, "Let's get out of here."

* * *

It was too bad that Candace became disappointed that his urgency to go didn't mean what she'd assumed it meant. She had slammed his car door angrily when he said he wasn't coming upstairs to her apartment. But Marcus didn't have time to care. He wanted to get back to Tracy as soon as humanly possible. He sat in his car on a street that he guessed was near Tracy's place, waiting for her call. She said she lived on Drexel and he was near Washington Park, where he had run into her. He had stopped at a Walgreen's in Hyde Park to get a toothbrush and other provisions. He needed to get the nasty taste of the cigar out of his mouth once he arrived at her house. He pushed the presets on his radio, scanning all the stations impatiently. It had been an hour and a half and he was eager to pick up where they had left off.

He left the radio on an FM love station and leaned down in his seat, rubbing his eyes. He wasn't tired. He was pondering what he should do about Sean. If he warned Tracy, it would probably worry her and easily drive her away from the company. She had already said that she hated the job. For his own selfish reasons he didn't wanted her to leave, but he knew the situation was toxic for her. Elaine had her in a scheme, Sean was about to chase her around the office and he was pressuring her to see him openly. He thought she should've had her fill of secret affairs, after the experience she'd had with Brian.

Finally, his phone rang. He picked it up immediately. "Hello?"

"Hey, I'm home," she said. He was cheered to hear that she sounded happy.

"Okay, what's your address?" he asked, starting the car.

"What? You don't have me in your Blackberry?" Tracy said, joking.

"It would've been too much temptation to program in

something like that," he countered, smiling to himself. She gave him the address and he was only a couple of blocks away from her greystone. It didn't take him long to arrive at her door.

"Hey," Tracy greeted him, wearing a silky, two-piece lounging outfit in a cute African print. The top had the full print and the black pants had the print on the hems. It fit her body nicely and reminded him of the Tracy he first saw at the go-kart event. It also reminded him of something his mother might have worn.

"Come, enter my humble abode," she said, stepping aside theatrically to let him in.

Once she had closed the door and turned around, Marcus scooped her into his arms and hugged her, pressing his cheek to hers. He had been patient long enough, waiting ever since their embrace on the balcony to hold her again. He released her and took a moment to look at her, holding her arms out just like Kevin had when she was wearing an evening gown. Her eyes also feasted on him. Marcus was a bit more rumpled than when she had seen him last, but still scrumptious.

"Can I use your bathroom?" he said, not wanting to pull away, but wanting to freshen up.

"Oh, of course. It's right down the hall there." Tracy took his arm and showed him the way.

They were standing in a small entryway next to a dark cherrywood staircase that rose to the second floor. The hall was of ornate wood, with framed and matted black-and-white photographs she had taken herself during a photography class in college. The hall went straight back, with doorways on the right side and an immediate opening onto the living room. The bathroom was the only door in her hall that was on the left side, right under the stairs.

After he'd found his way, Tracy went back to the living room and stood absorbing the subtle romantic mood she'd created. She hadn't had time to shop lately and could only offer him something to drink. Tracy had placed two ice-filled glasses of pink grapefruit juice on the table. She was happy that she had at least finished decorating the living room, bathrooms and her bedroom. The kitchen and other rooms in her house still contained boxes of unpacked stuff and hadn't been upgraded in design from the previous owner.

Freshened, Marcus had a chance to examine Tracy's everyday surroundings. She had the kind of home he thought she would. She had developed a free style of traditional colonial, Victorian romantic and African-American influences.

"You do these yourself?" he asked, noticing the photos on her wall. Tracy came to look.

"Yeah, I had a photography course in college and I learned to do that."

"This your family?" Marcus moved closer to peer at the people in the pictures.

"Yeah." Tracy led him down the row. "That's my sister, Tai, reading in the park; that's my mother, cooking up a large Sunday dinner; and that one is Tai's son, Samuel, when he was just a toddler; and her husband, Kevin, in one of his classes, when he was a lot smaller. They're in town now for the holidays. Now they have three kids. We're moving my mother into another apartment. We wanted to get her a house, but she didn't want to," Tracy was chatting nervously. She thought Marcus had made his intentions clear on seeing her tonight, and she was too jittery to relax.

"I made you a drink. Well, pink grapefruit juice actually. It was either that or water. I'm sorry I don't have much." She put on one of the Christmas discs she had received in her gift bag, Jingle Bell Jazz. Marcus sat on the couch and watched her move about in her space.

"That's fine," Marcus said, ignoring the drink. "Stop fussing and come here and sit by me."

Tracy did as she was told. Though nervous, she snuggled

into the space he had made with his arm. He picked up her hand and played with her fingers.

"So, your mom got home okay?" he asked.

Tracy smiled, thinking of Sheila's delight over the party. "Oh, yeah. She had a really good time. She loved the food and talked to everyone just like a social butterfly. She won a raffle prize too, y'know."

"I know. I saw her with one. What did she get?"

"I don't know. She wouldn't open it. Said she was going to put it under the Christmas tree. She's like a kid when it comes to Christmas. It's her favorite holiday. Instead of us waking her up on Christmas morning, she used to wake us up, jiggling bells like Santa had just left in his sleigh." Tracy smiled at the memory and at the care her mother took in making their apartment a home.

"You were right about her being worried. When she was looking for you, she was frantic." Marcus frowned, remembering Sheila's face.

"I knew she would be. She told me that Sean was helping her look for me and you came over and told her where I was." Tracy she looked down at her hands, growing somber. "She really liked meeting you...thanks for being so nice to her."

"What? Thanking me? I really like your mother." Her comment and the way her eyes fell sadly to her lap made him think about the state he had found her in on the balcony. "Tracy, you wanna tell me what happened tonight that made you so upset?"

She shook her head, swallowing hard. "I don't even want to think about that. I'm here now with you and I'm happy."

Marcus nuzzled the top of her head, breathing in her hair's fragrance. He pressed further, thinking it could have been Elaine that had set her off after the comment she had made. But he didn't think it likely, because Elaine hadn't been anywhere near Tracy at the time. He recalled her looking at him before she dashed off and thought, uncomfortably, that he had been the source of her misery.

"Was it because of me and…and my date?"

"No, it was stupid. I overreacted again," Tracy said, cutting her hand in the air.

"No, don't say that. Your honesty, your realness, is what makes you better than anyone up in that joint. If that was your reaction, that was your reaction. And I know you to be a strong and feisty woman. If you became that upset, it couldn't have been nothing."

She sighed and looked at her hands, growing stiff in his arms at the memory of the harsh words used to characterize her.

"Well, I was a little sad about the way I had left things with us. And you were with that woman. So I was in the stall feeling sorry for myself." She paused and stiffened. "But it was Anne Duncan and her cronies who, I guess, really set me off."

She told him most of what she had overheard them saying, leaving out the part about neither Sean nor him being attracted to her and their being out of her league. But he noticed that her voice became really sore at the way they had talked about her mother.

"I mean, it was just so vicious, Marcus. I had bought Mama a nice gown, but she wanted to wear that and—"

"Shhh. You don't have to defend your mother because of a bunch of stuck-up hags who couldn't measure up to you and Sheila all put together." His hostility against them rose, making his face hot. "Screw them. Who the heck were they with? They probably paid some dudes to take them out."

"You didn't feel that way when you went out with Anne," Tracy said, in her too-honest fashion. She wished she hadn't when Marcus was quiet and stretched out his legs.

"Anne was just a rebound screw. She was around the office all in my face and I was coming out of a bad relationship," Marcus said, thinking that the relationship wasn't that bad—

it was just how it ended. But he would tell her that tale on another day. "Anyone who would seriously take her out would have to be just the kind of dude she was with. Some Wall Street nerd who was happy to have a woman. Any woman."

Tracy laughed, in spite of herself. It was fun to turn the tables and engage in vicious gossip. She felt innocent because she wasn't doing the gossiping. It was Marcus. "Well, they just made me feel so…alone."

"You have me," Marcus said, intertwining his fingers with hers.

"But I didn't right then. All I had was Mama and the way they were dogging her. I just couldn't stand it anymore."

"You had me *then*. You just wouldn't accept me."

"I know, baby, and I'm sorry I did that to us. I realized after you came to me on the balcony that I really do need you in my life, Marc." She wanted to get her feelings across. He had been so honest with her on the balcony and everywhere, that she attempted to say more. "Not just want you. I really need you."

He was her soft place to land. It was easy to be a tiger at work, but she wanted to be a kitten at home.

"You know I've been miserable these past couple of weeks when you wouldn't see me. When you said…you loved me, I thanked God for bringing you back to me."

He had her eyes, but he wanted more. He kissed her cheek and slid his mouth over to connect with her fleshy lips. Marcus released her hand and put his arm around her waist, pulling her body solidly against his. His other arm was around her shoulders. Tracy encircled his waist with her arms, pulling him just as close as he was pulling her. Their tongues lazily connected and roamed each other's mouths. This was the heaven they had waited for.

Her hand, wanting to connect with flesh, snaked along the exposed skin at his neck, and then, eager for more, she unbuttoned his shirt until the buttons were blocked by his vest.

She put her hand in his shirt and squeezed the hard, hot skin of his broad chest.

His hand had worked its way under her silky top and explored her hard, silky-smooth back. He pushed closer to her, his fingers traveling under the back of her bra until he had set the clasps free. Marcus's hand moved to the front of her body and gently squeezed her firm, round breasts, now free of their constraints. He trailed his lips from her mouth to the soft spot where her neck joined her shoulder and sucked lightly, his tongue making enticing circles on her skin. Her scent toyed with his brain and he pushed with his feet to move her down until her back touched the couch.

Tracy couldn't get enough of him either. Once he lay on top of her, she pushed his jacket off his shoulders with both her hands. Marcus helped her by interrupting his maneuvers to quickly shrug out of his jacket. His eyes bore into hers as he removed her top and tossed it aside, along with her bra.

All the while, Tracy worked on all the confounding buttons of his shirt and vest, so that when he lay on her again, their heated chests connected skin to skin. Her legs opened to him and he scooted into the space she created, kicking off his shoes in the process. Tracy held his head and pulled his face into hers, lathering his face with kisses, before resuming her business with his sweet and knowledgeable mouth.

Her body was inflamed as she felt his solid, manly arousal pressed exactly where it should be. Their ability to consummate their need for each other was only separated by four inconvenient layers of cloth: his pants and briefs, her slacks and panties. With his arms around her head, Marcus moved slowly on her while they kissed, enticingly miming the feature attraction. She pushed the unbuttoned clothing off his shoulders and slid it down his arms. Now, they were both naked to the waist and she pulled him back to rub her erect nubs against his chiseled chest as they kissed deeply.

Marcus pushed up on his arms to take in her feminine nudity. Though his desire was reaching a critical stage, he had to behold the woman he had wanted for so long. As he gazed and rubbed her breasts and flat belly, Tracy took advantage of his raised position to undo his belt and the top button. She unzipped his pants, wanting a view of his masculinity in all its rigid intensity. He pulled her remaining clothing off in one gliding movement and set about removing his own in the same manner. He watched her big, brown eyes turn into lustful slits as he pushed his fingers inside her wetness, his thumb expertly finding the button that made her moan passionately. Her hands slid up his chest and around his shoulders, coming down the sides to grip both of his powerful arms. She steadied herself as she pushed her hips forward, eager to aid the pleasure he was giving her. Shivers rushed through her body at his command of her sex. She now needed more than fingers to soothe her craving. She reached between them to grasp what she needed. Marcus's eyes closed in relief and longing. He wanted to taste her spicy moisture, but her passionate, gentle tugging prevailed over his delaying their connection any longer.

It occurred to Tracy that she had another room decorated as nicely as this. "You want to go to the bed?" she asked hoarsely, barely able to manage the words. Marcus seemed to be unable to speak at all. With a slight shake of his head, he reached on the floor for his jacket and found the condoms he had purchased earlier. "Later," he finally said, huskily. After he unwrapped one, Tracy took it from him and rolled it onto his sizeable hardness. She looked into his eyes as he guided her legs around his hips and entered her slick heat in one slow move. Tracy gasped, while a moan escaped Marcus's lips. He lingered a beat, amazed that he was exactly where he had fantasized he would be in his numerous daydreams. The long-lasting rhythm they created produced screams of ecstasy and fulfillment that trumped both of their most vivid fantasies combined. Later, as promised, there was a more leisurely discovery of their intense passion for each other in Tracy's bedroom.

Chapter 20

Kevin was glad to have another man to help with the heavy lifting, but he didn't know if he liked Marcus. As far as he was concerned, the dude had just appeared out of nowhere and Tracy was already acting like he was her husband. Tai and Sheila were ready to accept him immediately. Sheila, having met him already, knew his weak-kneed effect on Tracy. Tai was impressed that he was a major hottie, but down-to-earth and not stuck on himself. They sometimes fawned over him as if he was the only man in the room, which probably explained Kevin's surly attitude. Just days ago, he had been the only man in their lives. Sam and Lucas only cared that he was fun, and no matter how much heavy furniture he lifted, he still had the energy to pick them up, twirl them around and roughhouse with them. Madison, the baby, regarded him the same as Tracy: He was fun, but she didn't really want him to hold her. Tracy needn't have worried about her brother-in-law. By the middle of their trying winter move-in, Kevin had warmed up to Marcus's lively, yet laid-back personality.

Fortunately, with the holidays on the way, Tai had paid for one more month of rent on her mother's old apartment. They hadn't expected Marcus's help with the moving, and Tai had allowed time for Tracy and Sheila to transport smaller items and clothes and stuff during the month of January. Christmas dinner and the arrival of Santa had been held at Tracy's house. Sheila still cooked everything—she wouldn't have had it any other way—but Tracy had enjoyed playing hostess.

After everyone had departed, Tracy and Marcus relaxed in her living room watching television.

"Mama was so happy that you'd brought a tree for her place. I told you how she's like a kid about Christmas," Tracy said, rubbing Marcus's thigh. "That was a nice surprise. I told her, 'My baby is so thoughtful. That's why I love him.'" She gripped his chin and pulled his face to hers for a quick kiss.

"I love you. And I love your family," Marcus said, thinking about the events over the past weeks. "This was the first time since my mama died that I actually felt like I was having Christmas with a real family."

Tracy just snuggled closer to him, trying not to imagine how bad Marcus had it growing up.

"Aw, man, I hate that the holiday is over and it's back to work tomorrow," Marcus groaned.

"What are you whining about? You don't have to go in," Tracy said. Marcus had accumulated plenty of time off, and like any sensible person, he took a big chunk of it from the week of Christmas all the way until a couple of days after the New Year. Tracy, on the other hand, could only be off the days that the offices were closed. It wasn't so bad. Sean, Julia and Elaine were on vacation and barely anyone was around the office. Pam came in, saving her vacation time to add to her maternity leave so that she would have three months off when the baby arrived. She and Tracy spent most of the day talking and laughing with each other.

"Yeah, but it's not as much fun without you. What am I supposed to do with myself?"

"I'm sure you'll think of something." She cut her eyes at him. "Just don't go getting yourself into any trouble."

"I ain't Brian," Marcus said flippantly. His eyes met hers and he saw that the mention of Brian's name hadn't been well received. He felt her briefly stiffen in his arms. He rubbed her shoulder, saying softly, "I'm sorry babe. I shouldn't have said that."

"No. It's okay. I'm not still hooked on him," she said, alleviating what had actually been Marcus's first thought when he saw her uncomfortable look. "I just shudder to think about what a fool I had been behind that fool. I knew it wasn't right, but I was so busy trying to force a square peg into a round hole that I didn't even acknowledge to myself that he wasn't the one."

Marcus grew quiet. He picked up her hand, and turned it over. He cleared his throat and Tracy looked sideways at him immediately. She had come to understand that that noise meant he was going to say something that wasn't easy for him to spit out. She waited, but he fixed his eyes on the television.

"What?" she said, unable to stand the suspense any longer.

"You know," he started, his eyes finally connecting with hers. "I knew him."

"I know. You met us together. I remember you now at the go-kart thingy," she said, imagining that it was him in the park that day. Marcus narrowed his eyes and looked at her. He twisted his lips. As much as he wished it were true, he didn't buy it. She nodded and poked her fingernail in his thigh. "I do. You wore a blue shirt, with the sleeves rolled up and khaki slacks."

"Anyway," he said, stretching out the word. He didn't remember what he wore that day, but he was pretty sure, that if he was going to be on television, he wasn't wearing that. "I mean I know him. He and I serve on a board together."

Tracy shrugged, unconcerned. "Well, you can't stop a bad rash from spreadin'."

Marcus smiled at her impromptu colloquialism, but soon became quiet. He cleared his throat, alerting Tracy that there was more. "The thing is…we were friends kind of…I mean…we're still cool. I just haven't heard from him since I met you."

Tracy became tense. She didn't like what she was hearing. Marcus was nothing like Brian, but their friendship made her begin to wonder at his motives for pursuing her so quickly. She tried to recall seeing them together. It had never happened. Though they kept their relationship under wraps at the office, she and Brian had been to a lot of places together. "Wait, I do remember him hanging out with his friend Mark. Mark?" She finally turned the "k" into a "c" in her brain. Marc. Marcus.

"Um, yeah. We went to games together and stuff," he said, stiffly.

"So…you all would, what? Pick up women together?" she asked, knowledgeable about Brian's behavior and wondering about Marcus. Sean had said he used Cathy as his own personal dating ground.

"Nah, nothing like that," he said, but remembered that Brian would chat up girls and get a phone number almost everywhere he went. "We just went to sporting events."

Tracy looked at the television, not seeing the program at all. She wasn't angry, but she didn't really know how she felt. "You all…talk about me?" she asked apprehensively, giving voice to her worst fear.

Marcus hadn't thought of that. He could smack his forehead for being so callous. It was natural for her to think that he had pursued her because Brian had said she was an easy lay, or that he told him he was going to be cutting her loose and to take his shot at her. Neither of those discussions had ever occurred.

Now he wished he had kept his big mouth shut and just cut all ties with Brian. But he couldn't do that so easily. The way he felt about Tracy, he wanted to take it all the way to the altar. He knew that Brian would find out that he had married his ex-girlfriend and he didn't want her to hear about their friendship from Brain.

"No, Trace," he said, turning his body in to her. She still wouldn't look at him. "Our friendship didn't cut that deep. I didn't even know about you until I met you at the park. He told me after you left that you were his girlfriend. I only mention it now because…we might bump into him and I wouldn't want you to be surprised."

"So how long have you known him?" she asked, finding the courage to look in his eyes. She had to discern the truth.

"A little over two years," Marcus said.

"And in all that time, he never mentioned me? I mean, I only dated him for a year, but you knew him through our entire relationship." She squinted at the implications.

Marcus dropped his eyes. "I'm sorry, honey, but he never did."

"Oh," Tracy said in a breathy voice. She and Brian had kept their relationship quiet at the office, but there was no need for him not to mention her to one of his buds. She couldn't stand Marcus's closeness anymore or his scrutiny. She rose suddenly from her seat and headed toward the kitchen. Once there, she opened the freezer and took out an ice tray. She started to angrily crack the ice into a container. Marcus joined her in the kitchen. His hands were stuffed deep into his pockets. He leaned his rear against the counter and watched her perform her task. Her lips were tight. She found a glass in the cabinet and put the ice cubes in it, then pulled a grape juice out the fridge.

"What's up, babe? Are you mad?"

She put the bucket of ice in the freezer and tossed the ice tray into the sink. "Why? Do I look like I'm mad?" she said sarcastically, glowering at him.

"At me?" Marcus asked softly. He thought it could either be a stupid question or help him to find out what was going on in her mind. She started to move away from him and go back into the living room, but she stopped and stared at him.

"So, if Brian called you tomorrow and asked you to go out, you would?"

"No. Not if you don't want me to," he said. But he realized it wasn't right. Even if she did want him to, he couldn't see hanging out with Brian anymore.

"But you'd consider it?" Her anger at Brian was directed at the man she loved. She had never told him what a true snake in the grass Brian was—how he had ruined her promising career and dogged her with Millicent.

Marcus straightened his shoulders, more confident in his judgment. "Actually, I wouldn't consider it at all. No. I wouldn't see him again."

Tracy stared at him, but as she looked at his gentle eyes, she felt instinctively that what had happened with Marcus was mere coincidence. He saw her, he liked her, found out that she was his partner's girl, he put her out of his mind and then he happened to meet her again.

He'd never shown her anything deceitful in his personality and he would have every means to be, growing up in a household with Elaine. Marcus also took care of her in a way Brian never had. She had always been bending over backwards to accommodate him. She couldn't even imagine Brian taking time out of his schedule to move her mother. He'd suggest she hire movers.

She dropped her eyes to the soft drink in her hands to say what she had to say next. "You must've thought I was the biggest fool over him. When you met me again?"

"No, not at all," he said earnestly. He crossed the room to her and slung his arm over her shoulder, leading her back down the hall into the living room. "After I met you and found out you were his girlfriend, I thought he was the fool. To have an attractive, smart, successful woman like you and just take that for granted. That's just plain stupid."

"Apparently, we're a dime a dozen," Tracy said snidely. She then grew serious. It would be good for Brian to see that she was with a real man now, but she wanted no part of him. "I really don't want you to be friends with him anymore, Marcus."

"Hey, I thought that's what we were talking about. He and I are over. Given a choice between him and you, I'd pick you every time." With their conflict out of the way, he felt free to joke. "But he did have some damned good seats though."

"You shut up." She jabbed her elbow into his side. He feigned injured, holding his side and plopping onto the couch. She sat down beside him, placing her juice on the coffee table. "Viv can get us those same seats. All I have to do is call her."

"And make sure it's not on a night he's there," Marcus added, picking up her juice and drinking large gulps of it.

"Go get your own," Tracy said, pulling the glass from his hands. "But it couldn't be. Those tickets only come up in pairs unless they're having something where the box is reserved for staff. You have to claim them on a list." She peered at him. "Hey! You can afford season tickets…to anything! Why don't you get some?"

"To what? I'm not really into any one sport that much. Plus, I don't have the time to go all the time. Or try to hand off the tickets to somebody." Marcus shrugged, uninterested in her suggestion.

"The Bulls," she said excitedly, turning to him in her seat. "Get some for the Bulls. We can go a lot, or even Mama would go sometimes."

Marcus nodded amiably. "It's a thought. I'll see if we can get on the waiting list."

"Aww, man, what time are you thinking about? There ain't no waiting list for the Bulls anymore."

"Fine. I'll call tomorrow. We didn't exchange gifts, so that'll be my Christmas present to you," he said. Tracy had tied his hands on that one. He wanted to give her an expensive piece of jewelry or a new camera or something. It couldn't be a ring, or else she would probably flee in the opposite direction. And she said it was too late to rack her brain trying to figure out what to give the man who had everything.

She demanded to know something he wanted and all he could think to say was, "You," until she became irritated with him. So, she had laid down the law: "No gift exchanges and I mean it. None of that we won't exchange gifts and then you bring a gift, Marcus. If I see a gift…we're through." Of course, she was being dramatic, but he got the message. Besides, Christmas had never been that meaningful for him. He received most of what he had on his Christmas list from Elaine, and so did Sean. The difference was that she strived harder to find something Sean hadn't asked for that would surprise him and really make him happy. Just like his mother, Karla, used to do for him.

"All right!" she squealed, standing up to pump her fists in the air. She turned back to him elated and sat astride his lap. She wrapped her arms around his shoulders. "Now you just think of something I can get you and we're straight."

Marcus smiled at her enthusiasm, and leisurely clasped his hands around her waist. He had had no idea she liked basketball this much. "I think I got my gift right here."

"Somehow…I knew you'd say that," she said, pulling his head to her and kissing him deeply.

While they were opening up, Marcus had meant to tell her that she wasn't the only fool for love. He was going to fill her in on what had happened with Hannah, Sean and him. But after she sat in his lap and began to kiss him, he was of one mind. He would later come to regret that omission.

Chapter 21

Over the holidays, Sean and Ashleigh had enjoyed themselves on a nice vacation in Aspen, skiing, partying, enjoying the spas and hanging out in their cabin. But Sean wasn't pleased with the amount of money Ashleigh spent shopping for knickknacks for their eventual home together. To Sean's dismay, she wanted a Valentine's Day wedding with all the romantic trappings he usually found to be over the top. But it was the bride's day and he was just a pawn.

Sean had attempted to put his obsession with Tracy out of his mind. But now Anne Duncan sat in his office, whining about the tongue-lashing she had received from Marcus.

"And what did he say to you exactly?" Sean looked bored, but his blood was boiling.

"Just that if I can't get along with all the executives and show some respect, then maybe I need to move on," she said in her annoying, nasal voice. "He said that he, and everyone else, has dealt with my bad attitude long enough and he was putting the warning letter in my personnel file. He said that if one more incident reached his ears about me, I'm gone. He can't do that, can he?"

"You're not union or civil service, you're an exempt employee. We can fire you at will," Sean said, oblivious to the dread growing on her face. "Which executives have you been rude to?"

The woman looked down uncomfortably. Sean already knew the answer from Marcus's rage. He also hadn't gone through their employee policy of meeting with her along with the human resources director if she requested. "To whom have you been insubordinate?" he asked again.

"Nobody," she said, not really looking him in the eye.

"So Marcus just came back from Christmas, gunning to pick on you out of the blue?" Sean didn't really like Anne either. She was one of Elaine's favorites for some reason.

"Well, I haven't warmed up to Tracy maybe, but I haven't really gotten a chance to know her." She put her hands on Sean's desk. Sean stared at them until she removed them.

"And in the meantime, you've been rude?" His brows went down and his eyes narrowed.

"No, I would never," she said too quickly.

"You know, I think you're lying," Sean said evenly. "You didn't speak to her when you saw us coming back from lunch and you're always glaring at her during our executive meetings. You got a problem with Tracy?"

Anne shook her head and looked at her hands.

"Because if you think this is another time that you, Anne Duncan, know what's better for Cathy Booker Foods than Elaine, Marcus and me, why don't you just come out and say it?" Sean sat up straight in his chair and leaned forward. He watched her. Her eyes were watery. She had expected his help and yet had got another chastisement. "You know, I'm one of the people he spoke of that has just about had it with your attitude. Now, we better see the improvements he mentioned or you can find another post."

"Yes, sir," Anne said quietly. She glanced up at him to see if she could go.

"Go on. Get out," he said.

When she left, he thought about Marcus. Obviously, Marcus and Tracy were still seeing each other, ever since that night at Elaine's. They played it real cool, because he had no idea until the Christmas party. He didn't buy Marcus's story about going out for a smoke any more than he thought Tracy's disappearance at the same time was just a coincidence.

Sean couldn't understand why Tracy would like someone like Marcus over him. He thought that maybe it was just the fact that he hadn't made his attraction known and plus he had a fiancée. Perhaps, if he could get her in a setting that would make her more inclined to see him more as a man, and less as a boss, she could fall for him. He would just have to put that theory to the test...and soon.

Chapter 22

Long before the majority of the staff arrived at work, Tracy sat at her desk utilizing her favorite relaxation tool, the panoramic view from her window. Today, she had run on the treadmill alone in the executive gym for the first time since she and Marcus had become a couple. Marcus was in Peotone with Kelly and a couple other members of his external relations staff. He was meeting with a prominent pastor and several community leaders in a downstate Illinois town. The black kids in the area were in desperate need of stimulating activities for the upcoming summer and Marcus thought that Cathy Booker Foods could sponsor a summer day camp. They were proposing activities, assignments, guest speakers and field trips to stimulate the youths' interest in all types of careers. Once it was rolling, Marcus planned to be a speaker himself, presenting topics on food science.

It was three weeks after the New Year and she and Marcus had enjoyed nearly a month of bliss together. During that time, she hadn't worked up the nerve to tell him the real deal between Elaine and her. He was still under the illusion that she was required to get some dirt on Ashleigh, and even that topic had never come up.

Tracy didn't think Marcus would be angry about her revelation. Well, at least not at her. He would probably hit the roof at Elaine though. She just didn't want to see the disappointment in his eyes. She wouldn't want Marcus wondering how she could allow herself to be used like that. And if he heard about the half a million dollars—that Tracy never cared about anyway—he would probably begin to wonder how influenced she was by the trappings of wealth. She thought about the night they got together. When she told him about the things Anne Duncan and her friends had said about her wearing designer names, he offered an irate excuse on her behalf, saying, "You can buy what you want to buy with your money. It's none of her business."

But it wasn't like that. This was Elaine's crap. Even though the clothing she wore was expensive business attire, she wondered if Marcus noticed that she never really wore that kind of stuff when she wasn't at work. If she were that kind of diva, she would wear similar stuff at home. Her jeans were from the Gap. She didn't go in for those new ones that cost three hundred to five hundred dollars and more. *For jeans?* To her it was absurd. She did mix in a designer piece or two, but that was her style prior to Elaine's ministrations. And even then, it was because she liked the style and had found the item on sale. To his credit, Marcus had commented that he liked the way she looked at home. He said it looked more like the woman he fell in love with when he first saw her in the park. She smiled to herself to think that a guy like Marcus, whom many women desired, could believe in love at first sight.

But now that she was back in the office and knew that Sean was in, she was beginning to feel the pressure of keeping such dirt to herself. She stood up and unenthusiastically flipped through Elaine's calendar. The witch was on an extended holiday in southern France with her husband, but she was not unreachable. Sean had been in for the last couple of weeks, but he had yet to resume his managers' meetings. She had to do a little more of attending board meetings in Elaine's stead, but so far, only two boards had held meetings. The last time she talked to Vivien, she said she had talked to some people for a new job for Tracy, but she said to call her in mid-January because her contacts were slow to get back from the holidays. Tracy looked at her watch. It was barely eight o'clock in the morning, but she picked up the phone to leave a message for Viv to call her.

A knocking at the door interrupted her phone call.

"Come in," she said, placing the phone back in its receiver. Sean opened the door.

"Good morning, Tracy. I'm glad to find you in," he said, coming into her office but standing near the door. "I hope you don't have a busy schedule today, because I'm going to need to steal you away from Elaine."

"No. She hasn't called me with any instructions yet, but the morning is still young," Tracy cracked, knowing it was safe to joke a little bit about his mother with Sean. She walked around her desk. "I was going to work on a speech she has to give in February, but it can wait. What do you need?"

"I should've given you advance warning, but I guess I wasn't really thinking that I wanted another brain during this meeting, until this morning." He moved farther into the room. Tracy nodded, ready to assist. "I'm flying out to Key West today and I want you to attend this meeting with me. I have all the things you need to bring yourself up to speed during the flight."

"Oh," was all she could say. Astonished, she unconsciously smoothed her skirt and returned to her desk, picking up som paperwork just to have something in her hands. She knew this happened all the time in the corporate world; she just hadn't expected it to happen to her. Sean's request shouldn't be seen as anything out of the ordinary. She glanced at him. He didn't present himself as anything but the usual, composed and unreadable Sean.

"So I take that as a yes?" Sean asked, with amused eyes.

"Um, how long will we be gone?" She had to call Marcus.

"It's a day trip. We'll be back tonight," Sean said, mildly irritated. He wasn't used to having to explain himself. He stood in front of her desk. "Look, we're on a private flight that leaves in about an hour. I'm running late as it is. Actually, I called Elaine this morning already and asked her if it was okay that I take you along. Is there a problem?"

"Of course not," she said, feeling silly for letting Elaine's junk get in the way of her performing her duties properly. But she knew there was no way Elaine would refuse a request like that. This played right into her plan. And numerous times Tracy had come into the station at CMT and found out that they had a breaking story that she had to hustle for. But she wanted to call Marcus. "I guess I won't need luggage or anything. Let me just gather my stuff and I'll join you in a minute."

She thought she had said it in a way that would alert anybody to leave. But Sean said, "Fine," and sat down on her couch. She couldn't talk to Marcus under this scrutiny. She gathered her coat from the closet and picked up her purse and briefcase. "What meeting is this?" she asked, stalling for time as she went to her desk.

"It's pretty exciting actually. You'll like this one," Sean said, looking rather pleased with himself. "Of all the food joints they have in Key West, they don't have a soul food restaurant. We're meeting with a brother who's going to open one, and we might be able to supply him with some specialty items for the menu. It could be lucrative for CBF."

Upon hearing the acronym, Tracy thought of how Marcus had switched to calling the company Cathy, just like she did. She couldn't leave town without calling him. She dashed off a note and folded it up. "That does sound good," she said, but wasn't really paying close attention. She kept up the conversation to keep his eyes from the note she was dashing off. "That's a new market for Cathy, right?"

"Yep. It could open up a whole new clientele for us. I met this guy sometime last year, just casually you know, but we hit it off. Imagine my surprise when he called me before the holidays and told me what he was planning. I thought of you this morning and how well we worked together on the Down-Home Grown deal. You're quick as a whip in thinking of the things I can't. I know you don't like to hear it, but you're a great substitute for Elaine."

Tracy threw her hand at him and kissed teeth. "I am so over that now. I'm resigned to my role."

She folded her note and came to stand next to the couch. "Okay, I'm ready."

"All right, let's head out," he said, standing and opening her office door for her.

"Where's your coat? It's pretty cold out there," she said, stopping at the door. She thought she saw her chance to make a quick phone call.

"All my stuff is in the car. I just came upstairs to see if you were here and get you," he said, dashing her hopes in one fell swoop. "Besides, we won't need them where we're going."

"Oh, that's right. Let's go then." She went through the door and made a beeline for Pam's desk. "Let me just put this over here and I'm off."

The note said: "Call Marcus and tell him I'm on my way to Florida with Sean, but I'll be back tonight. Tell him to call me on my cell. I'll try to call him if I can break away."

Pam was the only one she could trust with this information

She placed it right on top of her in-box, knowing that Pam always looked in her in-box first thing in the morning. What she didn't know was that Pam had delivered the baby the night before and she wasn't coming in for the next three months.

Chapter 23

The weather in Key West was sunny and balmy. It was oppressive to Tracy, because she was wearing a black wool suit with a long fluted skirt, black tights and high-heeled suede boots. She carried her coat on her arm and it was just making her arm hot. She had studied the little information Sean had. The guy had faxed a couple of sheets about his menu, his background and the demographic study of his potential market. Sean had filled her in on the things he thought Cathy Booker Foods could prepare and ship with few modifications to their plants.

"I hope it's air-conditioned where we're going. I'm wilting in this heat," Tracy said to Sean as they waited for their car outside the small airport. Sean looked at her, acting as if he had just noticed her discomfort, but he had anticipated this diversion in his head.

"Oh, we have some time before the meeting. Why don' we go shopping for you to get some more comfortable clothing?" He touched her arm sympathetically.

"No. I don't want to go into the meeting looking like a tourist," she said. From what she could see of the island, there were no large buildings, other than resorts in sight. "Maybe if I can get a pair of stockings, I'll feel better."

"They have some really nice shops in town. You'd be surprised at what you can get," he said, looking at his watch. "Do you see anybody holding up a sign with my name? Gerald said he was going to send a car for us."

"Nope, not unless it looks like a regular taxi," Tracy said, futilely looking around again. If a car was there, they'd see it. The airport was small, and from where they were standing, you could see every car in the front drop-off and loading area.

"Me either. He's not off to a great start. This is very unprofessional. He knew what time our plane landed," Sean said, stepping forward and hailing the next waiting cab.

"Now, don't go getting angry at him before we've even met with him. Maybe we should just wait a few minutes." The cab came to a stop in front of them and Sean opened the door for her.

"I've waited long enough. Besides, I know the way to his house. Let's go do some shopping," Sean said, before scooting in the car beside her. Tracy noted Sean's surliness. Ever since the confrontation at Elaine's house, she had noticed an impatient and mean side to his personality. She thought he was rather spoiled.

Sean took Tracy to Barney's, where she'd find an assortment of warm-weather business attire. Unbeknownst to her, she made the mistake of leaving all of her stuff with him while she perused the racks and then tried on her choices. He found her cell phone in her purse and turned it off, then deposited it deep within a pocket in his briefcase. He had a feeling that at some point during the night, she might try to sneak off and make a phone call to his bothersome cousin. He didn't think of his intent as unscrupulous; he just knew he wouldn't want to be disturbed. If all went as planned, he would find it for her when they went back to Barney's in search of the mobile.

They went from the store directly to the meeting with Gerald Harper at his lavish vacation home. They met on his veranda. Just as Sean expected, Tracy was a great help in suggesting ways that the two companies could fit together. Her expert handling of the situation made him think of all the ways he could fit together with her. But he had to tread carefully here, lest he scare her off. He saw her peeking at her watch when she thought no one was looking.

At six o'clock, when Gerald proudly suggested that they take a trip out to his site to get a feel of the layout, Tracy glanced at Sean meaningfully, but he just shrugged. Normally, he wouldn't go in for this sort of thing himself. The guy's setup really had nothing to do with their product, except that, so far, Gerald's chattiness was playing right into Sean's plans. This was almost exactly how it had worked with Hannah, except that time, he had been at home. He would've loved to have Tracy on his home turf, but that was too risky. She was no Hannah. Tracy would probably smell a rat immediately. But he could imagine making a great impression on her at his place.

"What time is our flight?" Tracy asked quietly as Gerald walked a few paces ahead of them, leading them to the barren storerooms of his restaurant.

"We've got time," Sean said, looking at his watch. He attempted to sound as bored as Tracy. "This has got to be the end."

Tracy cut her eyes at him, whispering, "I wouldn't be so sure."

Indeed, Gerald talked about his restaurant and equipment for another half hour. And to Tracy's annoyance, Sean asked a lot of questions, the same way he did at staff meetings. Which was really surprising, given that the man was addressing almost all of his conversation and attention to Tracy. Once in a while, she had to turn from him to stifle a yawn. It was nearing eight o'clock by the time they sat down in the few chairs he had in his office to draw up a plan that could lead to a contract. Sean would have to develop a dollar amount on the products, and both sides' lawyers would need to go over it, but it seemed to be a done deal.

"So, Gerald, everything looks good," Sean said. To Tracy's relief, he was wrapping up. She was tired and hungry and missing her man. "I think we missed the last flight out. Can you suggest a place in town where we can get a couple of rooms?" Sean asked. Tracy had been pleasantly smiling at Gerald, happy that their business was drawing to a close, but when Sean said this, her face turned stony and her head whipped around to Sean.

"You two can stay with me. I've got lots of room," their host answered, thrilled at the prospect of company. "Plus, y'all got to be hungry. I can whip us up a fantastic, down-home dinner and you'll get an idea of how I expect everything to look and taste when I open my restaurant."

"That sounds good to me. I know I could eat a horse, and I'm sure Tracy could eat a foal," he joked and looked at Tracy. She folded her arms over her chest and gazed at her new shoes. Her lips were tight.

"Uh, does your bathroom work yet, Gerald?" she asked with as much control as she could manage. She was furious.

"Oh, yeah. It's right down the hall there and to your left," he said, then she could hear him continuing his conversation with Sean. "I had to have the plumbing done first thing, you know, because I'm working here some of the time. You know how that is."

As she marched down the hall, all she could think about was slapping Sean. He said that they were doing okay on time and then, instead of telling her that they'd missed their flight, she heard about it as an aside. Plus, why didn't he just rush this guy along? Sean let him talk about minutiae all day, like it was the most fascinating conversation in the world. Once inside the bathroom, she dug into her purse for her cell phone. She had to call Marcus and tell him about this crap.

Tracy felt through her bag and then felt again. She started to panic. She pulled everything out of her purse one item at a time. She began to be filled with dread. Where the heck was her phone? Her attaché was out there with them. But she didn't remember putting it in her case. The last time she remembered touching her phone was throwing it in her bag at home in the morning. She inhaled deeply to calm herself and stuffed all her items back in the purse. "No wonder Marcus hasn't called me. I don't have my phone," she muttered to herself. She hoped that Pam had reached him so that he would at least know why she was out all night. Well, he wouldn't know why she was still gone, but she could explain that in the morning. But she would excuse herself sometime during the night to call him.

She returned to the men, her face still tight. "If we're going to spend the night here, I'll need to go to the store to get some toiletries," she said, not caring that she'd interrupted their conversation.

"My wife has some things in the house that you could wear. You're taller and smaller than her," Gerald said, appraising Tracy's body. "But if it's just something to sleep in—"

"No offense, but I'd really prefer to buy my own things," she said, looking at Gerald as though she'd had enough of him. He immediately fell silent and nodded his head. He busied himself gathering up his papers. She turned to Sean, with the same icy look. "I'm going right down the street to the strip. You two go ahead. I can take the shuttle back to Gerald's." With the island being only ten miles long, the shuttles ran through every street in Key West. Gerald's restaurant was right off the strip and Tracy could walk back to Barney's. It was just his house that was farther away.

"No, no. We can take you. It's no problem," Sean said quickly, feeling his plan to keep up with her slip away.

"Really, I'd prefer it." She had reached her breaking point with all the togetherness.

"Tracy, can I speak to you for a minute?" Sean said, jerking his head in the direction of the front room. "Excuse us, Gerald."

Gerald nodded and waved a hand in agreement. Sean led Tracy down the hall and into the dining room. When he was sure they were out of earshot, he asked her, "What's wrong? You look really mad all of a sudden."

Being the hothead she was, Tracy let loose. "You said that we would be back tonight. I counted on that. Then you two dragged on with the meeting talking about nothing really, until we missed our flight. Now, I'm supposed to go to his house and sleep in his short, fat wife's stuff without any toiletries? Am I supposed to wear her panties?" She didn't mean to dog another woman and had no evidence that this was true about Gerald's wife. She was simply angry and at the end of her rope. She had found a way to get it across to Sean that she had been terribly inconvenienced. "Look, I had to sleep in someone else's clothes at Elaine's, but don't think this is a situation I want to keep repeating."

Sean opened his mouth to respond and then saw the fire in her eyes and closed it. He waited a minute, with her staring at him angrily, before he found a response. "I'm sorry, Tracy, this is just how it happens sometimes in business deals. He's presenting us with a whole new market and I don't want to be rude. He wants to look at the place. We look at the place. He wants to talk for hours on end about his equipment, we talk about the equipment. You can't rush these things. You see that he asked us about our ability to produce our corn-bread mix in a way that he can make it fresh daily in his kitchen. That happened here, just now." Sean emphasized, leaning toward her and gesturing at the back rooms. Her features didn't soften, but she glanced in the direction he was pointing. "Now, he gets to cook us dinner and he's invited us to stay at his house. Businesswise, that's pretty good in my book. The closer you get to them, the more likely they are to accept the terms of the contract. You understand?"

She didn't say anything, but her look was a little less harsh. She folded her arms across her chest and looked at her shoes.

"I don't want to stay over any more than you do, but that's the price of doing business in the corporate world. It happens all the time. I thought you were ready for this. Elaine thought you were ready for this. We're in a high-stakes meeting. Yet, you were rude to Gerald in there. Why are you acting this way?" Sean watched her for her reaction. He was getting through to her.

His voice wasn't berating. It was pleading for her to understand where he was coming from and get with the program. She felt thoroughly chastised, and dropped her angry posture immediately.

"I'm sorry," she said quietly. "I guess I'm tired and hungry and…I do have a life, you know. This just interrupted my entire day. I don't like having no control of what's going to happen to me, like this."

"I know that, Tracy. That drive is why you're here right now," he said. His face was relaxing a bit too. The corners of his mouth curled up at her. "Even that attitude you're giving me is what I want…what we want at CBF. Just be yourself and follow your hunches. I wouldn't have you act any other way," he said, thinking that he meant to have her.

Tracy smirked a bit at his compliments. Though it didn't seem like she was making that big a difference to her, Sean, Julia and Elaine were always telling her that she was doing a great job. Marcus said so too, but he was her sweetie, he was supposed to say that. "Well, I'm still not sleeping in another woman's stuff again."

"So you're not going to go ballistic on me again? And you're going to try and relax, even if Gerald is telling us how great he is?" Sean touched her arm briefly.

"I'm cool. I'll get with the program," Tracy said, starting to walk to the back room now that she had been told how to behave. She was ashamed for getting so snippy. It was just that she had never really been in love before and she physically ached at not being able to be with Marcus tonight. Add to that the fact that she hadn't talked to him and didn't know if he knew where she was. She was sick to her stomach from worrying about him worrying.

"If it makes you feel any better, I don't have anything either and I'm sure as hell not wearing any of Gerald's drawers," Sean joked in a whisper. Tracy chuckled deeply from the belly. Sean did have his moments. In the office, he usually intimidated her, but whenever they got one on one, she actually felt comfortable with him and liked him. And despite the way Elaine had made her worry about him, he had never shown her anything but respect—as an employee and as a woman.

"All right Gerry, you want to go with us while we shop?" Sean said, taking charge of the situation when they returned.

Chapter 24

Marcus and his crew had returned to the office at around two. The first thing he did after he'd settled in, was knock on Tracy's door. His first trip away from her and he was missing her like mad. Well, half a trip. He had been thinking about how wonderful it would've been to have her along at the meeting. He had seen her sharp mind at work and thought that she could've contributed a lot, especially when the conversation was about helping black kids. That was her number-one cause. He remembered her saying that way back when he talked to her at the go-kart race.

When he didn't find her in her office, he went to her secretary, one of the only people around in the executive offices. Pam's husband had left a message on his phone that she had the baby the night before. Julia wasn't at her desk. Sean wasn't in. Gina said she didn't think she had come in, but she didn't call and leave a message or anything. Marcus knew that wasn't right because Tracy was preparing for work as he was heading out the door this morning. He spent most of his time at her house these days. Occasionally, they would stay at his place, but he didn't find it as homey as Tracy's.

He did most of the cooking. Years of being spoiled by Sheila's cooking, even as an adult, had made Tracy lazy in the kitchen. Marcus and Sean never had that luxury. Elaine had told them that she wasn't going to hang around the house cooking for them. She taught them how to follow a recipe and use the stove. Marcus was ten and Sean was eleven. They were free to grab some of the food she made for clients. Unless it was for a catered event, then they couldn't touch it because the portions had been made to exact order. They usually preferred to make their own food anyway. They were bored with the same old meals all the time. Marcus was more adventurous, having learned from his mother that experimenting with food was half the fun of cooking. By the time they were teenagers, he and Sean agreed that he was the better cook. Marcus took over the cooking duties by himself, with his cousin frequently requesting some of his favorite Marcus creations. Sean kept the house clean. When he thought about it, they had shared a lot together.

He called her cell phone a couple of times and when the voice mail picked up immediately, he knew her phone wasn't turned on. He sat at her desk and looked through her calendar, but didn't see any appointments for her or Elaine. Marcus called her mother.

"Hey, Sheila," he said, reminding himself not to alarm her. "Is Tracy over there?"

"No, is she coming over here today? It's a workday isn't it?" she asked.

"Yeah, but I had to go to a meeting downstate and she told me she had to leave work early to run some errands and stuff," he lied, after hearing a little worry in Sheila's voice. "And I couldn't remember where she said she was headed."

"Oh, well she's not here. I don't think she's coming over here. Try her cell phone."

Mothers had an annoying way of suggesting that you do the thing you would have obviously thought of. But Marcus played along. "I think she forgot to turn it on."

"Oh. Well, if she comes by here, I'll tell her to get in touch with you," Sheila said.

"Thanks, 'bye." He hung up, thinking that he did okay and Sheila didn't seem to think it was anything out of the ordinary. He went to the garage and saw her car. Now he was sure she was in the building somewhere. On his way back from the garage, he stopped by the cafeteria and didn't see her. He saw Julia eating with Sean's secretary, Lila. He stopped by their table, aiming to look unaffected, but numerous girlfriends had told him that his eyes always gave him away.

"Hey Lila, Julia," he said, taking time for a greeting. "Julia, you know where I could find Tracy?"

It was Lila who answered, frowning at Julia for confirmation. "She's with Sean, isn't she?"

"Yeah, yeah, that's right. Elaine told me when she called in," Julia said, nodding her head.

A funny feeling crept into the pit of Marcus's belly. "With Sean? Where?"

"They're in Miami," Julia said, more focused on her food. Marcus's eyes bucked involuntarily.

"Not Miami," Lila corrected. "They're at one of those Florida Keys."

"Key West." Julia nodded. She pointed at Lila, like this conversation had been their idea. "Once you said 'Keys' it came to me."

"Wha—" Marcus's throat was suddenly dry. "When did they go there?"

"This morning," Julia took over, now on more solid ground

ith her facts. "Elaine told me that Sean wanted Tracy to attend a meeting with him. They'll be back tonight."

Marcus didn't want to make himself conspicuous, but he couldn't leave without asking most of what he needed to know. "What meeting is this?"

Julia did stop fiddling with her food to look at him. Lila shrugged. "All I have is a guy's name on my calendar, but it doesn't say what it's about. It's a meeting Sean made on his own. He didn't give me all the information."

"Have you been able to reach him today?" Marcus asked, focusing his attention on Lila. He was beyond the point of caring what they thought anymore.

Lila shook her head. "No, but I haven't called him about anything either. Come to think of it he hasn't called me to ask about stuff. But he's got his managers' meeting on the schedule for tomorrow morning and he didn't cancel that, so I'm sure he'll be back tonight."

She answered with little interest, but Julia looked at him more shrewdly. "Is something wrong?" she asked, cocking her head at him. Marcus looked at her face, but his mind was a million miles away. Finally, he shook his head and left.

He remembered to call "thanks" over his shoulder after he'd gotten a few steps away from them. He went back to his office and took up his cell phone. He dialed Tracy's cell again as he walked over to Lila's office. Still no answer. He pulled up the calendar on Lila's computer and got the guy's name, Gerald Harper, but no phone number.

He thought about the greedy way Sean had looked at Tracy during the Christmas party and his mind began to race. This was almost the same crap he'd pulled with Hannah. Marcus was gone and Sean pounced. Marcus went into Sean's office and sat at his desk as though he could get clues as to what he was thinking from his perspective. Or perhaps he would find a notation that said, "Marc in Peotone. Seduce Tracy."

Though Tracy thought their stuff was under wraps, Marcus
had no delusion that Sean didn't know exactly what was up.
He could tell by the way Sean looked at him in passing.
Marcus also thought that it was mighty convenient for Elaine
to hire an assistant who looked just like Sean's type, right
before Sean was to wed a woman that she didn't like. He
didn't care what Elaine had told Tracy her job was at Cathy.
Marcus thought she was there to be an enticement for Sean.
Elaine probably wanted him to know that there were other,
better fish in the sea and she had found one. But what really
made Marcus's blood boil was that he knew Elaine didn't
want Tracy in her family any more than she wanted Ashleigh.
The way she had talked about Sheila clued him in that, to her
mind, Tracy and her family were from the wrong side of the
tracks. Elaine just wanted Sean to use her for his own pleasure,
forget about Ashleigh and then, hopefully, forget about Tracy.
He could kick himself for not really filling her in on how
wicked those two were. They were users from way back.
Selfish users.

Tracy wasn't a fool and she wasn't weak like Hannah had
been. Marcus knew she was in love with him and he had no
reason not to trust her. Everything in his body told him that
she wouldn't betray their relationship. Nevertheless, Sean
had charms. Marcus had never actually seen it in action, but
he'd witnessed his effect on girls. They were always left
wanting more of whatever flattery, or attention or kind words
he'd bestowed upon them in the wooing stage.

As his anger rose, Marcus was suddenly compelled to
move. He had to get a flight out to Key West right away. He
went back to his office to gather his things. On the way out,
he spied a folded note in Pam's in-box that had Tracy's handwriting on it: "URGENT." He picked it up and read it. He
stuffed it in his pocket. If he knew Sean—and he did—she
wouldn't be back tonight.

Chapter 25

"No, I'm serious. This idiot is screaming at the daughter of the publisher of *Black Enterprise* like she's lost her mind for not sending out a press release. Not that she didn't get them out mind you, but Anne wanted her to send it out before noon. And the girl comes to my office in tears. 'I can't do this job anymore, I don't want to work here,'" Sean said, imitating the young intern's voice. He paused to take a drink, peering over his glass at Tracy. Thanks to Anne's visit to his office, he had found an in to connect with Tracy. "I was afraid the next thing she was going to say was, 'I'm calling my father.' After all Elaine had done to court the magazine…hoping to get a cover story done on her. That's why the girl was there in the first place, with a pretty good stipend to boot. We didn't think we would have to share that information with Anne. Plus, dig this, it was only the girl's first week!"

"I'm surprised Elaine didn't fire her on the spot," Tracy said, shaking her head and frowning. She stretched out her legs and picked up the rather nice fruity drink Gerald had made for them. "Even if the girl wasn't the publisher's daughter, Anne has no right to abuse her subordinates. But, especially since she was an intern, she shouldn't have done that. Young people are taking these jobs to gain work experience. Positive work experience. Not to be abused as somebody's slave labor. If the releases were so important to her, she should've gotten them out her damn self. Or, or…used one of her regular staff."

They relaxed together on the veranda in the back of Gerald's spacious home. Their view overlooked the pool, and beyond a beautiful hedge mixed with bougainvillea, they could see the ocean. Gerald was far off in the kitchen, cooking up the promised feast. Tantalizing smells wafted toward them every few minutes, whetting their appetites. Tracy was actually glad to be there. She was relaxed and comfortable and Sean had turned out to be pretty good company. Gerald was an excellent host and an even better cook. He seemed to think of everything. He'd made the delicious fresh mai tais they were drinking, complete with slices of orange on the rim, and he had quickly prepared some crab cake appetizers with a scrumptious, creamy sauce. The table was set beautifully, with a floral arrangement cut from his garden, and delicate china and silverware. A small votive candle was the only light near them, with muted lanterns in the nearby yard.

"I know. I said the same thing. She's got a real bad attitude, and it just got worse while she was dating Marcus. I guess she felt entitled to show her ass," Sean said, shaking his head as though he were oblivious to the effect of his words.

Tracy almost dropped her drink. She didn't need any reminders that Anne Duncan had slept with her man. Also, she still hadn't called Marcus. She tried to continue the conversation like she hadn't been flustered to hear her baby's name. "So, why didn't she fire her?"

Sean shrugged. "I don't know. I'm sure Anne must have gone into Elaine's office and did a serious begging act to keep her job. Maybe Marc pleaded on her behalf too. The end result being that we have to deal with her today."

Tracy grew quiet. She couldn't imagine Marcus helping a witch like that to keep her job. On second thought, she could. Unlike Brian, if Marcus were seeing Anne, he would do everything in his power to help her. But Sean's words were making her think Marcus was more involved with Anne than he'd let on. She sipped her drink. It was packing more of a wallop that its mild appearance suggested. But Tracy was perceptive, even with her dulled senses.

If Sean's words were meant to warn her off Marcus again, he wasn't achieving his goal. They'd already discussed the heifer and if she had any doubts, she would ask him about her again. Tracy was in no position to cast stones herself. Marcus had seen the creep she had wasted too much of her time on, and he still loved her. Everybody made mistakes that they came to regret later.

"It smells so gooood," Tracy moaned, tired of the current topic of conversation. She would not sit here on a beautiful night talking about Anne Duncan, or any other creep from work. That included Elaine. "I thought the crab cakes were filling enough, but just smelling his food is putting me in the mood for more."

She stretched her arms over her head in total, complete leisure. Sean's eyes drank her in, watching her breasts strain against her top. Her flat, brown tummy was visible for mere seconds. Plus there were her words about being in the mood for more. It was all he could do to keep from adjusting himself at the sight of her in repose. He scooted down in his seat, stretching out his legs and held the cool drink unsteadily in his hands. He wondered if she knew how truly gorgeous she was. She didn't act like a lot of the pretty girls he'd known.

She was more natural and down-to-earth. Just like Marc. I really burned him that Marcus was probably enjoying endless hours making love to this super hot lady.

"Let me pour you another," Sean said, reaching for the glass pitcher of mai tais near his arm. Thanks to their large hurricane glasses, the pitcher was below the halfway mark. "It'll take the edge off your hunger."

"No. Nope," Tracy said, shaking her hand at him. "I think the edge is already off of everything too much as it is."

Sean hoped that was true. He moved the pitcher near her glass to pour, but she moved her drink away.

"Look, Sean, it's still half full," she said, holding up the glass to him. "You're not supposed to be encouraging your staff to drink. This could be a test, for all I know."

"The only test is...how many mai tais can Tracy drink?" He said, more flirtatiously than he was ready to be at the moment. He couldn't help it. With the exception of Gerald being there, this was going way better than he'd planned. Tracy was wearing a sheer, white blouse with embroidered flowers all over it and her lacy bra was just visible beneath. She paired that with a floral-patterned pastel skirt, which allowed an excellent view of her strong, shapely legs. Sean had bought himself a light-blue, short-sleeved rayon shirt and eggshell beige khaki shorts. They both wore sandals. She said that in this heat, her hair was bugging her on her neck. When she changed, she had pulled her crinkly Afro into a big Afro-puff in the back, with some tendrils of hair still framing her face.

"A lot, but you're not going to find that out tonight. I'd better go to the washroom." She stood up and then threw her chin over her shoulder in a way that made Sean's heart skip a beat. "While I'm there, I'm going to try to spy on Gerald's meal. I'm dying to know what he's cooking up next."

"You go get the dirt, Tracy," Sean said. He watched her hips sway gently as she walked away from him and his eyes moved down to the legs that seemed to go on forever. What he wouldn't give to have those wrapped around him at the end of the evening. He stood up and stretched.

Once she passed out of Sean's line of sight, Tracy did try to enter Gerald's kitchen.

"Gerald," she called in warning. Both of them had been given strict instructions to keep out.

"Tracy, you bet' not be trying to come in this kitchen!" he yelled back.

She stopped somewhere in the hall before she saw the actual workings. "I just wanted to know if I could use your phone. I forgot my cell phone."

"Oh, sure. There's one in the living room," he said, appearing in the doorway and wiping his hands on his apron. "Or, right back there in the den. The den's more private," he said, fully understanding about a person not wanting to get caught in a personal call with her boss around. She might want to talk about the boss or something.

"It's a long-distance call," she said. Her mother had taught her manners.

"Do I look like I'm hurting for money? Go on and make your call, girl. I swear, you Northerners." He went off muttering to himself as though truly offended.

Tracy chuckled and went into the darkened den. There was just enough light to find the phone and the leather office chair. She liked to talk to Marcus in the dark. Fortunately, the buttons lit up when she removed the phone from its base and turned it on. She dialed his home phone number. No answer, just his machine. She dialed her home phone, same thing. She dialed his cell phone.

"Hello?" Even with that one little word, Tracy thought he sounded quiet and different.

"Hey, baby, it's me," she said, happy to finally hear his voice. "What are you do—"

"Tracy, where are you?" Marcus cut her off, sounding frantic. His background noise was unusual.

"Didn't Pam tell you? I'm in Florida with Sean," she said, sitting up straight. This was her worst fear. He hadn't known where she was. She hated to make people worry about her.

"But where? What's the address?" He sounded rushed. Tracy hesitated. Why was he asking for the address? She must have been taking too long coming up with an answer. "Trace...what's the address?"

"Sir, you're going to have to turn off that phone," a woman was telling him.

"Just a minute, please," he said quickly, and then was back with her. "Give me the address."

"Marcus. Where are you?" Tracy asked, pressing the phone tighter to her ear.

"Now, sir, or I'll call the air marshal," the woman, that Tracy now guessed was a flight attendant, insisted.

"I don't know the address. We're in Key West," she said really quickly. Then Marcus's phone went dead. She stared at the phone in her hands. *Could Marcus be on his way here?* But why? She placed the phone back in its base and frowned at the room. She put her hands over her face and dragged them back. What was he thinking? She tried to think of what he was thinking. Did he get the message or not? Was he on his way to Key West or somewhere else?

She didn't want Marcus coming here, making a scene at Gerald's house over nothing. That would be too embarrassing. She hoped that wasn't what he was planning to do. She wished she'd shouted out the number to Gerald's before she was cut off, but she didn't know that either. At least, if he had the number, she could see what all of the urgency was about and allay any of his fears. She sat in the dark, stunned at the recent development. It was especially difficult to know what to do without knowing what he was doing. She shook her head. Was Marcus a jealous chauvinist? He was overreacting if she couldn't go off on a business trip without him calling in the National Guard. If he showed up at Gerald's nice home, bringing in all sorts of accusations and ranting, she would be through with him right on the spot.

In her news career, she'd witnessed stories where the woman recounted how her man started off like a fairy-tale lover. He did everything romantic and sweet that you could think of, but then he flipped and told her what to wear, who to talk to, where to go. Finally, they'd end up beating the woman into submission. Tracy would be damned if that was going to happen to her.

But even as she thought this, she didn't think it could apply to Marcus. He had the most gentle eyes and manner that she'd ever seen in another human being. *That's what those other women thought too, right up until the time he started whopping their asses,* the mean side of her brain offered. She sighed. Thinking about it wasn't going to solve anything. She stood up, resigned to put it out of her mind when her heart leapt in fear. She sat back down with dread. What if he was at her house and had found the contract between Elaine and her? He would be livid, thinking that's…no. The contract didn't say anything specific about her other deal. It just said, "may receive bonus of up to $500,000 for work considered outstanding and above and beyond the duties as assigned." That was ambiguous enough. At least her heart slowed down, but her questions still weren't answered. Gerald poked his head in the office.

"My dear, dinner is served," he said dramatically like an English butler. He snapped out of the joke when he considered her surroundings. "Oh, why don't I get that lamp for you. I'm sorry, I—"

"No, Gerald, I wanted it dark. Plus, I'm finished with my phone call now," she said, coming out of the room. She linked her arm in his, determined to get back on track with her relaxing evening, but her nerves were on edge.

"You talking to your man?" he asked, looking up at her. He was much shorter than Tracy.

"Now, Gerald. I went in there for privacy. If I wanted you to know everything and everyone I was talking to, I would've made the call right in the kitchen, so you could hear," she flirted.

"Yeah, but who's paying for that call," he said, enjoying her teasing. She wasn't what he had expected when she came with Sean. He thought he was going to have to deal with two pushy, know-it-all Northerners. Instead, Gerald thought he'd made two new friends.

"Oh? You're not going to pay for it if it was a man?"

"No, I'll pay. I got to pay my phone bill anyway. I'm just saying I have a right to know," he said, not seriously. He had walked Tracy back to the table where he'd created lovely dishes of plump juicy shrimp and rice with a kind of tomato sauce, with bits of herbs and onions and whatever. Tracy wasn't good at identifying all the ingredients in food. It looked like jambalaya, but not as soupy as she was accustomed to seeing it. He unlinked his arm from hers and pulled out a chair for her.

"Oh, my goodness. Gerald." Tracy turned to him surprised. "This looks so good."

"Isn't it incredible?" Sean chimed in, already leaning over his plate to smell it. Tracy did likewise. "It reminds me of the meals Mar— The meals I used to have when I was growing up."

"I'm glad you all are pleased. No one is allergic to shrimp, I hope." He looked around, but was confident from their appreciation that this was not the case.

"No," and "Not at all," were Sean's and Tracy's simultaneous responses.

"What do you call it? I mean, what is it?"

"It's a jambalaya, but it's my own version. Anyway, we can

talk about the dish while we eat. The best appreciation you can show a cook is to eat his food, not talk about it," he said, placing his napkin in his lap. "Let's pray."

They bowed their heads and found that Gerald was not only thankful for the food the Lord had provided, he was thankful for the good people at the table and for the upcoming business deal. He asked for the Lord's help in making sure that their bond was a strong one, formed in His glory and for the good of all who benefited from it and came to it. Tracy agreed with this, but added her own silent prayer that their lovely dinner was not interrupted by a crazed, jealous boyfriend and that Gerald's home not be sullied by anything negative like that.

Tracy's first bite of the long-awaited food was so luscious that she had to pause and moan. She didn't think Cathy Booker Foods could produce anything that would help this man's restaurant. Her nerves forgotten, she ate the rest of it in a haze, like she'd gobbled it down in a parallel universe. She barely contributed to Sean and Gerald's conversation, but just ate and looked at the beautiful view and soaked in the setting. There was wine with dinner, but Tracy stuck with the water. She became aware of the existence of other people as Gerald stood to clear the plates. Both she and Sean tried to help, but he insisted on doing it alone. He told them to wait for their desserts and coffee. Dessert? Gerald was too much.

The dessert turned out to be an irresistible peach cobbler, with a vanilla-bean whipped cream. The coffee was rich and silky on her tongue. Everything was wonderful. Gerald didn't join them for dessert. He wanted to wash up all the dishes, change the linens and turn down their beds.

"Ohhh," Tracy lamented, holding her coffee cup close to her nose. "I'm sorry I called his wife short and fat. She's the smartest and luckiest woman in the world."

"What makes you say that?" Sean asked, lazily. His deep voice aimed for the soothing undertones Marcus produced so easily. He'd had the wine with dinner and he was enjoying the effects of the combination of the drinks and the visual stimulation before him.

"Just look at him. She's not even here and he's handling a houseful of unexpected company better than most women I know. He's a great chef, and he's an able provider. Yeah, he's a bit short, but I could get over that. He really knows how to treat a lady," she cooed. Despite her experience on the phone with Marcus, she was back in a relaxed mood. She assumed Marcus hadn't found out the address or he wasn't coming here in the first place.

"Doesn't your man know how to treat a lady?" Sean asked in a sultry, quiet voice.

Tracy blew a breath out and leaned her head back on the chair. "I don't know. I guess so. Not like this." Then she caught herself. She raised her head and glowered at him. "Wait, who says I have a man?"

"Gorgeous girl like you? Without a man? It's not possible," he told her, taking his time. Tracy shrugged and laid her head back again. Sean linked his hands together at the back of his head and gazed at her.

"Well, it's possible," she said, flatly.

"No way," Sean said. "Plus, Gerald said you were talking to some dude in the office."

"When? He ran to tell you I was talking to a guy?" She looked annoyed.

"He said it at the table, just a while ago. You were so in love with the food, you weren't paying attention to a thing we said, huh?" He kicked her foot with his.

Tracy chuckled and sipped more coffee. "Nope. I was in heaven. Left all my cares behind."

"What kind of care could you have in the world?" Sean asked, tilting his head at her.

"Oh…I got troubles. Troubles, troubles, troubles," Tracy

trailed her words off, obviously affected by the liquor in her system.

"What kind of troubles, Tracy? The kind a man couldn't solve?" Now Sean's fingers made a pyramid in front of his mouth. He idly caressed his bottom lip.

"Huh! He'd have to be Superman to solve my problems," she said flippantly. But even in her haze, she noticed the direction the conversation was taking.

"Well, he wouldn't have to be Superman or even a super man; he'd just have to be dedicated to ensuring your utter and complete happiness." Sean looked down for a moment, then back at those big, brown pools she called eyes. "Which, I'm assuming your man is willing to do. Or else, why be with him?"

"Is that what you do for Ashleigh?" Tracy replied, trying to steer this discussion back in more safe waters. One minute he was her cool boss; now he was getting a little bit too intimate.

"Ashleigh's not Tracy," Sean said, leaning forward on the table and resting his head on his hand. He was taking her in. "She gets treated the way she wants to be treated. But you'll get treated the way a queen is supposed to be treated."

Tracy could ignore his advances no longer. She sat up straighter and frowned at him, placing the cup she'd been cradling on the table. With her sitting up, Sean put his hand on the back of her chair. "Whoa, wait a minute, Sean. What are you talking about?"

"You and me, kiddo," he said softly. His fingers trailed lightly across her back and came down her arm, until he was holding her hand. "What couldn't I give you in this world? What couldn't I achieve with you by my side?"

Elaine was right on the money. Tracy leapt up, bumping her leg on the table in her haste, but Sean still had her arm. He rose with her.

"Sean, I am not in for that," Tracy said, pulling away from

him. He tugged her gently, but she wouldn't allow her body to come back to him. His grip on her hand was firm, but not painful.

"Tracy, listen. Please…just hear me out." He didn't raise his voice, but he was desperate to convince her. He might have jumped the gun, but he was tired of waiting and looking at her. Especially knowing that Marcus had attracted this mouth-watering beauty. How could Marc woo her and not him? "Haven't you ever thought of me in that way?"

"No, Sean," came her quick reply. With a violent motion downward, she yanked her arm out of his grasp. Sean was surprised, and in the moment it took him to recover, Tracy made tracks for the house. Sean caught up with her before she reached the door and grabbed her shoulders. He turned her around and pinned her to the wall beside the doorway. His arms on either side of her head and his body blocked her escape.

"Tracy, listen to me. Just listen to me, love. I'm not trying to hurt you," he said with his face just an inch from hers. She started to cry. Two plump tears trickled down her face. She was so nervous, scared and bewildered that she didn't think to call out to Gerald who was right upstairs. "I'm offering you a life you've never known. A love like you've never known. We would be so good together…if you'd just give me a chance."

He pushed his torso into hers and she found the strength she needed to shove him off of her. It came back to her where she was and she called out, "Gerald!" as she dashed into the house. Sean was right on her heels and he grabbed her from behind, hugging her body tightly in his arms.

"Calm down, Tracy. I'm not trying to…to." He didn't have the words, because he knew his body was transmitting another message to her, hotly pressed against hers. The doorbell was ringing like crazy and Gerald came rushing downstairs. Sean let go of Tracy and she ran, meeting Gerald halfway up the stairs to cry in his arms.

"What's going on here?" Gerald asked, holding Tracy and looking angrily at Sean.

Sean turned from him, embarrassed at his aroused condition and aware that the scene must look crazy. The doorbell was still ringing maddeningly and it was soon followed by pounding. Gerald told Tracy that he had to answer the door. She could come with him if she liked.

Tracy shook her head and sat down on the stairs, sobbing into her hands. Gerald gave Sean an evil look as he passed by him. "I don't think I want you to stay here tonight Sean," he tossed over his shoulder on his way to the door.

Sean approached the stairs.

"Stay away from me, Sean," Tracy had the presence of mind to warn him. She pointed a finger at him and looked very lucid on this point.

"This is way overblown. I was simply trying to—" He opened his hands in a submissive way.

Almost as quickly as Gerald had gone down the hall, Marcus was in the room. Assessing the situation quickly, he walked right up, grabbed Sean by the shoulder, turned him around and punched him in the mouth. Sean fell to the floor at the bottom of the stairs. He didn't even know what had hit him until Tracy screamed, "Marcus!"

But Marcus was on Sean before he had a chance to recover. He punched him again and again. Sean was dazed and trying to cover his face, while making weak attempts at punching back. Gerald and Tracy pulled Marcus off Sean, but he was fighting them to get back to the business of punishing his cousin. "Let me go, Tracy," he said through his anger.

Sean sat up dazedly, blood dripping from his mouth. He touched his jaw and stared in wonderment at how this could've happened. He didn't know where Marcus had come from. He hadn't expected Tracy to just freak on him like that. And now Gerald was looking at Sean like he never wanted to see him again in life. Sean couldn't do anything, but start laughing. Sitting there on the floor, a bloody mess, with all of them watching. He chuckled and then laughed at his plight. This had been the worst night of his life.

"You see him laughing?" Marcus said, infuriated, trying to get away from his two captors. He was strong and dragged them a few feet, but they held on tight, pulling him back with all their weight inclined in the opposite direction. Gerald looked at Tracy behind Marcus's back.

"This is your boyfriend, I take it?" he said, smiling a little bit. Tracy looked at Gerald, but didn't find humor in the situation.

"Marcus! Stop it!" she yelled. He still tugged, such was his anger toward Sean. "Marcus, forget him. I need you right now."

They felt a slight release of his tension, though his chest was heaving up and down and his eyes were angrily fixed on Sean. Then they felt his entire body relax against their restraint. They didn't know how much strength it took to hold him back until they stumbled back into the hall with Marcus in tow. They figured it was safe to let him go. Marcus bent at the waist and put his fists on his knees. He winced and shook out the hand that had hit Sean over and over again. Tracy could see his knuckles swelling already. Sean's laughter dwindled to a whimpering whine. His nose made a squeaky noise too. Behind Marcus's back, Tracy mimed for Gerald to get a wet towel to Sean. She realized after seeing Marc's hand, that Sean might require medical attention.

Tracy moved Marcus into the kitchen. "Oh, Marc, why did you do that?" She felt sorry that she was at the center of all this confusion. She ran some cold water in the sink and put his hand under the tap.

"What did he do to you?" Marcus said, his eyes roaming over her entire face. His other hand was on his hip.

"Nothing. He didn't do anything, baby," she said, turning to get some ice. He grasped her arm.

"You were crying. You've been crying. Just look at your ce," he said, wanting to know the truth, no matter how bad was. Tracy swiped at her tearstained face with her free hand.

"No, Marcus. He did try something, but—"

"I'll kill him." Marcus released her arm and was headed ck to pummel Sean. Tracy ran in front of him and shifted l of her body weight behind her two stiff arms that pushed ainst his chest. She slid along the tiled floor, unable to atch his power.

"No, Marcus, I won't tell you what happened if you're ing to fly off the handle and fight again!" she yelled. He opped. He was breathing heavily again. He shook his head, ving to calm himself. "Now calm down."

Marcus looked at her like he was finally seeing her.

"Sit down!" Tracy pointed to a chair. But Marcus stepped rward and scooped her up in his arms. He clutched her to s chest.

"Oh, baby," he sighed into her hair. His words were delivered on ragged breaths. "Oh, Tracy. I was going to kill him."

"I know you were, sweetheart, and I love you for that, but he's t worth jail and all that mess," Tracy said, snuggling her face ainst him. She was so happy that he was with her. She released l of her pent-up tension in a fresh flow of tears. "It was just a oposition. He tried to…to…I don't know. But it wasn't like…" e just let the words fade out. She would have to tell him later, hen he was calmer, exactly what had gone down this evening.

Incredibly, they heard Sean calling through a nasally hine. "Marcus! Marcus!"

Marcus looked at Tracy and shook his head. Her eyes idened with fear. Then, just as incredibly, Tracy saw Marcus ll his eyes up to the ceiling, drop his tough posture and aswer with a sigh, "What, Sean?"

"I need to go to the hospital!" He didn't sound like Sean. Marc. I need you to take me to the hospital!"

Marcus squeezed Tracy and smiled down in her face. She had one eyebrow raised, and didn't know whether to smile back. "Do you think I should take that fool to the hospital?" he asked her, amusement in his eyes.

"Please, Marcus." She smiled freely then and pushed him in the stomach with her fist. "Please do."

"Okay," he said, kissing her forehead. "But only because you said so. Not because he deserves it." He went back to the running water and stuck his hand under. Tracy stood in the middle of the floor, not sure which way to turn. She wanted to tell Sean that Marcus would take him, but she didn't want to leave Marcus's side for one minute.

"But first, could you please see to my hand? It hurts like hell."

Tracy sprang into action, finding a large dish towel and lining it with ice from the freezer. She tenderly wrapped the bundle around his hand. He stole frequent kisses from her lips while she was helping him. Gerald came in the kitchen looking harried.

"I guess I'll run him to the hospital," he said quietly, looking at Tracy. "I tried to tell him not to ask your friend, but he…"

"I'll take him. I don't give a hoot," Marcus said, looking annoyed at the little man who was trying to talk like he wasn't in the room.

"Oh?" Gerald looked surprised. He looked from Tracy to Marcus, thinking she'd worked wonders on him in the little time she'd been with him. She shrugged and shook her head, meaning it wasn't me. They just have a dysfunctional relationship.

"I'm Marcus by the way. Marcus Hansen Booker," he said, looking pleasant enough for Gerald's frown to lift.

"Booker? You too?" He moved closer to Marcus, finally realizing that Sean and Marcus looked somewhat alike.

"Yeah," Marcus said. "Can I borrow your car, by the way?"

Chapter 26

Tracy rode along with them to the hospital to ensure that they idn't stray into any conversational category that could lead more fighting. She sat in the front of Gerald's Lexus and ean lay down on the backseat, holding an ice pack to his face nd nose. His supine position was not an indication of his juries, it was more of a reflection of how tired and worn own he was. Tracy turned in her seat to keep an eye on Sean.

Once they got underway, she thought she had her work cut ut for her. Marcus kept glancing in the rearview mirror, ying to peer at the groaning Sean.

"Do you have any idea what a damn fool you are, Sean?" Marcus asked. Of course, Sean didn't answer. "Did it ever ccur to you that not everybody is just totally bowled over by ou? Every woman is not just wasting time with the man ne's with, waiting for the chance to get with you."

He paused and looked into the mirror. "You know, some-ing occurred to me. This goes to show what a big idiot you

are. I think it's mighty strange that Elaine hired a beautifu
assistant after she heard you were getting married to Ashleigh
Don't you find that peculiar? Tracy looks like just your type
And Elaine hates Ashleigh. I'll bet she was hoping that Trac
would lure you away from Ashleigh and you fell for it hook
line and sinker. You are such a mama's boy."

Tracy stared at the side of Marcus's head, shocked that he'
come to the right conclusion on his own. Her mouth hung
open. They were a strange clan. Tracy wondered what kind
of world Elaine had brought them up in.

"Who says Elaine doesn't like Ashleigh?" Sean said
through the muffling towel.

"I hate to bust your bubble here, pal, but Elaine can't stand
Ashleigh. Did you think she would? You think she'd let
white girl walk away with her pride and joy? Take your pick
That's either you or the company," Marcus said, taking
pleasure in his tongue-lashing. "She even asked Tracy to dig
up some dirt on Ashleigh. Didn't she, Trace?"

Tracy's gaze dropped from the side of Marc's face and she
peered through the darkened car at Sean.

"Tell him, Tracy," Marcus said, hoping she wasn't trying
to spare Sean's feelings.

Sean sat up a bit. He looked at her with his one opened eye
"Did she do that?"

"No," Tracy said quietly and looked down into her lap
Marcus's head whipped toward her, eyes flashing angrily
wondering why she wouldn't tell Sean the truth. She touched
his arm, before he could say another thing.

"Actually, Marcus's hunch was one hundred percent right
Elaine wanted me to be a visual enticement for you to leave
Ashleigh," she said, watching as Sean righted himself to listen
to her. Marcus nearly drove off the road trying to look at her

"Day in, day out, your eyes were supposed to be on me
She offered me a million dollars. At first I told her to get lost

he seemed like some sort of crazy nut. I wanted no part of
er or her million bucks. But then things started to get rough,
nancially, and I remembered this lady who'd offered me a
ob at nine thousand dollars a month, not the luring
ing...but the real assistant's job." Tracy could tell they
eren't following her. Marcus was parked near the hospital
mergency doors, but no one exited the car. Tracy sighed a
eep breath. "Let me begin at the beginning. I met Elaine at
e health club. I had just lost my job at CMT and she was
ollowing me..."

It was nearly half an hour before she finished her entire
tory. Sean was sitting in rigid disbelief and Marcus was
tunned. She fiddled with her hands in the silence that
ollowed her tale. She was most concerned with Marcus's ac-
eptance of her reasoning. She looked at him, but he stared
traight forward through the windshield.

"I'm sorry I didn't tell you, Marcus. Even when you asked
e point blank that day in the park...I just couldn't." She
hook her head sadly. She needed his eyes, and she wasn't
etting them.

"I've been such a fool," Sean croaked from the backseat.
My mother's been playing me like a...I've been so stupid.
ll these years, Marc."

Tracy looked at him. He looked more in pain from his dis-
overy that he ever did from the pounding Marcus had given him.

"What'd I tell you?" Marcus said quietly, rubbing his
orehead with his hand. "She's played you like this even while
ve were growing up. She's made you into this...I don't know
vhat to call you. I don't even recognize you anymore, Sean."

"Then she offers a girl a half a million dollars to—" Marcus
tarted, but Tracy yelped in protest.

"A girl? So that's what I've been reduced to now in your
yes? I haven't done anything, I didn't sleep with anyb—"

"I know, sweetheart, I'm sorry. I just fell into talking to

Sean like we used to," he explained, pushing up the armrest between them and holding his arm open. "Come here, babe."

She moved snugly into the space she loved and was rewarded by a kiss on the forehead.

"Look, Tracy," Sean said, in a low, muffled voice. "I have a way to get you your money, but it's going to take a little collusion on our parts."

"I don't even want the money, Sean. I just wanted the job all along. Now, I don't even want that," Tracy said wearily.

"No. After all you've been through, you deserve the money." Both of them seemed to be saying the same thing and were overlapping each other.

Finally, Sean spoke alone. "Please. I want you to have it. And you and Marcus can go and live in peace far away from Cathy Booker."

"Who says I'm giving up my ties to Cathy?" Marcus asked facetiously.

"Marc, please. You've been wanting to leave CBF almost since the day we opened the doors. Take your shares of the company and go. Have fun in life. Get married. Whatever. If I were you, I'd get the hell out." Sean opened the door and walked to the emergency room doors. Tracy started to get out to fill out the forms that she knew Sean couldn't see or write on. Marcus pulled her back to him.

He spoke down into her round face. "Why didn't you tell me? Didn't you know that you could tell me anything?'

"I was going to tell you, but then I didn't know how you would look at me if you knew I accepted such a crazy assignment."

"The same way I'm looking at you now. I absolutely adore you, Tracy." He trailed a finger from her forehead down the side of her face. His fingertip left a burning trail on her flesh as it traveled down to the base of her neck. He was staring at her with nothing but unabashed love and longing. He dipped his head to sample her lips. His hungry lips found the spongy, yielding mounds and teased them with small tugs. She responded by pressing closer and opening her mouth slightly more to him. His tongue made a smooth entry through her parted lips and traveled along her teeth. Her mouth opened wider and his tongue was welcomed by hers in a gradual slow caress.

Tracy was so happy to be in his arms again, that she pressed harder against him. He squeezed her back until she felt him jump and break their kiss. He winced. "I'm sorry. It's my hand," he said, removing his arm from around Tracy.

"Come on, you'd better get looked at too." She got out on her side, and he got out on his, but he wrapped his arm around her shoulders once they were back together. She held him around the waist. It was a beautiful night in Key West.

Chapter 27

It took some convincing on their parts to make Gerald allow Sean to stay. But with everybody saying it was okay, he relented. It wouldn't have been a problem for Sean to get a hotel room, but he was as much a victim of Elaine as everyone else, if not more. The next morning, over breakfast, it was Marcus who extolled the virtues of Cathy Booker Foods to get the deal back on track. Sean told Marcus that a small, specialty project like this could be just the kind of thing to launch his own company. Nothing was inked in stone yet between CBF and Gerald. Plus, Gerald loved the idea, as long as Marcus could be up and running in time for his opening. Marcus said to give him a week to think about it, crunch the numbers and see what he wanted to do.

When they got home to Chicago, Sean called Elaine in France and told her that he was breaking off his relationship with Ashleigh. Marcus and Tracy were at his house, listening to his side of the conversation. Elaine couldn't even hide the excitement in her voice. He told her that he was in love with Tracy and that he wanted to marry Tracy. Just as everybody suspected, she didn't like that prospect any better than the first one. He stayed on a while, convincing her that he wasn't rushing into things. Tracy and Marcus could hear that she was getting very angry, but he kept up the ruse until Elaine hung up. Just as they figured, within seconds, Elaine called Tracy's cell phone. Tracy picked up, turning the speaker on, so they all could hear.

"Hello?"

Elaine was hot under the collar. "Just what hell do you think you're doing?"

"What are you talking about, Elaine?" Tracy said, playing her role.

"You marrying Sean was not part of the deal," she shouted at her.

"Screw your deal. Sean and I...we're in love. We just became close in Florida and I didn't mean for it to happen, but I fell for him. I guess I'd been kind of falling for him all along," Tracy said convincingly. She rubbed Marcus's leg, soothing him in case he really couldn't stomach this game. "And don't try anything, Elaine. I know all about your sneaky tricks."

"Look, Tracy, I'm going to wire the money to your account today. If you want to touch one penny of it, or if you touch one penny of it...you walk away from Sean, do you hear me?"

"Don't bother, I'll just send it back," she lied. By now, she was beginning to know Elaine almost as well as the boys did.

"You'll have it by this afternoon. Just think of the things you can do with that kind of money. And think, Tracy...think hard. Do you really love Sean? Or is this just a long-awaited screw between two young, healthy, attractive people? It's fine to enjoy Sean sexually, although that was not part of our deal, but I don't think you want to marry him. To tell you the truth, I always thought Marcus seemed more like your type."

At actually hearing Elaine's underhanded, scandalous words, both men were seething. Marcus raised his eyebrows at Sean, like, "See? See what a deranged witch you have for a mother?" Sean looked away, sadly.

Tracy did not want to get into discussing Marcus with Elaine. "Don't tell me what I'm feeling or who to love. There's no reasoning with you. I'm hanging up now."

"Tracy, wait!" Elaine called. Then she waited. "Tracy?"

"I'm here."

"Remember, you have a bit of a hot temper. Go to the bank at around one today and get your statement. Sleep on it tonight and tell me what you think in the morning. I'll call you tomorrow. As a matter of fact, Howard and I will be coming back as soon as we can get a flight back. Live with the account until then. I know you'll want to discuss it with Sean, but don't even mention our arrangement to him or I'll sue you for everything you embezzled from the company. All the clothes, all the jewelry, the furs, everything. I'll say you stole it." She paused for dramatic effect.

The men looked up shocked. Marcus started to stand, but Tracy had worked this scenario out in her head ages ago. She didn't bat an eye. She pressed down on his leg to keep him in his seat. Feeling he was going to say something, she shook her head "no" to him.

"You hear me?"

"I hear you," Tracy said dryly.

"You haven't told him already, have you?" Elaine said, suddenly worried.

"What? How could I tell him that I was here to lure him? That would end us before we even had a chance to begin. If he knew you were behind his attraction to me, he'd hate you and me."

Sean was impressed by the natural way Tracy played Elaine. He wished he'd been less angry and was able to deliver his lines like her. He thought Tracy was wrong, though. If he'd found that out, he would've still loved her, the same way Marcus was doing now. He would have still directed all of his anger toward his mother. Tracy was one in a million and, like Marc, he would let nothing jeopardize that.

"Good, then that's fine. I didn't mean to strong-arm you, I was just worried that you might be a fool in love."

"I'm not in love according to you," Tracy snapped back.

"Whatever, Tracy. I'd better go and do this. It'll give you something to think about other than screwing my son's brains out. Oh, and by the way…you're fired."

The guys sat speechless. Tracy smiled and shrugged, holding the phone at the end of her hand. That was the Elaine she knew, through and through.

"Well," Sean said, in a breathy voice. It felt like he'd been kicked in the gut to actually hear his mother say the things she'd said. He was tormented. How many years had she manipulated him, administering his life like he was a marionette?

He glanced at his long-suffering cousin and realized what a remarkable man he was. He was actually a man. His own man. But he wasn't gloating. He looked as though he'd been drop-kicked too. At least Tracy was consolingly rubbing his back.

"Well, that's that," Sean said. Marcus looked over at him, his expressive eyes unable to hide the hurt he felt for Sean. Or was it pity? Sean wondered. At this point it didn't matter. "So, once we have proof that she's transferred the funds into your account, I'll be able to nail her."

"What makes you think it's going to be from a Cathy account, Sean?" Marcus asked.

"Elaine doesn't have that kind of cash on hand. She spends too much. She's got it tied up in mortgages and whatnot. I'm sure that all the staging for Tracy was done with her own money, or else I would have noticed the huge expenditures," Sean said, comfortable in his knowledge of how his plan would play out. "She said you'll have the money today. If it were her own money, it would take her a while to scramble for that kind of cash."

Sean stood up and went to his bar. It was early afternoon, but he needed a drink. "You can keep all that stuff she got you, by the way."

"I don't want it either. Except maybe one suit," she said thinking of the great suit Melvin had produced for her at the last minute.

"Keep the lot," Sean said, waving his hand. "Sell it. Give it to your friends. Like I said, it all came from Elaine's personal money, so do what you like."

"What's going to happen once we confirm the money is in there?" Tracy had been too distracted when Sean first told her the plan to give it the appropriate attention.

"When she gets back in the States," Marcus explained to her, "Sean is going to have the information about which account was used for the unauthorized transfer of funds. Not one of us can take out that kind of money without board approval and an itemization and more meetings than you could shake a stick at. Anyway, once he confronts her with the unauthorized use of funds, either she has to pay it back or she has to resign and face prosecution for embezzlement of funds."

Tracy became alarmed. "She'll say I embezzled it."

"She doesn't have that option," Sean said, picking up where Marcus left off. "The money you get will be yours, clean and clear. That contract you have—the one that you say she insisted on—protects you from that claim. Plus, we know the truth. I'm going to tell her I know everything."

"If Sean is right, and I believe he is," Marcus said, going to the bar to get himself some water, "Elaine won't be able to come up with the money. Sean and I can tell her we'll pay it to keep her out of jail, but on the condition that she resign and give up some shares a little over the value of our assistance."

"That would make her the minor shareholder and you two the controlling interests," Tracy said, catching on.

"Exactly," Sean said. "And I do want to continue the company. I think I'm good with Cathy Booker, even if I got into it because of her. I just don't want to have to work with her on a day-to-day basis," he said rather defensively, wondering if his whole life had been built around a lie.

"You *are* good with Cathy, Sean," Tracy said, boosting his confidence. "I've seen you at work and I don't think she could be in any finer hands."

Sean smiled at her compliment, but his face hurt in that position. He went to sit next to her on his couch, slumping all the way down like he was exhausted. It was all he could do to try to talk to Elaine in a normal voice. She could've attributed his different sound to their long-distance connection.

"You are right for the company," Marcus agreed. "Without Elaine in the way, there's no telling what you can't do."

"Thanks, Marc," he said and sipped his drink. Then he grew somber. "Marc, I'm sorry I've been a shit to you over all these years. I—"

"Don't worry about it." Marcus had given his glass of water to Tracy and was putting ice in another glass to make one for himself. He pointed at Sean's face. "I think we're even."

"Yeah." Sean laughed. "But next time, don't store up your hostility toward me. Release it like I did, bit by bit. I'll be marred for life."

He wouldn't. He was being dramatic, but Tracy did regard with some concern his bruised and fractured jaw, his left eye swollen shut, the stitches above his eye and his overall puffy face. He wasn't going into the office for at least a few weeks. Marcus had a bandage wrapped around his fist. If they came into the office together, coupled with Tracy's firing, no work would get done with the level of gossip. It was already bad enough that all of them were off today and Sean had cancelled his managers' meeting.

"So," Tracy started, not knowing how to bring up the topic. "What's happening with you and Ashleigh?"

"I told her what happened, everything, and she understood. She was very upset, but willing to forgive. Since...nothing happened." Sean looked at Tracy, meaningfully. He had apologized countless times and even more after he returned her cell phone. But even as he completely understood what Elaine had tried to do, he found Tracy's entire persona magnetic. "But I postponed the wedding and told her we need to cool it for a while. If I was willing to throw everything away for a chance with you...Not even for a sure thing, but I was willing to dump her for just a chance...I figured she ain't the one."

"Don't feel that way. You got wrapped up in Elaine's—" Tracy pleaded for Ashleigh, but Sean cut her off.

"She put you in my sights and dressed you the way I like to see a woman dressed, but you didn't do one thing different from the way you would normally behave. Did you?" he asked.

"No, not really. Except hide my relationship with Marcus," Tracy said, thinking about it.

"So, I was attracted by Elaine's illusion, but I fell for you," Sean said, and saw Marcus's jaw getting tight. "Wait, Marc, before you come over and bust my other eye. What I'm saying is that, the way I felt about Tracy...the way I *feel* about her even now, is more than I ever felt for Ashleigh. I nearly ruined my career, my reputation, my relationship, pursuing her. What I need to do is find someone I feel that passionate about and who feels the same way about me, so that I can introduce her to my cousin and his lovely wife."

Sean's jumping the gun in their relationship caused them to look at each other shyly. It was what they both wanted, but neither had voiced the thought. Tracy dropped her eyes, saying, "That would be nice."

Marcus's heart thumped against his chest. "It would, wouldn't it?" he agreed, huskily. He would've gotten down on one knee and proposed to her right there if it weren't for Sean. He was already defeated enough. Marcus didn't need to rub his nose in it. But he made a plan in his head to get the ring, plan the evening and do it right. As soon as all the preparations were in place, he was going to ask her. He, instead, turned his attention to Sean.

"You know, you're going to do great things with Elaine out of the picture. You really should go ahead with that deal with Gerald. After Elaine's gone, you'll have opened up an entirely new revenue stream with made-to-order restaurant preparations."

Sean peered at him, raising his head a little bit. "And what about you? What are you going to do?"

"I want to stay involved with the foundation, but I'm giving up the food service industry. Elaine's shares will pay me extra dividends. I want to open the same kind of thing Gerald is doing. Except I just want to manage it, while I work on art like my mom did," he said. He looked only at Sean for his next idea. "My girl has family in Minneapolis and I think we might move there."

Tracy stared at Marcus for a minute, not sure she had heard what he said. When he finally looked from Sean to meet her eyes, she sprang from her seat. She ran to him and hugged him, wrapping her legs around his waist. "Really?! We can move close to Tai and the babies and Kevin?"

"Whoa, baby, you got to get down," he said, holding her butt. "My hand."

Tracy unwrapped her legs, but squished his midsection tightly. She turned her face up to his for a kiss and he complied, but briefly—there was still Sean.

"Of course. Anything for my lady. I got nothing to tie me here," Marcus said.

It was what her whole family really wanted more than

anything in the world. They just hadn't been able to afford Sheila's move and Tracy had had no success finding a job in that market. But it was their ultimate dream to be in close proximity once again. She'd never told Marcus this, but he instinctively knew that if he had a nice family like that, he'd really miss them. With Tracy's newfound wealth and Marcus's saying he would leave Chicago, there was nothing stopping her now.

"What about your boards and the foundation and…" She wanted to exhaust all possibility that he might back out.

"That's why they invented air travel," Sean piped up from the couch.

Marcus pointed to Sean and raised his eyebrow. "See, what the man says is true. I can get back here for those things."

"Hey! What about my Bulls?" she said, suddenly remembering that for the first time in her life, she had season tickets to the games. She poked out her lip.

"Air travel," Marcus and Sean said together. They laughed.

Everything with Elaine went down just as Sean had planned. She was caught totally off guard by the way they had all schemed to trap her. She, at least, didn't have to worry about Sean's marrying Ashleigh, but now she had no relationship with Sean other than a professional one. She was left with a few shares, but not enough to have any say.

Tracy and Marcus moved Sheila in March, and then themselves to Minneapolis in April. Sheila eventually conceded to getting a modest four-bedroom a couple of blocks away from Tai. She enjoyed the role of a full-time grandmother and took care of the baby when Tai went to work. She saw Lucas and Samuel almost every day, when Tai or Kevin stopped by to pick up Madison. Sheila was enjoying having so many people to cook for and prepared yummy meals that they could either eat there or take with them.

Marcus and Tracy went to the town as an engaged couple,

but got married once they were there amongst family. Since Kevin and Tai had used all of their vacation time over the holidays, they wouldn't have been able to come to Chicago for a wedding anyway. Vivien had pulled some strings to get Tracy some occasional freelance production work with a station in St. Paul.

Tracy was surprised to find out that Marcus was a very good artist. His paintings were compelling and intriguing, but he also sculpted and created mixed media. They had purchased a luxurious four-bedroom home, with a den, library, game room and sewing room. There was a small guest house at the back of their yard that Marcus used as a studio. He planned to sell his works at the outdoor summer art fairs, including those in Chicago.

Tracy stood on the back porch with a mug of coffee in her hand. She watched her husband concentrate on another inspired work of art. The door was open to the guest house so that he could enjoy the breeze created by the various trees surrounding their yard. She moved to the porch swing and sat down, gently rocking herself. Her eyes caught sight of a hummingbird sampling one of her flowers. She looked out at Marcus, taking his shirt off so he could be free to move and splash as he needed. When she was going through the torment of losing her job, Brian being a rat, the secret scheme and not being able to see Marcus and all, she had questioned God. Where was He in her life? Why had He taken her to this hell? But all along, He was reviewing His chart and staying the course. He made her strong enough to endure all that and arrive at the heaven she was in now. She thanked God that she had met Elaine.